Hyperspace: The World Between Worlds is a work of fiction. Names and characters are fictitious, and the incidents described won't happen until the stars are right and Cthulhu rises from his eternal slumber. Any resemblance to actual persons, living or dead, is entirely coincidental.

Edited by Jody Calkins
Cover art by Kasia Słupecka
Graphic Design by Sebastian Koziner

ISBN-13:

Published simultaneously on Yuggoth and Carcosa.

HYPERSPACE

THE WORLD *BETWEEN* WORLDS

by Lee Stephen

For Sandy, who allowed me
to explore a universe that has
inspired me for so very long.

This was an absolute dream.

Table of Contents

TABLE OF CONTENTS

Chapter One

I WATCHED WITH solemnity as the young human danced, kicking its hips out as it covered the bottom of its face with a hand fan. Its narrowed eyes were upon me, the creature blissfully unaware of the many imperfections of its form. Delta, for that was the name by which it was referred, chose not to wear the special garments that day—the most beautiful scarlet and golden-weaved garments that I'd prepared for it for this very performance—despite my urgings that they would have furthered its attempts to appear desirable. Instead, it opted for a hideous silver jumpsuit. Its decision to wear such a mundane garb when there existed such a resplendent alternative left me baffled and disappointed. Even in a training session such as this, attention to the minutest of details should be adhered. Every tug of thread, every jingle of every accessory must be accounted. But it insisted that it had not the time for such perceived trivialities. This was, as it so *humanly* phrased it, "just stupid practice." And so I watched, offering the occasional nod of affirmation that it so earnestly desired to see. I was there to please, and so I pleased.

As Deity's perfect creation, we Zepzeg struggle to comprehend such apathy toward outward appearance. Our species was formed from the very first crystals that were birthed into the cosmos—no carbon-based lifeform can rival that which is our natural luster. But even with such luster, we toil in our beautification chambers to achieve perfection—polishing our exteriors, chipping away what rough edges we should find undesirable, sculpting and refining the curves of our crystalline bodies. Making our luster shine brighter.

But for humans, there is no such luster. There is no such pursuit to attain perfection, for there is no hope of ever attaining it. Even their religions are founded upon the acknowledgment of flaws and inclusions. Like most species in the cosmos, humans do what they must to survive, and they do little more.

Delta extended the hand fan and pirouetted slowly, ending the choreographed turn almost a quarter's way too quickly, though it hardly seemed to notice. Shrouding the lower portion of its face again, it bent its knees and half bowed in my direction. I nodded in the acknowledgment that it sought, and it continued.

My name is Velistris, and I serve as communications specialist on board the *Illustré*, under the command of Captain Aurora Ultraviolet. Aurora is what humans refer to as an *aunt*, at least as it pertains to its relationship with Delta, which calls itself Aurora's *niece*. There are two such nieces on board the *Illustré*, and together, they make the full complement of the vessel's human crew. Neither niece seems particularly fond of the other, both sharing a common mother but different fathers. Delta is in a growth state that is referred to as a *teenager*. I do not pretend to understand the biological purposes of gender as it pertains to humans— nor age, which is curiously both celebrated and maligned in human culture.

Zepzeg do not age as humans do. We grow, we shatter, and we are reborn in our pieces. Though all Zepzeg have different life experiences, we are all fractures of the same original crystal. Shattering is our means of reproduction; therefore, we have no need for males or females in our species. Though my human companions refer to me as a female, it is merely for their own sense of comfort and familiarity.

Finishing its performance with a deft ballerina bow, Delta lifted its head to look at me. "So, what do you think?" it asked.

I do not enjoy lying, but I do so when I must. "You were splendid," I told it.

It stood upright and whipped its dark hair from its face. I was proud of that hair. I helped Delta straighten it and craft it to fall just above its shoulders. I treated it with the finest oils from the Zepzeg homeworld. It is not hair meant to be whipped with such reckless abandon. It is meant to shine and cascade like dark water. I must confess that for all their inferiority, hair is the one attribute of human beings that I envy. Being made of crystal, we Zepzeg cannot possess hair. It is the one part of the human body that I find magnificent.

With a wink, Delta said, "I knew I'd do well."

"Shall we try now with your garments?" I asked. "You would look so lovely in them."

"On a scale from one to ten, how would you say I did?"

It is a fan of scales. "A ten, naturally," I answered. It is always my answer. Delta does not seem to notice.

It cocked its hips and smirked. "I *am* a ten, aren't I?"

It was not. "You will surely impress at the ball."

Without so much as a word, it bounded for the door.

"Where are you going?" I asked.

"To tell Aunt Aurora that I did perfectly!"

It was gone from the room even before it finished speaking, its words reverberating down the *Illustré*'s corridors as I was left alone in its chamber.

The dance that Delta had been attempting to execute was called *Gold Moon Rising*—a dance that, once mastered, can be quite glorious to descry. It was Delta's intention to perform the routine at the engagement ball of Aurora and its fiancé, a human male named Bryce Lockhart. According to human custom, the Earth age of sixteen is one of great significance for human females and a point at which they "come of age," a term that I admittedly do not fully understand. Having reached said customary age, Delta was eager to perform

at Aurora and Bryce's engagement ball. The process of
engagement and marriage is also customary among humans,
and it seems a great inconvenience for what little benefit
it provides. Bryce resides in the Hyades Cluster, far from
our own, rendering it utterly unable to provide Aurora with
any tangible benefit save what Aurora calls *moral support,* a
polite term that humans use when no actual help is granted
yet the perception of help must be maintained. Presumably,
the benefit of being married to Bryce Lockhart will manifest
after their wedding, at which point it will invade our personal
space on the *Illustré* and take partial ownership of all of
Aurora's possessions. Once more, the benefit escapes me.

Thoughts on human relations notwithstanding, I was eager
to assist in Delta's preparation and beautification for the
engagement ball. Despite Delta's propensity to disappoint on
a technical level, I related to its desire to achieve perfection—
even if only by humanity's inferior standards. It shares this
desire with Aurora, who has entrusted me with all of its beauty
treatments for many Earth years. Like its niece, Aurora is a
human considered by many of its species to be quite comely.
I consider it a privilege to serve as its beautician. Though
the engagement ball was still many weeks away, I very much
looked forward to helping Aurora and Delta shine.

Aurora and its nieces descend from a line of human royalty,
a fact that I find very much to my liking. It was Aurora's *great
grandmother,* as it calls it, that established the first human
colony in the Ragnarok Cluster—one of the largest and most
bountiful star clusters in all the cosmos. It provided the
human species a foothold with which to sprout. The ancestral
female, known by the name Corinda Rhea, was awarded
great wealth for its deeds. It was a wealth passed down to its
heirs, all of which learned to live without the want typical of
such a flawed and struggling species. As one unaccustomed
to associating with underprivileged rabble, I must say that
I find the manners and outward appearance of Aurora and

Delta quite pleasing, all lesser possibilities considered. There is no greater joy for a Zepzeg than to associate with beings that strive to match our level of refinement.

Unfortunately, that sentiment cannot be echoed for the *other* members of the *Illustré's* crew.

As I stepped delicately out of Delta's room as to not scratch my crystal legs on its doorframe, I was nearly touched by the passing monstrosity that is Hank-is-Handy. Hank-is-Handy is a Vorck, and there exists no semblance of grace or couth among them. They are hideous, top-heavy creatures with wrinkled, pink skin, lipless mouths of long, unsymmetrical teeth, and pale, protruding, white eyeballs. They are utterly disgusting, and I quickly retreated back into Delta's room as to not be touched by its rubbery, odorous skin. Stopping in its lumbering tracks, Hank-is-Handy turned its thick neck in my direction.

"Excuse me, Velistris."

Its voice—how grating and harrowing was its dreadful voice! Were this not a trusted member of the *Illustré's* crew, I might shed crystals in fright every time I heard it. Naturally I said nothing, lest I be forced to endure it again. I simply dipped my head in acknowledgment, and it trundled along.

Of all the species in the Lernaean Cluster—the cluster in which we reside—the Vorck are quite possibly the most brutish. Of course, no species in our cluster can match natural Zepzeg splendor, but some do try. Humans can hide their hideousness quite well with our assistance. Something must also be said of the Zevolt—fearsome dragon-like beings with imposing bodies and a unique fearlessness. Many a cluster has fallen under their terrible reign. The Automata display a lovely symmetry, though that can hardly be counted to their credit as they are living machines incapable of being born into such beauty. And, of course, who can forget the Mendeku, a hardy insectoid species that are firm in appearance, though they sadly lack the social intellect to engage in any sort of meaningful civility. All of these species, and quite possibly more, display a certain level of nobility in their evolution, even if they cannot match our delicate, crystalline forms.

But the Vorck? The Vorck are disgusting in every which way, from their thuggish bodies, to their croaking voices, to the foul must that seeps from their pores. I suppose one must pity them a measure, for they spent much of their existence as slaves in another cluster before breaking the chains of their masters and retreating to our own. It is for this reason, perhaps, that they were unable to develop proper manners or at least technology that could remedy their dreadful appearances. At the very least, they have an excuse for their miserable state.

As Hank-is-Handy marched past, I watched as Elyse—Aurora's older niece and half-sister to Delta—followed in its wake. Elyse is wretched, so far as humans go, showing no regard whatsoever for those it has forced its mish-mashed appearance upon. It wears the most gaudy garments, it paints its face pale like a corpse, and most horrid of all, it has techno-dyed its hair a most revoltingly unnatural green color. All would be tolerable if it weren't for its insufferable personality, selfishly caring more for its own "artistic independence" than for those, like myself, who must look at it. I do not care for it at all.

As it walked past me, it cracked what humans call a smirk, a befuddling expression that means neither good nor ill. I hissed back—I could not contain myself. Its smirk grew wider! Was it a curse? An expression of pleasure? How is one ever to tell?

I waited until Hank-is-Handy and Elyse were past me before stepping back into the hallway to resume my walk to the bridge—no doubt where the two were heading, as well. The walk is not far, praise be to Deity, lest I tire my fragile legs.

The *Illustré* is of typical size for a space yacht—large enough to give each member of its crew space of their own, yet not so large as to become inconvenient. I am in what humans would call my third year as part of its crew, all of which was spent in the roles of communications specialist and beautician. Hank-is-Handy is also in its third year, all of which have been spent as the *Illustré*'s engineer and security officer. As for Delta and Elyse, neither has an official capacity on board this vessel beyond their roles as genetic carriers for their species. While Elyse spends much of its time with Hank-is-Handy in engineering doing whatever it is they do, Delta at least makes itself useful by allowing me to experiment on its skin and hair with an assortment of creams, masks, and treatments.

It is a baffling juxtaposition, that of engineering and beauty. I have heard Hank-is-Handy state on many occasions that it does not matter how the *Illustré* gleams in the starlight, if it does not run properly, then it is of no use. It is hard to imagine such twisted logic. If one has not used their life to glorify Deity with their pulchritude, then what is the point of existence at all? We all must die—what a waste it would be not to die beautifully.

I stepped onto the bridge, whereupon I was immediately attacked by Riley—a chaotic, slathering creature that humans call a *dog*. It took all the restraint I could muster not to shriek as it slapped its slime-coated tongue against my legs. What joy humans find in having their bodies licked by these disgusting creatures, I will never understand.

"Riley!" shouted Aurora from the center of the bridge, where it was seated. "Get in your kennel." Aurora had one installed inside a wall in the bridge—thankfully on the side opposite my station.

Relieved as the monster was called away, I examined my legs, where Riley's saliva dripped down to the floor. *I must cleanse my legs of this*, I thought at once, though I knew that there were far more important matters at hand. Registering Delta's voice as it prattled on to Aurora, I folded my hands together and approached.

"And she said I did perfectly!" the teenager said. "Would you like to see the dance now, Aunt Aurora?"

Raising a finger, I said, "Perhaps with the garments." I saw Elyse roll its eyes from the back of the bridge, where it was standing with arms folded beside Hank-is-Handy. That hideous green hair. How I fought to tear my sight from it. The subject of human genetics is so confusing to me. How such a deviant as Elyse could spawn from the same genetic material as a vibrant human like Aurora Ultraviolet is beyond my comprehension. Aurora was tall, slender—when it walked, its stride was alluring, even by human standards. In contrast, Elyse walked with its neck forward, slouched with sunken shoulders like some sort of bedraggled hermit. Aurora's hair fell over its shoulders in coppery red curls, whilst Elyse's chemical-green clumps were pinned up in the most haphazard of buns, its bangs hanging so lowly over its eyes that I found it miraculous that the creature could see. From Aurora, such radiant, near-flawless natural skin. From Elyse, a white plastering that did little to hide its multitude of blemishes. Should not natural selection have weeded out such a malformed creation? It still mystifies me today.

"I would very much like for you to see me dance, Aunt Aurora," said Delta. "I know you'll be impressed."

"I will, Delta," Aurora answered with a smile. "We'll be docking for refuel soon, and you can show me then."

Delta protested, "But I want to show you now!"

From the back row of the bridge, Elyse addressed its aunt and half-sister. "So this all sounds wonderful. Listen, Aunt Aurora, we're going to need to pick up a few linkages when we dock. We're down to one spare."

I was suspicious that it thought everything sounded wonderful.

"Umm, excuse me?" asked Delta, craning its neck to look at Elyse. "Can you not see that we're talking here?"

"Oh, I'm sorry! No, I didn't see."

Once more, suspicion. Had I eyes, I would have narrowed them.

Elyse opened its mouth to speak, but Aurora silenced it with a raised hand. "We'll get more spare linkages *and* watch the performance while at dock."

"When you talk about watching the performance, you mean 'we' in the singular, right?" asked Elyse. When Aurora shot it a warning stare, it sighed and said, "I can't wait."

Looking past Elyse to Hank-is-Handy, Aurora angled its head. "Is there anything else we need while we're there?"

I could swear, even from a distance, that the Vorck was drooling. "The spindrive is working good. The forward screen generator is dirty. It needs to be cleaned."

"I trust the two of you will handle that, then?"

"Yes, we will."

Aurora raised an eyebrow. "Is this something we'll need to cool down for?"

"We will deactivate all screens to clean it. The spindrive can remain operational. We will not slow down."

"Sounds good, Hank."

There was immediate disapproval on Hank-is-Handy's face the moment Aurora called it by its nickname, a concept that is purely human. Among the many curiosities of the Vorck species is their peculiar naming convention. They are under the terribly misguided mindset that one's name must in some way, shape, or form advertise its usefulness. *Hank-is-Handy*, for example, is a direct reference to its desire to be appealing as an engineer, or at the very least, an instrument of general upkeep and maintenance. There is often an attempt on behalf of Vorcks to make a play on words or to appeal to the simplicity of the human brain with rhyme or alliteration. *Rusty-is-Trusty, Dan-can-Cook, Chip-Flies-Ships.* All are examples of what one would expect to find at a trading hub or any outpost where Vorcks are loitering about looking for work. It has always eluded me what a Vorck would do should they change their occupation. Perhaps they would change their name as well.

Being grown in pods, the Vorck do not have family structures or any particular affinity for customs—nor do they possess genders, the lone characteristic shared between our two species. There is very little variation between one Vorck and the next. So far as Hank-is-Handy is concerned, it has at least acquired some of the manners that make humans tolerable. And I do suppose that its work in the engine room—as frivolous as it may be—is of modest quality.

Facing me from its chair, Aurora said, "While you're up here, Velistris, make contact with Duvall Station and advise them of our approach. I want the refueling process to begin and be completed as quickly as possible."

"Of course, captain," I said dutifully as I approached my communications station. Gliding my crystalline fingers over the holopanel, I sent a subspace ping to Duvall Station, a human-operated refueling depot in the sparsely inhabited Currier Belt.

As a human of prominent genetics, Aurora is often asked to partake in a variety of missions of diplomatic nature. Aurora's concern for expediency in this instance was related to an assignment of great importance concerning two of the more prominent species in our cluster. They are called the Broodmasters and the Dacians, and they are a pair of species with a great history of rivalry and bickering. The former are revolting blob creatures whose minds are filled with lust for ascendency rather than adornment. They are powerful, telepathic beings, able to control their broodling spawns to accomplish their will. Their minds are a terrible, terrible weapon, forcing any beings they deal with to consider their own thoughts carefully, lest they find themselves hypnotized by the Broodmasters' mind-altering influence.

As for the Dacians—winged beings with a striking resemblance to the monsters humans refer to as *gargoyles*— they possess a unique power of the mind as well, though it is far more subtle. Whilst the Broodmasters use their powers to control the brain, Dacians control the heart, able to stir all manner of emotions inside whatever tortured soul they set their sights on, be it fear, lust, anger, or something else. I have heard Elyse refer to these beasts as *space vamps*, though I still fail to understand the reference and was not particularly bothered enough to seek clarification.

The subject of this particular strife between the Broodmasters and Dacians is one of territory, specifically the star system of Gryamore. Though not a particularly habitable system, it is, nonetheless, one abundant in mineral resources. During a time when both species lived alongside each other cooperatively, they shared this system, each claiming an equal number of planets to mine for resources. There was but one world in this system—the fifth planet from Gryamore itself—that remained unclaimed. Now that the two species were locked in a state of disagreement, they both wished to lay claim to this world, knowing that its owner would own a majority of the planets in the system, which would tip the scales of power in their favor.

It was Aurora's task to serve as mediator in this dispute, ultimately determining which species would be able to lay claim to the world whilst simultaneously ensuring that said diplomatic winner would not use their newfound galactic edge to obliterate the other. It was a responsibility that had caused Aurora a great amount of stress, especially considering its general disdain for both species. I, of course, could not care less which species inherits this world, nor did I care if one should obliterate the other. My concern was solely for the physical comeliness of Aurora and Delta, that by my delicate fingers, they might please Deity enough to allow them to be reborn as Zepzeg in the Life After. If completing this negotiation allows Aurora to refocus on the process of beautification, then I will help it as much as I am able.

The subspace ping was returned to me. Duvall Station had acknowledged. "They await our arrival," I spoke gently to Aurora. "They wish to know if there is any other service they can provide."

"Send them our thanks," Aurora answered me, "and that we'll need nothing more than to refuel and be on our way. The Gryamore V negotiation cannot wait."

"As you wish, captain." I replied to the station as instructed, then I closed the channel.

It is during these moments of general inactivity, when humans have set nothing in particular in their minds to accomplish, that I have learned the most by observing them. One of the innumerable physical benefits of being a Zepzeg is that we do not possess eyes as humans do on the fronts of our faces—they are deep within our lifeveins, viewing the outside world from inside our crystalline bodies. This makes it impossible for humans to ascertain when they are being watched by a member of our species. I have used this to my advantage on many occasions, angling my head away from my human companions while keeping my focus upon them. I have seen them when they do not know that I am watching.

Though I pity them for their ghastly physical appearances, there are certain aspects of humans that I admire. If I am being true to myself, perhaps I even envy them in my innermost moments of self-reflection. The look on Aurora's face in that very moment, as it leaned back in its chair and settled in to watch the bridge monitor, was one I had seen many times before. With its subtly tensed eyelids and near-perfectly straight lips, it could almost be mistaken for a moment of doubt. But I have known Aurora—I have known humans—long enough to know better. It was a moment, not of doubt, but of uncertainty, for there is a difference between the two. It looked as if it was asking itself not if it *could* serve as mediator in such a crucial task, but if it truly wanted to. As if it had a choice.

The concept of choice is strange to me. I, as all Zepzeg, have a purpose to glorify Deity through the beautification of myself and those around me. The sanctifying power of beauty is why my species builds chapels amongst the stars— the most magnificent and colossal of structures, ornate in every way, glimmering as to call those who wish to visit them, that they too might find sanctification through beautification. That they might elevate their humble forms to something worthy of Deity's favor. Forming beauty out of chaos is not a path pursued by *some* Zepzeg. It is a mission that calls us all.

But humans are different. Though I am unfamiliar with Aurora's god, I do know it worships one. And yet still, even with the fervency that I know it possesses, there are moments such as this when it seems that its path is its own to determine. How can one seek to please a divine being whilst simultaneously seeking out their own pleasures and purposes? It is a vexing conundrum, to be sure. At times, it gives me great, great sorrow for Aurora's twisted, primal state. Yet at times still, it gives me sorrow for myself. Had I not a predetermined purpose ahead of me, what would I choose to do? It sometimes concerns me that I do not know.

Perhaps, in a sad, ironic way, that is another condition that I share with Hank-is-Handy. When I stare at it, I see that it, too, is staring at the humans around it. It is far more difficult for it to mask its focus, as I can, yet still, the humans around it treat its intrusion with only mild disdain, as if they can relate to its simple, small-brained state of wonder. I often catch myself wondering what it is thinking. If it longs to have the creativity to carve its own path in the stars. If it longs to be known not for what it can do, but for who it is as an individual. To even entertain the thought, for a Vorck, would be tantamount to an evolutionary leap.

Opening its mouth, Aurora sucked in some of the atmospheric oxygen required for its survival, then blew the air out. It is a gesture that human beings call a *sigh*, and it can mean a great many things. The sigh that Aurora drew then, I believed to be associated with situational resignation. It is a sigh I hear from humans often.

"All right, Delta," Aurora said, turning its attention to its younger niece. "Why don't you go ahead and show me your dance right now?"

Delta's lips stretched broadly into a smile, and it clasped its hands together with excitement. Behind Aurora's chair, Hank-is-Handy and Elyse quietly made their way to the bridge door, slipping out just as Delta's routine began. No one else even seemed to notice they were gone.

The routine was horribly imperfect, as it had been in Delta's room, and far less alluring than it would have been had it worn its proper garments. Yet still, the dance caused it to smile, which in turn caused Aurora to smile—and for them, that seemed to be enough. When Delta looked upon me for approval, I, too, offered the best smile I could summon from deep within my lifeveins. I smiled because it was what was expected of me. Because it is what I must do. How strange it would be to not carry such certainty of purpose. I cannot fathom it. Perhaps, in its simple, small-brained state, Hank-is-Handy can. Perhaps some day, I will ask it.

But until that day comes, I will serve Deity as I was designed to—beautifying all those that I can, that they might be reborn as one of my own in the Life After. At the very least, it is a noble purpose to strive for—one certainly more significant than maintaining a starship's innards. But to each their own. If lubricating a spindrive gives Hank-is-Handy a sense of purpose, then all the better for it. At the very least, it will give it something to do.

As inconsequential as that something may be.

Chapter Two

ELYSE AND ME were unpacking a linkage when the spindrive stopped and the ship's proximity overload alarm sounded. Aurora then called us to the bridge over the speakers. We did not know what caused the alarm to sound. We went quickly to the bridge to find out.

I am not good at reading emotions. We Vorck do not possess them like humans do. They have many emotions. I have tried very hard to learn them. Elyse has taught me that when humans are afraid, their voices tremble. This is how I knew that Aurora was afraid when she called for us.

I am Hank-is-Handy. I am the engineer and security officer for the *Illustré*. I was hired by Aurora after the species called the Xk-13 destroyed my home planet. She needed an engineer, and it was my function. I now live with her and her human family and a Zepzeg and a thing called a dog. I serve a purpose on the *Illustré*, and it pleases me.

Elyse Genza is a thing Aurora calls a niece. I do not know how families work. Vorck do not have them. All I know is that I love Elyse, because I have heard her say, "you know you love me," many times. She says I am the only one on the ship that listens to her. For this reason, I try to listen hard.

Though I am not male or female, the humans call me a male. They say it is because of my name. My first name, before the Xk-13 destroyed my home planet, was Judy-Fixes-All. I told them about that name once and they told me they did not like it and they were happy I became Hank-is-Handy. I suppose this means that I am happy, too. I have tried hard to use the female pronouns when I speak of them. I believe it helps me to fit in. I have tried to use those same words in my thoughts, too. It helps me to learn. I believe that I have learned very much.

"What do you think's going on?" Elyse asked me as she walked ahead of me. She walks faster than me, but I run faster than her.

"We are going to the bridge," I answered her.

She looked back at me and performed an eye roll. "Obviously! But what do you think we'll see when we get to the bridge?"

"Aurora."

She did not ask anymore questions, so I know I must have answered them to her satisfaction. I answer many of her questions to her satisfaction. She says that is why she speaks to me, because I always tell her the truth. I do not think she knows that when I answer a question, I am also learning. All of her questions have taught me a great many things.

The Zepzeg that we live with is called Velistris. She does not think I am learning anything. One day she told me that I have a small brain. I told her that Zepzeg are weak and Vorck are strong. To demonstrate this, I picked up a chair and pulled it apart. She did not speak about my brain anymore. I know that I am learning many things. I know that I already know many things. But they are not things that humans and Zepzeg know.

For example, I know that when calibrating a neutron secondary, deviant oscillations can result in a loss of performance percentage equal to three-quarters of the oscillating frequency times the distance between the input and output registers measured in standard galactic microunits. I do not believe that Velistris or the humans know this, except for Elyse, who I have spent much time teaching to be handy. She knows more than Velistris thinks she does, too. I do not love Velistris.

When we stepped into the bridge, I saw why Aurora's words were trembling. Weak Velistris's body was trembling, too. On the bridge monitor, there was a Daldath Planet Smasher. It was very big—the size of a small planetoid. It is a destructive spacecraft that can pull a planet apart to mine its resources. I turned my head between the bridge monitor and Aurora to see if she would speak. She did.

"It got close enough to force us out of hyperspace! I need you on guns, Hank-is-Handy."

Weak Velistris was moaning in fear. This is because the Daldath destroyed her planet. I do not hate the Xk-13 for destroying mine, but Velistris hates the Daldath for destroying hers. She hates them, but she also fears them. She is weak. Zepzeg are weak. I walked behind the weapons console and charged the *Illustré*'s plasma blaster. If the *Illustré* engaged the Planet Smasher, the *Illustré* would be quickly destroyed. I do not care about death, but I do not wish for Elyse or Aurora to die. Velistris can die, though. That would be okay. "I am ready to fire," I told Aurora.

She held her hand up. It is a signal for me to wait. "Wait," she said. Perhaps she did not know that I understood the signal. "I just want you on standby. I don't know what that thing's going to do yet."

"We should leave at once!" cried Velistris. "Are not Hank-is-Handy and Elyse working on the forward screens? Even with them fully operational, we could be obliterated in a single blast!"

What she said was not true. With the forward screens operational, it would take two blasts, maybe even three.

The bridge door opened. The other niece thing, Delta, came into the bridge. The dog, Riley, was with her. Delta's mouth opened, and she sucked in oxygen in fear. It is another thing that humans do. I have a hypothesis that it helps them run faster. But maybe I am wrong. The dog did not seem afraid. It ran to Aurora and jumped on her leg. Aurora did not notice.

Delta is a human that likes Velistris. They spend much time together, mostly putting things on Delta's head or sticking it in water. Velistris does to Aurora many of the same things. Elyse does not like things on her head or having it stuck in water by Velistris. I am more like Elyse.

Elyse has told me that Aurora pretends to be unafraid of things so that she and Delta do not get scared, too. Humans do not like their young to be scared. We Vorck do not have young. We are commissioned into existence fully developed. "Everyone," Aurora said, "let's take a deep, slow breath."

I took a deep, slow breath, but the others did not.

"We're too close to it right now to enter hyperspace without having to override the proximity sensor," Aurora said. "But I think it may have pulled us out by mistake."

Starships enter hyperspace by using a spindrive. It is a device that spins a pocket universe into existence around a starship. This allows the starship to travel at speeds that would otherwise be impossible. When a ship has traveled to its destination, the spindrive deactivates, and the ship exits its pocket universe into the real one. This is how all starships in the universe travel. When two spindrives interfere with one another, both vessels must exit hyperspace or risk being destroyed. This is why all starships have a proximity sensor, which allows them to leave hyperspace before damage is done to the ship's components. It is possible that our spindrive interfered with the Planet Smasher's and both ships dropped out of hyperspace by accident. If this happens, and it is not due to hostility, the ships will separate from one another under thruster power, then reactivate their spindrives to go their own ways.

That is what she meant.

I watched the Planet Smasher in the bridge monitor to see if its thrusters would activate. This would show that the Planet Smasher was trying to achieve distance. This would mean that it did not mean us harm. I also looked at my console, which would detect thruster power being engaged. When I saw that its thrusters engaged, I knew that Aurora would be pleased. "They are engaging their thrusters," I said.

Aurora opened her mouth and released a great deal of air. Elyse has told me that humans do this when they feel relief. Humans do many things that I do not understand.

Many humans feel many different ways about death. Some are afraid of it. Some are not. Very few seem to look forward to it. There are some species that do not seem to think of death very much, and there are some that think about it a lot. The Zepzeg think about death a lot. They believe that if they spend their lives looking beautiful, something good will happen to them after they die. I do not understand it, but I have heard Velistris speak of it. They believe that they are born for a reason. The Vorck are born in a pod. Perhaps that means we do not have a reason to live except maybe to not die. I do not know what to think of it, but I think of it often. I have thought of it more since I have lived with humans. Aurora tells me that there is a purpose for me. I believe that my purpose is to fix things. This is why I am called Hank-is-Handy. But she does not think that is my purpose. I do not know how she knows. Maybe her god told her. I know that she has one. She whispers to him in her room. I have heard it many times, but what she says does not make sense. She believes that all species were made by her god. She believes that it is the only one. I suppose this makes the human god the Vorck god. But I do not know why he grows us in pods. Perhaps one day I will know.

No one spoke in the bridge as the Planet Smasher moved farther away. Aurora gave no orders. Everyone only watched it until it was far enough away to enter hyperspace. Only when it disappeared from the bridge monitor did anyone talk again. "All right, crew," said Aurora, "stand down, back to work. Let's hope that's our only proximity overload for the trip."

Velistris did not say anything. She simply walked to the other side of the bridge and looked at the wall. She did not look scared, but she looked upset. The Daldath bother her very much. She does not like to deal with them. Aurora does not like to, either. The Daldath are difficult to deal with. But they are strong. I do not like the Daldath, but I do not hate them. I do not think of them unless they are attacking.

Elyse hit me on the back with her hand. She does this when she wants me to move. "Well, back to the old grease farm," she said. It is what she calls the engine room. I did not say one thing or the other. I only followed her as she walked out of the bridge.

"Have you ever seen a Daldath?" Elyse asked me as we walked through the ship.

I had. But she spoke before I could say so.

"I've never seen one in person, but I've seen pictures. They look…" She shook her head. "Disgusting."

I do not feel disgust, so I did not understand what she meant. She continued to speak of it.

"They look like…some big, exposed internal organ with spider eyes. Except they're like, crab eyes. Then they're all hooked up to this machine, with tentacles, and hoses, and all kinds of things attached to it. It's like this twisted mix of machine and living thing. It's so macabre." For two point one seconds, she said nothing. "Honestly, I think they're kind of zin."

Zin is a word Elyse uses when she likes something. Most humans do not like disgusting things, but some do. Elyse likes them a lot. She likes many things that Aurora and Delta do not.

In describing the Daldath, Elyse did a good job. I do not know how Daldath are born, but at some stage in their life cycle, they become one with a machine. Perhaps they need it to survive. Perhaps it is why they are hungry for minerals, always. They do not care about other species or their worlds. They seek only minerals. Many species hate the Daldath. I understand why they do, even though I do not hate them.

There is one species that Elyse hates, and it is the Collectors. They collect many things throughout the universe. One tried to collect Elyse because she had green hair, but Aurora set her free. This was many years before I joined Aurora's crew. Aurora and Delta do not understand why Elyse keeps her hair green. They do not like it. Elyse has told me that she keeps it green because her mother did not like it, too. Sometimes, humans do things to anger other humans. I do not understand this, but it makes Elyse happy. Elyse does not like it when I click my teeth, so in order to anger her, I once did it for a whole day. It did not make me happy. It did not make Elyse happy, either. Elyse is a human with many contradictions. This is why I learn from her. If I can understand her contradictions, maybe I can understand all humans better.

As we walked into the engine room, she continued to speak of the Daldath. "What do you think they were doing out here? There aren't very many good planets in the Currier Belt."

"Maybe they are looking for a good planet," I answered her. "Perhaps they were on their way to one when we forced each other out of hyperspace." It is not common to see Daldath. They are always moving from world to world, ripping each apart for its resources before moving to the next. The planets they leave behind are broken husks.

"I'd like to talk to a Daldath one day."

It did not seem like a smart idea, so I asked her, "Why?"

She did not answer. Instead, she asked more questions. "Do you think they can suck a person dry like they suck a planet? Could they, like, stab them with some kind of stylet and drink their blood through a straw? Do you think the body would get all wrinkled and caved in? Would anyone even know it was a human afterward?" She shook her head, which sometimes is good and sometimes is bad. "That would be *wicked* zin." This time, shaking her head meant good.

Elyse does not like the things that Aurora and Delta like. Many times, she likes things that they think are bad, like skin drawings, a drink called honeypop, and pictures of things that are dead. I have heard Delta call her a grungy weirdo. Aurora says it means a person that is different and sometimes messy. I suppose I am also a *grungy weirdo*, just like Elyse.

The engine room of the *Illustré* is large. It contains four sections for four different parts of the ship. One is the spindrive chamber, which is where the spindrive is located. Another is the forward screen generator, which is where we were replacing linkages earlier. The forward screens protect the *Illustré* from harm with an invisible energy shield. Another is the blaster turret bay, which maintains the *Illustré*'s only weapon, a top-mounted plasma blaster. The final section of the engine room is the thruster bay, which contains the turbines and burners that allow the *Illustré* to move in space without the spindrive.

The engine room contains many parts. Most of the important ones are very big. I can move some of them, but for others, we use a crane or a gravity lifter. All of the very big parts are too big for Elyse to move, so instead, she fixes wires and components that I cannot reach. Sometimes, she crawls into small holes to fix things that I cannot. It would be very hard for me to maintain the engine room without Elyse, so I am glad that she goes into it with me. It is a feeling that makes me feel good. Elyse says this is called *gratitude*.

Feelings for a Vorck are different from feelings for a human. A human makes many decisions based on feelings. Vorck do not. We do not feel many things at all, but sometimes we feel anger. Elyse is trying to teach me good feelings. She says teaching me good feelings helps her to learn good feelings, too. I think that me and Elyse are not very different in all things.

The hardest feeling for me to feel is amusement. Humans say many things that they say are funny. When a human is amused, they make many quick noises from their mouth that they call *laughter*. I have been trying very hard to master laughing. I believe that I am getting very good at it. I think that next time I laugh, humans will think that I am laughing as good as them.

Elyse walked to the forward screen generator chamber. It is where we were unpacking a linkage before Aurora called for us. As we walked to the linkage, I heard the spindrive engage in the spindrive chamber. It sounds like a hum. That meant that Aurora activated the spindrive from the bridge. We were on our way to the Gryamore System again. Elyse sat down on the floor beside the linkage to finish unwrapping it. We had unwrapped several linkages already, but some remained.

For a moment, Elyse sat quietly on the ground. She does this sometimes when she is about to speak. I have learned to notice it. I was correct this time in predicting it, too. "You know how Velistris always says she hopes she's the most beautiful she's ever been when she dies?"

I did. "Yes."

"I hope I'm a mess."

Her words did not make me feel one way or another. Vorcks do not care how we die. We do not think of death very much at all.

Elyse did not say anything else. She only leaned under the linkage and continued removing its wrapping.

Many times, Elyse gives me things to think about. She gave me some that day, too. I did not know why she thought of death. Maybe the Planet Smasher made her think of it. I also do not know why she hopes to be a mess when she dies. Perhaps by *messy*, she meant covered in grease or engine lubricant, as she often is when she works in the small holes that I cannot reach. Or perhaps, she hopes to have her insides torn apart by a creature, or to be liquefied or exploded. That would not matter to a Vorck, but for a human, I believe that her thinking is strange. But if that is her wish, then if I am there when her time for death comes, I will pull her apart like I did the chair in front of Velistris. Humans do things that other humans wish when they love them. I love Elyse, so I would do this for her. I have not thought about how I would do it. Perhaps that is something I should do. Or perhaps I will ask her what she would want me to do. I will think on it.

Me and Elyse worked in the engine room for many hours. After we unwrapped the linkages and put them away, we did a walkthrough of all of the sections. I do this every day, and most days she comes with me. Most days, she speaks to me. Sometimes, we talk about the engine room. Sometimes, she talks about Aurora or Delta. Many times, she talks about changing her hair from green to purple. I always know when she will talk about this, because first she always asks me if I have ever wanted to try something new. Then she says, "I think I want to dye my hair purple." But she has not yet done it. Humans say they want to do many things they do not do. I have tried to do this myself to fit in more. Last time we spoke of this, I told her that I wanted to become a rock. She told me that I was "off to a good start" because my head was "as thick as one." I felt my head, but it was not thick like a rock. I believe on that day, she was confused. Many things that humans say and do confuse me.

I still have much to learn.

When we finished in the engine room, we went to our separate quarters. Elyse has filled her room with many things that she likes, like incense, things that she has painted, posters with no color of humans doing things, and jars of small, dead animals. I do not have anything in my room except for a bed and an enzyme transfuser, which I connect to the attachment points on my chest. These points are where I was connected to the growth pod while I was in development. All Vorck are fed through them throughout their lives. We cannot eat or drink, though I have tried. Elyse once gave me a human food called *cuminash*, which is made of mushed up potatoes and a spice called cumin, but I could not swallow it. She says it has a good taste, but I do not know what taste is, and the cuminash did not give me any feelings. I think I would like to taste something someday. But I know it is something I will never do.

Perhaps I am more human than I thought.

For many hours, I stood in my room, attached to the transfuser while my body was replenished. Sometimes, I looked around. But mostly, I was still. When the transfusion was finished, I walked to the other side of the room for a while. Sometimes, I look at the wall. Sometimes, I look at the transfuser. Aurora put a mirror on my wall, so sometimes I look at myself. She has told me to use it to find the worth in my eyes. Because of this, I look at my reflection often. But I have only seen my face.

Aurora says that all beings have a soul. Of all the things I do not understand about human beliefs, this is what I understand the least. She says that my soul is inside of me. But I have never felt it. Perhaps one day it will move, and I will feel it. Until that day, I will continue to look at the mirror to see if I can find what Aurora wants me to find. Perhaps if I watch hard enough, I will find it. Or perhaps, I will just be Hank-is-Handy.

That is okay with me, too.

Chapter Three

THE FIRST THOUGHT that entered my mind when I heard the *Illustré*'s klaxons blaring through the hallways was, "please, let it not be the Daldath!"

Warning! Proximity overload detected. Warning! Proximity overload detected.

It is an automated and dreadfully voiced message that can mean anything at all. Perhaps we'd just been attacked by pirates. Perhaps we'd passed too closely to an asteroid. Perhaps Hank-is-Handy in all its moronic wisdom improperly calibrated the sensors. How I prayed that it was the latter!

The last time such an alarm had sounded, I had been in the bridge with Aurora. We had seen together the gigantic, horrible Planet Smasher appear in our bridge monitor as the *Illustré* dropped out of hyperspace. I have a history with those reprehensible beings—one I never wish to relive. As my delicate, crystalline spindles carried me toward the bridge, all I could think was that the Daldath must've had a change in heart and decided to destroy us. My body was unpolished, my angles desperately in need of a smoothening. I was in no condition *whatsoever* to meet my end!

As I carefully crossed the threshold to the bridge, I saw Aurora sitting squarely in the captain's chair, its hands gripping the armrests in the white-knuckled way that humans do when situations are dire. I could not restrain myself. I had to ask at once. "Is it the Daldath?"

Aurora barely afforded me a glance. "I don't know what it is. Look!" It pointed to the bridge monitor, where I immediately turned my beautiful head. There, directly in front of the *Illustré*, were the flashing bright lights of space combat. A mere second later, Aurora addressed the rest of the crew through the speakers. "All hands, you are needed on deck! Where is everyone?"

Without wasting another moment, I hurried to the communications console—my station on the bridge. There was no time to waste. Death loomed before us, and I quickly needed to act! Situating myself into my custom-made polyfurrite harness, I activated its built-in sliding vanity mirror.

Aurora was prattling on about something or other behind me—to be honest, I was scarcely paying attention. Something about the forward screens, and thruster power, and evasive action. It was all quite irritating.

My heart stopped as I inspected my lower-right cheek line, whereupon I discovered the most garish of blemishes. I'd buffed there only two days prior! This was a catastrophe.

You may be wondering what happens to a Zepzeg when it dies unbecomingly. Well, I shall tell you, for it is no small matter. Upon death, if we have not pleased Deity in the way in which we've bodily prepared, we are stripped of our consciousness, our bodies left behind as hollow shells, no lifeveins to be found and left for all eternity to drift as litter among the cosmic dust. Perhaps we drift into a star. Perhaps we are devoured by a singularity. Perhaps we are collected by some interstellar craftsman, cut down into fragments, and sold as fashion effects. It is quite possible that I, myself, have seen my own lifeless brethren dangling from the necklines and earlobes of those who've received my beauty treatments. Perhaps even Aurora's own jewelry collection has the remnants of a Zepzeg that failed to pass Deity's muster. Forgotten in boxes, covered in dust, our luster having long faded into oblivion. Oh the humility of such a fate! May I never be forced to endure it.

The *Illustré* shimmied as its reverse thrusters engaged, the tremors rattling the frame of the mirror as to render it useless for the purpose of seeing one's reflection. That blemish, that unholy imperfection! I could envision my shards now, dangling from the inflated proboscis of some Yaddith gypsy or stapled to the nipple of some asymmetrical Venge strumpet. The absolute horror!

"Not too close, not too close!" Aurora was yelling from its chair, gesticulating wildly with its hands as if someone was there to hear it. It was right then that I noticed Hank-is-Handy and its grimy counterpart, Elyse, manning their respective consoles at the back of the bridge. In the midst of my impending damnation, I hadn't even noticed their entry. I turned my head to the bridge monitor, where the most peculiar space battle was unfurling. Ships—the smallest, bluest little ships—were buzzing about furiously in every direction, as if we'd suddenly passed through some sort of swarm. What manner of havoc was this?

Delta came skedaddling through the door, its eyes wide with fright as it slid into its station, which was, of course, purely decorative, for Delta serves no purpose aside from aesthetics. Behind it, that slime-tongued little monstrosity, Riley, followed. "Aunt Aurora, what's happening?" Delta asked. Despite the very real prospect of displeasing Deity, I was delighted that I might hear whatever it was that I'd missed whilst my focus was averted.

"We got pulled out of hyperspace again!"

"By those things?" Delta asked, pointing to the ships. I would have rolled my eyes had I possessed them. As if *things* could mean anything else.

Hank-is-Handy answered—out of turn, naturally. "Many small ships are attacking a medium one. Perhaps we passed too close."

As clear as Hank-is-Handy said it, I could see it. We were definitely not the target—or at least, the intended one. The bridge monitor zoomed in on the cosmic fracas, where the medium-sized ship—a clunky, purple thing so hideously lacking in appeasing curvature that I wondered, "Why even build it?"—was being assailed by a squadron of smaller spacecraft.

"Hank-is-Handy, are any of these things pulling up on the database?" Aurora asked.

"No. They are unknown."

The purple ship was sparking and shaking. Though it fired upon its adversaries, there were far too many of them to be overcome. It was only a matter of time until it would be destroyed. All the better, for then we might be able to resume our journey. But alas, it was not meant to be.

"Some of the smaller ships are turning to us. We are being scanned."

"What are they scanning?" Aurora asked.

Much to my surprise, it was my own station—communications—that was showing signs of being scanned. "It appears they are accessing our language files," I said dutifully. It was a clear sign that they wished to communicate. Sure enough, within seconds, a hailing prompt was received. "We are being hailed."

Aurora wasted no time in placating their request. "Put them on, Velistris!"

"As you wish, captain." Passing their request through to the bridge monitor, I watched as the view of the star battle disappeared, replaced by not one window, but four smaller ones all across the display. In the center of each window was a being, each indistinguishable from one another, each bouncing up and down like springy little stalks of grass—or in their case, stalks of green, twisting flesh. At the top of each stalk stared a single, bulbous eye. The very moment I saw them, I recognized them—they are among the galaxy's most disreputable and annoying pirates. "The Vorticella," I said, unable to hold back the words.

Behind me, Aurora sounded surprised. "You know these things?"

"Yes. They are merciless pirates who hail from the Ragnarok Cluster, among others. I have never seen them in our cluster before, but I have seen them."

"What's your three-word assessment?"

Quite firmly, I answered, "Unrelenting little pests."

As they bounced up and down like little springs, the one-eyed creatures spoke through the *Illustré*'s onboard translator— the very one that they themselves had accessed. They spoke in four distinct voices—one proper, one vigorous, one shrilly, one drab—as if the translator had tried to ascribe to them personality but only succeeded in creating a cacophonic mishmash. Each spoke one after the other, their thoughts seemingly in unison—as if they were one body made of many.

"We are the noble Vorticella!"

"You are unfit to cleanse the dust beneath us—"

"—you meek and inferior beings."

"Jettison your cargo or die!"

Aurora said, "We have no cargo that would be of any worth to you. Please allow us to go on our way!"

I feared for a moment that Aurora might try something magnanimous and attempt to rescue the purple ship, but thankfully, its priorities were in check.

The beings answered, "We have scanned your ship."

"You have many valuable components!"

"Please jettison these components so that we might collect them."

"Or face annihilation—whichever is preferable to you!"

Aurora spoke, its voice growing firm. "You may find us more formidable than we appear, Vorticella. We are not to be trifled with."

Their stalks stood erect, their unblinking eyes stared onward. "You have made your choice."

"Prepare for joyous vaporization!"

The monitor went black, the four windows disappearing

as the space battle once again took front and center on the bridge monitor. As the purple ship struggled to break free from the collection of pirate spacecraft, four of them broke off to approach the *Illustré*.

Aurora's response was immediate. "Launch the twins!" Behind it, Hank-is-Handy's knobby hands worked the weapons console.

The twins, more properly referred to as Castor and Pollux, are fully-automated strike craft. Many ships carry such small spacecraft to assist in combat situations such as these. Not all are unmanned, of course, but being as the living arrangements in the *Illustré* are so cramped, it is the only option that makes any sort of practical sense, lest we sacrifice our own meager chambers to house egomaniacal fighter pilots.

I watched as Castor and Pollux were deployed, their slender, aerodynamic forms streaking off toward the rapidly approaching Vorticella fighters. I have always appreciated humanity's consideration toward the aesthetic when it comes to their space fighters. Though a spacecraft need not have a pointed nose or sleekly curved wings in the vacuum of space, it makes for a much more delightful visual display than, say, a hideous cube or some other obtuse eyesore. If one must joust, joust with style.

I am not a fan of combat. It does not cater to my areas of expertise. I do enjoy, however, seeing the occasional space pirate explode into particle-sized bits. And it is for that reason that I watched lustily as Castor and Pollux veered in formation to begin their initial attack run. Bursts of plasma streaked back and forth as the twins engaged, their Vorticella targets turning to intercept. At the same time, Hank-is-Handy fired the *Illustré*'s own plasma blaster, targeting one of the Vorticella just as it made its turn for the twins. There was a great explosion as the Vorticella fighter was struck, its fragments dispersing in every direction.

"Aurora," said Hank-is-Handy from its console, "the medium spacecraft is disappearing."

"Disappearing?" asked Aurora incredulously. "What do you mean?"

The bridge monitor shifted to show a close-up of the purple vessel that the Vorticella had been attacking. As sure as Hank-is-Handy was an idiot, it was disappearing from sight! A different kind of spindrive, perhaps? No, that was impossible. This spacecraft was cloaking! In the next second, it had vanished, its discombobulated pursuers scattering in every direction as if terrified one of them might smack into the invisible ship.

The monitor zoomed back out, the full scope of the battle returning to our sight. Castor and Pollux were still weaving, plasma was still streaking in every direction as they and the *Illustré* engaged the Vorticella. But now, a horrible twist had befallen us! The pirates that had been in pursuit of the missing purple spacecraft—a far greater mustering than the four adversaries we'd been facing—turned their sights toward the *Illustré*. In disappearing from view, that miserable purple ship had made us the pirates' sole target!

From its honorary display station, Delta gasped. "Are they all now coming for *us*?"

Aurora was quick to divvy commands. "Focus fire on those first three! There's no time for evasive action—drop them as quickly as possible!"

I understood what Aurora must have been thinking. The more spacecraft the *Illustré* had to defend against, the worse were its chances to survive. Even if an outright charge against these three put the *Illustré* in more danger, it was imperative that the Vorticella's numbers be diminished before the full brunt of their force reached us.

"Hank-is-Handy, how many new fighters are approaching?" Aurora asked.

"I detect nine."

Nine! With the three initial fighters that remained, that made twelve in totality. How was the *Illustré* to defeat such a ravenous pack? My molecules trembling, I held on tightly to my console station.

This is, of course, where the less diplomatic of my counterparts have a chance to excel. For as savage as Hank-is-Handy may be and as aesthetically irrelevant as Elyse has made itself, when it comes to the primitive art of warfare, there are few who can match the synchronicity of their simple minds. Just as Castor and Pollux pivoted around to find another Vorticella fighter, Hank-is-Handy managed to blow two of them out of the stars just as they lined up their weapons to fire upon the *Illustré*. The Vorticella's shots smashed against the *Illustré*'s forward screens, dissipating into nothingness. Elyse, meanwhile, was sliding its hands furiously up and down its own console station, which controls both the direction and power of the screens as well as the general allocation of power to the ship's systems.

All of this, of course, frees up Aurora to do what it does best, which is pilot the *Illustré*. It is not often that the good captain must take manual control of the ship's thrusters, but when it must, it is as fine a captain as the most apt of starpilots. From what I have perceived, piloting the *Illustré* involves each hand taking hold of some sort of lever and maneuvering them either forwards and backwards or to the left and right. From my vantage point, it has always seemed quite complicated, and it is something I wish to never attempt myself. Aurora has stated that its aspirations are for Delta to someday take on the role of starpilot and captain, though I can attest from firsthand experience that the young human has a long way to go—though to its credit, it does try.

Just beyond the two ships that Hank-is-Handy had destroyed, a third blast erupted. Castor and Pollux had hit their mark. With the four Vorticella fighters that had initially attacked us vanquished, there remained only the nine that had been pursuing the purple spacecraft.

"There are too many for the twins to waste time double-teaming," said Aurora. "Set them to solo mode!"

From the back of the bridge, Elyse acknowledged it with an affirmative, "Solo mode activated!"

As the two strike fighters broke out of formation to engage independently, Aurora brought the *Illustré*'s nose around to face the Vorticella fighters. But alas, the fighters had already fired, and a wave of energized plasma struck the *Illustré*'s forward screens. They flashed—how the very ship itself trembled! In a single tidal wave of fire, the entire forward screens had been rendered inoperable!

"We've got trouble!" said Elyse.

Aurora's voice was determined. "Yeah, so do they!"

Few species can match the bluster of humans. In my experience, I have learned that few humans actually believe they are ever going to die, despite the overwhelming evidence—such as their consistent dying—that suggests otherwise. Aurora is no exception, though at least its bluster is accompanied by a measure of skill.

With its hands yanking on its joysticks, it brought the *Illustré* rolling around, then pitched its nose down, which offered Hank-is-Handy an open field with which to engage the top-mounted plasma blaster. And engage, it did, firing off a series of shots that smashed into no fewer than two of the Vorticella fighters—though the exposure was not without consequence. With the screens already diminished in power, the wave of plasma blasts that struck the *Illustré* had little to penetrate before doing actual damage. As the ship shimmied, an array of red lights appeared on the spacecraft's damage indicator. Just before the Vorticella fighters would have smashed into the ship themselves, they split into a variety of directions.

"Another down!" Elyse said, announcing a kill that was made by one of the twins, before its voice grew more distressed.

"But Castor is damaged!"

"Damaged?" asked Aurora.

The green-haired monstrosity faced it. "Not destroyed, but badly wounded! Too badly to fight."

"Five fighters remain," announced Hank-is-Handy. "They are coming near again from many angles. I cannot engage them all."

"Put Castor in kamikaze mode!" Aurora said. "Hank-is-Handy, take as many as you can."

I watched as Elyse grimaced. It had grown quite fond of the twins, and it was clearly not pleased with the prospect of sending one of them on a self-destruct mission to ram into an enemy fighter. For a moment, it hesitated.

"Kamikaze mode, *now*!" yelled Aurora.

Blowing its hair from its face, for it had become quite disheveled in all the sudden commotion, Elyse said, "Kamikaze mode activated."

Once more, Hank-is-Handy fired, and once more the *Illustré* was struck from various directions by the Vorticella fighters. More red damage indicators appeared. How violently the ship was shaken! Was this the end? Was I truly going to meet Deity now? Was my one blemish too much for it to overlook, for one blemish is all it takes to fall out of Deity's favor! What an inordinate burden we must bear!

"I have missed!" announced Hank-is-Handy. "They are too agile in close combat."

Plasma fire struck the *Illustré* once more, throwing poor Delta from its console. The rest of us were jostled at our stations—hair was strewn about the humans' faces. Aurora flung its red curls out of its eyes. "Is Pollux even engaging? Where is Castor?"

"Pollux can't find position!" answered Elyse. "Castor's too slow to ram any of the fighters!"

The twins were failing. Hank-is-Handy was missing. The Vorticella were swarming around again.

It was truly the end.

Suddenly, just as two of the Vorticella fighters were curling around to come at the *Illustré* head on, something appeared out of the darkness just off the starboard bow. Its angle brought it on a direct intercept course with the pirates. We held our breath in the bridge as it unleashed bolts of energy at the approaching fighters.

The purple ship. It had reappeared—and it was helping us!

In a bright flash, one of the unsuspecting Vorticella fighters was struck, careening sideways into the one beside it—two destroyed in a single blow!

"Take Castor off kamikaze," ordered Aurora, the firmness returning to its voice. "I want all forces targeting those last two fighters!"

"Kamikaze mode off!" proclaimed Elyse joyfully. In front of it, Hank-is-Handy targeted the last two fighters and unleashed the *Illustré*'s fury with the ship's blaster. Plasma blasts soared toward the Vorticella fighters. Castor and Pollux reengaged. The dark, purple ship joined the fight.

For what must've been thirty seconds, the space around us was alight with all manner of weaponized energy, with bolts and blasts streaking to and fro as the last Vorticella fighters struggled to outmaneuver the veritable avalanche of fire beading at them. At long last, they got the message. This was not a fight they were going to win! The two pirates tore off, their little ships abandoning their attack as they hastily retreated.

On our bridge monitor, their one-eyed, peduncle forms appeared as they hailed us. Their interchanging voices, indistinguishable from the ones we'd heard earlier, spoke in shared unison. "Two species against one!"

"How cowardly, how dishonorable!"

"The noble Vorticella will not soon forget this."

No sooner had they finished speaking did their loathsome figures disappear from our monitor, their ships fading in the distance as their powerful thrusters propelled them away.

There was scarcely enough time to register the Vorticella's hasty retreat before another impending threat emerged—this time from the purple ship that had lent its assistance. Climbing back behind its console, Delta pointed ahead at the bridge monitor and shouted, "Look!"

The spacecraft was vibrating, the sparking and shimmying of its hull growing more violent with each passing moment. It was about to explode!

Grabbing hold of the controls, Aurora shouted, "Hold on!" before shifting the *Illustré* into full reverse. Despite the dreadfully pitiful whine of the *Illustre*'s damaged engines, our ship thrust backwards out of harm's way.

I must admit, as I watched the purple ship slowly erupt, I felt the smallest tinge of guilt for whatever crew was meeting their demise on board. There was no question that the proximity overload that'd pulled us into their little skirmish with the Vorticella had saved their lives, and in turn they came to our aid to save ours. Were it not for them, I would surely have met Deity with that damnable blemish. Perhaps it was sadness that I felt—primarily a human construct but one that I've occasionally experienced. The poor, poor beings on board that vessel. I hoped, for their sake, that they were beautiful.

It was right then, in the seconds before the ship exploded, that we saw a small, spherical pod jettison from its hull. Though we all saw it together, Delta clearly felt the need to do its favorite thing and point out the obvious. "An escape pod!" It'd barely gotten the words out when the purple ship exploded, its pieces bursting into shrapnel and peppering the *Illustré*'s hull.

Within seconds of the shockwave passing us, Aurora asked its elder niece for a status.

"No additional damage from the explosion," Elyse answered. "Same goes for the twins. I'm recalling them now."

"Where's the escape pod?" Aurora asked, rising from its chair to survey the space before us. Nothing but remnants of the destroyed ship could be seen.

After a long pause, Aurora received an answer. "I have detected the pod," said Hank-is-Handy. Moments later, the bridge monitor shifted to show the spherical pod drifting aimlessly away.

"The moment the twins are in, position the *Illustré* to retrieve that pod. Whoever is in there risked their lives to save us. We're not leaving without returning the favor."

Aurora was, of course, erred in its sense of fairness. We had already saved the being in the pod once when we were dropped out of hyperspace. It was the purple ship that'd returned the favor by intercepting the Vorticella that were attacking us. In my perfect mind, all was fair and the two parties could depart—us to our negotiation and the being in the escape pod to starvation in the void of space—with no feelings of indebtedness one way or the other. Such sound reasoning surely would not dissuade Aurora, however, and so I kept the wisdom of my deductions to myself.

Within minutes, Castor and Pollux had returned to the ship, and we were on our way to retrieve the utterly helpless pod.

It is never a surprise when I encounter species that, up until the time I encounter them, had only existed in clusters far, far away. Take the Zevolt, for instance. They ruled the Sassanid Cluster with an iron claw before their reign was upended and they abandoned the Sassanid for surrounding star clusters. The larger species in the cosmos are always moving from cluster to cluster, be it to find new territory to settle, to escape rising threats in their previous clusters, or simply to explore for the sake of exploration.

So understand, then, that it was not at all unusual to come across an unknown spacecraft such as the purple one that'd helped us battle the Vorticella. Space is an infinitely vast expanse, and even though species tend to gather and settle inside star clusters, there are countless species the galaxy over that exist in the many pockets of habitability that are scattered here and there. Humanity, in fact, is one of them. I could only assume that the inhabitant of the pod we were rescuing would be another.

The wonder with which humans approach unknown species has always fascinated me, for despite their knowledge that the cosmos is filled with all manner of life, they still act surprised when new life is discovered—as if they actually believed for a time that all life had been catalogued and there was nothing new to set their eyes upon. All three humans displayed this same wild-eyed exuberance as they hurried through the hallways toward the small docking bay, where a tractor beam was already retrieving the pod.

The lack of wonder concerning these things is another attribute I share with Hank-is-Handy, who always looks like an emotionless, wrinkled ape regardless of what is set before it. Though I do not take pride in sharing any attribute with the Vorck, this is, at least, one in which we can look upon humanity with a shared curiosity and perhaps even envy. To be moved or startled by every new discovery. I cannot fathom it, but a small fraction of me wishes to.

And as for Riley, that little monstrous dog, well, it seems surprised about everything.

The spherical escape pod was already in the retrieval bay, which is a small, sectioned-off portion of the docking bay specifically for holding things that have been dragged aboard from the inhospitable interstellar medium. It was not a particularly large sphere—neither myself nor Hank-is-Handy would fit in it, though I imagined a human could, given their limber composition.

Despite the assistance provided by whatever creature was inside the sphere, the humans still approached it with an air of understandable caution. I, of course, would not go near the pod, choosing instead to stay many meters behind my human counterparts. With its hand near the holster of its pristine, white hand blaster, Aurora signaled for Hank-is-Handy to stand ready. Retrieving an obtuse and unsightly construction device called a *phase hammer*, Hank-is-Handy recharged it and stood beside Elyse, its soulless eyes seemingly transfixed on the slight indentations that identified the pod's imbedded door.

"Stand ready, everyone," Aurora said. "I'm sending the invite." Walking to a console set aside by the interior retrieval bay door, it moved a lever down and up two times, sending a pair of resonance pulses into the pod's hull.

Though not a purely human custom, the act of sending a pair of resonance pulses into the hull of a rescued vessel was nonetheless invented by them. Humans have a phrase that the females have repeated many times that goes, "knock before entering." It is a phrase often shouted at Hank-is-Handy upon its entering their chambers when they are unprepared, never more vehemently than when one of them is changing clothes or has emerged from one of their strange water dousings. The act of cleansing oneself with water is quite curious to me. We Zepzeg, of course, do not permit grime and general muck to touch our perfect, crystalline skin; therefore, we need no such water cleansing as the grime is buffed off at once. Humans, however, seem to seep some sort of oil from their pores, most noticeably after they have done something strenuous, though it seeps regardless over time. Every day, all three of the humans strip themselves of their garments and—for lack of a better way to put it—drench themselves to remove the oil from their bodies. It remains quite astounding to me that humans have not cured this ailment or at the very least found a way to alter their genetic code to prevent this oil from developing in the first place.

I have suggested many times to Aurora that Hank-is-Handy be watered off, as perhaps this would tame its stench, but the captain has made it abundantly clear that partaking in such a ritual is Hank-is-Handy's decision alone. The insufferable Vorck despises being wet, so I see no salvation from its olfactory torture in any near future. I once witnessed Elyse position a bucket of water precariously on a shelf near the top of Delta's chamber door, which with some sort of string line caused it to dump its contents atop Delta's head upon it entering its room. Elyse got great joy in the act, so I can only presume that it must have found Delta's skin oil quite unpleasant to its sensitive nostrils and decided that it needed a cleaning. Delta, of course, was quite incensed about the matter and shouted colorfully at Elyse in return. The two did not speak for days. Perhaps such an experiment would work to clean Hank-is-Handy. Though if I were to attempt it, I might consider a mild acidic—not enough to make a mess, but perhaps just enough to kill it.

But I digress.

Almost two minutes passed after the pair of resonance pulses were sent, that particular custom apparently unknown to the pod's occupant. Aurora leaned closer to the pod, but then glanced back at me. "Velistris, you've never seen anything like this before, have you?"

With the widespread clientele that Zepzeg possess, there are few vessels in the cosmos that we haven't seen. This, unfortunately, was one of them. "I have never seen such a pod or a ship."

"All right, Hank-is-Handy, what do you think?"

"Perhaps there is no life in it," the Vorck answered. "Perhaps it was too close to the ship when it exploded."

I decided to insert my superior wisdom. "It is likely a visitor from another cluster—a cluster with no such custom of sending two resonance pulses to indicate an invitation." It was such an obvious answer, but humans do not often grasp the obvious. The obvious, on the other hand, is all the Vorck grasp at all.

It was at that very moment that a tremendous and awful hissing sound emerged from the pod. All of the humans leapt backward as steam blew from the indentations on its surface. Slowly, the door began to protrude and lift.

"Everyone, get back!" said Aurora, waving its arms to indicate to Delta and Elyse that they were to do precisely what it told them to do. Humans do not perceive well and often require a variety of audible and visual cues to follow instruction.

Delta ran hastily away, positioning itself partially behind a crate and craning its neck out to see as Riley followed behind it. Elyse, quite diametrically, took two simple steps backward.

No sooner had the protruding door slid upward than two small, furry creatures darted from within it! One blue and one pink, the two long-eared critters zipped like little electric bolts past Hank-is-Handy, chirping wildly as the Vorck turned with as much speed as it could manage to catch them, which was to say, no speed at all. The three humans whipped their heads around to follow the pair of creatures. Delta naturally screamed in terror whilst Riley barked and gave chase. Aurora shouted orders to surround them, Elyse retorted with some sort of gibberish, and for a moment, all was thrust into pandemonium.

Being the most astute of all potential observers, I was, of course, the only one to notice the waist-high creature emerging from the pod behind the distracted throng. There were no discernable legs on the plant-like being, which had the body structure of misshapen, hunched over moss. Its leafy flesh was many shades of purple, much like the spacecraft that'd been destroyed, and a pair of small red eyes glowed from within its mouthless, hooded body. As it slid from the pod like an upright gastropod, it waved some sort of body-length, flagellum-like appendage from side to side. As the only crew member with my wits still about it, I felt it my obligation to draw attention to the creature before it devoured one of the humans. Lifting my delicate arm, I pointed at the pod. "Behold. A lifeform emerges."

The equanimity of my delivery was of no use whatsoever. The three humans spun toward the escape pod with such heedlessness that their collective motion startled the creature, prompting it to slink back to the corner of the hangar with surprising deftness. As its oversized flagellum swayed wildly back and forth like a warning arm, it croaked lowly and repeatedly, obviously some form of underdeveloped communication. The two small, furry creatures were promptly forgotten by all parties but Riley, who'd disappeared after them further into the ship, barking like an idiot. As for the rest of us, we watched this new, strange creature as its red eyes surveyed us. It continued to croak on.

Raising its phase hammer, Hank-is-Handy asked Aurora, "Would you like me to kill it?"

I prayed that it would, for this creature seemed an irredeemably primitive mess.

With a calm hand extended, Aurora said to the Vorck, "Hold still for a moment." Despite its words to Hank-is-Handy, its eyes were solely on the lifeform. Taking a slow, steady step forward, it opened its palm toward the being and said, "My name is Aurora. Thank you for saving our ship." Its words were careful, precise. "We mean you no harm."

Clearly cowering in fright, its body trembled as its red eyes shifted from person to person. Its flagellum retracted as it continued to croak.

Elyse, in all its green-haired daftness, actually approached the thing. "Do you have a name?"

"Elyse..." warned Aurora, eyes shifting between its rebellious niece and the lifeform.

Kneeling down mere feet from the huddled creature, Elyse looked back at Aurora and rolled its eyes. "Come on, look at the thing. It's terrified." It looked back at the being as it croaked in response. "He's attacked by the Vorticella, his ship explodes, all of a sudden he's sucked into here and surrounded by all of us. He doesn't know what to think." Slowly, Elyse's lips curled upward. "I actually think he's kind of cute."

From far behind us, Delta shouted, "You would, you weirdo!"

"I really don't think you should get that close," said Aurora again.

"Ugh." Elyse looked back at it. "If it wanted to attack us, it would have already—"

It attacked! Its flagellum lashed out, coiling around Elyse's body like a constrictor. The next thing we saw was Elyse being jerked toward the being as a gaping mouth appeared. Elyse's head was enveloped, and the two of them, now attached, tumbled across the docking bay floor.

"*Elyse!*" shouted Aurora as Delta gasped behind us. Hank-is-Handy raised its phase hammer to fire, but Aurora quickly stopped it. "No! You'll hit her!"

The pair rolled across the floor, Elyse's muffled screams scarcely audible as it fought to pull its head from the being's mouth. Elyse kicked, grabbed, and tugged at the creature's mossy skin until at long last, after planting its feet against the creature, it summoned the strength to free itself. With a revolting *slur-plop*, Elyse yanked itself out. Its head covered in a most disgusting purple ooze, Elyse scampered away as the gastropod slithered back to its corner.

Grabbing Elyse by the arm, Aurora dragged it back to safety, ooze flying about as Elyse slung it desperately from its head. Hank-is-Handy wasted no time; the brute lifted its phase hammer and aimed it at the now huddling plant creature. As the Vorck prepared to fire its savage death device, the creature waved its flagellum frantically back and forth.

"I not meaning harm! I needing learn speaking!"

I could scarcely believe my resonance nodes! The being... it spoke! In the most pitiful, simplistic, simpering little voice, it spoke! There was no mouth visible, no means by which it could produce such a sound. Was this telepathy? Sorcery? Madness affecting us all? Aurora heard it, as well, its eyes widening as it stared at the trembling, purple thing.

Naturally, no revelation could dissuade the oafish Hank-is-Handy from committing to violence. With the phase hammer ready, it prepared to strike the creature right between its eyes.

"*Wait!*" Aurora shouted loudly, abandoning its gunk-covered niece to practically leap in front of the phase hammer mere attoseconds before Hank-is-Handy would have pulled the trigger. "Stop! Don't shoot!"

Behind Aurora, the cowering creature trembled.

Hank-is-Handy was defiant. "I will pulverize this creature's dumb plant head."

I was flabbergasted. Since when did the amoebic brain of Hank-is-Handy learn such a word as *pulverize*? It was so descriptive—far more so than the typical monosyllabic drivel it spewed.

Unfazed by the Vorck's evolutionary leap, Aurora said, "Hank-is-Handy, *put that weapon down now!*"

There is a little secret among the more learned that Vorck are susceptible to verbal coercion. When confronted with bluster, they often relent. As soon as Aurora berated it, Hank-is-Handy powered down the phase hammer and lowered it to its side, though in its eyes, I detected a glint of anger.

"Seriously?" asked Elyse, whose moist green locks were plastered down around its head. Pointing its finger accusingly at the plant thing, it said, "That thing just *ate* me!"

Once more, the being spoke, an eeriness to its disembodied speech. "I not eating. I very much learning! I speaking in way you understanding. I talking very good, yes?"

Elyse slung a glop of goo from its head to the floor. "I mean, what even *is* this? Is it acid? You don't know! What if it melts my skin?"

"Elyse, enough!" said Aurora.

"Aunt Aurora—"

"I said *enough*!"

The plant being interrupted, its flagellum waving as its red, glowing eyes looked Elyse's way. "I not being made of acid. You being foolish, indeed! You amusing me."

"I'm glad sucking on my head is to your amusement, thing!" Elyse snapped.

Aurora approached the being, crouching down to its level though staying considerably farther away than Elyse had, obviously concerned that it might mess up its hair, which I must say looked immaculate. Tilting its head a bit as if to scrutinize the creature, Aurora asked it, "When you...sucked her in...were you trying to learn how she communicated?"

Dare I say, the thing's red eyes seemed proud. "You being correct! I learning much from her mind. I learning all sorts of things."

Casting a look back at Hank-is-Handy, Aurora said, "You see, Hank-is-Handy? It wasn't attacking; it was trying to communicate."

Even I had to admit, it was an impressive biological feat. This was far superior to its irritating croaking. Hank-is-Handy, of course, did not look impressed.

"What's your name?" Aurora asked.

"I being Blepharisma," the thing answered.

So childlike, this thing seemed. I felt that Aurora sensed it, too. After seeming to mull over its thoughts, Aurora said to it, "Thank you for helping us in combat, Blepharisma. You saved our lives." Aurora now spoke to it as if it were part child—a clear indication that we shared similar sentiments. "Blepharisma," Aurora whispered to itself, turning its head away. "I feel like I've heard that before."

"Everyone always attacking me," Blepharisma said. "Nobody liking me. Everybody hating me. I needing a friend very badly. I enjoying potential friendship with you. Please agree to being my friend. Yes?"

Looking back at the thing, Aurora asked, "Why does everyone hate you?"

"I knowing not why everybody being hating me. I trying being likeable. I trying giving gifts. I trying everything. But they not liking me. You liking me?"

Once more, Aurora mulled—though this time, not for as long. A smile of sympathy emerged on its lips—more a decision, it seemed, than an emotion. "Yes, we like you."

Elyse wiped its hair back. "Unbelievable."

"*We*. Like. You," Aurora said, its voice low and threatening as it cast a warning look back at Elyse.

They locked eyes for a moment before Elyse sighed. "Of course," it said in defeat. "Yes, we like you."

Oblivious to their subterfuge, Blepharisma said, "I being very, very grateful. I liking you very much. You pleasing me!" Dare I say, there was genuine joy in its glowing, red eyes. It was quite pitiful to see.

Hesitating for a moment, Aurora extended its hand. When Blepharisma looked at it curiously, Aurora said, "It's a pleasure to meet you, Blepharisma. My name is Aurora. Welcome aboard the *Illustré*." It smiled. "It's customary for new friends to shake hands. I'd like to shake yours." When Blepharisma's flagellum protruded to reach it, Aurora said quickly, "Just, please don't inhale my head. I like my hair the way it is."

It overjoyed me to hear! I'd worked so hard on it.

The flagellum touched Aurora's open palm, and the captain wrapped its fingers around it. With a single, understated shake, it smiled then let the flagellum go. Nodding its head sideways in the direction of the ship's interior, Aurora asked, "So you want to help me find your two little friends who scurried off into my ship?"

"They being my blue pet Slarb and my pink pet Gralb! I being happy to find them."

Rising to its feet, Aurora gestured for Blepharisma to follow. "Come, then. Let's track them down before Riley gives them a heart attack." As it turned to depart, Aurora offered the rest of us a look of placation. "If you all don't mind, we've got to get back into hyperspace. After the four of you secure Blepharisma's escape pod, I want Elyse and Hank-is-Handy to give me a status on the engine room. I need to know how badly the Vorticella damaged us. Delta and Velistris, as soon as you two are done helping here, I want you to prepare one of the suites for our new guest. Any problems with all that?"

A foolish question for it to ask, for I have presented to it many problems in the past, none of which were adequately remedied.

Elyse raised its hand. "Umm, yeah, can I clean off, first?"

"No."

"Seriously?"

The captain's eyes narrowed. "Every minute here is a minute we're not in hyperspace. Not only is the negotiation waiting, but the Vorticella could come back at any minute. I'm sorry, but a shower can wait." It took a half step back before it smirked. "Besides, it's a good look for you."

Beneath the still oozing…ooze, Elyse glowered. I must confess, I felt a tinge of sympathy for the creature. I myself could have never tolerated being covered in such goo for any period of time.

"Any other questions?" This time, none were posed. "Very well, then. Come on, Blepharisma, let's go." With no further words to us, Aurora led the being out of the docking bay.

Several seconds passed after Aurora left before Delta emerged from its hiding place to approach Elyse. The younger female's eyes latched upon its slime-drenched elder. With a final check to ensure that Aurora was out of its earshot, Delta released a cackle the likes of which only a human could produce.

Wiping its face and slinging glop down, Elyse shook its head murderously. "Oh, you laugh."

Delta did so—repeatedly. So much so, in fact, that it prompted Hank-is-Handy, in all of its insufferable obliviousness, to try its own hand at laughter in a manner that sounded absolutely horrifying. "Ha." Its unblinking white eyes swiveled from Elyse, to Delta, then back to Elyse again, who it then pointed to. "Ha. Ha. Ha."

"Sure, why not?" asked Elyse, though I suspect its words were that strange thing called *sarcasm*. "Take a good look, everyone. Laugh it up. Get it all out your systems."

"You look lovely," said Delta. "The best you've looked in years."

"Ha. Ha. Ha. Ha. Ha."

Elyse snarled at the Vorck. "Oh, shut up, Hank-is-Handy. You don't even know what you're doing."

"Ha. Ha. Ha."

Eventually, their superfluous banter ended, and we began the process of securing Blepharisma's escape pod for proper travel. Delta and I, of course, supervised the ordeal. Elyse and Hank-is-Handy did adequately in their work, though I did offer several suggestions, none of which were adhered to or seemingly appreciated. Humans are quite a selfish species, I have learned, stubbornly insisting on doing things their own way even when in the presence of perfect creations willing to offer their insight. I sometimes wonder why I bother at all. They could have at least thanked me for supervising their efforts, though naturally they showed no gratitude whatsoever. At the very least, they performed their tasks without torturing me with their typical, miserable grumbling.

I suppose I should have at least been thankful for that.

Chapter Four

THERE ARE THINGS I do not like. I do not like hamburgers.
I do not like being wet. I do not like Velistris. These are all
things that other people like, but I do not like them. I have
learned that different humans like different things. Elyse
likes hamburgers, but she does not like being wet. Aurora
and Delta like being wet in Velistris's water bowl, but they
do not like hamburgers. Aurora and Delta also like Velistris,
but me and Elyse do not like her. I think Elyse does not like
more things than Aurora and Delta do not like. I do, too. This
is why I like Elyse.

I do not know what makes a human like something and
then not like something. I do not like hamburgers because
I do not like food. I do not like being wet because it makes
things slippery. I do not like Velistris because she is weak. All
the things that I do not like, I do not like for a reason. But
humans are not like this.

When Elyse first saw Blepharisma in the docking bay, she
liked him. But then he ate her head, and she did not like
him. When we went to the engine room, she talked about all
the reasons why she did not like him. The big reason was
because he ate her head. But the more she talked about why
she did not like him, the less it seemed she did not like him.
After we counted everything that was broken in the engine
room, she was very quiet for a long time. She was quiet all
the way until we finished, when I followed her to her room
so she could get clean. But before she went into her room,
she said to me, "Do you know how it feels to feel like you
don't have a friend in the universe?" I said I did not, because
I am not good at feeling things. Then she said, "That's how

I felt before I met you." When she said the word, "you," she was talking about me. But I do not think she was thinking about me. I think she was thinking about Blepharisma.

Elyse does not like it when I go in her room, so she told me to wait outside while she got clean. Then she shut the door. I stood in front of it for an hour. Mostly, I did not think about things. But sometimes, I thought about what she said to me. Sometimes, I can predict what a human is going to do. I predicted that when Elyse opened her door again, she would tell me that she liked Blepharisma again. But she did not. What she did was make a loud breathe-in sound, then say, "Have you seriously been staring at my door from like an inch away that whole time?"

I said, "Yes. Do you like Blepharisma?"

She said, "What?" I think it is because humans do not hear good. So I repeated what I said louder.

"Yes! Do you like Blepharisma?"

If a human does not understand something, they blink their eyes a lot. This is how I knew my question confused her. "No," she answered. "I don't know. Why?"

"It is my prediction that you like him again."

"Do you see my hair right now?"

I do not know why she asked me this. "I see your hair."

"No, I mean seriously, do you see it?"

I did. I do not know why she did not believe that I saw it. I also saw that it was different. It was smooth over the back of her head and very dark. It looked wet, but it was not dripping.

"I can't wash this gunk out. I shampooed, I rinsed, I repeated, I repeated, I repeated. It's like, *attached* to my hair. Look at this." She put her hands against the sides of her head and pressed her hair together. When she lifted her hands up, her hair went up. When she moved her hands away, her hair stayed up. "It *does not come out.*" She put her hands on her hair again and pushed it back. It went back. "It's like, pliable. I hate to say this, but I think I'm going to have to see Velistris." Elyse does not like Velistris. She released a sigh breath and leaned against the doorframe. "I'm so frustrated right now."

For a few seconds, she stayed quiet. But then she spoke again. Her voice was more quiet than when she spoke before, and it was slower.

"Why did you think I liked Blepharisma?"

I knew the answer. "When you asked me if I ever felt like I did not have a friend in the universe, I think you were thinking of when Blepharisma asked Aurora to be his friend because no one liked him. I think this made you think of sad things. I think that you think that you and Blepharisma have both experienced sad things, and I think this makes you like him." I waited to see if my answer was right.

Elyse looked away from me. She always does this when I have a right answer. "Maybe." She got very still, like she does when her brain is working hard. "I want to go talk to him."

"Why?"

"To yell at him for sliming me," she answered, but I predicted she was not being truthful. My prediction was correct. "And maybe to ask him what he's done. Where he's been. How he got from whatever floating rock he was born on to inside our spaceship. To see if maybe the universe rejected him because it doesn't understand him. To see if he's like me."

I listened, thinking on her words as she said them.

"Aunt Aurora's not really his friend. She was trying to control a situation, just like she tries to control me." She repositioned her body against the door. "Just like everybody tries to control me. Tries to tell me who to be, what to do. What my last name is. When all I really need is just for them to accept me for what I am."

I observed Elyse's eyes as she looked to the side. She likes to have green hair, but I find her green eyes more interesting to watch. Sometimes, I believe she sees things that I do not see. I thought for a long time that her eyes saw differently and that she was perhaps observing radio waves or invisible lifeforms, but over the years I have learned that her brain has the ability to project images over her eyes. She sees things that her brain wants her to see. My brain cannot do this. I can only see what I see. Elyse can see what is not. I wish I could see the not that she sees. Perhaps then I would feel as I suspected she was feeling then.

"Do I have worth, Hank-is-Handy?"

I knew the answer again. "Yes."

She looked at me. The side of her mouth curved up, which is a sign that humans are happy. But she was happy only a little. "You wouldn't lie to me, would you?"

"No, I would not."

"You love me even if I have depressing posters hanging on my walls and dead things in jars?"

"Yes, I love you." She told me that I did.

The curve in her mouth went higher. My answer made her more happy. "And that's why I love *you*."

I do not always like being a Vorck. I think there are many things about life that I do not experience, such as feelings. I knew she was feeling many things, but I could not feel them. Most of the feelings that I feel are the bad ones, like anger and irritation. I would like to feel love. I know that I love Elyse, but I do not feel that I love her. I have tried to feel love the way that she feels it. I have told her this, and she has told me that she loves me, anyway, and that she knows that I love her. I know that I love her.

But I want to feel.

"Well," she said. She stood up from the doorframe. She said nothing else for a moment. "I'm going to Blepharisma's room. You want to come?"

I did not. "We must report to Aurora the damage to the *Illustré*."

She looked away. "Yeah, that's probably smart."

Her assessment was correct.

"Look, why don't you just go talk to Aunt Aurora yourself? You can give her the full rundown better than I can."

"What will you do while I am reporting the damage?" I predicted that she would use that time to speak to Blepharisma.

"I'm going to go talk to Blepharisma."

I was correct.

"I'll be fine."

My two jobs on the *Illustré* were engineer and head of security. It would not be safe for me to allow Elyse to visit an unknown lifeform alone. "I cannot allow it. It would not be safe. I will deliver the report to Aurora, then we will visit Blepharisma together."

She argued. She often argues. "I'll be fine. He's harmless."

"He ate your head."

"You know as well as I do that he was trying to read my brain waves or something to communicate better. You heard him croaking and making all those noises before he did it. It's not like he chewed on me. After I talk to Blepharisma, I'll see if Velistris can wash my hair. I'm not wild about it, but what else am I going to do? I can't go around like this all day."

"You may function better if you remove your hair," I said. It is a suggestion I have made many times. She has never listened. I predicted she would not listen now, too.

"Yeah. No."

A confusing response. Perhaps she would consider it. "You cannot visit Blepharisma alone. We will give our report to Aurora, then we will visit Blepharisma together." Elyse performed an eye roll. It indicated she was not happy. "If you do not wish to accompany me while I give the report to Aurora, you may stay in your room until I return."

"Thanks for your permission."

"You are welcome. Is that what you wish?"

"Yeah, that's what I wish."

I turned my body down the hall to walk to Aurora's quarters alone. "Goodbye, Elyse."

"Goodbye, Hank-is-Handy." Several seconds after she spoke, I heard the door to her room close.

I walked away to deliver my report.

The things Elyse said to me gave me many things to think about. I wanted to think about them, but I knew I had to think about the damage report. And so I stopped thinking about Elyse.

Humans sometimes have great difficulty not thinking about things. There have been things that have made Elyse sad, and I have told her, "Do not think about them." But she does not have this ability. I have not spent much time around human males. Perhaps they are different. I have heard Aurora talk about the brain of Bryce Lockhart, the human male she is going to marry, which is another thing humans do that I do not understand. She has sometimes said his brain is like an empty box. I thought once that perhaps he did not fully develop. I learned later that it meant he was not thinking about things that she thought he should be thinking about. Aurora, Elyse, and Delta are always thinking about everything. Sometimes, I cannot focus on all of the things they think about. So instead, I think about the engine room. It is easy for me to think about the engine room, because I am good at fixing it. That is why I am called Hank-is-Handy.

I wish I could think about more things. I would like to think about the things that Aurora, Elyse, and Delta think about. I think if I could think about them, I could understand what it is like to have so many feelings. But sometimes feelings are bad. Maybe it is good that I do not have many of them.

Aurora's door was not all the way closed when I got to it. I did not know if she did it on purpose or if the door was broken. When I got by the door, I could hear her speaking to someone inside of it. I was not going to enter while she was speaking, as I have heard that interruptions are a word called *impolite*. I do not understand this word, but humans think it is important. All Vorck say what needs to be said. We do not worry about words like *impolite*. But humans worry about it. So I did not walk in, and I did not knock. I stood outside of her room and waited.

Her words were quiet. I thought maybe she was telling someone a secret. When she did not give the other person a chance to talk, I predicted that she was speaking to her creator. I have found that oftentimes, when humans speak to their creator, they do not give their creator a chance to talk back. They only continue to talk to him until they are finished, then they get up and do something else. I have heard it described as impolite when humans do not give other humans a chance to talk. But maybe it is different when they are talking to their creator. Maybe he does not talk much. I do not know.

Aurora asks her creator for a lot of things. She asks him to keep the *Illustré* safe a lot. I think it is because humans do not want to die. She also asks him to keep Bryce Lockhart safe. Maybe she thinks he is going to die. Many times, she asks him for directions. I predict that she does not think I am a good navigator. She asks for this many times, so I try hard to get better at plotting courses. Maybe I need to do better at telling her where we are so she does not think we are lost. I have thought about this many times, but when I tell her where we are, she always says, "I know that." Perhaps she is confused. Humans get confused about a lot of things.

I think that Delta and Elyse perhaps did not fully develop, because Aurora is always asking her creator to change their hearts. Sometimes human hearts get sick and doctors give them new hearts that they have grown. I think that maybe Delta and Elyse need new hearts. I have asked Elyse many times if her heart is damaged. Sometimes she says yes, and sometimes she says no. Humans do not always know things they should know. I do not know how Aurora wants her creator to give Delta and Elyse new hearts. Perhaps we will meet him at a space station.

Aurora sometimes talks to her creator about me and Velistris. When she talks about Velistris, she asks her creator to make her stop trying to clean all her blemishes and accept that she will always have them. I do not think Velistris would like to hear those words. Aurora believes that only her creator can clean blemishes good. She asks many times for Velistris to understand this. If I had a creator, I would not ask him to help Velistris. I think a better thing would be to make her not talk anymore.

When she talks to her creator about me, she always asks him the same thing. She says she wants him to make me see that me being handy is not what is important. This does not make sense to me. If I was not handy, I would not be Hank-is-Handy, I would only be Hank. I do not think anyone would want to live with a Hank that is not handy. She also asks her creator to show me that I have a purpose. I also do not understand this, because my purpose is to fix the engine room when it is broken. I think that sometimes she forgets that I am handy. I think that Aurora forgets many things, like where she is. Maybe this is why she always thinks she is lost and that I do not have a purpose.

But I think that maybe Aurora thinks that I should have a different purpose. If so, then I do not know what that purpose is. I am only good at being handy. Vorck do not have many purposes, but we are good at the ones that we have.

I wish that I could talk to the human creator. Sometimes I have tried, but he has never talked back. I have tried asking him questions like, "How many teeth does Hank-is-Handy have?" I know that I have sixteen teeth, and so I wanted to see if he knew the answer. But he did not speak at all. I have also asked him to make things move, but I have never seen him do it. I do not know what to think about the human creator. Maybe I will try talking to him again. Maybe I should talk like Aurora and not give him a chance to talk back. Maybe he will send me a subspace message some day on my console panel. I have never gotten a subspace message from anyone, though the humans get them often from other humans far away. I think I would like to get a subspace message one day.

"Amen," Aurora said. I could hear the word, even though she was speaking quietly. It is a word humans only use in prayer, and I believe that it means that their message is finished. I have not used it in my own prayers. Maybe that is what I am doing wrong. I will remember to try it if I speak to their creator again. "Hank-is-Handy?" Aurora asked. I could hear her walking to the door, so I knocked, because I am supposed to. "Ugh," she said when she got to the door and opened it. She looked down at where the door had not closed all of the way. "I'm sorry, the door mechanism must've gotten jostled when the Vorticella attacked. Can you fix it for me?"

"Yes," I said. I always say yes when she asks me to fix something. It is my purpose, even if she sometimes forgets it.

She waved sideways with her arms and stepped away from the door inside her room. She does this when she wants me to enter, but in case I did not understand, she said, "Come on in. What do you have for me?"

"Me and Elyse have completed our walkthrough of the engine room," I said.

"Let me hear it." As I stepped inside further, she tried to shut the door, but it did not close all the way again. "Yeah, this thing's off track pretty good."

I did not think the door broken was good, but sometimes humans like strange things. I predicted that she would want me to fix it, anyway. "The *Illustré* was damaged badly in the attack. We have replaced all damaged linkages with replacements, but we are now out of them. The thruster and spindrive chambers are back to operational, but all radiators in the forward screens are still broken. The forward screens will not be operable until we can repair them."

"How are the radiators for the plasma blaster?"

"They are functional."

She nodded her head, which means that she is thinking. "Can we swap out the forward screen generator radiators for the ones in the blaster turret bay? We're more escapees than fighters—I feel like we need the screens a lot more than the plasma blaster."

"I will swap out the radiators."

"How is Castor?"

"It is badly damaged. It is not suitable for launch until it is repaired." Castor is one of the strike craft on board the *Illustré*. The other one is called Pollux. It is not their real names. Their real names are Gemini-1 and Gemini-2. Elyse named them Castor and Pollux, because humans from Earth used to call some stars by those names. She told me that long ago, before humans went to the stars, they thought that the stars made different shapes. I do not understand this concept. When Vorck look at the stars, we see only stars. She showed me a picture of the star shape they called Gemini, but it did not look like anything to me. Star shapes make no sense to me in space travel. Perhaps this is why humans do not use them anymore. Elyse knows a lot about ancient human history because her family is considered historical. She was proud that she came up with the names of Castor and Pollux. She said we will fix Castor no matter what. I told her I would help her because I love her and because it is my job to do what I am told to do.

After I told Aurora the report on Castor, she seemed to be thinking again. "What if we..." She stopped talking. Sometimes humans do this when they are thinking about what they are saying, which does not happen much. "Never

mind. Make a list of everything Castor needs to be repaired—
as well as everything else that's broken. I'll make sure we get
the order in. Are we good to go into hyperspace?"

"Yes."

"Good," Aurora said. "I have a subspace conference call
with my Broodmaster liaison, but I don't want to start it until
we're underway."

"I understand," I said.

Humans tilt their heads sometimes when they are curious,
a trait they share with dogs. "I know you can't spend much
time around Broodmasters in the flesh. Would you like to sit
in when I make the call?"

Her words were correct. Vorck minds are easily controlled
by Broodmasters, so we do our best to avoid them. Some
people think the Vorck were slaves of the Broodmasters in
another cluster, but no one knows this for sure as Vorck do
not keep history like other species. It is not common for any
species to see a Broodmaster, but especially Vorck cannot
see them or their minds may get taken over. The chance to
see one was an opportunity that I did not want to refuse. But
I also knew that Elyse wanted to visit Blepharisma. It was a
difficult choice. "I would very much like to see the liaison,
but I cannot."

Aurora looked surprised. "Why not?"

"Elyse wishes to visit Blepharisma, and I told her I would
go with her. I must not allow her to visit Blepharisma alone."

It seemed that my words pleased her, because she smiled
a little bit. "You're turning down the chance to safely
communicate with a Broodmaster so you can keep Elyse safe
from Blepharisma?"

"Yes."

"Well, next time Bryce needs some pointers on priorities,
I'll be sure and send him to you."

I did not know what she meant.

"Why in the heavenly stars does Elyse want to visit

Blepharisma after what he did to her? Did she ever get that stuff out of her hair?"

"She did not," I answered. "She will ask Velistris to wash it out for her." When I said it, her smile got bigger, but I did not understand why. "She wishes to visit Blepharisma, I think, because he makes her think of herself."

When I gave Aurora my answer, her smile went away. "What do you mean?"

I told her what Elyse had said. "Elyse told me that you were not really Blepharisma's friend and that you told him you were in order to control him, like you try to control Elyse, too." My words made Aurora's face look strange. "She said that everyone tries to tell her what to do, who to be, and what last name to have." I do not understand what humans call last names. I believe it has something to do with a human's prior genetic carriers. Vorck do not have these, so we do not have use for last names. Elyse says her last name is Genza, which is the last name of her prior male genetic carrier, but Aurora and Delta say her last name is Greengrass, which is the last name of her prior female genetic carrier. The way humans name themselves does not make sense to me.

"She said all that?" Aurora asked.

I did not know why she would think that I lied. "Yes."

"Did she tell you anything else?"

"She asked me if I thought she had worth. I told her that she did and that I would not lie to her because I love her." I predicted that Aurora would want to know all of what I said to Elyse, so I told her.

Aurora became very quiet. She looked at me for a little while, then she turned and walked the other way. She then stood on the opposite side of the room looking at the wall. I look at walls in this way many times, too. Then she said, "Thank you for telling me this, Hank-is-Handy."

I did not know if I had provided Elyse with the correct answer, so I asked Aurora, "Was what I said to Elyse correct?"

She tilted her head up and down, as humans do when they mean to say yes. "What you said to her was wonderful."

"Good."

"Hank-is-Handy, will you tell me if she says anything like that again?"

"I will."

She turned around to look at me. "Thank you. I don't want her feeling that way. No one on board this ship should ever feel that way." She was quiet for a moment. "Hank-is-Handy, I don't think you should tell her that you told me what she said. I'm not sure she would like it. So just keep this conversation between us, and let me know if she says something like that again, okay?"

I did not understand why Elyse would not be happy that I told Aurora what she said. I told Aurora, "I understand," anyway, because I would follow her orders.

"Thank you. Now go swap out those radiators so we can get back on our way."

There is one thing about humans that is a great mystery to me, and it is their desire to keep secrets. The keeping of secrets does not make logical sense to me. If knowledge about a thing might assist others in one's species, why would that knowledge not be shared? One thing that humans suffer with is a condition called *embarrassment*, and it seems to be a reason why many secrets are kept. Vorck do not experience embarrassment, so I cannot understand this. Embarrassment is a very difficult concept to understand. Sometimes humans are embarrassed when they do not do good work. Sometimes they are embarrassed when other humans look at them. I do not know if it is good or bad to look at another human when they are embarrassed, nor do I know how to tell if a human is embarrassed.

I believe it is possible that Elyse was embarrassed when Blepharisma ate her head, but I do not understand why. I believe it had something to do with the residue that was on her head. I predicted that the residue on Elyse's head was something that was funny, mostly because Delta laughed at it, so I laughed like Delta laughed. But Elyse did not think it was funny. I believe embarrassment may be when one human thinks something is funny but another human does not. Perhaps Elyse was embarrassed because the residue made her hair heavy and it was stuck all over her head. I think that this must be another reason why it is better to not have hair than to have it. It is one less thing to be embarrassed about. I have told Elyse many times that it would be to her advantage to remove her hair, but she has never done it. Humans do not do many things that would benefit them. They are a species that likes to be embarrassed and suffer. This is why they are not good at giving advice.

Humans experience pride, which is another emotion that can lead to embarrassment when hurt. Human pride has always been a mystery to me. We Vorck have a great deal of pride, so it is a feeling that I understand well. But humans have so little to be proud about. They are weaker than many species and they have hair. These are not things to be proud about. If they were more like Vorck, they could have good reasons for pride. But humans are too much like themselves.

When I got back to Elyse, I told her everything that Aurora said about the engine room, but I did not tell her what I told Aurora about her. I did this because Aurora told me not to, and I am a worker on her ship. It made no difference to me who was told what. The exchanging of information and knowledge is good. I believe that secrets are bad. I will not keep secrets unless Aurora or Elyse tells me to. I would keep Delta's secret, too. I would not keep Velistris's secret.

I told Elyse that before we visited Blepharisma, we had to get the engine room fixed. I told her that after that, we could visit Blepharisma together. She did not look happy or sad. We then went to the engine room to swap out the radiators.

I have heard humans talk about something they call their happy place. It is a place where they do something that humans call *relax*, a physiological state where they allow themselves to become vulnerable to attack. I have never relaxed, but humans like to relax a lot. Elyse says her happy place is listening to old human music. This does not make sense to me, because it is not a place. Humans never make sense. Aurora says her happy place is on the bridge, when nothing is happening and she can look at the stars. Delta says her happy place is when her head is in Velistris's water bowl. I have seen her do this several times. Her eyes close and she leans her head back, exposing her throat to danger. If I had a happy place, it would not be in Velistris's water bowl.

I do not think I have a happy place, because I do not think relaxing is good. But if I wanted to be a weak Vorck that relaxed, then my happy place might be the engine room. I would look at everything and if something is broken, I would fix it. This is no different from what I do now, except I do not relax. I do not think I would like to relax. I think it would cause me too much stress.

It took me and Elyse several hours to switch the damaged radiators in the forward screen generator room with the good ones from the blaster turret bay. Radiators are very big components, so we must use the crane lift in the center of the room to put them into place. Elyse says that she likes to use the controls, so I let her. She is very good at it for a human.

Elyse did not talk about Blepharisma or her feelings while we worked. I like it when she does not talk about her feelings, because I do not understand them. Sometimes when she speaks of them, I tell her that her feelings do not make sense to me and I would very much like it if she spoke of something else. When I first did this, it made her express more feelings, the strongest of which was anger. I have since learned that humans have an override command which will make them follow orders without expressing negative feelings. The command is called *please*. I do not know how it works or how all humans have this command, but when I use it, they always do what I tell them. Now when Elyse talks about her feelings and I do not wish to hear them, I say, "Your feelings do not make sense to me. I would like it if you spoke of something else, please." The command makes her smile, initiate a physical encounter called a *hug*, then apologize to me. She then does what I ask and talks about something else.

I do not think humans are aware of this override command, so I do not use it often. I fear that if they become aware of it, they may find a way to deactivate it, and I will have to hear about their feelings all of the time.

On this day, I did not have to use the override command because Elyse did not speak. I like it better when no one speaks. If I was the captain of the *Illustré*, I would make it to where nobody spoke unless there was an emergency. Then we would speak to let others know about it. I believe this would be a better work environment. Perhaps a ship in which no one speaks is the closest thing I could have to a happy place. I believe a ship like that would make me very pleased.

When we finished, I told Aurora that the *Illustré* could enter hyperspace, then me and Elyse went to visit Blepharisma.

We do not get many guests on board the *Illustré*, but we get them sometimes. Mostly they are lifeforms that need to be taken from one place to another but do not have their own ship. Aurora says it is a good way to make money. I agree. There are seven rooms on the *Illustré*. Me, the humans, and Velistris live in five of them. That means there are two more that travelers can live in while we take them from one star system to the next. One of those two extra rooms was given to Blepharisma.

Elyse did not say anything as we walked to Blepharisma's room, but I think that she was thinking things. I was thinking things, too, mostly about what it means to be a friend. Elyse believes that I am her only friend. I desired to see how she would react to another lifeform, such as Blepharisma, that she thinks could be her friend.

Blepharisma's room was on the port side of the ship, which is the same side that me and Elyse have rooms on. Delta and Velistris have rooms on the starboard side, which also has an extra room. Aurora has captain's quarters which are above the bridge. It is bigger than our rooms, but she is the captain.

I could hear the two small creatures that Blepharisma had making their animal calls, even as we approached his room from the hall. They are strange sounds, like whistles and yips. They are not like the sounds that Riley makes. When Elyse got to Blepharisma's door, she raised her hand to knock, then she stopped. I asked her, "Why are you stopping?"

"I'm just trying to think of what I'm going to say," she said to me.

Humans think about this a lot. It is because humans try to achieve desired results through their speech patterns. Vorck do not care about this, so we do not worry about what we will say. We will just say whatever is true. Elyse knocked on the door, then she waited.

When I think that I may be in combat soon, I carry a tool that is called a phase hammer. It is a ballistic pulse tool used in construction. It could easily kill a lifeform like Blepharisma or anyone else on the *Illustré*. I carried it when we went to the docking bay because I did not know what Blepharisma was. I still did not know, so I carried it with me again.

The door did not open, but the two animals' calls got louder and faster. I recognize this as fear. I looked at Elyse. "Perhaps he does not know the human custom of knocking on the door."

"Yeah, well, he's about to learn the custom of breaking and entering." She knocked again. "Blepharisma! It's me, Elyse. The girl you slimed in the docking bay. Open up, I want to talk!"

Blepharisma spoke from the other side of the door. "I not knowing how to open door!"

"Hit the big yellow button next to the door with your... uhh, tentacle!"

A few seconds passed, and the door opened. Hot and moist air hit me and Elyse. I did not care, but Elyse made her face twist in a way that I recognize as disgust. She made a sound that is not a word that also means disgust.

Blepharisma was in the middle of his room, which was not fully lit. His two small creatures were behind him in the back corners. They were hunched down and shaking. I have seen pictures of things that humans call *rabbits*. They reminded me of them, except I have never seen blue or pink rabbits.

Elyse entered his room and waved her hand in front of her face, which was still showing disgust. "God, is it muggy enough in here for you?"

I stood in the open doorway to block it in case the lifeform tried to escape.

"I being most comfortable in heat and humidity!" Blepharisma said. "Captain Aurora being most generous in making atmosphere in my room to my liking. I being very grateful!"

"Well, at least I don't have to worry about frizz, thanks to you."

I did not understand Elyse's words.

When Elyse spoke to him again, her words were very firm. I think it was because she thought a lot about what she would say before she entered, so she was not nervous about saying it now. "So I don't really consider you sucking on my brain a proper introduction, so let's try it again. Hi. I'm Elyse Genza. It may or may not be a pleasure to meet you, answers pending." She held out her hand, and Blepharisma touched it with his tentacle, just like he did with Aurora in the docking bay.

"I being Blepharisma!" he answered.

"Yeah, so about that."

I have heard Elyse say those words many times. It is usually when she believes that she knows more than someone else. I predicted that that was the case again.

"Is Blepharisma *your* name or your species name?"

"I not knowing what you mean."

"My name is Elyse. I'm a human. This is Hank-is-Handy. He's a Vorck. Your name is…what?"

His red eyes stayed on her. "Blepharisma."

"And you are a…?"

"Blepharisma."

Elyse raised one of her fingers in the air and jiggled it. She does this a lot when she thinks she is right. "But see, that's the thing, because you're not. You're not a blepharisma. A blepharisma is a single-celled organism—a ciliate protist, I looked it up. I hate to break it to you, pal, but you're not a ciliate protist, and you've got a heck of a lot more than a single cell. Are you suggesting to me that you *evolved* from a blepharisma? That you are in fact the blepharisma's ultimate form?"

"I not knowing any of the things you are saying," Blepharisma said. "I always being Blepharisma. I never not being Blepharisma. You making me very confused!"

"I mean, look, we all evolved from something."

"I not knowing evolving."

Elyse crossed her arms and shifted her hip out. I have heard Aurora call this a *sassy* look when she has seen Elyse do it. She always uses that word when she talks about Elyse. I do not know what it means, but it does not sound like a good thing. "All right, let's try this another way. What is your origin? Where did you come from?"

"I coming from Ragnarok Cluster."

"No, not what *cluster*, what…" She stopped talking for a moment. "Okay, you're from the Ragnarok Cluster, that's great. That's *something*." I saw Elyse wipe her face with her hands. This is when I noticed moisture seeping from her human pores. Humans are always seeping something, but they seep more when the atmosphere is warm, as it was in Blepharisma's room. "Why do you call yourself Blepharisma?"

"It being my name."

Behind Blepharisma, the two animal things stood up on their four legs. They were taller than human rabbits, but not by much. They still made their animal noises, but not as much as they made them before.

"What do you call other things like you?" Elyse asked. I predicted that I knew his answer.

"Blepharisma."

My prediction was correct. Elyse laughed, but I did not understand why. I decided not to laugh this time, as she did not like it when I laughed in the docking bay. "Okay, so the name of you and every member of your species is Blepharisma, so that must mean you have some sort of collective identity. Collective identity, but not consciousness, as you're obviously speaking to me now as an individual." She tapped her cheek with one of her fingers. "So what do we call you?"

"I not understanding—"

"Yeah, yeah, I know that, bear with me. I mean, your name's got to have meaning, right? I can't just call you something random, like, I don't know, Russell. I could shorten Blepharisma to Bleph, or Blephy, but that's so mundane. It's like calling a goldfish Goldie."

Her meaning was a mystery to me.

"So you're attacked, your ship explodes, you get rescued, and now you're just out here floating away on our little luxury yacht in outer space. Shipwrecked on an interstellar island like a modern day Robinson—" Elyse sucked in a breath of air and snapped her fingers, a strange thing humans do when their brain is unexpectedly successful. "That's it! Oh man, that is *so* zin."

"What is so zin?" I asked.

She pointed to Blepharisma. "Defoe. After Daniel Defoe, the author of *Robinson Crusoe*."

"I do not understand," I said. I could not tell if Blepharisma looked confused, because I do not know how a Blepharisma looks when it is confused.

"*Robinson Crusoe* is a book about a guy who gets shipwrecked on this tropical island on Earth. It's way old, but it's been remade a million times. On Mars, in Alpha Centauri, in the 'Unknown Cluster,' in the tenth dimension. There was even this stupid one about him getting sucked into a black hole, it was ridiculous. But the root work, the *original* work—it's iconic. Yeah," she said, nodding with certainty, "we're rolling with this one. It's too good to pass up." Pointing at Blepharisma, she said, "Henceforth, your name is Defoe. Defoe, the Blepharisma. Theoretically."

"I not understanding any of this," Blepharisma said.

Elyse did not look like she cared. "All you need to know is that from now on, your name is Defoe. You're from a species called Blepharisma, but your name is Defoe. Got it?" She looked back at me, too. "That goes for you, too, Hank-is-Handy. You're calling him by his new name, as well."

I have learned that humans do not like to be told what to do, but they like very much to tell others what to do. It did not matter to me one way or the other what we called him, so I agreed. "I will call him Defoe."

"That's zin, baby!" She smiled. She looked very happy. That made me happy, too. Defoe was not looking happy. He was not looking anything. She turned to him again. "Okay, so the suck on my brain thing. Let's talk about that."

I have learned over the years that of all the humans on the *Illustré*, Elyse cares the most about asking questions and getting answers. Aurora has seen many things in the universe already and she is much older than Elyse and Delta. I have learned that the more a human experiences, the less they show feelings about new experiences. Though Elyse has experienced many things, too, she has not experienced as much as Aurora and, therefore, she has more questions about things. Her talking to Defoe is an example of this. Though I do not know to what extent Aurora spoke to Defoe after she left the docking bay with him, I predicted by listening to his conversation with Elyse that she had not asked him as many things as her. Elyse is always looking for new knowledge, and she does not believe that most things are the truth. She calls herself a skeptic, which means a human that does not believe many things unless they see evidence or hear good explanations. Elyse asked Defoe for many explanations during their talk.

The first thing she asked about was why he ate her head. He told her that he learns about new things by absorbing information from them, and that this can only be done when he puts them in his mouth. To show this, he put a wrench I had on my work belt in his mouth. When he spit it out, he told us all of the metallic compounds that it was made of. He said he can absorb knowledge from a lifeform in this way, too. This was how he absorbed some of her language. He asked Elyse if he could absorb more knowledge from her to show her how it worked, but she did not want him to. She said it is not nice to eat someone's head without their permission. Defoe said he would not do it again.

Elyse asked him many questions about his species, but he did not know many answers. He does not know why his species is called Blepharisma. There are not many Blepharisma in the galaxy, he said, so they do not see their own kind very often. Elyse said that she thinks he evolved from the lifeform, blepharisma. She said that a vorticella is also a very small lifeform, which she believes the Vorticella evolved from. She believes this is why they call themselves the Vorticella. She said that if the Vorticella did this, it would make sense that the Blepharisma did, too. Though I am very different from Defoe, I understood how he could not remember why his species was named what it was. We Vorck do not keep a good history of our species. We do not know what species enslaved us many eons ago or how we set ourselves free. We only know that we are now what we are. I believe Defoe is the same way. That is okay with me.

She also asked him about the two small animals, which he called Slarb and Gralb. He said that all Blepharisma have a Slarb and a Gralb, and that they have a symbiotic relationship. We observed as the two animals ingested some of his moss skin. Eating pieces of Defoe as he grows seems to serve two purposes. One is to keep Defoe from growing too large. Two is to sustain the Slarb and Gralb. In return for eating parts of Defoe, they provide food for him in the form of their waste materials. Elyse showed more human signs of disgust when she learned this. Defoe explained that the Slarb and Gralb each process his skin in different ways, so their waste materials are different and provide sustenance to him in different ways. Because they depend on each other, a Blepharisma will die if his Slarb and Gralb die, and a Slarb and Gralb will die if their Blepharisma owner dies. Their symbiotic relationship causes them to live a very long time, so death by natural causes is a rare thing. The only other form of sustenance that Blepharisma require is water, the same as most carbon-based lifeforms in the galaxy.

Blepharisma also do not like bright lights and they do not like cold temperatures. This is why Defoe wanted his room to be dark, warm, and humid. It was not as humid for me, because I was standing in the doorway, but it was very humid for Elyse, who was standing in the room to talk to him. Her skin and hair were shiny with moisture after only ten minutes, and she dripped of the pore seepage that humans call sweat. She did not complain, however, which was a surprise to me, as Elyse enjoys complaining about a lot of things. Perhaps she thought complaining about Defoe's room would be impolite. I do not know.

I wondered for a long time if Elyse would ask Defoe about potential friendship. I was not surprised when she did. "Why does everybody hate you, Defoe?" she asked. Defoe said he did not know, then Elyse said, "Come on, now, there must be a reason."

Defoe answered her, "Maybe it being because I being dangerous, dangerous pirate."

"Wait, you're a *pirate*?" she asked. This news was surprising to me, too.

"I being most ferocious pirate! I pillaging all sorts of spaceships for many, many years. I having a most lethal Darkboat."

Else performed a head tilt. "Darkboat?"

"Darkboat being the name of my ship before the Vorticella destroyed it."

"And how many ships have you pillaged in this Darkboat?" she asked.

"I not knowing how many. Number being far too many to count."

She said to him, "I'm going to go out on a limb here and say that that number is zero."

Defoe suddenly got angry. His eyes glowed brighter and he whipped his tentacle from side to side. Elyse jumped back to me, and the Blepharisma spoke. "Stopping your speaking! I pillaging many, many ships! I being dangerous, dangerous pirate. You making me angry by saying, 'zero.' Answer being many more than zero! I not liking you saying, 'that number is zero.' You stopping saying zero. Please, good friend?"

This is why I went with Elyse. I wanted to protect her in case it got angry. It got angry, so I reached for my phase hammer. I was going to pull it out when Elyse put her hand over mine. Aurora has done this to me many times. She does it when she does not want me to get my phase hammer out. So I kept it lowered. Elyse still looked at Defoe. "Okay, I'm sorry. I was just joking about zero. I'm sure you must've pillaged...lots of ships."

It did not make sense to me that Elyse would change her mind so quickly about what she thought. Then I thought that perhaps she was trying to make him believe something that was not true, like when Aurora made Defoe believe that she was his friend. I predicted this was the case.

Defoe's eyes got less red. He stopped whipping his tentacle. "I being very, very relieved. I liking you very much again."

Her words worked on him.

"I'm glad that you like me. I like you, too," she said. I predicted that she would want to talk to me later about what had just occurred, when Defoe was not around. I would have to wait to see if my prediction was correct. "It must be hard being a pirate, what with so many people not liking you and all."

"It being very, very hard," answered Defoe. "Being pirate very hard occupation. But I being very good at it."

I saw Elyse rub her hands on her face. Then she rubbed her hair and pushed it back. It stuck down good, like when Defoe ate her head in the docking bay. This was because of the heat and humidity. I predicted that Elyse would not stay in the room for very much longer, but my prediction was not correct. She continued to speak to him. "What is it like being you?"

The way she asked that question was different from all of the others. Sometimes when a human wants to say something important, they lower their voice in an effort to make their important words harder to hear. This does not make sense to me. When I want to say something important, I say it loudly so that everyone can hear. Humans do the opposite of what makes sense for many things. Elyse's voice was low when she asked Defoe what it was like being him. I considered using the override command and saying, "Speak louder, please," but then I thought that perhaps she wanted to be difficult to hear for a reason I did not understand. It did not matter, because Defoe was able to hear her.

"It being very dark and very lonely," he answered. "I thinking sometimes that people not liking me because I being different. I having hard time communicating from my Darkboat because I not knowing others' languages through video monitor. I having to be there with them to read their brainwaves liking I did for you. They hearing me only make natural speak-sounds, then they saying, 'Open fire!'"

"So you can't talk to anyone unless you read their brainwaves first. That must be so hard, knowing what you want to say but not having anyone understand you when you say it."

Defoe's body looked like it shrunk, but it did not. Humans do this sometimes with their shoulders when they are sad. I could not predict that Defoe was sad, because I cannot yet predict a Blepharisma. But then he spoke, and it sounded sad. "I living life alone in space wanting to talk but having no one to talk to. I talking lots to Slarb and Gralb, but they non-sentient and do not talking back."

For a moment, Elyse got quiet again. This was a sign that she was thinking with her brain. "I was your first human contact, wasn't I?"

His tentacle waved back and forth a bit. "You being correct," he answered.

"In that case," she said, "it was an honor sharing my brainwaves with you. A slimy honor, but an honor no less." Elyse placed her hands against her hips, which is a thing humans do when they are bored. "Well, I think I've interrogated you enough for one day. It was a pleasure meeting you, Defoe. And naming you. And being your friend."

I wondered if she was really being his friend or if she was doing what Aurora did and only saying it. I decided I would ask her after we left.

Elyse did a human wave gesture with her hand and said, "See you later." Defoe lifted his tentacle and did the same gesture back to her. This did not seem to hold significance to Elyse. She turned around to leave the room. But I thought Defoe waving was an important clue. She did not explain the human custom of waving goodbye to him. He did it because she did it. Many predators mimic, but sometimes prey do, too. I did not know which one Defoe was. What mattered was which one Defoe thought himself to be.

Or perhaps the wave meant nothing at all.

The door to Defoe's room closed, and me and Elyse walked down the hall. After several steps away, she put her hands on her head and spoke to me. "I am *soaked* and my hair feels gack-nasty."

"It was hot in the room," I said.

"It was hot, muggy, musty, and *disgusting*. I want Velistris to wash my hair, but I have *got* to take a shower first. My whole body reeks."

I did not want to talk about the state of her body, because I did not care about it. "Did you mean it when you said that Defoe was your friend?"

Elyse got quiet. This is how I knew that she did not know. "I don't know," she said. My prediction was correct. "I mean…I *think* so." She stopped walking and looked back at where his room was in the hall. "Hank-is-Handy, he's like a child. Did you notice his temperament when I showed skepticism that he was a pirate? That was like a temper tantrum."

I did not know what a temper tantrum was.

"He learned to talk from me, that much we've established, but what else did he learn when he sucked on my brain? Can we trust him? Does he trust us? He said all that stuff about

Slarb and Gralb, but we have no way of knowing if any of it was true. I don't know, I feel like we need to get to the bottom of it." She looked at me. "Do you think Aunt Aurora would let him work with us in the engine room? I guess kind of like a helper?"

"I already have a helper," I told her. "It is you."

"Yeah, I know, thanks. But you know what I'm saying, right? We get him to help us there, then we watch him to see if we can figure him out. It'd be a lot less conspicuous than always popping in his room." She did a sigh breath. "And I *really* don't want to stand in that putrid sauna again. You know what? I don't think we even need to ask Aunt Aurora. If she finds out he's helping us and she doesn't like it, we can always just apologize. It's easier to apologize than to ask permission."

I was thinking about a question. I decided to ask it. "Is what you want to do different from what Aurora did?" I did not have a moral judgment one way or the other. I was just curious.

"What do you mean?" she asked.

"When Aurora said that she was Defoe's friend, you said that she did not mean it and that she only wanted to get a desired reaction from him. If you tell Defoe that you want him to help in the engine room, but you really want to observe him to make a judgment on him, are you being different from Aurora at all?" Elyse looked at me by moving only her eyes. She does this many times when I am correct about something.

The corner of her mouth moved up, and she shook her head. She then hit me on the shoulder in a way not meant to initiate combat. "Yeah. I guess it is." She did another sigh breath. "Gotta learn from the best, right?" She did not say anything else regarding Defoe. She only walked ahead of me toward her room to get clean.

I had many things to think about as I stood in front of Elyse's door and waited for her, which was a very long time. Mostly, I thought about tactics to kill Defoe if he became a predator. But sometimes, I thought about Elyse and her feelings. I did not know if she wanted to be Defoe's friend. I did not like that she wanted him to help in the engine room. The engine room is mine, not Elyse's. But I love Elyse, so I will support what she wishes. I have been told by Aurora that this is how love works, and I do not want to do it wrong. Perhaps Defoe will be good in the engine room. If he does not do good or if he becomes a predator, I will kill him with my phase hammer. I think that maybe that would make Elyse sad, because Defoe would be dead and then Slarb and Gralb would die, too. But sometimes lifeforms must be sad. I decided that if I had to kill Defoe, I would do it quickly so I could focus on Elyse being sad. Perhaps I would put my arm around her. I have seen humans do this when other humans are sad. I believe it helps their bad feelings to end.

I was thinking about many other things when I heard Elyse shout from her room, "Holy zin!"

I raised my phase hammer in case she was in danger, then I knocked on the door and went inside. I looked around her room, but I did not see her. This is how I knew she was still in the bathroom. "Provide your location, please," I said.

"I'm in the bathroom!"

"Are you in danger?"

"No!"

I had predicted that she was in danger because she shouted, "Holy zin!" My prediction was incorrect. "I heard you shout," I said.

"Yeah, yeah, I know!" Her words were loud and fast, but not scared. Humans sometimes give this response when they are happy about something. It can cause much confusion at times. Sometimes I do not know if they are shouting because there is danger or because something good happened. Vorck only speak loud and fast when there is information that must be heard quickly and by many other Vorck. I think this works better than what humans do. "Hank-is-Handy, you've got to come in here!" she said from behind the door to her bathroom. "You're not gonna believe this!"

Her words indicated that she would show me incorrect information. I do not know why she would do this, but sometimes humans do things that do not make sense. Perhaps she wanted to verify incorrect information on the *Illustré*'s engine to serve as a test of knowledge for Delta or Velistris. Perhaps she wanted to see if they could work in the engine room, too, with Defoe. I lowered my phase hammer and opened the door to the bathroom.

"Are you seeing my hair right now?" she asked me for a second time that day. I believed that I saw her hair, just like I believed that I saw it the first time. She did not believe that I saw it then, too. I do not know why she kept believing that I couldn't.

Sometimes, I do not understand humans at all.

Chapter Five

IN ORDER FOR a human to maintain optimal refinement, a very strict regimen must be adhered. Diet, as one would expect for any carbon-based lifeform, is a critical part of the process, as is exercise to tame their fledgling metabolisms. After diet and exercise, of course, comes the most enthralling part of the process for any Zepzeg: the direct application of beauty products. It is exciting to apply products to a human, particularly onto their hair, which all Zepzeg find marvelously fascinating. Oh, to descry their lustrous strands after we have worked our artistry! It is a wonder to behold.

For a perfect being such as myself, the administering of beauty products is not only an act of embellishment, it is evangelism. Aurora and Delta, the two humans who have me to thank for their beauty, are as much my congregation as my clientele. With every blemish I mask with concealer, with every suffusion I apply to their tendrils, they grow closer to the flawlessness required to become a Zepzeg in the Life After.

Though physical comeliness is considered essential by both Aurora and Delta—praise be to Deity for providing me with lifeforms whose priorities are proper—Delta's emphasis on beautification makes it a far more appealing acolyte than its aunt. This personal emphasis seems to correlate with age, as sadly it seems that human female wisdom tends to peak in what they call "the teenage years," after which they lose sight of what matters on the outside and instead waste their time on unimportant, inward development. Truth be told, I find that Aurora both undervalues and underestimates Delta in many regards, not the least of which is Delta's efforts to succeed Aurora as captain someday. I have seen Delta on many occasions rehearsing the role of captain in the bridge when no one save myself is there to see it. I have even witnessed it watching video files of past encounters with hostile spacecraft in an effort to study and learn. I believe that an extension of trust to Delta on the part of Aurora would be beneficial to the younger's development, though sadly I have not seen such trust extended. Were Delta given a chance to prove itself, I believe it might surprise pleasantly. But I digress.

Because of Delta's devotion to its appearance, I spend considerably more time refining its form than I do Aurora's. While Aurora will typically visit my chamber every other Earth week, Delta's visits can range from multiple times a week to, occasionally, multiple times a day if there are various issues it wishes to address. The frequency of its visits delights me greatly! If only more humans had its commitment to their outward appearances, they might not be such a broadly hideous species.

On this particular day, Delta wished to have its hair washed. It pleases me so that it has allowed me full control of its hair care regimen, as any opportunity to mold human hair is one that I relish. I must say that I have become quite skilled at it. I confess that I have convinced it to believe that it must receive far more hair treatments than it truly needs simply because I love combing my crystalline fingers through its strands. Human hair takes on an alluring hue when wet, darkened yet glistening like starlight. Many an hour have passed with Delta's head in my shampoo bowl, the poor thing oblivious to the fact that its conditioner was rinsed out long before and that I just enjoyed watching water pass over its scalp. I cannot take such brazen liberties with Aurora, who is far more likely to say, "Speed it up," when my efforts begin to linger.

The particular treatment I was giving Delta was called

a citrus blossom suffusion, and it is quite popular among the more prone to opulence. It consists of a thick, sweetly fragranced cream that is applied to the hair, then allowed to sit, after which is a series of gentle rinses. This is a custom routine, of course, as all humans possess different hair types and require different processes. I feel I have quite mastered Delta's routine, to the point where I could almost do it blindly, though I could not imagine depriving my receptors of a moment of pleasure.

"Do you think I will do well during my performance at the ball, Velistris?" Delta asked me as I ran my delicate fingers through its scalp.

"I believe you should practice while wearing your garments," I said. "You must be fully prepared in every conceivable way, lest you falter and disappoint yourself." It was a gentle way of answering its question, *no*. But I was proud of those garments.

It looked at me with a familiar blankness before finally answering, "If you feel that I must."

"I do."

"Do you think there'll be a lot of boys there?"

It is obsessed with the idea of finding a male companion. "I am certain," I answered. "Are they not customarily at such events?" I knew that they were.

"I suppose so."

I have learned that the heart of a human female burns with lust, as apparent by the wanton fervency that both Aurora and Delta possess—the former for its fiancé, the latter for the as-of-yet unknown male suitor that it hopes to find. It is one of the chief reasons that I designed its garments in the manner that I have. The attempt to lure a biological mate is one that I confess to not fully understanding. Delta wished for its garments to be quite revealing when it brought the concept to me. It wished for any viewing males to have near-full visual access to its body. Yet I have found in my exhaustive study of human culture that human desire seems to peak when presented with things it *cannot* fully see. It is nonsensical on various levels—the concept of trying to lure in a being that wants what it cannot see by increasing what it *can* see, thus diminishing its desire—but no species in the galaxy ever pretends that humans make sense.

"Is the treatment taking well?" it asked me, looking back at me with its dull, aqua eyes as I stood overhead behind it.

"Yes. Just a short while longer and it will be finished." I had, of course, finished some time earlier, though Delta did not know it. Taking hold of the spray nozzle with a hand, I glided the running water over its scalp to give it the impression that there was work left to do.

Across the room, the door opened. I naturally expected it to be Aurora, as it pays visits to my chamber multiple times throughout the day, mostly to talk about mundane things such as whatever intergalactic or personal quest it has undertaken, but occasionally to discuss more substantive issues such as fitness routines or eyeliner. I was so certain that it was Aurora that I did not bother to turn my receptors away from Delta's magnificent, shimmering head. Imagine my surprise when it was not the captain's voice that I heard, but that of its stuffy other niece.

"Why, hello there, Delta, Velistris," it said.

Out of the corner of my receptors, I saw the lumbering form of Hank-is-Handy standing behind it in the hallway. With one must always come the other—as if dealing with a single one of them wasn't tortuous enough. Naturally, such justifiable disdain could not be expressed publicly, so I simply looked their way to offer a cordial dip. "Good evening, Ely—" The moment I saw it standing in the doorway, my lifeveins froze. A jolting shiver struck up my spine! So taken aback was I by what I beheld that I allowed the nozzle of my sprayer to drift over poor Delta's face. With a panicked sputter, it lifted its head right out of the bowl.

"Velistris!"

I was, of course, mortified, and I quickly dropped the nozzle and grabbed a towel to pass over Delta's face—but my eyes immediately returned to its older half-sister and the cause of my errant aim—for I could not believe what I was seeing. Its hair. Its green, techno-dyed hair! It was…

…it was magnificent.

Gone was the tied-up homemaker's bun, replaced by shoulder-length waves that cascaded down its head like bouncing ribbons. And the green—oh, the green! No longer did it lend to the appearance of chemical manipulation. Far from it! It was the color of dark teal, from the tip to the root, as natural looking as human skin. What decadence! What luster! What manner of sorcery was this?

My wonder was immediately replaced by shard-shattering fear. What had it done? Who could have helped it? How had it become so beautiful without *me*?

With its face dried, Delta turned its head in Elyse's direction. Gasping, it spoke. "Elyse! What did you do to your *hair*? You look…"

Don't say it, I thought! How I pleaded in my head for it not to say it!

"You look beautiful!"

I could not bear for it to behold Elyse a moment longer. "I am not finished," I said, placing my hand on Delta's forehead to sternly push its head back in the bowl. Though I dared not say it—how I hate that I even thought it—I feared that Elyse's hair would overshadow my own work on Delta's. Opening a canister of Aruvian milk paste, I applied it liberally to the top of Delta's scalp.

"I thought you said I was almost finished?" it asked me.

"With the first treatment," I answered. What more could I say? "There will be several stages to today's work—all to perfect a routine that will leave you looking extravagant for the ball, of course." I rubbed it into its hair with vigor.

All the while, its eyes tried to watch Elyse by the door. "You must tell me, sister, how your hair looks so exquisite!"

It thought it looked exquisite. I rubbed harder. I had to penetrate the roots! Naturally, Elyse sashayed into the room with all the modesty of a queen. "Eh, it's no big deal. I was just messing around a bit in front of the mirror."

From where its gargantuan form blocked the door, Hank-is-Handy opened its colossal and stupid mouth. "It happened when—"

Elyse snapped the Vorck a glare. The monstrosity immediately ceased talking, staring at Elyse with all the awareness of a block of wood. A secret! Elyse had one that it didn't want us to know. Their covert communication was as plain as day, surely Delta had seen it! But of course not. Its head was still in the bowl, its eyes staring up at the ceiling as I rubbed in the paste. It had seen nothing. With my lifeveins still shivering, I looked at Elyse again. "You said you were messing around in front of the mirror. Messing around with what, if I may ask?" Colugel. There was no doubt that it was using some variant of colugel. That was the only explanation for the firmness of its ribbons.

"I couldn't even tell you, to be honest," it answered. "I just mixed together whatever I had." As I smoothed back Delta's pasted hair, Elyse approached to stare down at it. "What are you putting in there?"

It was no secret. The bottles and canisters were right there. "An Aruvian milk paste mask."

It winced. *Winced*! Half-tilting its head in the awful way humans do when they hear something they dislike, it offered the most placating pseudo-smile I'd ever seen.

"What?" I asked, for I could not help it. "What is wrong?"

It looked surprised to have been asked. "Oh! Oh, nothing. Nothing at all. I think that's umm…that's a good idea. That should look, uhh…really nice." Without another word, the accursed female turned away from me. Really nice? What was *that* supposed to mean?

"Is there a problem with using paste?" I asked, though I regretted asking the moment the words came out.

"Nope," it replied, moseying to the banister that ran along the near wall. Leaning against it, it tossed its head back, causing its mesmerizing teal tendrils to toss over its shoulder in a way that was so utterly intentional. "Is that all you're putting in?"

It was all that I'd planned. "Of course not!"

"Thank goodness."

Thank *goodness*?

Not even Delta could let that remark slide. "What more should she add?" it asked Elyse. Of all people, Elyse!

I, of course, could not allow it to answer. "A shot of jiculum foam, for flexibility and bounce."

Once more, Elyse winced. "Does that really go with milk paste, though?"

"Of course it does." I had used them in tandem many times. This vile creature had no idea what it was talking about. Grabbing the jiculum foam sprayer, I gave it a proper shake before taking aim. Out of the corner of my eye, I saw Hank-is-Handy step aside at the doorway, allowing another to enter the room. I turned my head to it fully. It was Aurora and its petulant beast, Riley! The moment my captain set foot inside, its gaze went to Elyse.

"Elyse! What happened to your hair? It looks *fabulous*!"

I pulled the trigger on the foam sprayer. I felt the nozzle dispense.

Delta shouted!

Jumping up from its chair, its hands reached up to sling foam from its face and forehead. The young human screeched at me! "*Velistris!*" I'd done it again! Not looking at what I'd been doing, I sprayed the poor creature right between the eyes. From its perch against the banister, Elyse released the most sinister of smirks.

"Oh, my dear!" Dropping the sprayer, I once again grabbed a towel as foam dribbled from Delta's face to the floor. "I don't know what's come over me." But I did. I did know. It was all that troublesome twit Elyse's fault. It'd sabotaged me by looking beautiful without my assistance!

Snatching the towel from my hand, Delta ran it across its face to wipe itself off. Beneath streaks of foam that remained, it glared at me. There was nothing I could say. "I apologize for my awkwardness today. Please, place your head back in the bowl and I will finish my work." Beneath the chair, Riley began to lap up the foam that'd fallen. I dared not stop it in the slim chance that the foam might poison and kill the beast.

"I swear, Velistris," Delta said, "if you spray me in the face *one more time...*"

"I assure you, Miss Delta, it will not happen a third time."

"It'd better not." Glare still fixed, it leaned its head back with a measure of hesitance.

Gently, I dabbed the remaining streaks from its face with a moist towel. Placing my hand against its forehead, I grabbed the foam sprayer again to apply a thick layer to its scalp. As soon as it was down, I grabbed a comb to pass through its strands. The mixing of the ingredients was critical! This was a step I could ill afford to bungle. Still, I could not help but look Aurora's way as it approached Elyse to investigate. No doubt the captain was sensing the same level of foul play that I was. I was sure it was determined to get to the bottom of this.

"Did Velistris help you with this?" it asked.

"No," Elyse answered. "I just decided I wanted to try my hand at it myself. I don't think it was too bad for a first try, do you?"

Aurora looked elated. "That might be the best looking hair I've ever seen."

"Ow," said Delta, whose hair I was relentlessly combing.

"Can you soften up a bit?"

Flustered, I set the comb down before I made the poor girl bleed. I gave the mask a good, smoothing pat. "We must now leave it to set for a while. Please, remain still."

"And what's all in this?" Delta asked me.

"Aruvian milk paste and jiculum foam."

From its perch, Elyse said, "Interesting concoction."

"It is not a *concoction*." Can you believe it would use such a word? This detestable creature was vile to its core. "This is an enhanced routine that I've quite mastered."

"Ah, well," it said, "it'll be interesting to see how it turns out."

How I wanted to snap at it. How my lifeveins burned with indignation! The audacity of this creature to mold more beautiful hair than I, then to condescend about it. Could Elyse beautify a being to Deity's light? Could any human? This creature was toying with its eternal condition. As I observed Aurora marvel at the wretched Elyse's hair, asking it to pivot and lean so it could get a better look, I could not help but consider the ramifications of such blatant heresy.

Salvation is the Zepzeg's and the Zepzeg's alone to give. Humans are one of the many misguided species that believe they can achieve immortality via their own means. For some, it is in their works. For some, it is by their faith. All of it is rubbish. There is but one means of salvation and one alone: by the perfection of outward appearance as administered by the Zepzeg. If they were Zepzeg, they would understand this to be true. But they are not. How I wish that I could show them what it was like to be an image of perfection—to let them taste what it means to be crafted from the bosom of creation itself. To experience Deity. This is why the burden of the Zepzeg is great. It is only by our deeds and discretion that other beings in the cosmos can attain salvation. It is our right to dispense such beautification and immortality, not theirs. Their ignorance about this is maddening, but not wholly undeserved. It is hard to pity beings at times who are so lost.

Therein lies the danger of such a reckless being as Elyse. My purpose on the *Illustré* is to administer beauty to those worthy enough to receive it. I consider Aurora and Delta worthy; therefore, it is my duty to make them beautiful. It is my divine mission. The challenge of turning such grotesque creatures into symbols of perfection is daunting enough—I can ill afford a false prophet to lead them astray. Human hair is magnificent. It is the primary reason why salvation for humanity is possible. It is I and I alone who must be made its caretaker.

I listened as Aurora prattled on about it. "Those waves are gorgeous," it said. "It all looks so lustrous."

The waves were gorgeous—and it was so lustrous. Just gorgeous and lustrous enough to earn them eternal damnation. I had worked so very hard on Aurora and Delta. Their souls mattered a great deal to me. I was not about to let them perish without a fight.

"I should like to know your routine," Aurora said.

It was time to speak up. "I believe I can create superior results to what you behold in Elyse." There is only one way to prove one's worth to a human. It is a primitive custom, but one their whole species' history is predicated upon. "Perhaps we should have a competition."

"A competition?" asked Aurora curiously.

"I shall refine your hair, and Elyse shall refine her own," I said. "We shall see whose turns out the best."

Delta's eyes narrowed and it leaned back to look at me. "Why wouldn't you use my hair?"

"Silence, child." Aurora was a fully-developed human. If it decided that my work was superior, Delta would follow its lead. The opposite was not necessarily true. "I shall refine your hair, Aurora, and we shall see whose is superior."

Aurora looked at me in the way it often does when it thinks

it understands me. It has a way of narrowing its eyes that is distinct among its human counterparts. It is almost as if it is trying to peer through my crystalline skin to my very lifeveins. Lifting its chin, it addressed Elyse, though its gaze stayed on me. "Elyse, would you be open to such a challenge?"

"Hell yes," Elyse answered. "That would be totally zin."

"Language, niece."

It does not like the word, "hell," spoken by its nieces. I have found that some humans relish profane speak, while some are quite taken aback by it. Aurora falls into the latter category. Elyse rolled its eyes in the insipid way that it does, but it said nothing.

"I look very forward to this competition," Aurora said, offering me a smile. "I'll schedule an appointment soon."

I am not often a fan of competition. It seems a cruel trick, considering whoever is competing against a Zepzeg is competing against perfection. But as with all undesirable tasks, one must do what one must. It would reveal Elyse to be the false prophet that it was, and that was what mattered.

Pushing up from the banister, Elyse tossed its hair through the air and smirked at me. Oh, how I detest a smirk! Was it happy? Was it being difficult? What a vexing species humans are. "Well, this was fun," Elyse said. I disagreed. "I supposed I'd better head to my room to work on my recipes."

Not once had I ever heard a human refer to a hair treatment as a *recipe*. It furthered my theory that Elyse knew nothing of hair care whatsoever—though that much was evident to any creature with eyes. Something peculiar was afoot. Just the same, if it was threatening to leave, I was not about to stop it.

"Lates," it said as it walked to the door, tossing up a parting wave that was as halfhearted in care as it was lackluster in execution. "Let's go, Hank-is-Handy." Together, the two departed down the hall.

I am ashamed that at the time, I could not restrain my relief that they were gone. "I fear there is little good to come from that one."

"What makes you say that?" Aurora asked, assuming Elyse's prior stance against the banister. Brushing its own curly strands from its forehead, it tilted its head and looked at me.

"The way it parades in here, flaunting its hair like it is the envy of the cosmos. Does it not aggravate you?"

From below, Delta nodded its head. "Oh, it aggravates me very much! But she did have nice hair."

I lifted my head to look at Aurora in an attempt to gauge its reaction. To my surprise, it did not bear one. With one eyebrow arched, it simply looked at me and said, "It?"

It took me a moment to realize what it was referencing—but realize, I did, and I lowered my head in shame. "I apologize, captain. It was not intentional." There have been times when I have forgotten the significance of pronouns when speaking with my human crewmates, most often when my lifeveins burn with emotion. This was one of those times.

Aurora said nothing. It only looked at me for a moment longer before smiling. "Don't worry, Velistris, I understand. I've been botching Hank-is-Handy's moniker myself, lately. I'm sure Elyse would forgive you had she heard."

The captain has stressed to me many times the importance of using proper pronouns in speaking with humans. It is admittedly a struggle. I have been told that humans find being referred to as "it" to be rather insulting, so I have tried my best not to address them as such. With some humans, that is easier than with others.

"I sent you a com-panel message," Aurora said, its sudden topic change indicating that its visit to my quarters had had a purpose. "I had a chance to talk to our Broodmaster liaison earlier today. I have the full meeting on holodrive, I was wondering if you could take a look at it and let me know what you think."

How I wished I could have been there for it. Aurora usually

invites me to such conferences. It made me wonder, had I done something wrong to be excluded? Naturally, I kept these thoughts to myself. "Of course, captain. I will watch the recording at once."

"There's no need to hurry. I'll swing by later tonight for you to work on my hair, if that's all right with you. We can discuss the video then."

"I will be prepared with my full assessment."

It smiled. "I look very much forward to it." Rising from the banister, it dipped its head in my direction, its coppery curls dangling in front of its eyes before it brushed them away. How it made me long to treat them! "Well, I'm afraid I must be going. I have a video appointment with a Flight Wares sales rep to order new components after our run-in with the Vorticella. You know how Flight Wares can be. A late customer is a former customer."

Flight Wares was one of the many corporations that provided ship components to vessels such as the *Illustré*. I was well aware of their lackluster service. If their products weren't so economical, I'm certain that Aurora would have no use for them at all.

"Hopefully we can pick up the new parts when we refuel in the Goode System." After the heaviest of sighs, it tried its best to offer me a smile. "Send me a message when you finish the video and I'll come by. Take your time with Delta, though. We've got quite a ways left to go and it's no hurry."

I was appreciative of its understanding. Artistry must not be hastened. "As you wish, captain," I said in reply.

With a final wave—one with far more eloquence than the halfhearted gesture from Elyse—Aurora left my quarters, its canine counterpart in its wake.

There was much time to pass before I would be free to watch Aurora's video conference with the Broodmaster liaison. The mixture in Delta's hair needed time to set before getting rinsed out, which gave the young human ample time to discuss things with me. Mostly, it talked about the competition between myself and Elyse, making known its befuddlement as to how the green-haired human could have *possibly* crafted hair so ravishing on its own. It speculated on what Elyse could have used and how it could have acquired such products. As with any topic of interest, I engaged as best as I was able—though I do confess to my thoughts being elsewhere.

It greatly concerned me that Aurora had not invited me to partake in the Broodmaster video call. I was its trusted advisor. I should have been there. Was its trust in me waning? Did it feel more confident in its own diplomatic instinct than in mine? If so, that was cause for great alarm. I *am* its diplomatic advisor. I must be present at such critical junctures. I must!

Yet I was not.

Only fueling this existential crisis was the ordeal with Elyse. If Aurora and Delta were deceived into believing that they could be made beautiful without my assistance, then what other false doctrines might they succumb to? Worse yet, what would my purpose be aboard the *Illustré*? If I could not be trusted as their beautician, and if I could not be trusted as their diplomatic advisor, then with what could I be trusted? Would they expect me to prepare meals for them? Partake in menial tasks such as cleaning the hallways? We have scrub bots for that. What if there was nothing for me to do at all? What if...

...what if I became irrelevant?

As the most relevant being on the ship, such a thought was incomprehensible. But humans are often an incomprehensible lot. I had to account for their lack of intelligence. I had to show them, beyond all shadows of doubt, that I was the most worthy among them. And there was only one way to do that. I had to be victorious in my competition with Elyse.

This was by far the most dangerous circumstance the crew had ever faced. This was for the sake of their souls. I had to win, at all costs!

There was a sudden, violent sputter! Jettisoning myself from the reverie of my thoughts, I flinched and looked down at Delta, whose hair I'd just begun to rinse and who I was now—once more—spraying in the face. Aghast, I released the trigger on the nozzle, though the damage was already done. With the whole top side of it dripping, it leapt out of the chair and whipped its wet head to face me.

"*Velistris, you buffoon!*"

I was mortified. I was statuesque in fright! I did not know what to say. All I could do was muster what little courage—what little dignity—I had left. "I apologize." I heard my own words oscillating. It is something that does not oft happen. "If you will please allow me to finish, I will make your hair look—"

"Allow you to *finish*?" it shouted, wiping its hair back, then running its hands down its still-dripping face. It slung the droplets to the floor with genuine spite. "Finish what? Hosing me down? Dousing me with foam? Thank God, you were not using your aerosnips, or I might have a *hole* in the middle of my face!"

"I would have never done that to you." I cared for it far too much. Did it not know that?

It snatched a towel, which it ran over its face with vehemence. "Pardon me if I'm a little skeptical of that!"

"Please. Your hair is unfinished. If I may—"

"You may not *touch* my hair—maybe ever again! You are awful at your job, Velistris. Awful! Awful!"

Those words. How they fractured me.

"I will do my *own* hair today," it said, its face a vibrant shade of red. "Or perhaps Elyse will do it. Her hair looks better than you ever made mine look. No one needs you, anyway!" It turned for the door.

How I wanted to stop it. How I wanted to plead to it! But I was too shaken. My lifeveins felt numb. This was not just any human speaking these words. This was a human at the peak of knowledge and understanding. This was a teenager.

The door slid open. Delta stormed out. Seconds later, the door slid back shut.

I was alone.

I pivoted my delicate head to look about the room. Water pooled on the floor from where I'd misfired and where it'd dripped. Evidence of the crime I'd committed. Proof of the eternal damage I'd just done. I had but one job: to save the souls of the humans I cared so very much for. To bring them to Deity not as gruesome beasts, but as refined creatures worthy of being Zepzeg in the Life After. All of my time, all of my efforts went into perfecting my craft. For them. Their salvation depended on it. And I had failed them.

I do not know how long I stood frozen by the water bowl, staring at the mess I'd created. Where I'd only moments before fought to muster courage and dignity, I now fought to muster anything at all. Delta was angry because I'd sprayed it in the face. How I wished a wet face was the extent of my sin. I had betrayed its trust in me, and in doing so, sabotaged my own efforts to beautify it to salvation. If they did not reach perfect beauty, it would be my fault. It would be my fault alone.

There was but one thing left that I could do. Sending out a prompt for the scrub bots to clean the water from the floor, I set to work immediately at my product station. I needed to earn back their trust. I needed to earn back their faith in me. I needed to create the best hair treatment that I could possibly prepare. It would not be good enough for Aurora's hair to look stunning, or magnificent, or lustrous.

It had to look perfect.

Aruvian milk paste would not do. It was effective, but not exquisite. Colugel was far too common a product and could serve me no use. The same could be said for jiculum foam, despite its high cost on the market. No—this was no time for the typical. I needed the absolute best. The rarest. The most costly. From the beginning of the treatment to the end, every step—every product—needed to be the grandest. I would compile my list, I would prepare my ingredients, then I would allow it to set before applying it when Aurora visited me later that evening. That would give me time to watch its video conference with the Broodmaster. There was so much to do.

Unaccustomed to such stress, I took a moment to worship Deity by admiring myself in the mirror and thanking it for my beauty. Such acts of worship are of the utmost importance, particularly in dire times such as these. How I needed Deity's guidance now. More than ever!

Aurora's hair would be beautiful. The most beautiful in all of the cosmos. I could ill afford to settle for less.

With my full array of products before me, I prepared to battle for Aurora and Delta's souls.

Chapter Six

I DO NOT OWN many things. Vorck do not collect possessions like other species do. We do not work to profit but to survive and have purpose. There are many species that do like to collect things. The Collectors like to collect things. That is why they are called the Collectors. Humans like to collect a lot of things, as do the Zepzeg, though most of what they collect are things to wear. I have found that dogs like to collect many things, but I do not understand why it is important to them, because they usually chew and destroy what they collect. What they collect is also from other people, so sometimes collecting things is not good. But Vorck do not collect things. We do not have sentimental attachments. There are very few things a Vorck owns that he cares about. There are only two things that I own that I care about. One is my phase hammer, because it is a useful tool and also a weapon. The other thing that I own and care about is not a thing. It is the engine room of the *Illustré*. Even though the *Illustré* belongs to Aurora, I take care of the engine room. I feel like it belongs to me. I like to be in control of it.

"All right, so this is a linkage. We use it to connect power sources to different components of the ship. They're pretty heavy, but Hank-is-Handy can move them without any help."

The words were Elyse's as she spoke to Defoe, the Blepharisma that she decided should work in the engine room. I did not agree with her decision to bring him to the engine room. It is not Defoe's engine room. It is mine, and I know how to run it.

Defoe waved his tentacle thing as he followed her. "I being very familiar with linkages! Blepharisma Darkboats have many components that must be connected, too."

I looked into the blaster turret bay, which was next to the forward screen generator bay, which is where we were standing. Blepharisma's two animals, his blue Slarb and his pink Gralb, were touching the different ship parts there. I did not want them touching things. I did not want them in the engine room at all. I was afraid they might bite something and break it. Then maybe they would die, and if they died, maybe Defoe would die. I did not want that, because Elyse likes Defoe. If Elyse did not like Defoe, maybe it would not matter so much.

Elyse decided that she did not want to ask Aurora if Defoe could work in the engine room. I think this is a bad idea. Aurora likes to know what is going on in her ship because it is her ship. It is not Elyse's ship. She did not pay the credits for it.

Humans make many judgments on things. Sometimes they make judgments on people. This is what they call trust. Aurora has always had good trust in me because I do good work and I always let her know what is going on. But Elyse did not want her to know about Defoe. I was afraid that if Aurora found out that Defoe was working in the engine room without her permission, she might not have good trust anymore. That would give me many feelings that are not good. I have worked hard for many years for her to trust me like she does. This is why I thought inviting Defoe into the engine room was a bad idea.

I was right in my prediction that Elyse would like Defoe. She liked him even more now because of what he did to her hair. I do not understand how Defoe made Elyse's hair look good. Elyse does not understand it, either. When she went to wash his plant slime off her head the last time, she said it came out easy, then her hair dried and looked different. She did not do anything to it at all. One bad thing Defoe did is that I think maybe he made her brain sick. She continues to say, "I can't believe how my hair looks," even though she looked at it many times in the mirror. I did not know why she would have such a hard time believing it when she can see it. I believed very much how her hair looked.

Elyse has never cared about her hair much. She does not like to care about things that Aurora and Delta care about. She thinks this makes her different and that different is good. I did not understand why she cared about her hair so much now. Maybe it was because it looked very different. Elyse usually has it squished into a very small ball on her head that humans call a *bun*. But there was no bun now, and her hair had many curves and waves in it and it also cascaded down her back. She liked this, but I did not understand why. I think it would make it easier for an enemy to grab and hold while they cut off her head. I think that not having long hair would decrease a being's chances of having their head cut off in this way.

I watched as Elyse told Defoe about the linkages that are always breaking and how we always need more of them. These are not things that Defoe needs to know about. I do not trust Defoe and I also do not like Defoe. I think he is bad for the ship and I wish he would stay in his room. But Elyse told him to come here, so it is not his fault. Perhaps when she is not looking, I will crush his plant head with my phase hammer. If she asks me what happened, I will say that he slipped. I think this would be a good thing to say because when people slip, they hit their head a lot. But I do not want to lie to Elyse. I do not think it is something she would like me to do. Then maybe she would not trust me much, too. If Aurora and Elyse did not trust me, then I would have many bad feelings that would make me want to leave. If I decide to crush Defoe's plant head with my phase hammer, I will do the right thing and tell Elyse the truth. I think that would make her feel better.

It is difficult for me to understand why Elyse likes her hair so much now when she did not before. Humans have very hard emotions to understand. I like things because they are good and I do not like things because they are bad. It is very easy to know what I think about things for that reason. But humans like things they do not like and they do not like things that they like. I have tried hard to understand the way that they think. I think that sometimes humans make themselves not like things if they think they cannot have them. I do not think Elyse ever thought her hair could look like it looked now, and so she decided not to like it or to care. But then when it looked the way she thought it could not look, she decided to like it.

Humans have many feelings about themselves. I think that pretending to not care about her ugly hair somehow made Elyse feel better about it. Now that her hair was not ugly or a bun, she cared about it a lot. Humans care a lot about the things they like about themselves. Vorck do not think this way. I care very much about things I do not like about myself, such as my need to have a head. If I did not need a head, I would not have to worry so much about an enemy cutting it off. But I do need a head, so I think very often about ways to not let enemies cut it off. I think this decreases my chance of losing my head in this way, which is a good thing for survival. A Vorck cannot live for very long without a head. I predict it would be less than a week. If I only thought about the things about me that were good, such as my strong arms, then I would not think about my head very much. Enemies would exploit my carelessness and would try to cut it off. So it is good to care about things you do not like about yourself. It gives the enemy less things to exploit.

I think I will find something that Elyse does not think she is good at and help her get good at it. I do not know what it will be, but I will think about it. I think making her feel good about a thing she does not feel good about will make her happy. I will think hard of all the things she is not good at and pick the one that is easiest to help her with. It will be hard to think of the best thing because there are many things Elyse is not good at. Maybe I will make a list and show it to her. I will call the list, "These are the things you are not good at." Then she can look at the list and tell me which one she wants to improve. I think this is a good idea that she will enjoy.

Elyse was explaining more things to Defoe when Delta walked into the engine room. Delta did not have good-looking hair when she entered. It looked wet and pushed back over her head. I think if I was a human that had to have hair, I would like to have wet hair a lot. It would be easier to get out of the way, and it would be more difficult for an enemy to grab while they tried to cut off my head.

When Delta saw Defoe in the engine room, her eyes got big like they do a lot when humans see something they do not expect. "What's *he* doing in here?"

"Umm, excuse me? What are *you* doing in here?" Elyse said. "Why are you wet?"

Defoe looked at Elyse and Delta but did not say anything. Delta put one of her hands on her hip, which is something that Elyse hates. She calls it *attitude*, and she does not like it when Delta does it. I watched Delta to see if she would say something that would make Elyse angry, but she did not. She only said, "How did you do it?"

"How'd I do what?"

Delta's body did not move, but her eyes moved. First they watched Elyse. Then they watched Defoe. Then they watched me. Then they watched Elyse again. That is when they stopped moving. "Your hair. How did you do it?" Elyse was quiet for a moment, which made Delta speak again. When she spoke, she blew out a breath like she was very tired. "I'm wet because Velistris sprayed me with the hose again."

Elyse made a small laugh sound. "I'm sorry?"

"I don't even want to talk about it," Delta said. "I'm *done* with Velistris. I'm over her. She's the *stupidest* person on this ship."

What Delta said surprised me. She does not usually say smart things like that. "Weak Velistris is *weak!*" I said. I could not help it. Elyse looked at me in the way humans look at things they do not understand. Then she looked at Delta.

"How did you get your hair to look like that?" Delta asked. "You must tell me, sister."

Human females are competitive about the way that they look. I have found that if a human female discovers a new way to look, sometimes they do not like to tell other females about it. I do not understand why. For this reason, I predicted that Elyse would not tell Delta the truth about her hair. My prediction was incorrect.

Elyse squinted her eyes very hard. "Do you *really* want to know?"

"Yes," answered Delta. "I must know. I *must* have hair as beautiful as yours. I would do anything."

"*Anything?*"

"You know I would."

Based on past experiences with Delta, I believed this to be true. "Defoe," Elyse said, "come here, please. I'd like to introduce you to Miss Delta Bluewater."

The Blepharisma approached on his big slug foot.

"Defoe?" asked Delta.

Elyse answered, "That's his name. Defoe."

"How'd he get such a human-sounding name?"

"Because I named him. He didn't have a name until he met me. It's after Daniel Defoe, who wrote *Robinson Crusoe.*"

Delta looked confused. "Who, who wrote *what?*"

"Never mind." Defoe came next to Elyse, who put her hands on her hips the same way that Delta did. "Defoe, Delta would like hair like mine. Would you like to help her?"

"I being very happy to!" answered the Blepharisma.

Taking several steps away, Delta said, "What's *he* have to do with it?"

"Oh, he's *everything* to do with it."

"How?"

Humans do not like to give good answers. I think they would get along more if they answered questions better.

"Do you trust me?" Elyse asked.

"No," Delta answered. "Absolutely not. I do not trust you one little bit!"

"You want hair like mine, right? You'd give *anything* for it, right?"

Delta did not look like she wanted to answer. "I'd give... most things. Please, sister, just tell me what he has to do with your hair."

"You should tell her," I said to Elyse. "That way, she does not think she is being attacked." I knew it would not make Elyse happy for me to say it, but I thought it needed to be said. I think that Elyse thought this was fun, but fun should not hurt other lifeforms or get them in trouble, unless they are unimportant lifeforms. Unimportant lifeforms can get hurt and it is okay.

"Attacked?" asked Delta. Her eyes got big and she pointed to Defoe. "Wait a minute, is that thing going to *eat* me like he did you?"

Elyse looked at me with an angry face. "Thanks a lot, Hank-is-Handy!"

I did not feel bad that she was angry. I love Elyse, but she was not making a good choice.

"I'm not getting eaten by that thing!" Delta said. "If you think that, you're crazy!"

"Okay, listen," said Elyse, as she held up her hands. "So yes, it happened when he ate my head. Or after he did, to be more precise. At first, I couldn't wash that slime from his mouth out of my hair, but then after a while, it just came out on its own, like it lost its hold or something. I don't know if it dissolved, if my hair absorbed it, or what, but after I shampooed and dried off, it looked like *this*. Seriously, I didn't do a thing to it. Do you honestly think I could make my hair look like this on my own? It even darkened my techno-dye!"

Delta got quiet for a moment. Her eyes did not make it easy to tell what she was thinking or feeling. She looked more closely at Elyse's hair. "It does have quite the shine."

"It's not just the shine. Feel it!" Elyse walked closer to Delta so that Delta could touch her hair.

"It's so soft," Delta said with a quiet voice. "It feels like silk!"

The smile on Elyse's face got bigger. "And *all* you need to do to get this soft, silky shine…is to let my friend here 'treat' you."

Sometimes I do not like being in charge of security. This was one of those times that I did not like it. I would rather have done different things than what we were doing, such as run forward screen diagnostics or lubricate the turbines in the spindrive chamber, but I could not do them because I needed to make sure Elyse and Delta were safe. Even though I did not fear Defoe, I could not leave the two humans alone with him. I wished that we could do something else, so I said, "I wish that we could do something else."

"I know, shut up," said Elyse.

"This is important!" said Delta.

I disagreed that it was important. If the engine room does not function properly, then the *Illustré* will not fly properly. I believe that this is more important than hair. But they did not believe it.

"Did it hurt?" Delta asked. "When he did it?"

"No, not at all," Elyse answered.

I watched Delta get quiet for a moment. This is because she was thinking. Then she said, "Let's do it."

Elyse's eyes got big. "You're gonna do it?"

"Let's do it!" She bent her knees like she was preparing to get hit hard. "If you're telling me it doesn't hurt, let's do it."

"It doesn't hurt at *all*."

Humans do not like to feel pain. For a Vorck, pain is something that is expected in life, so we do not fear or have feelings about it. We do not have pain receptors like humans do. If I was engaged in combat with an enemy and it cut my arm off, I would feel pain but I would still be able to function. I have seen some humans lose limbs in combat. They do not handle it as well as a Vorck. Humans are not weak like Zepzeg, but they are weaker than Vorck. This is why it did not surprise me that Delta did not want to feel pain.

Delta performed a head nod. "All right, let's go. Let's go, before I change my mind!"

I watched Elyse clap her hands. I do not know why she did it, but she only did it once. "You ready?"

"I'm ready!" Delta closed her eyes very tight and her body tensed up.

Elyse looked at Defoe. "Defoe, are you ready?"

The Blepharisma looked at Elyse with its red eyes. "I not understanding what is happening, but I being ready!"

"Suck her brain."

I got my phase hammer ready in case I needed to kill Defoe. Defoe reached out with his tentacle arm and wrapped it around Delta. When he did this, she opened her eyes and opened her mouth and sucked in a breath that sounded surprised. Defoe looked like he puffed up big and he rose up over her. The tentacle pulled Delta forward as Defoe ate her head.

I began to think of something as I watched Delta try to get away from Defoe, who had her head in his plant mouth. I began to wonder what information he would get from her brain. Many species do not like the Broodmasters because they can read brains, but it did not seem very different from how the Blepharisma read brains, except that the Blepharisma had to eat peoples' heads. I wondered if this was why Defoe understood everything Elyse was telling him in the engine room. Perhaps he got all of this information from her brain. Perhaps he felt like he needed a friend because Elyse felt like she needed a friend. What if all of Defoe's thoughts and feelings were Elyse's first? What if Defoe was like a reflection in a mirror to Elyse and she did not realize it? I did not know enough information to form a prediction as to whether I was correct or incorrect, but I decided that I would never let Defoe eat Aurora's head, just in case. I would not want it to know everything about the ship.

Defoe's tentacle arm let go of Delta, and she moved quickly to get her head out of his plant mouth. When it came out, it had the same slime on it that Elyse had when she was in his plant mouth. Delta's hair looked wetter than it was before but also sticky and heavy, and it was stuck all over her face. The only part of her face that I could see was her mouth, which was open and breathing very hard. Delta took some steps backward but then fell down on her butt. I have seen humans breathing the way that she was breathing then. It is called *hyperventilating*. Very quickly, Elyse knelt down beside her.

"Delta! Are you okay?"

Delta was performing hyperventilation breaths very hard. Her breathing was the only part of her that moved.

Something moved behind me. I turned around to look and saw the Slarb and Gralb. They hopped into the room that we were in and stopped when they saw me. I watched them for a second, then looked back at Delta and Elyse.

"Delta? *Delta?*" Elyse said. Defoe was not doing or saying anything. He just looked at Elyse as she said Delta's name over and over. He did not look puffed up or big anymore.

Delta opened her mouth and made a loud screaming sound. Elyse put her hand over Delta's mouth. "Shh! Shh! It's okay!"

Delta stopped screaming, then put her hand on the top of her head. When she felt what was there, she made a face that did not look happy at all. "You did it!" said Elyse. She pushed Delta's hair over her head and out of her face. "That wasn't so bad, was it?"

"This feels *revolting*!" said Delta.

"You look revolting," said Elyse. "But you're *going* to look great! That's what you want, right?"

It was what Delta said that she wanted. I heard her say it myself. It did not look like Delta was in trouble or would die, so I stopped looking at her and instead looked at the Blepharisma. He did not look any different than he did before. I do not know what he was thinking now that he had put Delta's head in his plant mouth. I do not know if he was thinking anything at all. But I was thinking very many things about him.

I have tried hard for a long time to feel feelings the way humans do. I have especially tried hard to feel Elyse's feelings and to also feel good feelings. It is something that is very difficult for me. Sometimes I think of it a lot even when humans are not there. But I have never been able to feel feelings the way that humans do.

I did not know if I was right that Defoe was feeling the things that Elyse feels because he ate her head, and I did not know if he would feel the things that Delta feels now that he ate her head, too. But I thought that if he did, it would not make me happy at all. It would make me very sad. I believe that this is because feelings would come much easier for him than they would for me. I have known all of the humans on the *Illustré* for many years but I have never felt their feelings. But Defoe does not know them at all. Perhaps he would be able to feel all of their feelings, or perhaps he would not be able to feel any of them. I did not know, and I did not have enough information to make a prediction.

But I recognized a new feeling in me, and it was one that did not make me happy. I recognized that I did not like Defoe even more despite not knowing if he could feel their feelings or not. I did not want him to feel their feelings at all, because I could not.

I know what this feeling is called, because I have heard all of the humans use it with each other. It is a word called *jealousy*. Sometimes, they use the word *envy*, too. It is when you have bad feelings about someone because they have something you wish that you had. I have heard those words used most by Aurora and Elyse when they talk about Delta. She is jealous and envious of many things, like she was jealous and envious about Elyse's hair and wanted hair like that herself. It is not a good feeling to have. Humans do not like it when other humans have jealous or envious feelings. This is what made me sad.

I love Elyse and I want to feel her good feelings. I wanted to feel them on my own because that would mean I grew as a lifeform and was able to understand other lifeforms, especially ones that I loved. I wanted to evolve as a feeler. I realized now that I had indeed evolved and that I was feeling a new feeling—but it was not a good feeling at all, and it was not a feeling that Elyse would feel. If Elyse cares about something that she does not have, she does not get envious about it. She makes herself not like it and it helps her to not feel bad about not having it. This is what she did with her ugly bun hair before Defoe ate her head.

But Delta does get envious.

In all of my years trying to feel the good feelings that Elyse sometimes feels, I recognized now that my greatest area of emotional evolution was to feel jealousy like Delta feels. I was jealous that Defoe might be able to so easily feel feelings, so much so that I began to think bad thoughts about him. For example, I thought right then that it might make me feel good to hit him in his plant head with my phase hammer.

But this is a bad feeling, too. Humans call it *wrath*. That I felt both envy and wrath did not make me feel good at all.

I wondered what Elyse would think if she knew that I was feeling all of these things. Would she be ashamed of me? Would she not want me to love her anymore? Did feeling these things mean that I was a bad human or a bad Vorck? I very much did not want her to know what I was feeling.

It also made me wonder why bad feelings are so easy. I know that I love Elyse only because she says, "you know you love me." But I do not feel love. I also do not feel happy, or excited, or amused. I have only ever felt feelings that humans say are not good, like anger, and sadness, and now jealousy and wrath. The more I thought about all these things, the more bad feelings I began to feel.

"Hank-is-Handy?"

I realized that Elyse was speaking to me. I looked at her.

"You okay, big guy?" she asked.

A reason that Elyse loves me is because she says I always tell her the truth. But I knew that if I told her the truth and that I was not feeling okay, then she would ask me why. Then I would have to tell her the truth again about how I was feeling jealousy and wrath. And if I told her that, she might have bad feelings toward me or not love me anymore. So I did the thing that she loves me for not doing. "Yes." I lied to her. It made my bad feeling worse. But I did not want her to stop loving me.

Delta was standing next to Elyse. Even though her head was still sticky and wet, she did not look scared anymore. I did not know how long I had been thinking about feelings, and I did not know if they had talked while I was not paying attention to them. Humans do this a lot, too. They call it *zoning out* or *daydreaming*. It is another thing that Vorcks do not often do.

Elyse spoke again. "We're going to go to Defoe's room and sit for a while, just in case it was the humidity that helped me wash that slime out. Do you want to come with us?"

Her question made me think two different things. The first was that I did not want to go with her. I wished to remain in the engine room. The second was that I still needed to protect her from Defoe in case he turned evil and tried to hurt her and Delta. I knew that as the security officer, it was my responsibility to protect her and Delta and the rest of the crew. Aurora has good trust in me because I do these things. So I knew that what I needed to do was go with them. But a thing happened to me that I did not understand. I knew the good thing that I wanted to do, but I did not do it. I did the bad thing that I did not want to do instead. "I will stay in the engine room. There are neutron secondaries to clean." There were not.

She smiled at me and said, "No problem. We'll just hang out there for a bit, then wash her off to see what happens." She raised her hand to perform a wave of departure. "Wish us luck!"

"Good luck," I said. It is what one is supposed to say to a human when they ask you to wish them luck.

The Slarb and Gralb went next to Defoe, who I looked at again. He looked the same way that he always looked, with his red eyes that looked at everything from underneath his hooded plant head.

"Let's go, Defoe!" Elyse said.

Defoe's tentacle arm waved around. "I being going!" He followed them out of the room on his slug foot, and his Slarb and Gralb followed behind him.

I was alone.

There are many things that I do not understand. This is especially true about humans and their feelings. But what I am supposed to understand is what it is like to be a Vorck. I have always been a Vorck. I cannot not be a Vorck. Vorck do what they want to do and they do not do what they do not want to do. Vorck always do things for reasons they understand. But I did not understand why I felt bad feelings toward Defoe, and I did not understand why they caused me to speak something to Elyse that was not true. I always wanted to feel feelings like a human, but I did not want to feel the bad ones.

I did not do anything in the engine room after Elyse and Delta left with Defoe and his Slarb and his Gralb. I did not lubricate the turbines. I did not check the connections on any of the linkages. I did not take an inventory of maintenance supplies. What I did was stand and think for a very long time. I could not stop thinking, even though I wanted to. It made me think of all the times I told Elyse to stop thinking about bad things when she thought of them, but she could never stop thinking about them. Now it was me who could not stop thinking about the bad things I did not want to think about. I wanted very much for something to happen that would make me think of something else. But nothing did. So I stood.

I do not know what happened to Elyse and Delta or if Defoe's plant slime got out of Delta's hair and it looked good. None of them came back to tell me. I have always heard Aurora say that she wished Elyse and Delta would get along better because they were half-sisters. Maybe she was getting her wish. If this was the case, then that made me happy a little bit. I realized as I stood alone in the engine room that I was also getting my wish, because I had wished that no one would speak in the *Illustré* unless there was something that needed to be said. There was no speaking at all in the engine room, because I was the only one there.

It was not as good as I thought it would be.

Chapter Seven

BROODMASTERS. Revolting. Disgusting. Utterly vile. It is hard to imagine how Deity thought fit to breathe such contemptible creatures into existence. Perhaps it was to serve as a contrast to ourselves—ultimate monstrousness juxtaposed to perfection. Perhaps Deity was just having a bad solar cycle. Whatever the reason, the Broodmasters are here, and it is the rest of us who inhabit the many clusters of the cosmos who must deal with them.

To see a Broodmaster—even on a video monitor—is to see the very definition of uncomeliness. They are grotesque blobs, dark and oily, with numerous growths and pustules protruding from their bodies. Though I have never stood in the physical presence of one, I have heard that they smell utterly foul. With vestigial tentacles swatting away the flies and other insects that are drawn to it, it is very difficult to imagine that an ounce of sentience exists within them. But therein lies the most dangerous aspect of these universally reviled monsters. They have evolved far past sentience, into the realm of mental manipulation. They read minds. They control them. They plant thoughts with such cunning subtlety, it can be hard to recognize them as anything but one's own. Through their swarms of offspring, many of which are born for no other purpose than to move them about and satisfy their every whim, they are able to control entire cities and starships. I have always struggled to understand the nature of human offspring, but I would far prefer that uncertainty of purpose than to experience the hopelessness of being a Broodmaster's child. They are born to serve. What a horrible, unfortunate existence theirs must be.

The video file that I was viewing was from earlier that day, when Aurora had been contacted by its Broodmaster liaison prior to the planetary negotiation. Their faces were side-by-side on a split display. To have Aurora's ravishing loveliness so close to the disgusting form of the Broodmaster only emphasized the creature's repugnance.

"It is a pleasure to meet you, Aurora Ultraviolet," it said, the surface of its gelatinous skin jiggling with every word that the computer translated. Translation systems are designed to attempt to match tone with appearance. It aims to make beings sound like one would imagine in one's own language. The result with this Broodmaster was terrible, like the reverberating echo of an internal organ had it possessed a mouth—deep, distorted, and ethereal. I could see Aurora's eyes wince ever so faintly as it heard the Broodmaster speak for the first time. Even as accustomed as it was to the many species who live in our cluster, the creature's harrowing voice affected it. "I am Corvus, Broodmaster ambassador to the human embassy."

Aurora dipped its head, likely with as much civility as it could muster. "The honor is mine, Corvus."

"I am sure that it is."

Communicating via video conference sets a Broodmaster at a distinct disadvantage. Without being in another being's physical presence, there is no way for it to exert its telepathic energy. It is a curious arrangement for a Broodmaster to agree to, and even more curious for it to propose, as was this case with this particular meeting. It did not make sense for a Broodmaster to initiate a dialogue without having use of its most powerful weapon: its mind. Or perhaps that was part of its deception, meant to give the illusion of fair play. Anyone who knew a Broodmaster knew better. Aurora most certainly did.

"We are still quite a ways from Point Maven." It was the name of the human embassy where the negotiation was to be held. "Might I inquire as to why you've chosen to contact me in advance?"

The Broodmaster's many eyes—some of which I am not even certain were functional—darted to and fro in random directions. "Yours is a lineage of great renown," it said. "My own ancestors knew of Corinda Rhea and her colony in the Ragnarok Cluster. I wished to see for myself how one of her descendants has fared. I see that you have fared well. Corinda would be proud, were she alive on this day."

"Flattery may work for some," Aurora said, "but I am not among them."

"Our reputation is not held in the highest esteem," said Corvus in response—a rare true statement from any Broodmaster. "It has been said that we seek to manipulate. I wished to dispel that notion by discussing Gryamore V in an environment where your mind is protected. It is a step of good faith."

Aurora's own eyes passed over the creature, no doubt drawn in by its repulsiveness. "I appreciate the gesture, though you must know that this type of communication is improper before such a consequential negotiation."

The Broodmaster let loose a garbled roar, its body shaking with violence as it bellowed, "*Improper!*" Aurora's eyes widened, as taken aback as I was, though within moments the Broodmaster's shaking had ceased. Its voice returned to normal as if nothing had happened at all. "I respect your concerns, Aurora Ultraviolet. The opportunity to speak with me over visual subspace communication is yours to accept or decline. We only wished for fairness, in light of the Dacians sending one of their own ambassadors to meet you."

One of their own ambassadors? I was certainly surprised to hear this, as apparently was Aurora. "A Dacian ambassador?" it asked, incredulously. "I'm sorry, I've heard of no such thing."

"Of course, you haven't," Corvus answered. "They would dare not request a meeting as we would. A Dacian ambassadorial ship left the Gryamore System one rotation ago. We are certain it is heading to intercept you."

"If the Dacians believe they will coerce me into siding with them, they are mistaken—as are you, if you believe the same."

A sound like a satisfied groan came from the monster. In its garbled, ethereal voice, it continued. "We long only for fairness, Aurora Ultraviolet. If the Dacians have the opportunity to meet with you in secret, so should we."

The look in Aurora's eyes was one I had seen many times before. It was one of utter insistence. "They will have no such opportunity. Any Dacian that wishes to pay my starship a visit will not find it as pleasant as they imagine."

"Surely now you understand why we reached out to you."

There was hesitance in the captain's eyes. I understood why. It was always a risk agreeing with a Broodmaster. One never knows what game they play. Lifting its chin in a manner akin to defiance, it said simply, "I understand, Ambassador Corvus. Thank you for bringing the matter to my attention."

"We do not wish to harm the Dacian species. We would gladly share the Gryamore System with them as we strive for peace and harmony, as we do with all of our neighbors in this cluster." The mere thought of a Broodmaster longing for peace and harmony was as laughable as it was preposterous. By the look in Aurora's eyes, I could tell it didn't believe it, either. "Remember this in the negotiation," the monster said. "It is only fair. Transmission over."

There was no opportunity given to Aurora to reply. The channel closed, and Corvus's side of the monitor went to black. With the Broodmaster gone, Aurora allowed itself a moment of composure, closing its eyes and pushing its fingers up through its hair. It looked exhausted. Captaincy is a burden that I cannot imagine. Opening its eyes a moment later, Aurora looked at the camera and said to the computer,

"Save to slot 419, transfer file to Velistris's holodrive at recording's end." Leaning forward, it reached out to turn off the camera.

There was a sudden commotion behind it! Aurora flinched, its hand still outstretched to end the recording as it turned around to look. It was Riley, that accursed creature. It was yipping against the inside of the captain's door, its paws scratching and scratching like it desperately needed to escape. I have seen this behavior in the beast several times. It is often when it needs to defecate—a process so disgusting, I can hardly understand how any carbon-based lifeform can deal with it. Rising from its chair, Aurora made its way hurriedly to the door to "walk" the monster. "I'm coming!" the captain told it, a hint of panic in its voice as if any moment, the dog's bladder might erupt in its quarters. Opening the door, Aurora trotted out with it to bring it to the hallway defecation chamber.

This was not a little scene I had expected to see, the beast having distracted Aurora just as it was reaching to turn the camera off and send the file. Nonetheless, there was nothing much for me to see other than the captain's empty quarters. So I folded my crystalline fingers together and considered the Broodmaster's message.

Broodmasters are quite difficult to gauge, even for Zepzeg, as their distinct lack of facial features and body language make all but their actual words a mystery—and their words have little to do with their intent. Just because a Broodmaster is not in range to affect one's mind does not mean there isn't manipulation at play. Every word that resonates from the gelatinous blobs must be inspected with the utmost caution. There was bound to be something of significance in the video, regardless of its short length.

My thoughts were interrupted as Aurora returned to its room, Riley leaping at its legs as if the beast's intent was to trip the poor captain. For the life of me, I cannot imagine why any sentient lifeform would desire such a pest! But humans appear to have a distinct affinity for dogs as companions. I waited to see Aurora alter its course for its communication console to turn off the recording, but quite to my astonishment, it didn't. Riley's distraction must have forced Aurora to forget to end the transmission and have it sent to me! I watched as the captain mulled about the room, leaning in front of the body mirror that hangs in the far corner to inspect its face, then to tease back its hair. Those gorgeous tendrils. How I longed to run my fingers through them later!

Suddenly, there was a flicker of light on the black side of the monitor, where Corvus had been moments before. The familiar sound of a communication prompt emerged. Someone was calling Aurora! Surely it would realize now that it'd forgotten to turn the recording off. But it didn't. Instead, it pranced to the monitor with the largest of smiles on its face, the likes of which I had never beheld. Dare I say, there was even a glow to its skin. I have spent many years of my life in the company of humans, long before I ever knew Aurora Ultraviolet or its crew. I have seen a plethora of emotional states displayed on their faces—anger, enthusiasm, boredom, amusement, even sadness. But never—not once—had I seen such a radiant expression as this.

My captain sat down in the chair in front of its console, reaching out to tap the display to accept the communication prompt. There, appearing in the blackness that only minutes before had displayed the most grotesque of creatures, there appeared the face of a human male—dark hair both atop its head and protruding ever so slightly from the lower side of its jawline in the form of what humans call *stubble*. The moment its hazel eyes made contact with Aurora's, the same glowing smile appeared on its face as the captain's.

Bryce Lockhart. This was Aurora's fiancé. Its nostrils expanding as it drew in a breath, it said, "Hello, beautiful."

Aurora melted. Right then and there, I saw it. Its pupils dilated—a thing that does not occur regularly on board the *Illustré*. Its shoulders relaxed in a way I'd never seen. Everything about its form, its face, its posture, seemed to surrender whatever burdens it was accustomed to carrying. All care was lost. In no other setting had I seen Aurora in so much peace. Its smile widening, it said to Bryce simply, "Hey."

I realized in that moment that no mind was given whatsoever to the fact that the recording was still on. In the midst of Riley's distraction and Bryce's sudden calling, the captain had simply forgotten that it needed to be turned off. What I was about to witness was not meant for me.

I should have turned it off. I should have respected what I knew would have been Aurora's wishes and stopped the playback right then and there. But I was drawn. Curiosity triumphed over decency, and I found myself nervously observing, as if at any moment one of them might realize I was intruding.

"Is that all I get, just a 'hey?'" Bryce asked. I found its statement contradictory, for its words sounded accusatory though were accompanied by a smile. Was a fiancé supposed to be addressed in a certain fashion? I did not know.

Aurora laughed—an odd response, I thought, to such a presumptuous and demanding question. "After the day I had, you're lucky to hear anything from me at all."

"What's going on?"

The captain ran its fingers through its hair, blew out a breath as if it was gasping for oxygen, then shook its now loosened curls from its face. There was such a haphazard look to its mannerisms. It was so unreserved. Unprofessional. Did it not care how its fiancé viewed it? "I had my first run-in with our Broodmaster ambassador today."

"Ooh," Bryce said, its smile widening to the point where I saw the white of its teeth. It looked amused, though

I was uncertain of what could have amused it. "Well, that explains it."

Explained what? I listened on.

"Yeah, it's…" Aurora's words trailed off, the captain shaking its head. "You know how it is."

Bryce nodded. "I do."

"I can already tell this is going to be a battle of trust." It laughed, a tad gently. "The problem is, I don't trust *anyone* involved in this."

Ignoring Aurora's statement, its fiancé offered a puzzled expression before saying, "I thought you weren't supposed to meet anyone until you got to Gryamore?"

"Yeah, that's what I thought, too," answered the captain. "I got word that the Broodmasters wanted an audience. Apparently they caught wind of a Dacian ambassadorial ship leaving Gryamore to rendezvous with us. Their concern is that it's coming to initiate some kind of secret deal."

"Really?"

"Yeah. Or so they think, apparently. It wouldn't surprise me. You remember my run-in with Vood."

Bryce nodded. "Oh, yeah. I remember."

I did not, which was quite surprising to me. How was it that this being knew more of Aurora's past dealings than I? I was hopeful that one of them would elucidate this past encounter, though as typical for humans, they moved on, leaving their words shrouded in mystery.

"Hank's ready for them if they show up, right?" Bryce asked.

"Hank's ready every minute of every day," Aurora said, laughing. Bryce laughed as well. "No one else knows about any of this, yet. I had the Broodmaster video call sent to Velistris as soon as it was finished, so when we get together later she'll give me her thoughts."

Evidence that it believed the recording had stopped.

Aurora flashed its eyes at Bryce. "My hair's getting a little *makeover* today."

At last! Something of substance would be discussed.

"A makeover?" it asked. "It needs to be made over?"

"I got recruited into a little hair-styling competition between Velistris and Elyse."

Its eyes widening, Bryce said, "*Elyse?*"

"I don't know what she did, but her hair looks *incredible* right now. I'm talking like someone on cinevision."

I did not like hearing those words, though after my incident with Delta, I could not help but listen with humility. It was clear to me that I had my work cut out for me. To heap such high praise upon Elyse's work was something I had never heard the captain do—not in any regard, let alone in regards to its hair. On any other day, I would scoff at the mere notion of competing with Elyse with such an important thing. But I now felt quite nervous. What if I sprayed Aurora in the face with water? What if I applied the wrong kind of cream to its roots? What if I became distracted and failed to let its mask set for long enough? These are catastrophic errors, yet I realized now that I was capable of them. I was capable of sustained imperfection. This would be no large issue with humans, who are quite acclimated to imperfection, but for a Zepzeg, it is unimaginable. This was no longer solely about the salvation of my crewmates. If I could not defeat rabble such as Elyse in hair styling, what did that mean for myself? What if I could no longer buff out every scratch on my pristine surface? What if Riley licked me and I failed to notice it? What if my crystalline skin clouded? In the eyes of Deity, I might as well be rusted metal.

Lost in my thoughts, I realized that I'd missed a portion of what they had said. I refocused my poor, fledgling attention. "What, you don't think I could pull off straight?" the captain asked with the wryest of grins I'd ever seen.

"You know I'd miss those curls."

"These curls?" It tossed its head back and forth, then placed its chin atop its intertwined fingers. A loose ribbon dangled down between its eyes—all the while, it smiled.

Bryce smiled, too. "Better not give me those eyes for too long or I might have to fly over there."

"You couldn't catch me if you tried," Aurora said, an odd coyness to its words. I was completely befuddled by this dialogue. What about Aurora's eyes would force its fiancé to fly to the *Illustré*, and what did chasing it down have to do with anything? Did these words contain some sort of hidden meaning that I was not privy to?

"I don't know, I've got a pretty fast set of wings."

"Not fast enough, flyboy."

"Then I guess I'd have to tractor beam you."

It pursed its lips. "Ooh, you'd tractor beam me?"

"Yeah, that's right."

"Tell me more about how you'd *tractor beam* me."

What kind of bizarre conversation was this? Were they discussing space combat? Was this the initiation of a duel? I had never heard of such a custom between two humans scheduled to be married, so I could only assume that this was some sort of unspoken tradition that I was unaware of.

They went on about this for quite some time, quipping back and forth about different ways they would defeat each other, all of it nonsensical. Yet with every word they spoke, their voices became lustier. It was not until this had gone on for over five full minutes that I began to suspect that their words were allegorical—very similar to Elyse's confounding sarcasm. It is utterly mystifying to me how humans are able to communicate effectively! How does one know when one is being literal or figurative? What grave mistakes that could cause! Imagine if Aurora had mistaken the threats of the Vorticella for an invitation to intimacy. What if they'd told us to lower our screens and the captain instead revealed its reproductive organs? How utterly awful and inconvenient it must be to be such a befuddling creature! It is no wonder that so many humans seek out Zepzeg to be their diplomatic advisors.

At long last and quite mercifully, their doublespeak came to a close. They transitioned into a form of dialogue that was more solemn and discernable. "I really miss you," Aurora said, its voice barely more than a whisper. Its eyes flickered downward before meeting Bryce's again.

Bryce matched the words in tone. "I miss you, too."

"Is it okay if I tell you I'm struggling right now? With the distance?"

The male's face remained firm. "I know."

"I know that...this is what we need to do. I know it's what we *must* do. You and I aren't the only ones this is going to impact. It's the unification of two houses. But at that same time, part of me wishes we could..."

"...we could what?"

"I don't know. Elope. Fake our own deaths. Just skip all the pomp and circumstance and just...be." Aurora looked down, its eyes once again shied away from Bryce.

Bryce looked at the captain, still. "You think you want that." It smiled a bit. "But I know you better. You'd get bored with me if you weren't the galaxy's premier representative of House Ultraviolet. You'd still want to be..." The words seemed to escape it, at which point Aurora smiled and spoke in turn.

"Gallivanting around the cosmos from one cluster to the next? Feeding my wanderlust?"

"You know it's you."

"It doesn't have to be."

After drawing in breath through its nostrils, Bryce said, "You're doing what you're doing right now because you spent your whole life working up to it. That's who you are. I'm marrying you knowing that. I don't expect it nor do I want it to ever change." It nodded. "And so I can wait. I can endure the distance, because I know once that gap closes, I'll be husband to the most outstanding woman the universe has ever known. A woman chosen by other species to negotiate matters of vast significance. Matters that impact everything. That's the caliber of woman I get to wed. This wait is hard, yes, but some waits are supposed to be. I'd include marrying Aurora Ultraviolet among them."

It appeared as if Aurora was trying not to smile, as if it was fighting hard to resist it. A smile emerged, anyway. It lifted its eyes to the monitor. "You know you're not too shabby yourself, right?"

"Yeah, a politician's kid," Bryce said with the faintest of smirks. "Don't know many people who'd get worked up over that."

"I would," Aurora said quietly. "If it was you, I would very much."

There was a pause. For several moments it lingered before Bryce spoke again. "I love you, Ro."

Ro? Had it mistaken Aurora's name? To my confusion, the captain answered amicably. "I love you, too."

There was a sudden chime behind me! At first, I thought it might be a trick of the audio on the recording, until I realized with horror that it was coming from my own chamber door. Aurora! It was showing up for its appointment. With the video still playing and the two presumably on the verge of saying something else, I had no choice but to quickly turn the console off. How I wanted to hear more! I was mesmerized by this manner of intimate talk between them. It was the kind of talk I'd never heard before. Other species do not speak this way. But I could not listen further without revealing my prying receptors to Aurora. As the video disappeared from my monitor, I said, "You may enter!" Indeed, it was Aurora who appeared when the door slid open. Folding my hands together as I faced it, I offered it a well-practiced smile of delight. "Are you ready for your treatment?" It was not what I wanted to ask. I wanted to ask what certain words and phrases meant. Why had Bryce referred to it as *Ro*? What exactly *was* love, a baffling concept to most species in the cosmos? But I could not ask these things. Not outright. Not without navigating the conversation toward them first.

But at least that, I could try.

Aurora was wearing a light blue, silk robe—one of its preferred garments when being treated. "I am ready," it answered my question. "What do you have for me?"

I directed it to my chair. "Please, captain, have a seat."

It did so. "Should I lean my head back?"

"Not yet. I would like to massage your scalp first."

Aurora smiled, though it was not quite so relaxed as how it'd smiled in the video. I realized in that moment that I would now forever judge every smile that emerged from its face to see if my presence could ever match that of its fiancé. I feared that answer would be *no*. "I'll take a scalp massage any day," it said, lowering into the chair.

I had warmed a small bowl of canoleil oil in preparation. It is common knowledge among the more learned that a scalp massage before a shampoo has tremendous benefits. Canoleil oil is a rare oil that comes from the canoleil blossom, found only on the Zepzeg world of Aeriel IV. It is a sweetly fragrant oil with fantastic exfoliating properties—arguably the best found in the natural world. It is also quite expensive. A pint of canoleil oil can match the price of a small starship. In the hands of the untrained, it is a terrible, terrible waste. As Aurora situated itself in the chair, I dimmed the lights in the room. Humans are a species that is naturally averse to bright lights, a flaw that I try to accommodate for when doing truly important work, as I was this day. "You may close your eyes if you wish."

It did. "I smell canoleil," it said, its smile widening a bit.

"Your receptors are functioning well," I said.

"Bringing out all the stops today, are we?"

I stirred a small hair painting brush into the bowl. "Only the best for my captain." I swirled the brush around to ensure it was saturated. "I will be applying several coats to your scalp. All of this should be absorbed by your hair, but if some were to touch your face, it would not be undesirable. Canoleil oil is just as beneficial for the skin as for the hair. You may allow it to sit, or I can rub it in if you wish."

"All sounds good to me."

"I will now begin." Swirling the brush around once more for good measure, I picked it up from the bowl and moved it over the captain's head. Holding out some of its red curls with one hand, I began painting them with the other.

I have found that there are two distinct moods to the captain when I beautify it—it is either highly talkative or not caring to talk at all. I could tell within a single minute of painting that this session would fall into the latter category. I did not know if that boded well for me or not. "You must be excited to finish these negotiations."

It was quiet for a moment before answering. "Must I?"

"I am sure of it."

"And why is that?"

It was my attempt to cleverly engage with it on the topic of my choice: its recent conversation with its fiancé. "What, with the engagement ball approaching and whatnot." Its strands darkened as they absorbed the oil—I found myself inclined to stare as I combed it back over its head.

"A ball is a ball," it answered, "nothing more. How I wish I could skip it."

I knew that it felt this way from the video, but it still saddened me to hear. One should never frown upon an opportunity to be the center of attention, particularly if one is beautiful. I was cautious in my reply. "You may feel differently about attending the ball after today's beautification. Your hair will be the most radiant of any human who has ever lived."

"Not all people define beauty the same way," it said.

Obviously, such a statement is preposterous, but I did not wish to offend it in such a noticeably fragile state. And so, I simply continued to paint, applying coat after coat of oil until its hair was slicked back with the richest of sheens. Such a wondrous shine, I have never seen on another human. After one final brushstroke to saturate, I placed the fingertips of my two hands against it and began to massage.

"Mm." It closed its eyes as it made the utterance. This is a part I know it likes. "That feels good."

The crystalline fingertips of a Zepzeg are far too sharp to rub against human skin without some form of protection, and so I utilize carbonester gloves to reduce pain and friction. Though I do find that they reduce a measure of fine motor skill from my hands, that is far more preferable than the inconvenience of bleeding scalp wounds. As I stroked its locks, I occasionally placed my hands against its forehead and brushed back—a subtle effort to keep oil from dripping onto its face and detracting from its pleasure. "Would you like to hear about the treatments I have in store for you today?" I knew that its conversation with the Broodmaster would eventually come, but I was far more inclined to discuss my own work first.

"Why did Elyse's hair fluster you so?" it asked, ignoring my question.

"I was not flustered."

"Quite the contrary, I've not seen you so flustered in all our time together."

Its words, though it pained me to hear them, were true. This was not something I wished to discuss. "It is my purpose on this ship to provide you and those worthy"—I did not mean to say the word, for I knew Aurora hates such terms, but it came out before I could stop it. I had no choice but to go on and pray it didn't notice—"with the utmost in beautification care. I wish to prove to you that your faith in me is not in vain."

"There are so many concerning things about your words," Aurora said, its eyes still closed. "How shall I decide which one to address, first?"

For a moment, my fingers stopped stroking.

"Your purpose on this ship is not to make us beautiful."

"I am aware, captain. My purpose is to serve as your diplomatic advisor."

"Nor is that your purpose." Its words surprised me to hear, and I angled my head. "Do you not believe that I could operate the communications station from my chair on the bridge if the need arose?" it asked. "Or that I could not provide myself and my nieces with beauty treatments if you were unable to? Perhaps they would not be the quality to which we've become accustomed under your care, but they would suffice nonetheless."

A low hum resonated from my core. It is a hum far too low for humans to perceive, but it is quite displeasurable to a Zepzeg. I believe it is akin to pain in a human's stomach as caused by stress. "Then what is my purpose, captain?"

"To share your life with us, and for us to share ours with you. To make ourselves better."

"I am making you better now."

"Putting oil in my hair does not make me better."

"I understand." I did not, for it was utter foolishness. "But once washed out and as a precursor to treatment, it will provide you with a most glamourous luster." Several dribbles emerged from its hairline. I stroked them back before they could reach its eyes.

Its eyes were opened now, though downcast, for I could see them in the reflection of the mirror across the room. "My hair does not require a glamorous luster. You are quite obsessed with luster, and sometimes I wish you'd cease being so."

I went still. I did not know what to say.

"I'm sorry," it said, its voice softening a touch. "That was uncalled for. Perhaps *I* am flustered on this day."

It most certainly was, and in a most demeaning way. I'd never heard it speak words so abhorrent. I resumed my stroking of its hair, as much a means of restraining my irritation as enhancing its experience.

Lifting its head, it looked at me in the mirror's reflection. "I am battling something deeply personal at present, Velistris. I would discuss it, but I'm not certain you'd understand. I'm not certain anyone here would."

Pressing my fingertips into its scalp, I moved them in small circles—an attempt to lull it into a vulnerable state. Its eyes closed, so I was hopeful that I'd succeeded. "You may try to explain it, if you wish." I knew the cause of its strife. How I desperately wanted to discuss it without the risk of revealing that I'd seen its video with Bryce. "I should very much like to hear whatever it is that ails you. Perhaps I could provide valuable insight."

"It is doubtful, but I will speak of it if you wish."

"Please do." I slid my fingers to the backside of its scalp, stroking just behind and below its ears. This is a spot I know it enjoys, as it often makes pleasure sounds when I engage it. I find that humans speak the most when they think the least, which is what I wished to encourage. I was hopeful that, distracted by pleasure, it would reveal its full conversation with its fiancé without caution.

"Mmm," it said. I had succeeded. Placing one hand against its forehead, I eased its head backward so that its glistening tendrils dangled into my wash basin. "I don't know," it said, a tad woozily.

It was on the verge of confession. I needed only to nudge it a little more. Sliding my hands around its neck, I slipped the top of its robe from its shoulders. With my carbonester gloves soaked with warm oil, I began to massage its shoulders and neck. "The increased comfort will make your pores more receptive to the oil. Please forgive me if this is undesirable." I knew it to be the opposite.

"Oh, my goodness," it murmured, closing its eyes as it now dipped its head forward. Though this defeated the purpose of my leaning its head back for the sake of keeping oil from its face, it seemed now not to care. I was unbothered by whatever oil dribbled to the floor. None of this was detrimental to the treatment, and if it elevated Aurora's ecstasy and made it speak more easily, all the better for me.

I lowered my own voice, as humans prefer this when speaking intimately. "Allow your tension to relent. Be at peace." Its head became quite limp. I am grateful as a being made of crystal to not have to bother with such inconveniences as muscle and tissue. They always seem in need of some sort of maintenance to operate properly. Aurora drew in the longest of breaths then released it through its nostrils. I continued to massage, knowing that it was only a matter of time until its will crumbled. I needed only to be patient.

At last, that patience paid off.

"I miss him so badly."

"You miss who, captain?" Obviously, I already knew the answer.

"Bryce."

It spoke in barely a whisper—an indication that I had properly intoxicated it with my touch. Humans are a strange contradiction when it comes to the disclosing of personal information. Though they often go to great lengths to keep their private lives secret, I have found that it is truly their desire to reveal as much about themselves as possible to any who might be inclined to listen. One only need know the right comforts to provide to prompt humans to speak more than they typically would—and often to a degree they later regret. Aurora is quite susceptible to massages, particularly when accompanied by warm oil. I have used this technique many times to get it to reveal aspects of various assignments that were supposed to be for its ears only. Aurora calls this manner of disclosure, *confiding*. I call it tactics. I did not ask it to elaborate on its last statement, for I knew elaboration would come on its own. Sometimes, it is best to wait humans out.

I was correct, as always. "I just want him here so much. I just want to touch him, you know?"

"Of course, I do." I had no idea.

"I talked to him today. It was almost…strange hearing him. Like I'm not used to it."

Human speech pattern also changes amid moments of pleasure. Aurora would have normally said it'd "spoken with" as opposed to "talked to" Bryce. Likewise, instead of "not used to," it'd have said "unaccustomed." It is a subtle change in them, but one that is perceivable. When their words are simplified, I find that more truth comes out. I listened as it spoke on.

"I don't even know if I'm doing the right thing."

Angling my head, I asked, "How do you mean?"

It rolled its neck as I massaged some nodules of tension. "I'm Corinda Rhea's granddaughter. It's my destiny to be traipsing about the galaxy, is it not?"

"It is right if you feel it is right." Humans like to hear such meaningless drivel.

"What if I just want to stay still? What if I want to just get married and retire in my late thirties? What if I just want to… stop? Am I even capable of that? Could I do it if I wanted to?"

I could scarcely imagine Aurora Ultraviolet stopping at anything. "And you are experiencing all these conflictions because of a video call?" Moving my hands up its neck, I slid them behind its ears, where I began to delicately stroke.

It moaned gently before answering, "I don't know. God, Velistris, you are so good at this."

Perhaps I was too good. I wished it to continue discussing its video call with Bryce, not my mastery of beautification and comfort. I slid my fingers from its trigger points and returned to massaging its scalp in order to keep it focused. "Tell me about love."

"Love?"

For the life of me, I do not know why humans do this. It is

infuriating when one wishes to get to a certain point. "Yes, love." As if possibly, by love, I'd meant hate instead! What a baffling mind they have.

"Love is…" It paused. "I don't even know. It's this…feeling. This attraction."

"There is magnetism involved?"

"I think I'm describing lust."

"And what is lust?" I know of the definition of lust, of course. But the *feeling* of lust, I cannot imagine. Zepzeg do not lust for anything—we were created, rather, to be lusted *for*. But *to* lust? That sensation, I do not know.

It seemed to be thinking. "If you're lucky, it's what comes before love." As if sensing that this answer would explain nothing to me, it continued on its own. "Lust is when one human finds another physically attractive, or appealing, or… desirable, whatever. But love is…just painful."

Painful? As if I could not become more confused than I already was! "So lust is preferable to love?"

It laughed, but only for a moment. "I really want to say yes, but honestly, no. Lust comes and goes, but love is forever. True love is forever. If you can find it."

"But what *is* it?" I hoped my frustration was not evident in my voice. "Is it a physical need that hurts when not provided for, such as humans experience hunger or thirst?"

"Velistris, you're asking the wrong person right now."

"I find that quite hard to believe, considering you are engaged to be married, which is supposed to be the ultimate human expression of love."

It sighed. "Love is when you care for someone so deeply, you'd do anything for them. You'd die for them. You'd live for them."

What a dreadful thought on all accounts! Was it speaking of love or slavery?

"It's when someone brings you so much joy, so much happiness, that you don't want to spend a moment without them. You can't even imagine it."

I tilted its head upright, stroking back its damp strands as it continued.

"Being with them becomes the most important thing in the universe to you. It becomes all that matters."

"But what are the *benefits*?" So far it had described physical pain, voluntary servitude, and addiction. These were not things to long for.

Once more, it fell quiet, as if thinking of how it wanted to answer. At last, it settled on something. "The benefit is having someone with you who is always looking out for you. Always trying to make the universe a better place for you, always trying to make you your best self. Comforting you when you're sad, rejoicing with you when you're happy, holding you when you need to be held. Giving you emotional support for the rest of your life."

A dreadful thought came to me. I could not help but ask it. "When you and Bryce are married, will he take over your beautification routines?"

Aurora laughed gently, though I did not understand why, for this was a serious matter. "Don't worry. Your job is secure."

Thank Deity!

"Can I ask you a question?" it asked me, which I thought a bit ironic.

I answered nonetheless. "Of course."

"Why did Elyse's hair *really* bother you so?"

I was taken aback somewhat by the return to that topic. I still did not wish to discuss it. "I believe I already answered that. I desire for you to have the utmost faith in me."

Its eyes still closed, it said, "That was a good answer. It was very direct. Very polished."

"Thank you."

"It was not true at all."

I ceased in my stroking, for at the moment, it'd caught me unprepared. "Of course, it is true."

"You're a terrible liar."

I disagreed with that assessment. I lied to it all the time, for a variety of reasons, and it scarcely seemed to notice.

It went on before I could rebut. "You looked downright scared. What about her hair scared you?"

"Were you not surprised to see such hair on Elyse?" Inwardly, I applauded myself for saying Elyse and not "that wretched beast."

"Of course, I was surprised. But I wasn't scared. So tell me what scared you."

I could not answer it truthfully, for to do so would put my evangelism at risk. I have found in dealing with humans, particularly in the realm of religion, that it is more advantageous to bend truth for comfort's sake. Humans desire comfort more than all other things. It is why they cling to the belief in an afterlife for themselves despite no evidence to support the claim. While telling Aurora "you are not good enough to receive salvation without help from a Zepzeg" would have certainly been truthful, it would not have landed me in its favor. It would have called such a statement *rubbish*, as they are keen to say, and quite possibly ceased its beauty treatments over it. Rather than risk that, I simply smiled and said, "I was scared you would resent me." Placing my hands at its forehead, I pulled them back tightly, pulling its strands back in the process in a way that I knew would feel particularly relaxing—and hopefully, distracting.

Its eyes did not close, a telltale sign that it was more keyed into what I was saying than the comfort I was providing. "Why would I resent you?"

There was certainly no cause for it to resent me. Quite the contrary, I consider my friendship its greatest achievement. But it wished for elaboration, and for the sake of the ruse, I had no choice but to provide it. "I have been a part of your crew for many years, now. You have paid me to be your beautician and diplomatic advisor. I feared you would consider me not worth the price you were paying." Anytime one can juxtapose the worth of friendship to the worth of money, they are certain to prompt a virtuous, if not somewhat defensive, reply.

"I would never do that, Velistris. I would never relegate your friendship to a credit amount."

You see?

"Promise me you'll never think me so shallow," it said.

I paused, purely for dramatic effect. "I am sorry if my concerns offended you. I will not have them again." Pulling back on its head, I maneuvered it down into the wash basin. "I will allow the oil in your hair to set undisturbed for a minute before I rinse and begin the next stage of the treatment. You may close your eyes."

It listened, shifting its shoulders back and forth as if to settle back in its chair. "Thank you for telling me the truth, Velistris."

"You may always count on me for that, captain," I said. Turning away from the basin, I began to rinse my own hands to cleanse them of oil.

Behind me, it spoke. "I was afraid you thought Elyse's sudden hair-styling prowess was threatening your ministry."

It knew me more than it let on. I felt I should have been surprised, but I was not—a testament to its occasional cleverness. Just the same, I felt a tinge of irritation, if for no other reason, because it considered me inconsequential enough to humor up until that point.

It picked up on my feelings. "I know your religious customs."

"They are not *customs*. They are truths. They are a divine calling to all in our species. I have striven and shall always strive for you to attain perfection. It is what I am tasked with so that you might find immortality." There was no sense in hiding that motivation now. "It is what I want to do."

"And you believe it is your right to dispense such proclamations of perfection?"

It spoke in truth. "You know that it is."

"Might I pose to you a possibility?"

"You may."

"How can an imperfect being dispense such proclamations?"

An imperfect being. The nerve! "I am quite perfect, thank you."

"I believe Delta would say otherwise after you sprayed her in the face."

Naturally, it would bring up that subject. "In that, I was imperfect in execution, not in motive."

"So you meant well?"

"You know I did."

It shifted its eyes to me. "And that matters to you?"

My hands froze beneath the rinsing water. Electricity pulsed through my very lifeveins themselves. My entire structure solidified. Slowly, I angled my head around to regard it. Its head was still in the bowl, its eyes closed again. There was no expression on its face other than solemnness. "I'm sorry?" I asked, uncertain if, for a moment, my voice might have oscillated again.

"Oh, never mind. It was a silly question. Please, continue your work." Once more, it shifted in its chair, as if the movement was intended to fill a void left by the silence. Drawing in a breath through its nostrils, it asked, "So what's going in my hair today? I'm excited to hear about it."

It had set a snare for me. A snare that I'd fallen into with reckless haste. Though I am often tactical in my responses to humans, there were no such tactics in play when I claimed that my motivations absolved me of any wrongdoing in the treatment of Delta's head. But in making such an assertion, I was stating that my thoughts and feelings mattered more than what I'd done on the outside. That what kept me in good moral standing was my intent, not my outward performance. To a human, such errant reasoning is normal. For a Zepzeg, it is blasphemous.

Walking to the wash basin, I grabbed the nozzle, warmed the water's temperature, then directed the nozzle over Aurora's scalp. As I ran my hands through its shimmering hair to loosen the oil, I found myself strangely unnerved. Yet I spoke on, as was my duty. "I will first infuse your hair with silk resin," I said, knowing to do nothing more than resume our charted course, "then polish it with a coat of mustberry cream."

"I've never experienced mustberries," it said.

"I know. Only the finest for my captain." With no further words between us, I began applying its treatment.

In the several hours that passed, the two of us spoke in a manner that I would call typical. We discussed the treatment, of course, and speculated as to how Elyse could have learned to craft such magnificent hair. We also discussed the video conference call with Corvus, the Broodmaster liaison. I shared with it my thoughts on the matter, cautioning it to treat Corvus's message concerning our Dacian visitor with skepticism until we spoke with the Dacian itself. One must always treat the words of a Broodmaster in that way. Of all the sad, pitiable creatures in our cluster, they are quite possibly the worst. I care little for anything they say.

But between our moments of dialogue, I found myself silently obsessed with the words I had spoken. The hand that I had played into, if such words could be used to describe it. It did not matter whether it was trickery or astuteness at play from Aurora. What mattered was my response to it. Without thinking—without hesitance—I had betrayed the very beliefs that I had always held sacred. It'd happened in the blink of the proverbial eye, as if it was tied to some intrinsic understanding.

But such an understanding would be ridiculous. It had been a slip of the resonators and nothing more. I must have become so accustomed to Aurora's line of reasoning that I had become momentarily blinded. I was sure this was the reason. I was sure of it.

Or was I sure of it?

It was during this line of thinking that I began to realize a dangerous thing about doubt—namely, that it takes very little of it to initiate growth. Aurora has recanted on numerous occasions a parable about "mustard seeds of faith" and how they can move figurative mountains if summoned. Though I know nothing of mustard or its seeds, I understand the concept. It means that even the smallest effort of faith will grow. I was now sensing from myself the very opposite. I was sensing a seed of doubt—as if the very consideration that the internal mattered was akin to my questioning my own beliefs. The doubt was small, as mustard seeds supposedly are, but it was present. That was all that mattered.

What if the internal *did* have weight?

It was a ridiculous thought, I am aware, but it was one that I simply could not shake from my consciousness. I had already shown earlier that I was capable of fallacy by spraying Delta in the face. Now I had shown that some of my thoughts could be fallacies, too. What if some of my *beliefs* were? I suddenly found myself mechanically rubbing mustberry cream into Aurora's hair with little thought or motivation to guide them. What if outward perfection was not the only thing that mattered, as I had so instinctively and mindlessly suggested? What if one's beliefs and convictions mattered just as much? What if they mattered *more*?

It was difficult to even confess the thoughts that ran through my mind as I massaged Aurora's hair, the repetitive strokes becoming just as therapeutic for me as for my dear captain. For a Zepzeg to have any such thoughts is blasphemous. We are taught that Deity would strike down a Zepzeg for even entertaining the notion that something other than outward appearance was of spiritual significance. Yet I was entertaining it, and I was not stricken.

The different species of the cosmos believe many different things. Some believe that all sentient beings were created by a divine creature or source. Some believe that they evolved from lower lifeforms. Some believe that reality itself does not exist and that we are all constructs of the same eternal cosmic illusion. Even among those beliefs there are offshoots. How was one to know which belief was true?

Despite my sullen wonderings, I still beautified Aurora's hair to the best of my ability. I mustered all the solemnity I could muster as I rinsed it, dried it, and molded it into the most vibrant, flowing ribbons that I had ever created. When Aurora finally looked in the mirror, many hours after I had begun my work, its eyes sparkled with excitement. On any other day, watching it toss its head back and forth, touching its curls with the wonder of a child, would have brought me the greatest of joys. But that joy was sullied by my thoughts within.

It was not long after my work had concluded that Elyse returned to my chamber for the judgment. Much to my surprise and disappointment, Delta was there with it, its hair also molded into something as beautiful as any hairstyle I'd ever crafted for it. Whatever magical thing Elyse had conjured up for its own hair, it had done so also for Delta, whose typically straight strands now fell in gentle, shimmering waves down the sides of its face. Its curls were different than Elyse's and not nearly as defined, but they were no less magnificent. They seemed perfectly formed for its face. A true work of art.

If only I'd cared. I was too distracted by other things.

When the time for judgment came, Aurora declared— properly, I believe—that the work I'd done on its hair was superior. I accepted its praise with the grace my crewmates have come to expect of me. I did wish to know how Elyse had done such fine work on it and Delta's hair, but neither human was inclined to share their secret. Not being privy did not bother me as much as I thought it would. My mind was too preoccupied with my thoughts. My conflictions. My seed of doubt taking root.

For the first time in my life, I looked upon another being with envy. But it was not Aurora, Delta, or Elyse. It was Hank-is-Handy. I watched it as it observed the competition, oblivious to any and all associated significance. It held no core beliefs of any kind; therefore, it was not tethered to any potential sources of catastrophic disenchantment. It was open to any possibility but attached to none. How marvelous that must've felt. How liberating and free. I knew not how to comprehend it.

I wished not to think of these things any longer, so as soon as the winner of the competition was declared, I requested that my crewmates leave my quarters so that I could have time to worship. They acquiesced, as they've grown accustomed to my dedicating time to such things. But though I did look in the mirror once I was alone, I did not worship. Instead, I only stared at my own face and form as it looked back at me. At that beautiful body that I'd sculpted specifically to appeal to humans, so that I might reach them and make them acceptable to Deity. How it looked…

…how it looked so unsettlingly different.

As I turned from the mirror, I did something that I never dreamt I would ever do. I covered it. I could not bear to look upon my reflection any longer. I could not bear to catch a glimpse of the perfection that I had striven for so desperately. I wanted only to sit in silence. To be alone. I felt, for a moment, that it might bring me peace.

How I wish that it had.

Chapter Eight

TO THE VORCK, a species is defined as either strong or weak. The strong species are the ones that fight good. The weak species are the ones that fight bad. This is how we determine who is strong and who is weak. The Vorck are strong because we are strong and because our ships are strong. The Zepzeg are weak because they do not have strong ships and their bodies can crack if they get hit hard. The Broodmasters are both strong and weak because they have strong telepathy but weak bodies. The Dacians are mostly strong. But most species are weak.

The Vorck will usually say about humans that they are stronger than weak species but not as strong as Vorck. Most Vorck would call humans weak. I would call them weak, too. But I am beginning to learn that humans are stronger than they look but not in ways that Vorck call things strong.

Since I began having bad feelings of jealousy about Defoe, I have felt many other bad things. In addition to jealousy, I have felt wrath, sadness, loneliness, and a strange feeling that I do not have words for but that prevents me from moving because I wish to do nothing. I do not have the strength in my brain to overcome these feelings. This is something I never experienced until now, and I do not like it. It makes me feel weak, but in a different way than the Vorck think about weak species. It makes me feel weak inside. It stops me from doing anything good, even work in the engine room.

But humans do not stop. Even though they feel these bad feelings, they continue to function. They walk and talk and do their jobs. I have seen Elyse sad many times, and sometimes she does not wish to talk to anyone but me. But she still works in the engine room and she still does the things that Aurora asks her to do. I do not know how humans have the strength in their brains to overcome these bad feelings. This is why I say that I feel like a weak Vorck. I also will say now that humans are stronger on the inside than they look on the outside.

Elyse and Delta have been talking a lot, which means that Elyse is not talking as much to me. She is happier than she was before, and I think it is because she has another human to talk to that she likes. I wish Elyse would talk to me as much as she used to talk to me. I thought I would like silence on the *Illustré*, but I do not like it anymore. I miss Elyse. I love her.

I believe that this is the first time that I have begun to feel love as a Vorck, but it is not a good feeling like I thought it would be. It is a bad feeling that makes me very sad. When Elyse works in the engine room with me, sometimes Delta comes with her and they talk. Sometimes Defoe comes with her, too, to help her with the tasks that I give her to do. I hate Defoe. I feel like he has made Elyse spend time with me less, and I do not like it.

I have not seen anything that tells me if Defoe absorbed information from Delta when he ate her head. The only thing I know is that she likes her hair now. Many days have passed since he first ate her head and made it look good. Elyse and Delta have both had Defoe eat their heads again since, but now they are not afraid to do it. The last time they did it, they held hands and did it at the same time, then after he spit them out, they laughed very hard together in a way that made me angry inside. I did not want Defoe to make them laugh. I wanted to crush his blue Slarb and his pink Gralb with my phase hammer. That would make me laugh very much. But I do not think it would make Elyse laugh. So I will not do it.

I do not know what to do. I cannot kill Defoe because it would make Elyse and Delta sad. But not killing Defoe makes me sad. I understand now why he said everybody hates him when we first met him in the docking bay. I hate him, too.

There is one other strange thing that has happened. I have not seen Velistris anymore. I used to see her a lot in the halls when I would walk one way and she would walk the other, and sometimes I would see her in the bridge with Aurora. But I have not seen her at all, and Aurora has not seen her much, either. She asked me once, "Have you seen Velistris?" I had not, and so I told her that I had not. But it is strange for Aurora to ask where Velistris is, because they are usually always together. I wondered for a moment if maybe Velistris had died or broken into pieces in her room and we did not know about it. At least that would have been good news on an otherwise bad week. But Velistris was not dead, so my week stayed bad.

On this day, the *Illustré* was to be visited by an ambassador from the Dacians. Aurora has talked to me about it. It is not a meeting she wanted to have and she did not invite the Dacian to come. The Dacian decided to visit the *Illustré* on its own. Aurora has seemed not as happy in the past several days as she usually is. I do not know why. Maybe it is because she does not want the Dacian to visit, but maybe it is because of something else. She has not told me, and I do not know.

One thing that has helped me not think about Elyse has been to finish replacing the damaged components in the engine room after the Vorticella attack. There were many things that needed to be fixed, and I fixed them. I did this mostly by myself, but sometimes Elyse, Delta, and Defoe helped, too. I did not want them to help because I wanted to do it alone. But I did not tell them that, so they did not know. It took me longer to do the repairs than it usually does, and I think it was because of the bad feelings I was feeling. But I got the work done. Getting work done makes me feel like a strong Vorck again, so I try to do it a lot. I have also thrown things a lot, and this makes me feel strong, too, especially when the things that I throw break into pieces. Perhaps I will throw Velistris if I see her or maybe Defoe or his blue Slarb or pink Gralb. It would be very hard to pick which one of those things to throw first. I will think about it and make a good choice.

I have been working on a list of things that Elyse is not good at, and it is very long. I labeled it, *"THESE ARE THE THINGS YOU ARE NOT GOOD AT."* I think it is a good list, and here are some of the things on it:

Not having hair
Punching a wall and breaking it
Running faster than a Vorck
Not getting hurt when you punch a wall
Being worried about not having a head
Using the psionic wrench to calibrate the targeter
Picking up big things
Liking things you do not like
Putting in good linkages when linkages get bad
Not burning in a fire
Compensating for spacetime differentials
Not having to eat
Opening a door when it gets stuck
Telepathy
Not bringing Defoe to the engine room

These are some of the things that I put on the list. So far the list has six hundred and forty-five things on it. I will try to put more before I give it to her.

I think it would be best to pick something from the list that Vorck are good at. Then I could help her better. Maybe I will help her to get stronger so she can pick up big things. I think that could help her a lot. Then if a big thing falls on her she will be able to pick it up and not die under it. I do not want Elyse to ever die. I think teaching her things to help her live longer is something that a good friend would do. I hope she picks that one when I give her the list. I think I will tell her to pick it.

There are many things I must do before lifeforms visit the *Illustré*. They are all things that Aurora makes me do. The first is to make sure all of the ship components are working good in case the meeting is a trap. I do not think the meeting with the Dacians is a trap and Aurora does not think that, too. But if it is, we still need to be able to fight good and escape fast. It took a long time to run all of the tests after I fixed the broken things, but all of them turned out good.

One thing I also do is make sure my phase hammer is fully charged and working the right way. This is so I can use it if a lifeform attacks. Then I will kill the lifeform and maybe blow it out of the airlock. I also have a robotic suit that I get in that helps me be stronger and fight better. It is made of many metals and moving parts that I get inside. It is also the same size and shape as my body so that it will fit good. Not all species use robotic suits to fight, but some do. Humans are one of the species that use it a lot. Aurora, Elyse, and Delta all have robotic suits on the *Illustré* and one of my jobs is to make sure they are all working and fully charged. I did that after I made sure mine was working and fully charged.

I do not think that Aurora will wear her robotic suit when the Dacian ambassador comes. I think that she thinks that if she wears it, she will look like she wants to fight. This is one thing that me and Aurora think different about. I think it is a good thing to look like you want to fight before you negotiate. I have found that it helps you win the negotiation. Humans do not always act like they want to win things. Maybe it is because Aurora is not trying to win this negotiation but to pick whether the Dacians or Broodmasters win it.

Aurora does not allow Elyse or Delta to be there when she negotiates, but sometimes she records a video of it to show Delta when the negotiation is over. I think she wants Delta to be like her one day and have her own ship and do things like she does. I think that is one reason why Delta is on the *Illustré*. Aurora does not think that Elyse can do things like she does, so she does not show the recordings to her. I think this is the right decision because Delta is more like Aurora than Elyse is.

When it was time for the Dacian ship to meet the *Illustré*, I went to the bridge.

The Dacians are a species with many strange ships. One of their ships is called a Lancet and it is very big and difficult to defeat in battle. They also have many smaller and medium ships. The most fearsome ship that Dacians possess and that they are most known for is called the Clusterboat. It is a medium ship that is made of many smaller ships that act as one. When the smaller ships are together, they share power which allows them to shoot stronger energy beams. Because the smaller ships all connect by their sterns, it is impossible to get behind a Clusterboat because there is no behind. Every direction has a gun that can shoot you. Once the energy screens for the Clusterboat have been depleted in battle, the smaller ships break apart and act like fighters. Their weapons are not as strong as they are when they are sharing energy, but because there are more of them, they can fly in formations and attack from multiple sides at the same time. It is very difficult to defeat a Clusterboat and the smaller fighters that break apart from it. I do not like them and neither does Aurora. I am glad that the *Illustré* has never had to fight one.

The *Illustré* had to drop out of hyperspace to meet the Dacian ship. When I saw that it was not a Clusterboat, I was glad. I think that Aurora was glad, too. I think this because when I said, "Sensors detect a Dacian Valebird approaching," she did a sigh breath and her shoulders got lower. Humans keep their shoulders very high when they are worried about something. I predicted that she was not as worried when she heard me say it was a Valebird because they are ships Dacians use a lot in diplomacy.

Velistris spoke from her station. "The Dacian vessel is hailing us." Aurora always takes Velistris with her when she does diplomacy. It is because the Zepzeg are good at knowing what a lifeform wants.

"Put him on the monitor," Aurora said, then she stood up. Humans always stand up when they tell someone to put someone on monitor. I do not know why.

"Yes, captain," Velistris said. She pressed the buttons on her console station that make lifeforms appear on the bridge monitor. After she pressed the buttons, the Dacian appeared.

I do not understand how other species in the galaxy think about Dacians. I have heard other species call them "strangely beautiful," but to me they do not look like other species that are called beautiful. They look like a thing that humans call gargoyles or demons and they are mostly purple, but some are black. They have wings like a gargoyle and sharp teeth, too. Gargoyles do not look like something that humans would call beautiful. I have also heard them described as bat things, but I have never seen a bat.

If one was to ask a Vorck if a Dacian is strong or weak, the Vorck would say that Dacians are strong. That is because they have powerful bodies that could kill weak species. I predict that if a Dacian and a human got into a battle, the Dacian would win and kill the human very easily. They would even be difficult for a Vorck to kill because they have many things on their bodies that are sharp, like teeth and claws. If I was a Dacian that had to kill a Vorck, I would try to put my sharp things into the Vorck's eyes to make them not work anymore.

Then I would get a sharp thing and cut off their head so that they would only have a week to live.

"Ambassador Ultraviolet," the Dacian said. Dacians are a species that can learn to talk like other lifeforms, so they do not need translators. The Dacian looked at Aurora with its small circle eyes. They were purple like the Dacian's skin, except that they were bright. Dacians have bright eyes that sometimes look like they glow. "I humbly thank you for meeting with me today."

I saw Aurora lift her chin up a little, which is another thing that humans do when they want to look strong. "There's nothing humble about the way you've chosen to meet with us. I must say, in fact, that it's quite displeasurable and *certainly* not customary."

When Dacians breathe in, sometimes their throats make a fluttering sound. It sounded like this when the Dacian breathed in after Aurora spoke. "I apologize, Ambassador Ultraviolet. I believe what I have to say will be of great interest to you. May I board your ship?"

"Might I know the name of the one so presumptuous as to think a face-to-face meeting necessary?"

"I am Thule of Clan Shallowcrest, humble servant of Queen Ugazra. I have been sent ahead of the negotiation at her behest."

The different species have different names for their leaders. Some use titles like president, emperor, or master. The Dacians have kings and queens. Queen Ugazra is the Dacian in charge of their presence in the Lernaean Cluster, where we live.

Aurora was quiet for a few seconds before she spoke. "Thank you for identifying yourself, Thule of Clan Shallowcrest. I will grant you and you alone access to the *Illustré*. My crew and I will await you in our docking bay. *Illustré* out."

Thule opened his mouth to say something, but his face disappeared before he could. Velistris has been trained to turn off the monitor whenever Aurora says, "*Illustré* out." Sometimes she makes the monitor go away before a lifeform is finished speaking. I believe this is a form of intimidation, but I would not be intimidated if my face disappeared from the monitor before I was finished speaking. It would make me not want to negotiate well.

"Clan Shallowcrest," Aurora said to Velistris. "What can you tell me about them?"

Velistris turned around to look at Aurora. "They are not a particularly large clan. They have few specimens of renown. I am unaware of any noteworthy connections between Clan Shallowcrest and Queen Ugazra beyond their general serving under her. Most Dacians who work for the queen belong to her own Clan Whitetalon."

Aurora did not make any reaction to what Velistris said. All she did was stand for a few seconds then walk back to her chair. She pressed the button that works the *Illustré*'s speaker system and said, "Delta, please come to the bridge." A few seconds passed, then Delta said she was coming. "Hank-is-Handy," Aurora said to me, "armor up and meet Velistris and me in the docking bay. I don't know what's going on, but whatever it is, I don't want us going into it unprepared." I told her that I understood, then Delta came into the bridge. Aurora looked at her. "Delta, I will be going with Velistris and Hank-is-Handy to the docking bay to meet the Dacian ambassador. I want you supervising the bridge while we're away."

Delta made her eyes get big. They always get big when Aurora tells her to supervise the bridge. It does not happen often, but it does happen sometimes.

"If you see anything peculiar from that Dacian Valebird or if any other ships appear on sensors, you are to notify me immediately. If a ship appears and it's a Clusterboat, you are to immediately thruster to a safe distance, then enter hyperspace. Don't wait for my permission—just do it."

"Yes, Aunt Aurora," Delta said.

Aurora looked at us again. "Okay, you two, let's go meet our new *friend*."

It did not take me long to get into my robotic suit. This is because I have gotten into it many times before. Even though I have been in it many times, I have never used it in a fight. I would very much like to use it in a fight someday. I think that the best way to see if something works good is to use it for the reason you have it.

Humans like to collect things they do not use. For example, Aurora has a laser rifle that was used by her great grandmother, Corinda Rhea, when she settled in the Ragnarok Cluster. Aurora has it on a wooden plaque in her room. I have seen her many times cleaning it and making sure that all of the parts are good, but I have never seen her use it or bring it on a mission. She says she values it greatly, but it is always on the wooden plaque in her room. Delta also has a collection of pendants that she has collected from many of the embassies we have visited, but I have never seen her wear them. Elyse has collected dead things in jars in her room, but I do not know why or what she would do with them that would have a purpose, so I think it is different than what Aurora and Delta collect. But if I had things that I valued, I would very much want to use them instead of not using them like humans do. I am hopeful that one day I will get to use the robotic suit that Aurora told me to put on. Perhaps if I use it and I like it, it will become a favorite thing like my phase hammer and the engine room. I will see what happens.

I saw Elyse in the engine room when I walked by it on my way to the docking bay. I also saw Defoe, but she moved him out of sight very quickly when she saw that we were passing. I think she did it so that Aurora did not see him in the engine room. Her attempt to hide him was successful because Aurora did not see him. It is good that Aurora did not see him, because she did not know that Elyse was bringing him to the engine room. I predicted she would be mad if she knew it. When I saw Elyse, she saw me, too, and she tilted her head. It is a trait that humans share with dogs when they are curious, so I said, "We are going to meet a Dacian!" When I said it, Elyse's eyes got big, and Aurora, who I was walking with, turned around to look at me. I think that maybe it was not a good idea to say what we were doing the way that I did, but I do not think about keeping secrets all the time like humans do.

I have asked Aurora many times since we rescued Defoe and his blue Slarb and his pink Gralb what she plans to do with them, and she has told me that she does not know. I think she will keep Defoe on the *Illustré* until the negotiations are over, then maybe she will bring him to a space station or try to find other Blepharisma to give him to. She has not said what rooms he can and cannot go into, which I do not like. Aurora does not like to make rules, but I think rules are good. They let you know what you can and cannot do. If I were in charge of a ship, everything would have a rule. If someone acted bad, I would tell them that a new rule is that they cannot breathe. Then they would die and would not do bad things anymore. Aurora likes to let people make decisions, then tell them after if their decision was good or bad. This does not make sense to me, but Elyse and Delta like it. Aurora likes to be an aunt that they like.

Even though Aurora does not know what she will do with Defoe, she has spent time studying him. She has asked me several times to help her do tests on him to see what he is made of. She does not think he evolved from the other lifeform called a blepharisma even though he calls himself a Blepharisma. She says he is half plant and half animal, which makes him unique because there are not many things like that in the galaxy. Aurora does not know that Defoe ate

Delta's head. I will not tell her. I do not think I should be the one to tell her. I think that the ones to tell her should be Elyse and Delta, but I do not think they will do it. So I suppose she will not know.

We were in the docking bay when the Dacian ambassador, Thule, docked with the *Illustré*. I have not met many Dacians, but I have met some. I do not like or dislike them. Aurora does not like them. Many years ago, she told me about a bad Dacian she met whose name was Vood. He tried to trick her into giving him places that she owned. He tried to trick her using mind powers.

The Dacians have mind powers, but they are different than the mind powers of the Broodmasters. Dacian mind powers are not as strong. Aurora says it is a form of hypnosis. It is a mind power that can make lifeforms do what they want them to do. She said that there are some animals from Earth that use hypnosis to hunt. One of them is something called a snake. I have never seen a snake before, but Aurora says they are dangerous animals that can make prey stand still by looking at them. This is also how Dacians hypnotize other lifeforms. They can then make the lifeforms calm or afraid. This is how they can get a lifeform to do what they want. The one that tried to trick Aurora into giving him places that she owned, Vood, did this to her while they were alone. This is the reason why she does not want to be alone with a Dacian. If there is another lifeform with her, then they can see that the Dacian is trying to hypnotize her. Then they can kill the Dacian and the hypnosis will end. This is also why I say that their mind powers are not as strong as the Broodmasters.

Because Dacians look like the things that humans call gargoyles and because they use hypnosis, humans sometimes call them a thing called *space vamps*. I do not think space vamps are real. But I know that Dacians are real, so I do not know why humans would not just call them Dacians, because that is what they are. Sometimes humans like to give things unnecessary names.

Thule was alone when he came through the docking bay door after his ship had connected to the *Illustré*. Dacians have large wings with hands on them that they walk on. A lot of times they walk on their wing hands and keep their feet in the air, which is the opposite of what most species do. It is another thing that makes them difficult to fight, because they can punch you with their feet and kick you with their hands. This is why it is better to just shoot them.

When Thule saw me in my robotic suit, he stopped and made another fluttering sound. "I hope my presence here does not frighten you, Ambassador Ultraviolet," he said. Dacians have a voice that sounds like a loud whisper. It does not make sense to me.

"If I may be honest, I'm not quite sure what to expect from you, Thule," Aurora said to him.

I think that my robotic suit was a good idea. It would probably make Thule afraid to fight with me because he might think he would lose. Dacians do not like to wear robotic suits because it would stop them from flying. They do not wear very much armor or clothes. He looked at Aurora again. "Is there a room on your ship in which we could discuss business alone?"

"Whatever you have to say, you may say it in front of my friends."

I looked at Velistris to see what she was doing. When lifeforms visit the *Illustré*, Velistris looks at them a lot. I think this is because she is trying to figure out what they are doing. Weak Velistris is not better than me at many things, but figuring out what lifeforms are doing is one of them. If I do not know what a lifeform is doing, I usually just try to kill it.

Thule made a hissing sound and he folded his toes together the way humans do with their fingers, then he bowed his head. "I will abide by whatever rules you deem necessary."

Aurora did not look happy. Her eyes were very narrow. Humans do this a lot when they are not happy. "State your purpose for this most inappropriate visitation."

I watched Thule's eyes very carefully to see if they were looking at Aurora's. They were not looking at her eyes. They were looking at all of us. When a lifeform has eyes that move around a lot, it usually means they are thinking about bad things, but for a Dacian, it is good. This is because they cannot hypnotize a lifeform unless they are focusing their eyes on them. "As you know, the Broodmasters have been a bane on this cluster for a millennium."

"To the contrary, I do *not* know and thus cannot speak for the state of the millennium."

"You must believe me, for what I say is true." Thule fluttered again then hissed. "Were it not for the Broodmasters, we Dacians would have far more prosperity and hope among our people. Their greed is a curse upon this cluster."

I did not disagree.

"The Broodmasters crave many things," Aurora said, "none more so than power and influence. Of this, I'm well aware. But your species is not so innocuous. I have had my own experiences with your kind that have been…less than ideal."

It was right then that a strange thing happened. I saw it when I looked at Aurora. She touched her head and made a soft hum sound. It was only for a second, then it was gone. She did not look around or say anything else. I wondered if Velistris noticed it, too. When she spoke, I knew that she did. "Captain?" Velistris asked.

"What is it, Velistris?"

"Are you all right?"

The look Aurora gave Velistris was confused. "Of course. Why wouldn't I be?"

I was confused, too, but what confused me was that Aurora looked confused.

"You touched your head," said Velistris, "as if you were in pain."

"No, I didn't."

Thule spoke before anyone could say anything else. "You speak of Vood." When he said the name, Aurora looked surprised. "He tried to coerce Ultraviolet Hall from you. He threatened the life of your suitor, Bryce Lockhart."

Ultraviolet Hall was on a moon in the Fomalhaut System. It was a luxurious place that Aurora and her family owned. As a gift, Aurora's twin brother, Henry, gave her full rights to the Hall. This was because Aurora liked it very much.

"How could you possibly know that?" Aurora asked.

"We have done our research, ambassador. I wish you to know that Vood has been dealt with and will never harm you again. This has been done as a gift to you."

I watched to see if Aurora touched her head again, but she did not. I do not know why she touched it the first time and made a hum sound. I predicted that it was not important, so I looked at Thule.

"I don't know how you found this information." Aurora said, "but I do not appreciate you prying into my private affairs in an attempt to curry favor." Her voice got louder than it usually does. This does not happen with Aurora often. "I've requested it once and I shall request it only once more: what is the true nature of this visit?"

"I wish to appeal to your sense of reason," said Thule. "Imagine a cluster purged of the Broodmasters' vile presence!"

Aurora's eyes got wide. "I beg your pardon?"

"This is what we hope to accomplish. These are hard words to hear, I am aware, but they are honest and true. With control of the Gryamore System, we would have the power to rid this cluster of the Broodmasters once and for all! Surely you see the benefit in this, ambassador. Surely, you must!"

I did not disagree with what Thule said, but it surprised me that he said it. It did not seem like a good thing to say before a negotiation. I predicted that his words would make Aurora mad.

"Surely *you* must realize the grand inappropriateness of speaking such words!" she said. "I've never heard something so abhorrent before a negotiation."

My prediction was correct.

Thule said to her, "I do not believe your ears so fragile as to have never heard such words before. This is a vast and dangerous cluster. There are many species it would be best without! We Dacians are not afraid to rid it of them. Humanity, of course, would be permitted to survive."

"Permitted? What a gracious host you are!"

I think that Aurora was speaking sarcasm words when she said it. It would not make sense for her to think Thule was being gracious.

Thule's body got tense and he recoiled a little. He made more fluttering sounds with his throat. "There will be grave consequences for giving the Gryamore System to the Broodmasters! Think wisely before you make such a decision." I noticed that Thule's eyes were not moving anymore. They were looking only at Aurora. "It would be wise to give us what we want, ambassador. It would be wise. It would be wise."

I think that Velistris noticed it, too, because she did a flinch thing. Aurora did not seem to notice it. She was looking at Thule and not doing anything. Then Velistris spoke. "He is hypnotizing her!" I predicted the same thing. I grabbed Thule very quickly because I was not far away. The loud sound he made when I grabbed him was like a hiss or maybe a gasp, which is a thing some lifeforms do when they are more surprised than being normal surprised. Thule began to kick and claw at my suit, so I threw him across the docking bay. His wings spread and he flew to the ground between us and the interior entrance to the docking bay. When Thule was away from Aurora, she fell to her knees. She looked unstable, which I think was because the Dacian was hypnotizing her and I made him stop.

"Vile heathens!" Thule said with a hiss. It was then that I saw two things at the same time. One was Thule reaching into a pouch around his waist. I think it was to get a weapon to shoot at us. The second thing I saw was Elyse watching from the door to the docking bay. She was very close to Thule so I wanted to make a good decision to keep her safe. I did not.

"Elyse!" is what I said, but I should not have said it, because it let Thule know that she was there. I reached for my phase hammer at the same time that Thule turned around to see Elyse, too. I was too far away now to use my phase hammer, so I ran to Thule to get closer, but he flew toward Elyse. When he got close, she screamed and tried to back up. I predicted that he would stick his claws through her weak human body and kill her. I am glad that my prediction was incorrect.

Just before Thule got to Elyse, Defoe appeared from the hallway beside her. I do not think Thule knew that Defoe was there because he acted surprised and tried to stop flying, but because he was surprised it was not a good attempt to stop. This was also when Aurora got up from the floor and looked at what was going on.

Something happened that I did not expect to happen. Defoe got big with his plant mouth and made it go over Thule. Thule kicked and screamed when his head went inside Defoe's plant mouth and he tried to get away, but Defoe did not let him go.

"*Blepharisma, no!*" shouted Aurora behind me. I did not look at her when she spoke because I was looking at Defoe, Thule, and Elyse.

Thule and Defoe tumbled across the floor like Elyse did when Defoe ate her head for the first time. Elyse screamed Defoe's name loudly. I do not think that Defoe was listening to anything going on because he was too busy eating Thule's head. Even though I knew it was keeping Elyse safe, I moved close to try to get Thule's head out of Defoe's plant mouth. But I did not have to do anything because Defoe spit him out. Thule rolled across the floor with plant slime on his head, then he went still.

"Blepharisma!" Aurora got up and ran to Defoe and Thule, but I do not know which one she was trying to get to. Thule was on the ground with Defoe's plant slime on his head, but he was not moving like Elyse and Delta moved after they got covered in Defoe's plant slime. I predicted that Thule was not moving because Defoe killed him, but my prediction was incorrect. Many of my predictions for the day were incorrect.

Defoe looked at Aurora with his red eyes. "I being very sorry if I causing a problem! I trying to not letting the Dacian kill Elyse. I sucking away his energy."

I did not think that Aurora looked like her normal self. She looked like she was having trouble standing and moving in the way that she usually stands and moves. I predicted that it was because the Dacian had tried to hypnotize her, and this prediction was correct. But she looked normal enough to talk in a way that was normal for her. "Why did you come to the docking bay? You knew what we were doing. You could have gotten yourself killed!"

It did not surprise me that Aurora was upset that Elyse had gone into the docking bay to see the Dacian. But it did surprise me a little bit that she was saying this now, immediately after Thule had attacked. Her breathing was very hard and fast and she was looking in every direction very quickly. I believed that she was in what humans call a *state of shock*, an event where humans become useless during a time when they need to not be useless. She was looking down at Thule and feeling for a pulse, which all living carbon-based lifeforms possess. She released a sigh breath. "He's alive, thank God." She looked at Defoe with angry eyes. "You could have killed him!"

Elyse spoke back with loud words of her own. "And what about you? That thing was hypnotizing you! We all saw it!"

I raised my hand. "I saw it."

Aurora raised her hand quickly, which is something she does when she wants me to be quiet quickly. "This is a tense diplomatic situation," she said loudly to Elyse. "That's why I had Hank-is-Handy with me! He was taking care of it. But you nearly became his hostage, or worse, his victim! Hostile or not, he was here on behalf of the Dacian queen! What's going to happen when he tells her that some unknown lifeform attacked him and nearly killed him on our ship?"

"But he attacked *you!*" Elyse said.

Aurora thinks of many things at the same time very well, which is something that not all humans can do. She likes to keep a situation in control even when it is out of control. This is why Aurora was saying what she was saying.

"I very much liking to say something," said Defoe as he waved his tentacle thing.

"And you," Aurora said to him. "Were you in the *engine room* with her?"

"Elyse being very generous in taking me there many times! I knowing all about how this ship works now. It is pleasing me greatly!"

Aurora's eyes got very big and she looked at Elyse. "Oh, *really?*"

Defoe's tentacle thing continued to wave around. "I still very much liking to say something!"

"Well, you're going to have to say a *lot*, because I'm going to have to take a sworn statement after you assaulted a liaison to the Dacian queen!"

"He is not a liaison to the Dacian queen."

Aurora did an eye blink and the room got quiet. "What?"

"He did not having a Dacian mind," Defoe said. "His mind being controlled by a Broodmaster."

When Defoe said the words, the room got very quiet. Aurora's eyes did not get small like they do for humans when they get angry, nor did they get big like they do when humans get surprised. She just looked at Defoe like she does when she looks normal. Nobody else said words, either, but I looked at their faces. Elyse's eyes did change, but her eyes were changing a lot. I think it is because there were a lot of things going on that made her feel a lot of different things. I could not tell what weak Velistris was thinking because Zepzeg do not have eyes. But all of them were looking at Defoe. I believe that weak Velistris was looking at him, too.

I do not know how much time passed before someone else said something, but I think it was maybe eight or nine seconds. There is something strange that happens to time when there is silence, especially if it is silence where someone should be talking. Even though only eight or nine seconds passed, it felt like a great deal more time had passed. Maybe even fifteen or sixteen seconds. To humans, this silence can be described as uncomfortable. I would describe it as eight or nine seconds that felt like fifteen or sixteen seconds. Eventually, someone did speak. It was Aurora. "What do you mean, his mind is being controlled by a Broodmaster?"

I do not know why she asked this, because I thought Defoe's explanation was very clear. Humans often seek confirmation for things that do not need it.

"Even though he being a Dacian," Defoe said, "his mind being manipulated and controlled through a Broodmaster."

"He's being *mind*-controlled?"

Once more, unnecessary confirmation. Defoe said, "Yes." I hoped this was the last time Aurora asked him to repeat himself so that we could get on with the conversation, because I felt like what he was saying was very important.

Delta's voice came over the *Illustré*'s speakers. "Aunt Aurora, the Dacian ship is leaving!"

I thought this was strange because the Dacian was still on our ship. Delta's words made Aurora's eyes change, but this time they got wide like a human's does when it is surprised. "The Broodmaster," she said. It was another time when humans make their voice quiet when there is something important to say. I do not know why humans do this so often. "He's on the Dacian ship!" Aurora did not say anything else. She only ran past the Dacian and to the hallway that led to the bridge. Elyse ran after her. I decided to follow behind them even though the Dacian was still on the floor, because I thought that maybe the *Illustré* would be attacked and that I would be needed on the bridge.

"Weak Velistris!" I said as I ran out of the room. "Guard the Dacian in case he attacks!" She did not listen. She never listens.

When we got to the bridge, the Dacian ship was gone. Delta got out of her chair quick. I think she was scared to sit in it. Aurora did not get in her chair like she usually does. She looked at me and said, "Are there any other ships on sensors?"

There were not, so I said, "There are not."

The bridge got quiet again. When I looked behind me at the door, I saw that Defoe was standing outside of it looking inside with his red eyes. Aurora talked to him. "Blepharisma, explain what just happened to me again."

Elyse, who was by him, said, "His name is Defoe—"

"I'll talk to *you* later," said Aurora with a mad voice. "Because believe me, we have a *lot* to talk about. But right now," she looked at Defoe again, "I want to know *exactly* what you perceived when you..."

"Absorbing?" Defoe asked.

Aurora moved her head in a way that was not a nod and was not a shake. She looked like she did not know how to move it. "Sure," she said.

Defoe answered her, "I seeing that the Dacian getting close to attacking Elyse. This making me very mad! I consuming Dacian to stopping him from attacking. Then I sensing something very, very funny!"

I did not know why he said the word *funny*, but I stayed quiet because I did not think it was important to bring up.

"I sensing second presence in Dacian mind. I having sensing this presence before, but not many times. I knowing it belonging to Broodmaster! This when I realizing that Broodmaster being controlling Dacian's actions. I thinking that maybe Broodmaster controlling from Dacian ship that just left. This very, very strange, indeed!"

"Could you possibly be wrong?" Aurora asked. "Could you possibly have sensed a presence that wasn't there or misinterpreted the Dacian's mind?"

"I never being wrong when I absorb! I being very, very good at absorbing!"

Aurora spoke words, but she was not looking at anybody when she spoke them. Humans do this a lot when they are speaking to themselves, which is a thing that many species do not do and find confusing when humans do it. "The Broodmasters told me they detected the Dacian ship leaving the Gryamore System to intercept us. The Broodmasters must've captured a Dacian ship and sent it to intercept us themselves."

"Why?" I asked her.

"There's only one reason that comes to mind—and it would be just like a Broodmaster to do it." She looked at me. "They're trying to manipulate the negotiation."

Some things did not make sense to me, so I asked about them. "Thule said many bad things about the Broodmasters. Why would a Broodmaster make them say those bad things about their own species?"

Velistris spoke for the first time. "That is the essence of the negotiation. Their aim is to make the Dacians seem unreasonable in a way that discourages Aurora from siding with them."

"Exactly," said Aurora.

Velistris continued to speak. "Thule made it abundantly clear that were the Gryamore System given to the Dacians, they would use it to wipe the Broodmasters from the cluster. As the mediator and ultimately the decision maker of these talks, there is no way that Aurora would side with such monstrous intent. She would have given the planet to the Broodmasters out of principle alone."

"Those slimy, untrustworthy cretins," said Aurora. "That video call with Corvus was them setting the stage. Phase one of their effort to sway my opinion."

Velistris pointed one of her weak fingers at Aurora and said, "During your conversation with Thule, there was a moment when you touched your head as if you were hurting. When we commented on it, you sounded as if you didn't know what we were talking about. Hank-is-Handy and I both took note of it."

"I don't remember reaching up to touch my head, but I remember you mentioning it. I thought it so strange. But now I wonder, was the Broodmaster that was controlling Thule attempting to reach into my mind as well? Thule mentioned Vood, the Dacian with whom I had my unpleasant run-in. I wonder if the Broodmaster drew that information from my mind in that moment to use against me through Thule's words."

"Shortly after that," Velistris said, "he attempted to hypnotize you. With Hank-is-Handy and me both present, it would have been a futile and foolhardy attempt. But perhaps we were meant to see it take place. Perhaps the Broodmaster was hoping that we would defend you and kill the Dacian in the process."

Aurora performed a head nod. "That would have both tilted my scales of judgment and killed off any evidence of their influence. Dead Dacians don't talk. We would have been none the wiser about their efforts to manipulate. When we would have reached out to the Dacian queen, which we surely would have, she would have denied it—but the evidence was before us in the form of my attacker."

Aurora and Velistris were both speaking many words that made sense. They are very good at making sense of things quickly. This is why they do diplomatic things together. I listened as they continued.

"The one factor they couldn't have possibly accounted for," Aurora said as she looked at Defoe, "was Blepharisma."

"How remarkably serendipitous," said Velistris, but I did not know what that word meant.

"Hank-is-Handy," said Aurora, "secure Thule in the other guest suite, then watch over him. I don't know how much he'll recall or what his last recollection will even be, but he's liable to be hostile upon awakening. Ensure he's in no position to threaten the ship when that happens."

"Yes, captain," I said.

Aurora took a step closer to Defoe, then she knelt down to be closer to his height. Defoe looked at her with his red eyes but did not say anything. "Everyone else, gather in my chamber. You as well, Mister 'Defoe.' We all have *much* to discuss."

It was difficult to predict what kind of discussion Aurora would have with everyone else. Her voice did not sound happy, or mad, or sad, or scared. It sounded like a mix of all of them and none of them at the same time. I recognize this as focus in humans. I wanted to be there when the discussion took place, but I also knew that securing Thule was important. It was also what I was ordered to do, so I had to do it. As everyone else in the bridge stepped toward the lift that led to Aurora's room atop the bridge, I stepped into the *Illustré*'s halls to do as I was told.

Chapter Nine

"I DON'T EVEN know where to begin."

They were not words I was accustomed to hearing from my captain, nor was I accustomed to the manner in which they were delivered. Aurora's head was in its hands as it leaned over the empty dinner table in its chamber suite. On any normal day, I would have marveled at the sight of such a rudimentary setup being used as a place over which to discuss business—for very few specimens, even among humans, would dare to attach such a meeting to their private chambers—but this was not a normal day or a normal week. This was a week laced with the most intense personal vexations for which I was little prepared to handle. The addition of this new stress, I feared, was simply too much.

It is very rare that Aurora leaves the bridge completely unattended. It often chooses Delta as temporary overseer while it conducts business elsewhere on the ship, though for a meeting of what was sure to be considerable magnitude, it must have considered everyone's presence except for Hank-is-Handy's critical. It is rare that official meetings are held here, as Aurora prefers to conduct business on the bridge save the most dramatic of situations, of which this current ordeal most certainly qualified. I did not know how it would begin to address this particular quandary, and apparently it didn't, either. No effort was made to shroud its exhaustion and confoundment as it simply propped its elbows on the table, quite sloppily I must say, with its hair dangling over its hands as they covered its face. It was not a look that served an Ultraviolet well.

Sitting around the table were Delta, Elyse, and the Blepharisma whose name was apparently *Defoe*, or so claimed its green-haired counterpart. The wretched other-niece had mustered quite the force of allies between Hank-is-Handy, Defoe, and most recently, Delta—much to my anguish and chagrin. I, of course, would not lower myself to sit at a table comprised of such miscreants, so I elected to stand by the wall nearest to my captain that I might hear it most clearly. And also to prove a point, which I fear may have been missed.

At long last, after what felt like an eternity, it lifted its head and spoke again. "I suppose I must first say what I *should* say, which is thank you to Mister Defoe for saving the life of my niece in the docking bay. Were it not for your quick actions in…enveloping Thule, Elyse would have surely perished."

And it was to be *thanked* for that?

"I being most happy to help," Defoe said, its flagellum waving about like Riley's chaotic tail during moments of joy.

"We have much to talk about and even more I must process, but I first wished to express my deep gratitude. I love my nieces dearly, despite the harsh judgment I will soon be passing down." It looked at Elyse as it said the words, its tone smoldering as its blue eyes narrowed. For its part, Elyse looked shamed. A good look for it. Aurora's gaze returned to Defoe. "Consider this invitation into my private quarters an extension of my newfound trust in you. Please do not make me regret it."

Its altruistic gestures always come with a warning. I do not fault it.

"How long have you been working in the *Illustré*'s engine room?"

Elyse fidgeted in its chair and said, "I—"

Snapping its fingers, Aurora shot the vile human a look it quite deserved. "I asked him, not you." It looked at Defoe again. "Please, answer my question."

Though there is still much I must learn concerning Blepharisma mannerisms, there are several attributes I have taken note of during my time with the newly christened Defoe. As with most lifeforms, its eyes seem a window of sorts into the soul, often displaying emotion in a way that correlates somewhat with human emotions. In the few times that I have seen Defoe annoyed or agitated, its eyes narrow much like a human's. They also seem to part outwardly in an exaggerated fashion when the being is saddened. I have also noted meaning in the gesticulations of its flagellum, which seems to wave with fervency in times of high intensity. It seems to mimic what would be detected in another lifeform's pulse, or as previously mentioned, the tail of a dog, all while simultaneously being used as an actual appendage with which to grab hold of objects or, occasionally, wriggle feverishly at someone as if delivering a lecture. As it began to answer Aurora's question, I found its flagellum waving side by side in a manner I recognized as excitement.

"I being working in the engine room for a very long time!" it said. "Elyse taking me there right away to teach me how engine works. I learning very much about human spindrive and spaceflight!"

"How do you mean, 'right away?'"

"The first day I being brought on board!"

And it was right there, with that statement, that my captain's anger crested. Slapping its hand on the tabletop with utter vehemence, it turned sharply Elyse's way. "You brought an unknown lifeform into our engine room and showed it how everything worked?"

"It's not like it sounds," said Elyse desperately.

"I eagerly await your elucidation."

The room fell silent as Elyse's guise of innocence fell. "I thought it might be an opportunity to learn more about him. To…make him feel like part of the crew, to be his friend."

"I liking friendship with Elyse very much!" Defoe said.

My captain's glare shifted to the Blepharisma. "I'll bet you are." It returned to Elyse. "And how exactly did you hide him from Hank-is-Handy?"

"Hank-is-Handy being very helpful, too!" said Defoe, answering before Elyse could. "He letting me learn many things with Elyse."

Oh, the size of my poor captain's eyeballs! I have never seen them bigger. Were they lasers, they would have fried Elyse's heart. "You dragged *Hank-is-Handy* into this?"

"I—" The wretched being sputtered, no words of meaning coming from its lips.

Aurora interrupted its senseless driveling with another pointed question. "Did you instruct Hank-is-Handy to keep this from me? I find it hard to imagine that keeping such a secret would be his idea."

As much as I wondered what the truth was, I also wondered if Elyse would possibly tell it. Humans despise losing face, and it was losing more of it with every passing second. At long last, and I admit somewhat to my surprise, it confessed. "Yes. Yes, I did. Don't blame him. He told me not to do it."

"You would have been wise to listen to him!"

"Defoe needed a friend, he…" It bit down on its lips, a gesture I have seen often when a human is revealing more than it wishes. I have always found it curious how humans' mouths act ahead of their brains. It is something that often gets them into trouble. "I wanted him to feel like a part of the crew."

Pushing its fingers back and through its hair, Aurora leaned back its head and produced a sound of frustration. "Elyse, he's not part of the crew!" It looked at Defoe with an expression of placation. "I don't mean that to offend you, but what I'm stating is true. The engine room and particularly the spindrive are *the* most important places on the *Illustré*, and we can't have guests gallivanting about them. So let's get this all out in the open, because it needs to be in the open.

Defoe, you are our guest. That is quite different from being a member of the crew."

For what it was worth, Defoe did not look offended. Truth be told, it looked rather oblivious.

"And Elyse, you had absolutely no right to make that kind of a decision on your own—at least not without consulting with me first. I find it most dissatisfactory that you would take it upon yourself to put the ship at that much of a risk, and to be honest, it makes me question the level of trust that I've extended to you."

"I *get* him," Elyse said, its teeth showing as it practically seethed the words.

As it should've, Aurora looked completely perplexed. "What do you mean, you 'get' him?"

"I get him. I understand him!" Fight was brewing behind those ghastly green eyes.

"How could you *possibly* understand him?"

Elyse slammed its hands on the table and leapt to its feet. The rapid and unwarranted gesture caused Aurora and Delta to flinch. I dare say, it even caught me by surprise. "Because no one likes him! Because he needs a friend! Does that sound familiar? It *should*!"

"Elyse—"

Aurora's words were cast aside as Elyse's eruption continued. "I've tried, and I've tried, and I've *tried* to convey to you just how lost and alone I've felt on this ship! I've tried to do everything you've asked me to do, I've tried to be the perfect little niece you wish God had made me, but I'm sorry, I can't. I am who I am—the rotten branch on the family tree, the black sheep of the Greengrasses!"

"Niece, would you please—"

"Maybe if everyone had appreciated me for what I was instead of lamenting over what I wasn't, I wouldn't be so messed up. Maybe there's nothing wrong with me. Did you ever think of that? Maybe I'm not a deviant, or a pariah, or a lost cause. Maybe nobody has just shut up and listened when I've tried to say something instead of judging me over the clothes I wear or the color I dye my hair!" It was at that moment that the horrid creature turned to *me.* "And by the way, Velistris, you can thank Defoe here for how good my hair looks, because *he* was the one who did it. Ask Delta if it's true—he did her hair, as well!"

Had I a mouth, I would have gasped! Was it saying that creature had styled its hair? Surely the Blepharisma could not be responsible for its lustrous tendrils! And Delta's? This was a nightmare! Could it be true?

"And do you want to know the really sad part about this?" Elyse's fury returned to Aurora as it pointed at its own hair. "The look on your face when you saw this was the first time I ever saw you look proud of me—as if that even mattered, as if shiny hair had *anything* to do with character, or value, or worth! Do you realize how sick that is? Do you realize how utterly *useless*"—Tears began falling as it formed the words— "that makes me feel? You don't care about my work in the engine room, you don't care about my opinion, you don't care about what I can contribute to or what I can accomplish. You care about..." Its eyes glossed over with liquid, and it looked down. "You care about my hair."

The whole room fell speechless. None of us knew what to say.

"You were right," it whispered through its heaving. "Hank-is-Handy, you were so right." Lifting its head again, it fired a glare toward Aurora that was akin to thrown daggers. "I should have *cut it off!*"

"Elyse, please go to your room," Aurora said, likely with as much dignity amidst this debacle as it could muster. "Do not do anything foolish. Please, just go to your room. I would very much like to talk to you later."

Its head lowered; the wretch actually laughed. "*To* me. How fitting your choice of words." It looked up again. "All you do is talk *to* me. No one bothers to actually engage." No other words were uttered. It simply rose from its chair, slammed it back into place, and marched into the lift that would take it back to the main level. It did not even bother to say bye. I was, of course, fine with that.

The silence that ensued was among the more ominous of any I could remember. Though the Blepharisma did not seem entirely aware of the situation's gravity, its body did seem to have shrunken some—perhaps a reaction to the tension around it, or perhaps it was just my imagination. I fully expected Aurora to be the first one to speak again, so you can imagine my surprise when the voice I heard was Delta's.

"I knew, too, Aunt Aurora," it said quietly, a touch of shame in its voice. Aurora looked at it. "I knew Defoe was working in the engine room. I didn't tell you—"

"Please leave," the captain interrupted, its voice more measured—more hurt—than it seemed to have been earlier when it'd addressed Elyse with such rage.

Now, it was Delta's eyes that shimmered. "I'm sorry." Looking down, it rose from its chair and hurried for the elevator, not daring to show its face to the captain or myself. Oh, the hurt it must've felt! I dare say I ached for it.

Then, as suddenly as the room had been thrust into chaos and shouting, all went silent and still. I stood beside Aurora, who looked as uncertain as to how it should feel as I felt myself. "Please accept my apologies, Defoe. This display was…not typical. I am greatly embarrassed by it."

"Am I being in trouble?" the Blepharisma asked. How childlike the question seemed. How strikingly human. Only years ago, I would have heard Delta ask the question in the same manner.

To its credit, Aurora tried hard to smile. It was unbecoming. "No. You did nothing wrong. I admit, there is much I feel I must learn about you, but you saved my niece from certain death at the hands of the Dacian. For that, I will forever be grateful."

"Elyse and Delta being good to me. I being very happy being their friends. I being your friend, too, right?"

"At this stage," the captain answered, "I would not hesitate to call you a friend. To all of us. And I thank you for that."

The creature's red eyes shone brightly, and it waved its flagellum about. "You making me very happy, good friend! You pleasing me."

Aurora leaned once more against the table, its former weighted and sloppy state replaced by the proper etiquette to which we've all become accustomed. "There is still much I must learn of your unique…abilities. But for the moment, those things must wait. I need to hear the full extent of what you experienced when you 'absorbed' the Dacian, particularly as it concerns his Broodmaster controller. What could you glean from what little time you had to absorb?"

I tried to listen intently to Defoe's answer, but as the Blepharisma spoke, I found Elyse's final revelation drifting to the forefront of my mind. *This* was the creature responsible for it and Delta's extravagant hair? How could that be? How was it possible?

"The Broodmaster controlling the Dacian was bad, bad, bad! He wanting to do bad things to trick my good friends. I not knowing why, but I knowing that he was using the Dacian to do tricking. The Broodmaster's presence leaving right away when it realizing I was there."

"So it sensed your presence?"

"Yes, it did sensing. Then it leaving very quickly! I making it very, very scared. I keeping it away from my good friends!"

It must have been the slime from its mouth that made their hair look so radiant. That was the only plausible explanation! There must have been some protein, some nutrient that provided the young females with their waves and rich lusters. How I envied Defoe for such a natural ability. How I hated it!

"Could you sense the Broodmaster's name?" Aurora asked, oblivious to my festering resentment. "Is there anything you could tell me about it personally?"

The Blepharisma's eyes parted outwardly. "I being very sorry. I not knowing anything else. It leaving before I could absorbing more."

"You said you'd sensed a Broodmaster before. How, if I may ask?"

"Broodmasters being very common in the Ragnarok Cluster. They being one of the first species I meet! They teaching me to absorb mind knowledge. They teaching me very much! But they not liking me."

Aurora blinked, an indication that its words had surprised it. "Did you say they *taught* you to read the minds of other beings?"

"I learning much from other beings. Even you being teaching me now! I learning how to be good friend."

"Where and how in the Ragnarok Cluster were you able to absorb knowledge from them? Broodmasters are quite difficult to see in person."

Its words were truth. Broodmasters hide their bodies from the outside world, choosing to live vicariously through their offspring, who serve at their beck and call.

Defoe looked sad again. It seemed a common look for the pitiable creature. "I not remembering where and how. I just knowing that I absorbing from them."

"I'm sorry, I don't mean to sound rude or confused, but how am I to trust that your information is accurate if you can't even remember simple details of your own past?"

Its eyes suddenly brightened, as if it'd had the grandest of ideas. "I could absorbing things from you then tell you what I knowing! That way you know my absorbing the very, very best."

Aurora raised a speculative eyebrow. "Would that involve enveloping my head?"

"Yes! Absorbing being very painless, I assuring you."

"I appreciate it, but I'll pass."

A wise decision, I thought.

"You said that you learn from every being you absorb. How exactly did you mean that?"

"I not knowing exactly how I mean it. I only knowing that I learn from everything I absorb."

Aurora leaned back in its chair and blew out a heavy breath upwards, blowing a loose curl from its face. "Well, you're a riddle wrapped in a mystery inside an enigma, aren't you?"

"I not knowing what that means."

"It means there is so much of you shrouded in mystery. The origin of your species, your species itself, your personal history. I do not typically lend trust to those I understand so little, but your actions have prompted otherwise."

"I being very sorry I not knowing more. I trying to remember very, very hard."

Aurora smiled, again, seemingly with pity. "It's quite all right. These are my challenges to deal with, not yours. For you, I have only gratitude."

I suspected that Aurora also had a touch of suspicion, but I knew it would dare not say it.

"I must speak with Thule, and I would like both of you to accompany me. Would you agree to that, Defoe?"

"I agreeing!"

"By the way, why did Elyse choose to call you that?"

Its eyes parted sadly. "I not knowing. I not understanding many things Elyse saying or doing."

Heavily, Aurora sighed. "Well, that makes two of us." Pushing back, the captain rose from its chair. "Well, let us not tarry. The sooner I get answers from Thule, the sooner we can begin to chart our course forward. Please, Velistris and Defoe, come." Gesturing to the lift, the captain made its way toward it.

There were so many thoughts that churned through my consciousness as I followed Aurora and Defoe through the *Illustré's* hallways. In the days since that accursed seed of doubt had been planted in my mind—the one that suggested the internal mattered as much as, if not more than, the external—I found myself becoming more and more disconnected from what I'd always felt was my purpose: to beautify others for the sake of their salvation. It had always been such a clear purpose—such a meaningful one. But that wicked seed was now growing roots, and I found it harder and harder to uproot them.

In order to understand this, you must understand what it is like to be elect. To know that yours is a purpose greater than any other and that you were molded in the image of your creator. That is the Zepzeg existence. We are representatives of beauty and can both attain and bestow it like no other. Or at least, that is the way it is supposed to be.

To doubt one's perfection is to doubt Deity, and that is sin. If I doubted the role of outward perfection in attaining salvation, then I lacked the belief necessary to be Deity's evangelistic servant. At the very least, the suggestion of such had occurred to me whilst I'd washed Aurora's hair. And now there was the revelation about the Blepharisma—that it was capable of beautification the likes of which I could not rival. It was more perfect than I at treating hair, yet Deity had not made it. Deity *couldn't* have made it. The Deity I knew was not capable of birthing such a repugnant-looking creature. But that was the Deity *I* knew.

There are humans that do not believe in a creator. They call themselves *atheists*. I find the prospect of a purposeless existence horrifying, and I could not imagine myself clinging to such a cynical belief system, or lack thereof. Yet I cannot help but feel a sense of understanding as to how they must feel, for at present, I felt more alone than I had ever felt before. If there is no Deity, then there must be no Life After, as the two are irrevocably connected. And if there is no Life After, then what is the purpose of life? To live and to die? To change the lives of others, but to what gain? For them to live and to die? If hopeless death—the Great Nothing, as we call it for those who do not reach the Life After—is all that awaits, then what is the purpose of doing anything at all? I cannot fathom the end of consciousness. Yet I have no recollection of the time before I existed, and it has not impaired my ability to live. Is that what it would be like to *not* be? Like remembering the time before one existed? When the mind ends, where does it go? What happens to a memory? For that is all that life is—a series of memories of moments passed, be they by decades or nanoseconds. Would my consciousness be forever trapped in its final thought? Would time itself cease to exist for me? Would my mind return to the time before I existed? The thought of that is so unfathomable. So harrowing.

I had little time to dwell upon those thoughts, as Aurora, Defoe, and I approached the room where the Dacian, Thule, was being held. Hank-is-Handy was there, lording over the captive like the monstrous brute it was. As I saw the Vorck, I wondered for a moment if Aurora would speak against it for allowing Defoe into the engine room. Typically, I would have wanted very much for the Vorck to be called out for being derelict in its duties as the *Illustré*'s security officer, but in that moment I found I cared little.

The Dacian's wrists and ankles were clasped together by magnetic clamps, rendering it quite unable to do anything of worth. The instant it saw us enter, it rasped and bellowed, "Vile human! Detestable fiend! I demand to know why I've been imprisoned on your spacecraft!"

"I would very much like to tell you," Aurora said, its voice measured yet confident. "We took you aboard our vessel under the assumption that you were a liaison to Queen Ugazra."

"*Deceiver*! I have no recollection of this!"

The juxtaposition of their tones was striking. The captain was a far cry from the disheveled mess it'd been in its chambers. It was completely in control. "There's a reason you've no recollection of it. You were under the influence of Broodmaster mind control."

Thule's elevated breathing stopped. It craned its neck. "What did you say?"

"You were under the influence of a Broodmaster. It must've stolen your ship in the Gryamore System. We were en route there to take part in a negotiation for control of Gryamore V."

Its purple eyes widened. "You are Aurora Ultraviolet!"

"I am."

With such modesty did it admit its identity. It is something I have grown to admire in Aurora, not because I agree with it, but because I recognize the restraint needed to do it properly. I would display no such humbleness were my name legendary. Thule rasped and recoiled. "And I am on board the *Illustré*?"

"You are."

Our ship is as well known as its captain, not for its prowess in battle, of course, but *because* of its captain. I paid close attention to the Dacian's body language. It pulled its wings in tighter against its chest—a sign of fear.

Aurora spoke again. "If you agree to cooperate, I will have my Vorck companion release your restraints. You are not here due to anything you have done. You have been thrust into this unwillingly by your Broodmaster neighbors."

It was more than clear that Hank-is-Handy did not approve of releasing the Dacian. It is not a fan of freedom, a remnant trait from their history as slaves. But it would not protest. It never does. Thule lowered its body subserviently and extended its wrists. "I will cooperate, Aurora Ultraviolet."

"There is no need to use my full name. You may call me Aurora." The captain looked at Hank-is-Handy. "Release him.

He will not harm us."

Hank-is-Handy did as told, releasing the magnetic clamps from the Dacian's ankles and wrists. Thule kept its body low even as it was freed, taking several steps back from Aurora in the process. It dipped its head to the ground, careful to avoid eye contact. It is a custom of the Dacians to avoid eye contact when wishing to convey respect or submission, the purpose being to show the recipient of their respect that they do not intend to use their powers of hypnosis. It is a custom not always followed, but the fact that Thule followed it said a measure about its diplomatic instinct. "How may I assist you, Aurora?"

The captain wasted no time. "I would like to know the last thing you remember."

"I operate a merchant vessel called the *Stravelter-karass*."

Dacian ship names are ridiculous.

"I was on the way to a trading hub—I had recently emerged from Gryamore's asteroid belt. It is the last thing I remember."

"Are you in any service to Queen Ugazra whatsoever?"

"No. I have never met the queen. She does not think highly of Clan Shallowcrest."

Ever so slightly, Aurora's eyes narrowed. "Are the Broodmasters your customers?"

Thule spat on the floor. "I would never stoop to sell my wares to such a fiendish species as theirs."

"The only trading hubs near Gryamore's asteroid belt are controlled by Broodmasters. Who are your customers, if I may ask?"

There was purpose in Aurora's questions. I could see it in the way it angled its head down, as if to peer into the Dacian's soul. As if it had suspicions. As it turned out, it was right to have them, for I could tell as soon as the Dacian's wings tensed that there were secrets it wished not to reveal. "There are many species in this cluster. I serve them all."

"What goods were on board your ship?"

It hesitated—another sign of its leeriness. "Microplasters."

"*Microplasters?*"

"You state it with such incredulity. Is it so hard to believe?" Aurora set its hands on its hips. "There is no shortage of microplasters in this cluster. Why tread on such dangerous grounds to sell such a common material? There must be numerous ways for your customers to purchase microplasters without treading so closely to Broodmaster territory."

"I only sell. I do not ask why."

"A convenient answer. I don't happen to believe it."

Thule rasped, "I carried many other materials. Carbonester, silicite, and cragsteel."

"Carbonester, silicite, cragsteel...none worth such effort when they can be purchased for so little anywhere in the cluster." It angled its head. "You don't wish me to discover your cargo, and now I am quite curious as to why." Keeping its eyes on Thule, who was still avoiding eye contact itself, Aurora asked, "Have you been properly introduced to the *Illustré*'s newest crew member? You've met him before, but I'm quite certain you don't remember."

It was referring, of course, to Defoe. The Blepharisma had remained silent throughout the whole of the conversation, as was proper. I noted Aurora's referring to Defoe as a crew member, a stark contrast to its prior statement that the Blepharisma was nothing more than a guest. I did not know if this was intentional to trick the Dacian, an innocent slip of the tongue, as humans say it, or if the captain was having a genuine change of heart regarding the creature. Ultimately, it mattered not to the captain's point.

"Did you notice the strange residue on your head?" Aurora asked.

Defoe's slime. It was still present on the Dacian despite what looked a haphazard attempt—no doubt by Hank-is-Handy— to clean it up. I will say this for the Vorck: it is quite good at cleaning. Though I am sure it cared little for the comfort of the Dacian, it no doubt considered any dribblings of the substance on the floor to be a slip hazard. Ever practical, Vorcks are—and not extraordinarily adept at rising up once they've fallen, though I suppose I can speak little on that particular skillset. It is not a strong suit of the Zepzeg, either.

Aurora continued. "That residue is what is left over after our friend, Defoe the Blepharisma, enveloped your head. He performed an ability that he calls absorbing, in which he drew information from your mind. With it, he was able to detect your Broodmaster controller." It lowered its gaze even more dangerously. "With it, he can tell me who your *real* customers are—and what you provide them. Somehow, I doubt it will be microplasters." When the Dacian said nothing, Aurora shrugged its shoulders. "As you wish. Defoe, would you kindly reacquaint yourself with our guest?"

"I being happy to!" the disgusting thing replied.

Reaching out with one of its feet, Thule said, "No! I will speak."

The most fraudulent of smiles emerged from Aurora's lips. It was outright rude. "How wonderful. So speak."

The Dacian's throat fluttered, and it shook its head like a distressed animal. "For years, the Broodmasters have sold us baited goods. They export them to us under the guise of a willingness to peacefully coexist, only for us to discover that they are devices of destruction—toxins that poison our citizens or hidden bombs that destroy our vessels. They have become quite adept at hiding their bombs from detection. Several of our ships, including a commercial carrier, have been lost to them." It lifted its lips to further bare its teeth—a sign of Dacian hatred. "We wished to return the favor. It was not goods that the *Stravelter-karass* carried, but proximity mines disguised as rescue beacons. We know that the Broodmasters would not willingly rescue anyone—but they would *certainly* arrive to steal their goods. We wanted to ensure that their deeds did not go unpunished."

Gasping, Aurora said, "You were out to destroy them!"

"They are vile creatures, deserving of destruction! What is the harm if a treacherous Broodmaster receives its due fate?"

"And what if one with a soul actually seeks to rescue the supposedly distressed vessel?" Aurora asked. "Or worse, what if a passerby from another species detects the beacon? They would be destroyed, not the Broodmasters!"

Thule snarled. "Wars are a messy affair. There will always be collateral damage."

"But you are not at war."

"Perhaps not outright," Thule said, "but the battle line was drawn long ago—and it runs through Gryamore V!"

Turning away, Aurora pushed its fingers through its tendrils in disgust. "How am I to make this choice when one answer is no better than the other? The Broodmasters seek sabotage, the Dacians seek vengeance. Is there not *one* worthy in this accursed lot?"

"You speak from a place of privilege," snarled Thule. "You do not share such close proximity with your arch nemesis."

"There are *many* species in this cluster that we do not care for," Aurora said, whipping around to face it with such hair-flinging velocity it made my lifeveins surge with energy. Oh, the bounce of those lustrous curls! If it hadn't been for its vicious tone, I could have admired them longer. "That does not give us the right to seek their destruction. For what it was worth, the Broodmasters were trying to sway the negotiation, not destroy you outright! What you have confessed to is a crime."

Thule snarled. "Crime is a human construct. The universe is a dark and dangerous place. It is not one that lends to cooperation. The strong survive; the weak perish! This is the way it has been long before your feeble species took to the stars."

"I have no choice but to consider you hostile. I apologize, but I must," Aurora said, tapering the emotion in its voice.

It looked down and adjusted its gloves—it often diverts its attention to such menial tasks when it attempts to administer order. "You will remain in our custody until I determine what to do with you. Hank-is-Handy, please replace the restraints on his wrists."

"Giving Gryamore to the Broodmasters would be a grave mistake, Aurora," Thule said, holding its appendages out for the Vorck to secure. At the very least, it understood its place in all of this. "This cluster cannot afford a looming Broodmaster threat. Gryamore would tip the balance in their favor."

Having turned away already, Aurora angled its head partway toward it. "In my experience, there is but one thing that cannot be afforded, be it in a cluster, on a planet, or in a ship. And that is self-justification. It is the first step one takes toward atrocity. I will not soon forget this conversation, Thule, and I thank you for it. It has been enlightening, to say the least." Aurora stepped through the precipice of the room into the hall, then turned back to the Dacian. "I'm afraid that for our protection, I must lock you in your chamber. Your needs will be provided for, and I will ensure that the communication console in this room is in proper working order. I will leave your ankles unrestrained that you may access it if need be." Its gaze swiveled to the rest of us. "The rest of you, please come with me."

I wasted no time in heeding its commands, for I wished to remain in the Dacian's presence for as little as possible. It was not that I disagreed with it—truth be told, I understood its point of view entirely. Humans have always lent unwarranted trust to the spirit of altruism. The denizens of the cosmos are not a cooperative bunch. No, I wished to leave the Dacian because I feared that in its frustration and wrath, it might strike out at us. It is better kept behind a locked door. I was glad that Aurora deemed it necessary.

As Hank-is-Handy engaged the door lock, Aurora faced us. "There are things we must all do—precautions we must all take, or we will fall into the snare of this complicated situation." It looked at the Blepharisma. "Defoe, it is not your fault that you have been given access to our engine room. It is a great privilege of which you have been entrusted. I only wish that that trust had been mine to give and not Elyse's. Nonetheless, her trust is now my trust, and I will lend mine to you as she has lent hers, for we are in a fragile state on this ship. We need all the assistance and cooperation that we can get."

Its red eyes upon Aurora, Defoe waved its flagellum. "I doing my best to help!" Always so cheery, it is, as if it is oblivious to the chaos around it. Perhaps it is. Or perhaps it simply does not extend care to such matters. I found myself envying the creature ever so slightly, as I have found myself envying Hank-is-Handy lately. Ignorance, I am learning, can indeed be bliss.

"I only ask that you not enter the engine room on your own accord for now. That is not a matter of trust, it is one of knowledge. Hank-is-Handy and Elyse better understand how the components of the engine room work and will be better able to guide you if present."

"That sounding good!"

"You may return to your quarters now." Moments after Aurora said the words, Defoe slithered away down the hall. The captain's focus turned to me. "I have a task for you of great importance."

Dipping my head as is proper, I said, "I will do all that you ask, captain."

"Stop sulking about and be present."

My lifeveins froze. I looked up at it again. "Captain?"

"Your behavior as of late has been less than desirable. You are never there when I need you, you are distracted from all of your tasks—it is like the confidant I've come to know and trust has been stolen from me, replaced by a listless husk. You are not acting like a Zepzeg. You are acting more like… more like Elyse."

I scarcely knew what to say—how to react. So many words had pierced my core lately, yet I was not numbed to it. Its words hurt as badly as Delta's after I'd doused it.

It leaned in closer to me. "Get over whatever it is you're fighting. This situation we're in is important, and there are no clear paths forward. I do not know what you need, and I do not know if I can help you find it, but whatever it is, solve it. I will solve it myself if I must, but I must first know what it is, so if it must be made known to me, make it known. Otherwise, get better. Right now you're hardly better than nothing at all."

I felt I could shatter right then and there. All I could offer was the promise of compliance. "I will be better, captain."

"You had better. There are many others in this cluster who would lend a fine hand to diplomacy. It is already clear you are not needed for hair. Be gone from me."

The insult! The appalling nature of its words! Even more appalling was that I could not contest them. It was speaking on behalf of its own experiences with me. The fault was my own. Lowering my head in shame, I turned around to return to my chamber. The last words I heard Aurora speak were to Hank-is-Handy, and they were as pointed as they'd been to me.

"And *you*. There is *much* that we must discuss. To your quarters, immediately."

Hank-is-Handy said nothing—a rare moment of wisdom from the imbecilic beast. I did not turn to see them go. I could hear the Vorck's heavy footsteps trundling away.

There was so much to process of what'd just occurred. It felt as if the *Illustré* was now at a tipping point. Elyse was in outright rebellion. Delta had been most heinously rejected from the equation. Even Hank-is-Handy was in line for a lashing. But my dear captain? What was I to make of this sudden change in it? While all of its lectures were indeed warranted, it was the manner in which they were delivered that raised alarm in me. This was not the calm and collected human to which I'd become accustomed. This was a human overflowing with emotion. While that may be well and understood for some, it is not Aurora Ultraviolet. It is not the kind of human that it is. Something was amiss, and I was keen to uncover it. But there would be a time for that, and it was not now. For now, the one that needed repair was myself.

It was right in claiming that I had not been myself. I had hoped that my deviations had gone unnoticed—that perhaps Aurora just thought me in a queer season—but it was evident to me now that something needed to be done to remedy the feelings that were churning in my core. Before I could figure out my dear captain, I knew I must first figure out myself. I feared it would not be an easy task. Many humans spend a lifetime attempting to sort out their self-perceptions and fend off what they call their *demons.* I have never understood those trials until now. Gathering up my courage, and dare I say my humility, I retreated to the solemnity of my chambers to address my fractures within.

Chapter Ten

I HAVE BEEN wrong many times. I have also been right many times. But I have not been wrong and right at the same time many times. On this day, I was wrong and right at the same time. It was not a feeling that was good.

I was in my room thinking about the words that Aurora said to me. She said them after she found out that Defoe had been in the engine room and that I had not told her. She was not happy that I did not tell her. I predicted that she would not be, and my prediction was correct.

Aurora did something that she does not do a lot, which is to get close to my face and shout loudly. She also pointed at me with her finger. I did not like or dislike when she pointed her finger. I think she meant for it to make her words stronger. But I did not like it when she spoke loudly. It made my head look down and away from her and it made my body feel small. When she walked closer to me, I stepped back until I was touching the wall with my back. Then I could not go back any farther. So I stood there and listened.

She said that I should have told her when Elyse took Defoe to the engine room. She was correct. She also said that I put the entire crew in danger, including Elyse, by letting her show Defoe how things work in the engine room. She was correct about this, too. She was correct about many of the things that I knew. This is why I say that I was right. But I was also wrong in that I did not do what I knew would be right to do. I warned Elyse about this, but she did not listen. My error was listening to Elyse. I listened to her because I love her.

I think that maybe I should not love Elyse. It has made me

have bad feelings and now it has made me get in trouble. I think love is a bad thing that makes Vorcks weak. I want to be a strong Vorck. So I will stop loving Elyse. I predict that it will not be easy, because I do not want to stop loving her. But I must do it if I am to serve my purpose on this ship. I want to serve my purpose more than I want anything else, even to love Elyse. If I do not have a purpose, then it would be most beneficial to the crew that I was not here. I would be using oxygen that could be used for other crew members. My not being there would increase the efficiency of the rebreather systems. If I cannot serve a purpose here, then perhaps I will leave when we go to the next space station to find purpose on another ship. Or perhaps I will go into the airlock and then go into space, where I cannot live for more than a few days. Then I would die and would not be using oxygen that does not need to be used. Maybe then the rebreather systems would work more efficiently. I will think about these things, then decide what to do. I will also try to do my purpose better, because I do not want to leave the *Illustré* at the next space station or go into space.

I picked up my phase hammer to bring with me when I left to go to Elyse's room. I did this in case she got mad when I told her I did not love her. If she tried to attack me, I would hit her with the phase hammer and she would be dead. This would not make me happy or sad. It would not make me have any feelings, and I think that is a good thing. I also brought the list I wrote of things that she is not good at. This way, she can make herself better at something if she wants to. I think having the list will be helpful for her.

When I got to Elyse's room, I knocked on the door. I wanted her to know it was me, so I said, "It is me." I waited for the door to open, but it did not open. I also waited for her to say something, but she did not say anything. I thought that maybe she did not hear me, so I knocked again and said, "It is me." When the door did not open and she did not say anything again, I opened the door console on the wall and bypassed the locking mechanism. The door opened but I did not see Elyse. Then I looked at the bathroom, and that is where I saw her.

Elyse was in front of the mirror, and she was looking at herself in it. I saw a pair of scissors and a lot of her hair on the floor. This is when I saw that she had cut most of her hair. But she did not cut all of it. It did not look symmetrical or like anything that Aurora, Delta, or weak Velistris would call good. I think they would have done a gasp sound if they had seen it. I did not make a gasp sound because I was happy to see Elyse's hair shorter and because Vorck do not gasp.

Elyse was looking at her reflection and her hands were outstretched against the vanity top. She was holding a pair of scissors in her hand, so I do not think she was finished. "We must speak," I said. I thought that Elyse would say something that humans say when they are told they must do something, like, "okay," or, "in a minute," or, "what is it?" But she did not say any of those things. I do not know if she heard me, because the things she said did not have anything to do with what I told her.

"Do you ever get tired?" she asked. Her voice was very quiet and hard to hear, like humans do when they are saying something important.

"No." I held out the list. "I do not love you anymore. Here is a list of what you are not good at."

She did not look at the list or take the list. She did not do anything at all. "I am so tired," she said. She looked down and her head turned to the scissors. Her shoulders shook, which humans do for one of three reasons. The first is if they are too cold. The second is if they are scared. The third is if they drink a lot of a drink called *coffee*. I predicted that she was shaking because of one of the first two reasons, because I did not see coffee in the room. "I am so incredibly tired."

"If you go to sleep, you will not be tired."

"I know," she said. Her voice got even quieter. "I think I've finally come to realize that."

I thought that all humans knew that they would not be tired if they slept, but perhaps Elyse did not know. I am glad she found out. "I will put down the list so you can see it. I will now go to the engine room to make repairs. Aurora says that Defoe can go to the engine room to work, but only if one of us is there."

"Don't worry," she said. "I won't be going there."

I do not know why she said she would not be going there. She goes there many times during the day. Perhaps it was because I told her I did not love her anymore. I predicted that this was the reason. "You can work in the engine room even if I do not love you."

"I know."

My prediction was incorrect. It did not make me happy or sad. I did not know what else to say, so I said, "I will leave you now."

When I turned to leave, she spoke again. "Hank-is-Handy?" I looked back at her. "Would you miss me if I was gone?"

I knew the answer to the question. "Yes." I knew it because I missed her when she was working with Defoe and when she was with Delta instead of being with me.

"Thank you."

"You are welcome." It is what one is supposed to say when a human says, "thank you." I do not know what it means. I turned to leave the room. When I was not looking at her anymore, I heard her make sounds that humans call *sniffling*. It is when they are very sad and make many small breaths with their nose. Being sad does not produce good work, so I turned around to her again. "You are sad."

Elyse stopped leaning against the sink and she knelt down in front of it. She put her head against her arms, which were now folded. She began to make tears, which is a wet thing humans make that prevents them from seeing clearly. I do not know why they do it, and I am glad that I do not do it. "If you want to leave, leave," she said. It was hard to hear because she was making the sniffling noises. But I am pretty sure that is what she said. I do not know why she said it, because I knew that if I wanted to leave, I could leave. Maybe she thought that I needed permission. Humans like to give permission a lot even when they do not have to.

"I want to leave," I said, because I wanted her to know that that was what I wanted.

"Then leave!" she screamed. She screamed it in a very loud voice. I think that if Aurora or Delta had heard it, they would have done a flinch thing. But Vorck do not flinch very often. That is why it is good to never do something around a Vorck that might make other beings flinch. Instead of flinching, the Vorck might try to kill whoever is doing the thing.

It was at that time when I realized that Elyse would probably not attack me and I would probably not have to use my phase hammer. I deactivated it with my finger so that I did not use it by accident. I do not want to kill anything by accident unless it is Velistris, Defoe, his blue Slarb, or his pink Gralb. "Good bye, Elyse," I said, then I turned to go away from the bathroom. I did not know what she would do after I left. Maybe she would take a shower to get clean. Maybe she would cry some more. I knew I could not help with either of those things, so I left.

I think that I do not know many of the things that humans go through even though I am feeling their sad and bad things a lot. I think that maybe feeling the good things makes the bad things feel worse because the bad things can be compared to the good things, and they are very different. I think that the things Elyse was feeling were very bad, and I think that it made thinking of the good things worse. So even having good feelings is bad, because the bad feelings will make the good feelings not be good anymore. Feelings are very difficult to understand. I think I understand them better than I did a long time ago when I did not feel many feelings at all, but I do not understand them as good as a human does. I think that I will never understand them as good as a human does. I think this is okay. Not everything is made to be like everything else. I think that if there is a human creator and he made all of the things that exist, he probably made them for different reasons. This means that they have different purposes. It also means that it is okay if two different lifeforms do not feel the same things. I used to feel sad that I could not feel the good things like humans feel, but it does not make me sad anymore. It makes me feel like a Vorck.

I was glad that I did not love Elyse anymore. I think that she was okay with it. I hoped she would use the list I gave her of things she was not good at to get better. That would make me glad, I think. It would be a good feeling, but it would be a good feeling that I liked. I was glad that I could at least go to the engine room now to work and not feel bad about it.

There was a loud noise in the *Illustré*. I heard it sound through all of the halls, and it made me stop walking. It was the alarm for the proximity overload. It meant that something pulled the ship out of hyperspace. The next thing I heard was Aurora on the speaker. "All hands on deck, get to the bridge now, get to the bridge *now!*" The *Illustré* shook. I predicted that it was because the ship had been shot. I ran very fast to the bridge to find out.

When I got to the bridge, Aurora was strapping into the harness on her chair. She does it when she thinks the ship is going to move a lot, like when it is under attack. I looked at the bridge monitor to see what was going on. This was when Aurora said, "It's the Vorticella! They just forced us out of hyperspace!"

On the bridge monitor, I saw several of the Vorticella fighters strafe past the *Illustré*. They fired again and their shots hit the ship. The ship shook again. Even though Aurora did not say it, I knew that she wanted me to get to my weapons console. I ran very fast to it and strapped myself into the harness there. I did this so I would not fall when the ship shook. I put my hands on the trigger controls for the plasma cannon and I activated it. This is when I saw the bridge door open and Elyse came inside. She was running, too, and the look on her face was scared.

Aurora pointed to the screen generator console and said, "Elyse, get on screens!"

Elyse did not say anything. She only ran to get to the screen console like Aurora said. Aurora did not say anything about Elyse's hair. I predict that this was because the Vorticella were trying to kill us. Delta and Riley came in after Elyse, then Velistris came. The ship got hit again and they almost fell, but they did not. They got to their console stations and strapped in like I did. Delta shouted, "Riley, in your kennel!" Riley moved quickly into the kennel built into the wall of the bridge. When he got inside, she pressed buttons and the kennel door closed.

This is when the plasma cannon became fully charged. "Plasma cannon charged," I said. "I am engaging." I pulled the trigger and began to shoot at the Vorticella on the targeting monitor at my station.

"Velistris," Aurora said very loudly, "open a channel!"

Behind me, Elyse said, "Forward screens are down to thirty percent! We're not going to survive many more strafes like the ones we just took!"

I did not pay attention to what Velistris said to Aurora about the channel, because I was trying to shoot at the Vorticella fighters on my monitor, but I think that she told Aurora that the channel was open because I heard Aurora say, "This is the *Illustré* sending a message to all Vorticella fighters! We are willing to negotiate! Please tell us your terms!"

The Vorticellas appeared on the monitor the same way they did before, except there were six of them instead of four. When they talked, they all had very different voices.

"Release to us Blepharisma—"

"—and you will be spared."

"We know he is on your vessel."

"Resist us and be destroyed!"

"Like the weak and inferior—"

"—beings that you are."

I looked on my sensors. I saw that there were over twenty fighters, so I said, "I am detecting over twenty fighters."

It was at this time that the door to the bridge opened and Defoe came in. He did not have a station on the bridge, but I think he came in because he heard Aurora tell everyone to go there. I think that she probably did not mean for him to come, but she did not think to say it when she said it.

Aurora looked at Defoe, then answered the Vorticella on the channel. "We have given the Blepharisma sanctuary on this vessel. If you're willing to talk, we would love to discuss this situation in a civil manner!"

Behind me, Elyse said, "We are *not* handing over Defoe!" I think she was angry because she sounded angry when she said it.

"There is nothing to discuss," said one of the Vorticella. The others then began to talk like they did the first time.

"Hand over Blepharisma—"

"—and your crew will be spared."

"Or force us to destroy you."

"Or perhaps you will destroy us."

"Either way, we do not care!"

"Only the threat of vaporization—"

"—makes existence meaningful."

Aurora made a loud sound that sounded like, "Argh!" Then

she said, "There *must* be some way we can work this out without bloodshed! Why is he so important to you?"

"He has information," a Vorticella said.

"Important information!"

"Information that we cannot allow to escape."

"Turn him over to us—"

"—or face annihilation!"

Aurora performed a head shake. "I am sorry, but I cannot turn him over to you. Whatever information he has, I am certain it is not worth his life! There is no question in my mind that if you had him, you would kill him."

The Vorticellas said, "You have made your choice."

"We are pleased you wish to fight!"

"Let us embrace death together!"

"And become dust amidst the stars."

The Vorticellas disappeared from the bridge monitor. I do not think there was anything else they wanted to say.

The ship shook again because the Vorticella fighters hit it. Behind me, Elyse said, "Screens down to four percent! One more pass and—"

Aurora interrupted her and said, "Divert all powers from the screen generator to thrusters!"

"*What?*" said Elyse. I think that this is because without any power to the screens, it would only take a few more hits to destroy the *Illustré*.

"Divert all power to thrusters! Don't question, do it *now!*"

"Diverting power to thrusters," said Elyse. She then did as she was told.

I saw Aurora grab the joysticks on the chair tighter. "Hold on, everyone!" Sometimes Aurora says to do something and not everybody does it. But this time, everyone listened and held on. I held on, too. Aurora pushed the joysticks forward. The *Illustré* moved forward very fast.

Even though the *Illustré* is not a warship, it is faster than many ships that exist. That is because Aurora made me install special burners in the thruster bay many years ago. She runs them through a neutron secondary, which gives them more power than they would normally have. All of the components are expensive, but she can afford them because she is rich.

I held on tightly as the *Illustré* moved forward very quickly. It weaved side to side and I saw enemy fire from the Vorticella fighters streak past. She moved the joystick from one side to the other so that the Vorticella fighters would continue to miss. They did. I tried to look at the sensors to see their positioning, but the fast movements made it hard for me to stay still and get a good look. This is why she told us all to hold on. The only one that could not was Defoe, but he was holding onto a railing with his tentacle thing. The ship stopped weaving and went straight, then it went very fast. This was because she maneuvered past the Vorticella fighters and was now trying to get distance. Now they were behind us and trying to catch up. They were also shooting.

"Hank-is-Handy, engage!" Aurora said.

I rotated the plasma cannon to face behind the ship. I saw many Vorticella fighters shooting from behind, but I also saw some veer off. I knew that they would try to approach from different directions. I wanted to shoot at them, but I could not, because I had to shoot at the fighters that were still shooting at us. So that is what I did. I missed the first few times I shot at them. This is because the Vorticella fighters are very fast and nimble. I shot again and I hit one and it got destroyed. I moved the plasma cannon to another one and hit it, too. It also got destroyed. "Two fighters destroyed," I said. The other Vorticella fighters fired at us, and Aurora made the *Illustré* move again. But she did not move fast enough. Two of the shots hit the *Illustré*, and it shook with much force. At the front of the bridge, Velistris's harness broke and she hit the wall. She made a loud shatter noise because a part of her broke off. The part that broke off was one of her arms.

"Hull breach, docking bay!" said Elyse.

That was not good news. That meant that the strike craft, Castor and Pollux, could not be launched to assist. But even if they could, Castor was still damaged. It was unlikely that a lone strike craft could have made any difference. At the same time that Elyse made the announcement about the docking bay, Delta said, "*Velistris!*"

Aurora weaved the *Illustré* again because the Vorticella fighters were shooting. I predicted that because Velistris was not strapped in, she would be thrown to the other side of the bridge and maybe break into more pieces. My prediction was half correct. The *Illustré* rotated quickly, and Velistris and the part of her that broke flew across the bridge. But she did not hit the wall and break, because Defoe reached out with his tentacle arm and grabbed her. He pulled her to him faster than I saw him pull Elyse and Delta before. His plant mouth opened big and he put her whole body inside of it. I think he did it so that she did not break. The *Illustré* moved again to avoid fire, and Defoe flew across the bridge with Velistris in his plant mouth. He hit the wall once, then his tentacle thing wrapped around a rail and he stuck to it.

I fired the plasma cannon again at the Vorticella fighters behind us. I thought that I fired good, but they moved before the shots could hit them. I predicted very quickly that soon, the fighters that veered away earlier would attack us from different directions. My prediction was correct.

The *Illustré* was struck again, and many red lights flashed on the damage indicator. It also shook worse than before.

"Major hull breach!" said Elyse. "Blast shields down!"

"Where?" asked Aurora very loudly as she made the *Illustré* do many spins and turns.

Elyse answered loudly, "My room! Oh God, my whole room is *gone!*" I continued to fire as Elyse hit many buttons on the *Illustré*'s system map. "I'm reading a blast door failure on one of the doors that's already down."

"Is it compromised?" Aurora asked.

"Not yet, but it might be soon!"

If the blast doors failed, it would put all of the living quarters at risk for a loss of life support.

Next, Elyse said, "Aunt Aurora, what about Slarb and Gralb in Defoe's room? If that system fails…"

Aurora said, "Yeah, they're not the only ones!" I knew she was thinking about Thule, too. The Vorticella fighters shot at us again, and Aurora turned the *Illustré* into a hard loop to avoid them. From her chair, Aurora got on the speakers. "Thule, I'm opening the door to your room. Move toward the front of the ship and find the bridge *now* or you're going to die!" I predicted that she hit the buttons to open his door from the bridge, but I could not see because I was shooting at the Vorticella fighters. I hit one of three that were clustered together, and it flew into the other ones and they got destroyed.

"Three fighters down!" I said.

From her seat where she was strapped, Delta said, "I'll get Slarb and Gralb!" She unstrapped herself, but Aurora yelled at her loudly.

"No! It's too dangerous!"

It was too late. Momentum made Delta hit the wall hard by the door, but she caught herself against it and hit the door to open it. "I won't let them die!"

Aurora looked back at me and said, "Hank-is-Handy, if there was ever a time I needed you to be perfect, this is it!" She activated the thrusters to full forward power and the *Illustré* flew forward fast. I rotated the plasma cannon around to search for more Vorticella fighters. I saw some, and I shot at them. They shot at us, too. Some of their shots grazed the ship, but none of them hit hard.

I was not perfect like Aurora wanted, but I did hit some of the Vorticella fighters as they got behind us. I was beginning to feel like I was learning the way that they moved and their tendencies. It made it easier for me to predict what they were going to do, and predicting is something I think I am good at. I shot again and destroyed another fighter, and the rest of them in pursuit broke in opposite directions. There were also two clusters of Vorticella fighters coming at us from different directions, so I told Aurora about them. "Vorticella fighters are coming from multiple directions. We will not outrun them. We must fight, captain."

"Then fight!" Aurora opened the channel to the rest of the ship and shouted, "All hands, brace for evasive action!"

I do not know if Delta, Thule, or the Slarb and Gralb heard her, or even if the Slarb and Gralb could understand what she was saying. I do not think Aurora knew, either. Aurora pushed one joystick forward all of the way and turned the other all the way to the side. It made the *Illustré* nose dive and rotate at the same time. The maneuver put the nearest cluster of Vorticella fighters in my line of sight with the plasma cannon. I believe this was what Aurora was trying to do. I pulled the trigger and shot several of the ones that were coming. "I register eleven Vorticella fighters on sensors!" I said.

At the same time as Aurora made another very hard turn, the bridge door opened and Thule came in. His wrists were still bound and he could not fly, but his ankles were free so he could walk. The momentum of the turn flung him across the bridge, and he made a loud and painful sound. "What's going on?" he asked, then he looked on the bridge monitor. His body recoiled like Dacians' bodies do when they are surprised. "What kind of ships are those?" he asked loudly.

"Vorticellas!" answered Aurora. She pointed to the communications station where Velistris had been. "Can you work a comm station?" she asked quickly and loudly. Thule said something, but I was busy shooting at more Vorticella fighters and missing them, so I did not hear it. I think that he said no, because the next thing that Aurora said was, "Well, learn *fast*! We're one man down and we need all the help we can get!" She slid open the drawer on her desk where she keeps important items and she pulled out the key to the magnetic clamps. She threw them quickly in Thule's direction, and he caught them with his feet.

I was not surprised that she was freeing Thule, because having him as a prisoner and dying was worse than having him free and surviving. I could not see what his reaction was when he saw her throw the key at him, but I did see him unlock the magnetic clamps quickly. He grabbed onto the railing around the communication console with his hands and began to tap at the touch screen with his toes.

The bridge door opened a second time, and Delta came in. The Slarb and Gralb were in her hands, and she ran to the kennel where Riley was. She opened the door and threw them inside it with him, then she said, "Please don't kill each other in there!"

"Delta, *hold on*!" said Aurora. I predicted she said this because the *Illustré* was going to turn hard again. My prediction was correct. Delta ran fast to her console and strapped herself in as Aurora engaged the spacebrakes and pulled her joysticks all the way back. Several Vorticella fighters streaked past the ship and I tried to shoot them. I missed.

"What does this station control?" asked Thule.

Aurora answered, "Comms! We need to send out an urgent distress call!"

The Dacian made a roar sound. "I do not know how to work this station!"

"We need Velistris there!" said Elyse from behind me.

Delta looked at her. "Part of her is already broken! She'll *shatter*!"

I believed that Delta was correct. I also believed that it did not matter, because a distress call would not help our situation fast enough.

Aurora pushed the joysticks forward hard once more, and the *Illustré* flew with as much forward thrust as it had left.

But I could see that the drives were damaged and that it did not have full power. I knew that it was only a matter of time until the Vorticella fighters destroyed us. If I had been allowing myself to feel feelings, I would have been sad for my human friends that would die. But I did not feel anything.

Shots from the Vorticella fighters flew past the ship. It was almost time for us to die. Aurora tried to veer the ship, but it was not enough. It was too late, and I predicted that our death was imminent.

My prediction was incorrect.

The proximity alarm sounded just before the shots from the Vorticella fighters reached us. In front of the *Illustré*, a very large spaceship dropped out of hyperspace and appeared. It was the Daldath Planet Smasher that we had encountered before.

The shots from the Vorticella fighters stopped, and I watched them scatter in all directions. Aurora altered her course, too, even though I think it was out of instinct because the Planet Smasher was still very far ahead. She made a gasp sound and said, "Oh my God!"

Sometimes humans call out to their god in moments of surprise. I believe Aurora did this because she was surprised to see the Planet Smasher. I believe the arrival of the Planet Smasher surprised her because it is not common for spaceships to drop each other out of hyperspace multiple times unless one spaceship is pursuing the other. But the Planet Smasher did not seem to be pursuing us. I knew it would be important to discuss why the Planet Smasher had now dropped us out of hyperspace twice, but I also knew that this was not a good time to do it. This was because we were engaged in a battle.

On the sensors, I saw a pair of Daldath warships drop out of hyperspace next to the Planet Smasher. "Two Daldath warships have dropped out of hyperspace," I said. Daldath warships are very dangerous and can destroy small vessels

like the *Illustré* and the Vorticella fighters very easily. I was
surprised to see them because they were not there the first
time that we met the Planet Smasher. I predicted that they
were there now as protection in case the Planet Smasher was
forced out of hyperspace again, but there was no way to test
my prediction.

I did predict that the battle would not last for much
longer because of the arrival of the Planet Smasher and the
warships. My prediction was correct. "The Vorticella fighters
are breaking off," I said. Space battles are very dangerous.
Most species do not like surprises when they are in a space
battle. I do not feel one way or the other about them, but
humans do not like surprises unless they are the ones doing
them. I believed that the Vorticellas did not like surprises,
too, because they were now leaving. Soon it was only us and
the Daldath. I knew that if the Daldath attacked the *Illustré*,
we would die very quickly, but it did not attack. It stayed in
space and the warships stayed next to it.

Sometimes when a bad thing or a thing that scares them
happens, humans get very still. I believe this is a response
that prey do a lot. Sometimes when a predator animal gets
close to a prey animal, the prey animal gets still so that the
predator animal does not see them. I think this is what the
humans were doing, too, but it did not make sense and I
did not think it would make the Daldath not see us. This is
because we were in a spaceship.

Blepharisma opened his plant mouth and Velistris came
out. She was covered in plant slime and slid across the floor
a little bit. I saw her move, so I knew that she was alive. One
of her arms was gone because it was what broke against
the side of the bridge. I saw it on the floor, too. Delta left
her station and went to Velistris to help her up because she
could not stand up on her own.

Aurora usually cares a lot when someone gets hurt. I know
this because she asks if they are "okay" and her voice gets

very loud and fast. But she did not do this with Velistris. I think it was because she knew that Velistris was not going to die and she was more busy with the Daldath ships. "Elyse, what's our status?" she asked without looking back at Elyse.

I looked at Elyse. She pressed many buttons on her console that told her all of the problems in the *Illustré*. Then she said, "We have several hull breaches, but most of the ship's systems are functional. The engine room took damage, but it was from power surges, not direct fire. Thrusters are good, the spindrive is good. Blasters inoperable."

"And the blast doors?"

"They held."

Aurora looked at me. "Hank-is-Handy, can the *Illustré* handle hyperspace with hull breaches?"

"Yes," I said. "The hull breaches will not affect the speed at which we can travel."

Aurora continued to look at the Daldath ships even though she was talking to me. The Daldath ships were not doing anything. They did not seem to want to attack. "Considering the fact that we've now dropped each other out of hyperspace multiple times, what is the likelihood that that Planet Smasher is headed to any system *other* than Gryamore?"

When she said it, many of the others on the bridge turned their heads to look at her. Thule did and Delta did, too. Velistris did not and neither did Blepharisma. "The likelihood is low," I said. Space is very big. It is not probable that any ship runs into the same ship more than once unless it is pursuing them, they are pursuing it, or they are going to the same destination. I did not believe the first two scenarios to be true. I looked down at the sensor where I saw that the Daldath ships were backing up. "They are moving away from us," I said, "possibly preparing for a jump to hyperspace."

Aurora did not say anything. She only watched the spaceships on the bridge monitor like everyone else.

There were many ramifications if the Planet Smasher was

on the way to the Gryamore System. Planet Smashers harvest all mineral resources from a planet's surface, but this destroys the planet. That is why they are called Planet Smashers. Nobody likes it when a Planet Smasher comes because it means a planet near them may get stripped of its resources and reduced to a husk. If the Planet Smasher was going to Gryamore, it meant that they were either going after a planet that the Broodmasters or Dacians were already living on or they were going after Gryamore V, which we were going to negotiate about. I think it would have been best if it was going to Gryamore V, because then we could just let the Planet Smasher destroy it and not have to negotiate anymore. But negotiations do not work like that. If Vorck were in charge, I think they would work like that. But Vorck are not in charge.

Thule looked at Aurora from the communications station. "We must destroy that Planet Smasher! It cannot be allowed to attack the Gryamore System. It may be a Dacian colony that falls!"

"Or a Broodmaster," said Aurora in a way that sounded not pleased. She performed a head shake. "We cannot destroy that spaceship. We are badly damaged, and even if we weren't, we're no match for those warships, let alone the Planet Smasher."

Banging his feet on the console, Thule said, "Then you must alert the colonies! You must alert your military! You must do this quickly so we have time to muster our defenses!"

It did not surprise me that Thule was getting loud and with angry feelings. Every planet in the Gryamore System is important to them and the Broodmasters.

"I shudder to think what might occur should your people and the Broodmasters muster in the same place," said Aurora. "I fear it would be a precursor to war. One so-called errant blast and all hope of civility would be discarded. It would be used to justify genocide." She turned her head back to the monitor, where the Daldath ships were getting farther away. "But you are correct in saying that we must do something. The Daldath must be confronted at Gryamore, if that is indeed their destination, or they will singlehandedly wreck any hope of peace in this negotiation. And if what must be done results in a joint mustering, then I pray that it ushers in a spirit of unity and not competition." She looked at me. "Hank-is-Handy, plot a course for Gryamore at maximum velocity. We must surpass the Daldath at all costs. I fear an agreement as to Gryamore V's fate must be determined quickly, before the Planet Smasher arrives at the system." She looked at Velistris, but she asked a question to either me or Elyse. She did not specify who. "Whose quarters are currently inaccessible due to the breach?"

Elyse answered the question because she was looking at that monitor. "My quarters, Defoe's, and Thule's are inaccessible. Mine is…destroyed."

Aurora gave an answer that was very quick. "Delta, move your belongings into Velistris's chamber and relinquish your chamber to Thule. Elyse, you will move in with me until the ship can be repaired. I am afraid I have no choice but to restrain you in Delta's room, Thule, much as you were previously. I wish I could extend to you my trust, but it has not yet been earned. In light of the recent complications with the Daldath, I hope you understand." Thule made a snarl sound that did not sound like a good sound, but Aurora did not respond to it. She continued talking. "Hank-is-Handy, you will share your room with Defoe and his…companions…for the time being. Will this be a problem?"

It would not be, so I said, "No."

"Thank you, everyone, for your understanding." She looked at Velistris. "Velistris, are you able to walk?"

Velistris spoke, but her voice echoed. I had never heard her with an echo voice before. Maybe it was because she was broken, or maybe because she was scared. I do not know which. "Yes, captain."

Aurora looked at Velistris's arm that was on the floor. "How long until it develops sentience?" Zepzeg have a very strange way of reproducing. When a part of them breaks off, it becomes a new Zepzeg. Zepzeg are usually very careful about when they do it and they make many plans before doing it. I do not think Velistris planned to hit the wall hard and for her arm to break off.

When Velistris answered, her head stayed down. "I do not know, captain."

"Well, we will deal with it as we are able. Delta, please assist her to your chamber to rest. I am sure she'll wish to be cleaned. Help her to the absolute best of your ability. As soon as you're finished, move your personal effects, then return to the bridge."

"Yes, Aunt Aurora."

"Go, now. Take her arm with you."

Delta and Velistris moved quickly.

Aurora spoke again. "Hank-is-Handy, secure Thule in his chambers, then assist Defoe with whatever he might require. He may desire a warmer temperature than what you're accustomed. I ask that you acquiesce."

"Yes, captain," I said.

"Elyse, please monitor the bridge while I go to my chambers. I must contact our fleet admirals to request their presence at Gryamore. If the Dacians and Broodmasters are to muster, so must we. Let us hope it is all for nothing."

I did not hope one way or the other, but I said, "Let us hope," anyway. Humans like it when you agree with them with words, even if you do not mean it.

"To your tasks, all of you."

She did not say anything else. She only walked to the lift that would take her to her quarters above the bridge. As Elyse moved to the captain's chair, I escorted Thule out of the room.

Chapter Eleven

I HAVE NEVER been broken. I have shed crystalline filaments. I have carved, and chipped, and smoothened my exterior. I have even allowed portions of my body to be removed for the purpose of reproduction. But I have never been broken.

Until that day.

While on the bridge during the Vorticella attack, the harness at my station failed and I was thrown against the wall. Zepzeg are beings unaccustomed to strain—and particularly unaccustomed to blunt-force trauma. Whereas a hardy being like Hank-is-Handy can absorb blows to the body, our crystalline bodies make us particularly vulnerable to physical stress. Having one's body thrown against the metal walls of a spaceship is something we are simply not physically prepared for. My body gave way, and I broke, right above what would be considered my right elbow. It did not hurt—for we do not have pain receptors as do most carbon-based lifeforms, but I felt it. I felt it reverberate through my lifeveins. I saw the arm immediately slide across the bridge as the *Illustré* moved. The next thing I knew, I was inside Defoe's body. Its sucking me in was likely the only thing that kept me alive. I was grateful, and I am typically grateful for nothing. It was uncharacteristic of me. Zepzeg are not supposed to fear death. But I feared.

Up until the point when it spat me out, I saw, heard, and knew nothing of what was going on in the battle. The Blepharisma must have clung tightly to whatever railing it'd attached itself to, for I scarcely felt it move. For a time I simply existed, swaying side to side in the primordial slime that resides within its body. While everyone else engaged in combat, I had only time to think. And think I did.

I knew instantly that the part of my arm that'd broken off was too big *not* to develop. I felt a strand of my lifeveins go with it. We call offspring produced from such accidental breakages *fracturelings*—though the term is only a descriptor, not a judgment on worth. I have heard humans use the term *mistake* for such unintended reproductions of their own kind. It is an unfair term for a being that had no say-so in the way in which it was delivered into existence. Likewise, my fractureling had no say-so. Fracturelings develop into fully functional Zepzeg just like the most carefully planned of our offspring. In fact, considering the size of the strand of lifevein that broke with it, it would likely mature at a greatly accelerated rate. Most Zepzeg take years, if not decades to mature. This one was liable to mature in a matter of months. But for this particular fractureling, that expediency was not a good thing at all. That was because the lifevein that would form its core was *mine*.

I was a spirit in torment. Over the past week, I had grappled with every forbidden thought. I had questioned every belief that I had been told could not be questioned. I had even come to doubt the existence of Deity itself. All newly born Zepzeg carry with them the recent thoughts, memories, and feelings of the Zepzeg from which they originated. The knowledge within our lifeveins is ancient—and consistent. We pass on a mindset of devoutness. This is how we maintain our perfection. But I did not pass on perfection, for I felt far, far from perfect. I felt withered. I felt disconnected and alone. I felt godless. So would, too, my fractureling feel withered, disconnected, alone, and godless—for those were the weights my lifeveins carried. It would be a Zepzeg born into sin. One that knew nothing of perfection, pulsing in the resonance of its mother's transgressions. A Zepzeg unlike any other in the worst possible way.

As I stared down at the fractureling, the shape of my former right arm already losing some of its definition, I wondered what kind of life it would have. If this was a Zepzeg born unto sin, so then would its offspring be born unto sin. It would be an entirely new strain. Practically a new species. Would it have served the galaxy best for me to kill it now? I could not bring myself to do such a barbaric thing.

I knew that I had an obligation—a duty, both to my species and to Deity itself—to reclaim my perfection as quickly as possible. My fractureling might have been born unto doubt, but it would still have me to guide it. If I could find my way to perfection again—if I could reaffirm the perfection that I *knew* was within me—then my offspring would have a chance to at least learn from me and to overcome whatever inherent predispositions it might have harbored against Deity's truth. The onus was on me. I had always been perfect. I could be perfect again. I had to be, if I was to salvage my daughter of iniquity. In the meantime, I decided to name it Wither. I could think of no more appropriate moniker for a creature whose soul was ushered into existence in such a deplorable state.

"How are you feeling, Velistris?"

It was Delta who asked the question. It had been assigned to my room in light of the attack on the *Illustré*. I was none too thrilled about the thought of sharing my room with it. I just wanted to be alone. "I am tired," I said—a statement that was true. The exhaustion within me existed on many levels.

To say that the arrival of the Planet Smasher had shaken me was a great understatement. The Daldath destroyed my home planet. There are no beings in the cosmos more deserving of our disdain—not even the wretched Broodmasters. The Daldath are bringers of ruin who do not care what they ruin. The thought that they might be paralleling our path to the Gryamore System was truly terrifying. Much like Thule, I wished them destroyed.

On a more localized level, I felt thoroughly enervated after my recent slime bath inside Defoe. I am fortunate that my crystalline skin is easy to clean, and I was appreciative that Delta assisted me in its cleaning. With only one arm, the task would have been quite difficult by myself. In that particular instance, I was glad to have Delta by my side.

Then, of course, there was the matter of Defoe itself. It was common knowledge by that point that the Blepharisma was capable of absorbing thoughts and information from those it enveloped. Being silicon-based, I did not know to what extent its power worked on me. I wished to speak with it, so I requested that Delta arrange it. "I should very much like to speak with Defoe," I said.

It nodded eagerly. I was glad that it wished to appease, even if I felt it a bit out of sympathy. "I'll fetch him right away!" Away it went, out of my quarters and into the hallway.

I took what few moments of solitude I had to consider the complicated situation that Aurora and the *Illustré* were now in. I speak the truth when I say I did not know how these negotiations could possibly proceed with a Daldath Planet Smasher en route to the system. A matter as complicated as that involving ownership of a planet would demand time and patience, neither of which we could now afford with the looming potential for war between the Dacians and Broodmasters. Thule spoke of the mustering of Dacian forces, as Aurora did human ones. Surely the Broodmasters would follow suit. With all three species' armies mustered in the same system at the same time, there was bound to be conflict—Planet Smasher or not. The Dacians, a species quite known for its bluster, would certainly find an excuse to challenge the Broodmasters. Where would that leave the negotiation? Where would that leave us? I supposed that only time would reveal how this situation would play out. I feared we did not have much of it remaining.

It was not long until Delta returned with Defoe in tow. I must admit, I had not been eager to spend time with the slimy creature up until that point, as I'd considered it quite inferior to my perfectly engineered form. But my prejudices, I found, were beginning to temper. I wanted to know what it gleaned from me. I wanted to know if it'd gleaned anything at all. So I asked. "You have spoken of absorbing information from the various beings you envelop." In retrospect, I should have begun my dialogue with an expression of gratitude toward the creature, or at the very least a customary hello. I did not think of it then. I wasn't accustomed to offering courtesies for those I considered inferior.

For what it was worth, the pitiable Blepharisma did not seem to notice—or at least, to care. "You being very different from most beings I enveloping. I having hard time reading you!"

So optimistic did its voice always sound. So chipper and innocent. It made me sad that so many thought ill of it. Myself included, at the time. "So you were not able to absorb anything from me?" I was more relieved than disappointed, but it would be untrue to claim that no disappointment abided within me. Part of me hoped to unlock some revelation or hidden truth.

"I not being able to read any thoughts or feelings," it answered. "I only being able to learn about your composition."

My composition. There was nothing it could tell me about that subject that I did not already know. The body is the most important part of Zepzeg culture. We care for it meticulously.

"But I learning about it very, very much! I learning more about your composition than other species' compositions. I being able to sense it through and through, right down to the microfractures!"

At that word, my thoughts stopped. Microfractures? Turning my head, I looked at the creature's red, glowing eyes. "By that, I assume you mean the damage to my arm and the other small scratches I've accumulated on my surface." Indeed, it had been quite the unfortunate week in that regard. There would be much to buff out and polish if I was to return to perfection. Even in the midst of my spiritual anguish, I desired the physical perfection that I knew was attainable. I desired oneness with Deity, even if I'd once struggled with doubt. Oh, that terrible, terrible seed. I wished to be purged of it.

"Oh no, I talking about things much, much deeper!"

Much deeper? What ever could it mean?

It waved its flagellum around as it explained. "You having many, many microfractures. You having many cracks and impurities! They not being visible from outside, but deep inside I see them lots, lots, lots!"

Throughout my body, there came a chill.

The Blepharisma went on. "You having a life source deep inside you." It referred to my lifeveins. "But it eating the crystal around it. It making it brittle and broken. It growing back, but it also being eaten, over and over and over. It making many small cracks and fissures deep inside! Too small to see and too many to count."

"Impossible." I did not intend for the word to be spoken. It simply came out. But truly—*truly*—what it claimed could not be.

"It being very, very possible! I thinking that if the life source being unable to eat the crystal, then it dying. I thinking the life source needing room to grow."

Room to grow? Like a plant breaking through concrete in order to reach sunlight? What it was saying was unbelievable. Irresponsible. If it were true, surely my species would have known it!

Or...or would they?

It went against Zepzeg culture to consider things inwardly as it pertains to the spirit. All of our focus was on the physical. All of it was on comeliness. From the moment a Zepzeg is born unto the universe, it is taught it is an image of perfection. An image that cannot be questioned. There is no need to look within—not with science, not with conscience. What matters is what we see in the mirror. In all of my hundreds of years of existence, in all of my learnings, I never recalled looking at one of my own kind through a microscope. There was no need to. We were told we were perfect. It defines us as a species in the universe. We were made perfect by Deity. By remaining perfect, we would join Deity in the Life After. That was it. That was everything. Defoe was mistaken or lying. It *must* have been. Mustn't it?

I turned my head to Delta. I no longer felt in control of my body or its movement. I was simply doing. "I wish to see myself. I wish to see deep to my lifeveins. Will you bring me the translucometer?" It is an instrument often used to examine hull components that may be broken behind the metal—a means of seeing through walls. I was ready to see through mine.

Delta's eyes parted sadly. It was aware of what was happening—of what my mind was considering. It wished not to obey. "Velistris, must we?"

"We must. I must."

"Nothing good can come of this for you!"

I reached out with my remaining hand and touched it on the arm. Humans can often be swayed by such gestures. "Please. I must know what is within me."

It opened its mouth to protest but stopped itself short. It knew I would not be dissuaded. There was a translucometer mounted in the hallway not far from our room. With its head down, Delta made its way out of the door to retrieve it.

In the minute that it took for Delta to return, Defoe remained quiet in the corner of the room. I do not know to what extent it was aware of what was happening, but I suspect that it was to some, as its eyes were parted in a way that was most forlorn. It almost looked afraid, as if it might be suddenly concerned that it'd done something wrong. The Blepharisma's flagellum was not waving—one of the few times I'd seen it still.

I do not have a heart as humans do; therefore, I cannot feel the rush of what they call *adrenaline*. But in periods of intense stress or anxiety, my lifeveins do emit a low, resonate hum. It is far too low for humans to perceive, but I have witnessed Riley perceive it. It causes the dog to angle its head and stare at me as if in its primordial mind, it wishes to know what is wrong. It is strange to me that of all the lifeforms on the *Illustré*, it is the most underdeveloped that is able to sense what all of the others cannot. I could sense my resonations as Delta approached with the translucometer. They grew more intense as it began hooking up the device, placing its circular sensor eye against my skin as its display was filled with blurred imagery. It always took a moment for the image to adjust to the depth that the user desired. As Delta made the adjustments, I watched the display intently.

I did not expect the image to find clarity as quickly as it did. It actually took me by surprise. Perhaps that was all for the better, for what I saw made me feel as if time itself had ceased. I saw my lifeveins. For the first time, I actually saw them. They looked like long, stringy filaments. Like the roots of a plant. I could see the boundary between lifevein and crystal, where the end of interior met the beginning of exterior. The part of myself that I could not see.

It was fractured. More than fractured. It looked splintered in every direction. A web of asymmetrical imperfection—brittle, broken, and never-ending. The Blepharisma was right. I was *far* from perfect. I was blemished down to my core.

I had thought that my imperfections were something new. That they'd begun when I'd sprayed Delta in the face with water. I thought that when I'd questioned Deity, they'd only worsened. But I was wrong. Deep within—at a place that could not be carved or polished—I was nothing but a mess.

Lifeveins are spoken of in a way that is magical. In a way that suggests they are some splendid treasure. But what I saw now was not magical or splendid. It was remarkably devoid of anything resembling beauty. It was like a collection of sinew fibers. Had I seen a lifeform that looked like them, I'd have considered it unworthy of Deity's light. But that lifeform was now me. I realized then the gravity of the lie I'd believed. There was nothing I could do to make myself acceptable. There was nothing I could do to achieve the perfection required. I was irreparably damaged from within.

I could not save myself. No Zepzeg could. If one was even to attempt to fix such deep fractures, it would mean exposing the lifeveins—something that would cause death. There was nothing...nothing we could do to achieve perfect beauty.

Something changed in me in that moment. Something was lost. I realized that I was no longer the master of my eternal destiny. I was no longer able to right my existence in a way that appeased Deity. I had feared that my fractureling would be the origin of Zepzeg imperfection. How wrong I was. We'd been imperfect from the very beginning. I looked away from the translucometer's viewer. I felt dead.

"Velistris?" Delta asked.

It was concerned. I could hear the concern layered deep within its voice. It was afraid for me. It pitied me. I did not answer it, for I did not know what to say. I had spent my entire existence aboard the *Illustré* trying to help Aurora and Delta achieve a perfection that I myself was incapable of grasping. Oh, the humiliation. Oh, the folly. What a fool I had been.

What does one do when they realize the full extent of their condition? How was it that the Zepzeg did not know of this imperfection, this disarray, deep within? They had to have known. They *must* have known. There was no doubt in my mind that at some point in our species' history, a Zepzeg peered deep within the framework of its brethren to see what lay on the inside. How then could they have remained silent? How could they have not sounded an alarm? How could they have allowed the lie of propitiation through beautification to propagate? I could not believe it. I would not believe it. This was the grandest conspiracy in all of the cosmos.

Yet what was I to do now? Would I be that one to alert my species? To what avail would it be? We served a Deity that we could in no way appease. Not if what we believed about that Deity were true. All of our toil—all of our lifelong struggle for perfection—was for naught. If such knowledge were to be known, it would cause the mass despondency of an entire species. I wondered if whoever that first Zepzeg was who peered at a living lifevein had considered that. If they'd realized the full gravity of what they'd seen, as I had. Could that have been what stopped them from telling others about it?

Yet still, others must have known. Others must have stumbled upon this knowledge themselves or at the very least, been made privy to it. Not once in my existence had I ever been implored to look within myself. My receptors were taught to look at others and at what I displayed to them. For the display was what mattered...not what was actually within.

The cause of their silence concerning this did not matter. Perhaps they were too scared to speak it. Perhaps there was too much profit in the business of beauty evangelism and cosmetics. Perhaps it was something else. None of it changed the reality that we were flawed in the eyes of our creator. Flawed to a degree from which there was no known remedy. I found that I suddenly did not care what this knowledge meant to the Zepzeg species. I was much more concerned with what it meant for me.

How could I possibly appease Deity when all of my works were in vain? Delta and Blepharisma were still there. Both had remained quiet as I lay there with my head rolled to the side and the energy sucked from my core. It was at that moment that I did something I hadn't expected to do. That I'd never done before. Extending my remaining hand out, I reached for Delta's. It did not seem to notice or mind the alien gesture from me. It only entwined its fingers with mine in silence. For the first time, I noticed its warmth. As a crystalline entity, it is a warmth I cannot provide. But I realized in that moment the value of it, for it tempered my consternation in a way that beauty products could never do. Beauty products merely touched the surface. My ailment was buried deep within.

I do not know how much time passed as I held Delta's hand, for time suddenly seemed a mystery to me. Such happens, I suppose, when the prospect of eternity is lost. I only know that in that time that I held its hand, I was provided a measure of comfort and dare I say, love, that I had never felt before. At least, not in the way that other beings describe it. Aurora and Bryce's private conversation— the one I had witnessed through video earlier—now made so much more sense to me, not in that I entirely understood what they felt, but in that I realized the nature of distance. I did not want to let go of Delta's hand.

But I knew that I must. The *Illustré* was in dire need of a focused and capable crew. The negotiation between the Dacians and the Broodmasters was about to take a horrible turn in the shadow of a new Daldath threat. Even in the midst of my heinous revelations, I knew that I had a role to fulfill, if not for me, for the lifeforms I suddenly realized that I very much cared for. And so I did what any crewmate worth their salt would do in such a time: I mustered what little constancy I had left to muster. I did it not for myself, but for them. I did it because I knew it was required. "Please give me some time to prepare," I said to Delta. "I must be ready for Aurora for when we arrive at Gryamore."

It did not protest despite its past propensities. It only squeezed my hand, then slid its fingers from mine. How I hated to let it go. In only a few moments, it and Defoe were making their way out of the room. I was left to my solitude.

I spent much of my remaining time in the room looking at Wither. I found that I suddenly cared very much for it. I was bothered far less by the means through which it'd entered the world. Such is the case, I suppose, when one realizes that sin is inherent. It would enter the world no different than I had. Perhaps, in a way, it would enter the world better for having me as its mother. I could choose to tell it the truth about sin, and perfection, and beauty, and Deity. But before I could do that, I knew that I must first learn the truth myself. I knew the truth insomuch as I knew it was not what I'd believed. What I did not know was what I was to do now. How does one overcome imperfection?

There was only one being that I knew—that I trusted—to provide me with that information. Aurora. It, like all humans, was rife with imperfections. It would have valuable experience in dealing with them. I needed to talk with it, desperately, not only for the sake of my own condition but to better equip myself for raising Wither. I knew that Aurora had much to deal with, most notably its contacting the human military concerning Gryamore. This was an important task that could not be neglected. I would have to give it time to complete it. I also imagined that it would talk with Elyse about the condition of its hair, which looked outright butchered in the small glimpses I'd managed to catch of it before the battle with the Vorticella rendered me useless. Yes, there were many things for the captain to attend to, and I was but one of them. But I was one of them. It had always implored us to go to it with personal issues, that it would be glad to listen and to help. I am sure it never imagined that message would be heard by me—but such was the way things had unfolded. I would give it some time, then I would speak with it. I might even forfeit the customary platitudes I hurl toward it in the effort to curry favor. I would certainly consider it. There were many things I had to consider.

I looked very much forward to what it would say of them.

Chapter Twelve

IT DID NOT take the *Illustré* a lot of time to reach the Gryamore System. This is because it has a very good spindrive that is very fast. Humans call this spindrive a Magellan Navigator and Aurora spent a lot of credits on it a long time ago. I like having it because it runs good even if other parts of the ship are damaged and because it can outrun a lot of other ships that might be bad, like the Daldath Planet Smasher we were trying to beat. The only bad thing about the Magellan Navigator is that it has many more moving parts than other spindrives so I have to do maintenance on it a lot. But to me this is not a bad thing. Humans sometimes think work is bad, but I mostly think it is good.

When we got to Gryamore, there was a repair freighter waiting for us. I think that Aurora told the human military that the *Illustré* needed it. It was good to see it, because it meant that the *Illustré* would get repaired more quickly than if I had to do it alone. I would not have had time to get it repaired before the Planet Smasher arrived, especially if we had to fight the Daldath.

The only bad thing about the *Illustré* getting repaired was that we had to leave the ship. The repair freighter was not very big, but there were enough rooms on it for everyone to share. Aurora stayed on the *Illustré* because she wanted to make sure things were getting repaired good. She said that there was no need for them to work in her quarters so there was no problem with her staying there. I told her that I could also stay and watch the ship get repaired, but she said she wanted me to go on the freighter. She said everyone would leave but Elyse, who she wanted to stay with her on the *Illustré*.

A good thing happened to Elyse while she stayed with Aurora in that she shaved all of her hair off. I think that there were many words spoken between Aurora and Elyse after the Vorticella attack. I think some of them were bad and some of them were good. I am glad that Elyse has no hair. I estimate it has lowered her chance of an enemy cutting her head off by eighty-five percent. It will also not block her vision when she gets wet, which is another good thing. I think that maybe I still love Elyse. I told her that since the list I made of things she was not good at got destroyed in her room, I would make her another one and that her not having hair would not be on it. She said that she did not want me to make the list again but that she knew I did it because I loved her. I did not know that I did it because I loved her. It is harder to not love someone than I thought. But I will still make the list.

Elyse spends a lot of time with Aurora. I wish she spent more time with me, but I am glad that she is not spending all of her time with Delta and Defoe because I do not understand them. I only understand Elyse and Aurora. I think that I also understand Thule a lot, and I have been spending more time with him.

When we got to the repair freighter, Aurora contacted the Dacians and reported to them that she had Thule. They said that they wanted her to give him back, and when she asked them why, they said it was to punish him for treason. This is because he told us about how the Dacians seek to punish the Broodmasters in the Gryamore System by setting traps for them in distress beacons. The punishment in Dacian culture for treason is death. She did not like this, so she told them, "If that is the case, then he shall remain in my custody." At first I did not want Thule to stay with us, but I think that maybe his staying with us could be a good thing. I do not believe he wishes to do us harm because then we would turn him over to the Dacians and he would die. I do not believe that Thule wants to die. I also know that he does not care about Gryamore anymore or who gets it. This is because even if the Dacians win it, he cannot go back to live with them or they will kill him. So I do not know what we will do with him.

I have spent a lot of time talking to Thule while Elyse has been with Aurora. He has many opinions about many things and I find that I agree with him a lot. Sometimes I do not even know why I am agreeing with him. One time he told me that I would think it was a good idea to break into the security station on the repair freighter and sneak food out of the pantry for him, and I agreed with him and did it. It is good to have someone that you agree with. Many people think it is good to not be around people you agree with all the time, but I think that advice is bad. I like it when people agree to do what I say they should do, and Thule likes it, too. I am glad that me and Thule are friends now. I know this because many times he says, "I am your friend, Hank-is-Handy. You can listen to me." So I listen to him a lot.

I do not think the people on the repair freighter like Thule very much. They look at him a lot and tell him to go somewhere else a lot, too. I do not know why more people do not like Thule. He is not bad like Defoe or his blue pet Slarb or his pink pet Gralb. I do not like them at all.

I did not have anything to do on the station, so I went to find Thule again to talk to him more. He was standing in one of the windows of the ship and looking out at space. I think it is confusing how Dacians walk on their winged hands and do things with their feet that other species do with their hands. But it does not make me think less of him. It just makes me think that he is different because he is a Dacian and I am Vorck. I think this is okay.

"Hello," I said to him. I said this because this is what friends are supposed to say. He did not say anything back to me, so I said it again but louder. "Hello!" He turned his head to me, so I know that he heard me. Dacians have big ears so they hear things good. Some people say that they hear too much, but I think it is worse to hear little. I am glad I have a friend who hears everything, that way he can tell me if an enemy is coming from behind to cut my head off.

Thule looked back at space for a moment before he spoke. "I have given countless years to these stars. All of it was for nothing."

I think he meant that he worked a lot in the stars, but I do not know for sure. I do know that Dacians do not live as long as many other species. Most Dacians live to the age of what Aurora would say is sixty years. So it was strange to me that Thule could not count the years, because it was a small number. "You have lived forty-two human years." I knew this because of biological tests that were run on him. But I also know that a year is different to a Dacian than what it is to a human. To a Dacian, age is not a constant. They will say that they are at the age of something, then they will say that that age has ended and they are at the age of something else. For example, Thule said after we got to the repair freighter that his, "age of vengeance," had come to an end and that his, "age of bitterness," had begun. Most Dacians have six or seven ages in their lives. It is very confusing and I do not understand it much.

"I have given my life to the queen—I have lived for her cause! And what now has it gotten me? I am a prisoner no matter who I am with. The Broodmasters, your captain, now my brethren themselves. There is nothing good in these stars, Vorck."

"There is radiant heat energy that can be used to power solar stations." I was surprised that he did not know this.

"I speak of fate! I speak of fairness and receiving what one deserves. I have done my good deeds, yet everywhere I turn leads to death. There is no future for me here, and so where shall I go?"

I did not know the answer. "Would you like me to get you something from the security station pantry?" It made him happy the last time I did it.

He looked at me and I thought he would say yes, but then he said, "No. There is nothing for me there, here, or anywhere."

I think that Thule would like Elyse.

"How do you stand it, Vorck? How can you tolerate your life of servitude? Do you not long to be released?"

I thought it was strange what he said because I never thought of myself as not free. If I wanted to leave the *Illustré*, Aurora would let me. She has told me this many times. But I do know what it is like to feel like a prisoner in my mind. This is because the Vorck used to be slaves and it is how we all feel. But I have learned that feelings can be wrong. "I am not a servant. I do what I want to do. I am a free Vorck that makes his own choices."

"Give me my drink."

I looked on the pedestal next to the window where he put his bottle of blood juice. It was there, so I gave it to him.

"Do you not see yourself?" he asked me as he took it.

I did not know what he meant, so I asked, "What do you mean?"

"You will do whatever one asks of you without question. You are a slave to *everyone*. It is what your...species...is."

His words were confusing me a lot. I did not see how giving him his drink made me his slave. I did it because it was something that I think humans would say is nice, and I think being nice is good when it does not get someone killed. "I am not a slave. Aurora has told me this many times."

"Would you believe it had she not told you?"

I did not understand what he meant again, so I said, "They help me understand what I am. Sometimes it is hard for a Vorck to see these things on their own. That is why they help me. I know that I am free because Aurora has told me.

I know that I love the young human, Elyse, because she has told me I love her. They have more experience with these feelings than me."

He tilted his head like many species do. "Is that how you believe that love works?"

"I do not know how love works. All I know is that it makes me feel many feelings. Some are bad and some are good."

"How do you know these feelings are love? Because a human told you they were?"

I showed him my phase hammer. "If I gave you this and you did not know what it was, I would tell you that it is a phase hammer. Then you would know it. In the same way, Elyse helps me know what love is so that when I have it, I will know it, too. It is very helpful for me to hear these things."

"If she told you that you were a space rat, would you believe *that*?"

"I can look in a mirror and see that I am not a space rat. But I cannot see love. It is not a thing that I can touch. I wish it was, because then someone would show it to me and I would know it. But I cannot do it that way. So I must rely on Elyse. I know that she would not lie to me."

He made one of his eyes squish and he made one of his fangs stick out. Dacians do this when they do not believe something and they wish to make it known. I predicted that he did not believe that Elyse would not lie to me, and my prediction was correct. "So fast are you to fall for the guises of humanity. Of all the species in this cluster, they are among the *least* trustworthy. Deceit is their currency, Vorck, and they spend it thriftlessly. They work all things to their advantage with little to no regard for the well being of those around them."

"Are not the Dacians doing the same thing? And the Broodmasters? That is what this negotiation is about."

He ignored what I said and continued to speak. "You would

be wise to leave these humans at your nearest opportunity, Vorck. They will sell you out the moment doing so benefits them! They and the Broodmasters are both vile, treacherous creatures."

I think that Thule was using a thing humans call *prejudice*, which is when one makes judgments based on tendencies and experience. I think that most times prejudice is good, but sometimes it is bad, like when one is being prejudiced with a human. It is not good to be prejudiced with a human because they are so different. I thought these things, but I did not say them to Thule. Instead, I said, "You and the Broodmasters wish to destroy each other. Aurora is here to make sure that you do not. Destroying things is bad. The only time it is good to destroy things is when you do not like them."

"At least we Dacians are honest about our intentions." He made a loud and raspy sound. "The Broodmasters would never confess to it, but they would do *anything* to be awarded supreme power in this system. They would attempt to destroy us just as we would attempt to destroy them."

"I do not think Dacians are honest about their intentions," I said. "You disguised bombs as distress beacons for the purpose of blowing the Broodmasters up. This is not an honest thing to do. You should just fight them outright." I know something about Dacians that I do not think Thule knew that I knew, and that is that Dacians can sometimes act like cowards when they think they are in a position to lose. It is only when they get strong that they strike. I do not dislike them for this because I think it is a strategy that can work, but I did not think it was fair for Thule to talk about honesty when he himself took part in these acts that humans would call cowardly. I predicted that he would not agree with my assessment, so I did not share it.

"We did what we must to combat a cunning foe," he said. "I do not expect a sub-creature like you to understand. You would rather ram into the enemy headfirst than attempt a winning strategy."

What Thule was saying was a little bit true. We Vorck do not like to do sneaky things. We are not good at them and we think they are for weak species to do. We like to hit things very hard. His words were referencing the Vorck supership called the Ram. It is a very big spaceship that we make very strong so it can ram into things and break them. This is why we call it the Ram. It is a good name that describes what the ship does very well. We like things that are simple and easy to understand. If a human made a ship that was going to ram things, they would have probably named it something that did not make sense, like *The Color Orange* or *Eat a Banana*.

I did not want to argue with Thule, so I said, "I think you will see that these humans are different if you are with them long enough."

"It certainly sounds like I'll be with them long enough," he said, "but I can only tolerate imprisonment for so long." He looked back into space again. "I must find a way to break free of them. You must help me, Vorck." When he looked at me again, his eyes were doing shiny things that I liked. "You must help me, Vorck."

I began to want to help him.

"You must—"

"He must *what?*" The voice was from Aurora. She walked up to us. He looked surprised to see her and the shiny things in his eyes stopped. When he did not answer, she said her words again. "He must what, Thule?"

He made some sounds that were not words, like what humans do when they do not know what to speak. Then he said, "He must show me how I can be of service to your most charitable crew. You have been gracious enough to take me into your care, after all."

"Care and custody are very different. Do not forget that you are in the latter." She looked at me. "Are you okay, Hank-is-

Handy?"

I did not know why she asked me, but I answered her, "Yes."

"You are aware that he was trying to hypnotize you, right?"

"He was not."

"Oh yes, he was. Did you not see his eyes?"

I did see them, so I said, "I saw them."

"And did you not notice anything strange about them?"

"They did shiny things that I liked."

"Right, that's called hypnosis."

I thought about her words. Now I understood why I liked the shiny things so much. "Oh."

She looked at Thule again and pointed a finger at him. "Let me be clear. If you so much as look at any of my friends in a way that might suggest you're even *thinking* about manipulating them, I'll have you blown out of the airlock. Do you understand? I'm the only thing standing between you and death in more ways than you realize."

Thule's body looked like it got smaller and he stepped back a step. "I will heed your words, captain."

"You had better, Dacian."

He did not respond to what she said. I find that many species do not respond to or acknowledge things they do not like. It is something that makes Vorck different. "To what do I owe the honor of your visit, Captain Ultraviolet?" Thule asked.

I was surprised to hear him say it was an honor. I did not think that he thought that it was. "Velistris and I will soon be leaving for Point Maven," Aurora said. "Because I have claimed captor's privilege, you cannot accompany us or you would be apprehended by Dacian Syscorps. I have no choice but to leave you here."

"I understand," Thule said.

"No, I don't think you do. I'm being forced to place my trust in you not to cause chaos while I'm away. It is not a trust I am eager to extend, as…well, I don't trust you. But I must do what I must, as bringing you along would result in your apprehension and execution, which is a punishment I do not feel is appropriate considering your government is the one that tasked you with your deeds."

Thule made a fluttering sound deep in his throat. "So you are threatening me. Behave or face punishment?"

"Is that not how law and order traditionally work?"

"Your graciousness knows no bounds," said Thule. I think that he was using the thing humans use called *sarcasm.*

Aurora performed a face sneer. "Your attitude could use a touch of work."

"If there is nothing else, may I return to stargazing and minding my own business?"

For eight or maybe nine seconds, Aurora did not say anything. All she did was make her eyes narrow very slowly, and her lips twisted a bit. When she did speak again, it was not to Thule but to me. "You mind your guard, Hank-is-Handy. The security team on this freighter leaves much to be desired. If his eyes look 'shiny' again, remember what that means. I won't hold it against you if you kill him. At least in your case, it would be justifiable." That is all she said to me. She turned and walked away.

One of the things that makes hypnosis hard to prevent is that it is hard to tell if you are being hypnotized. That is why I could not detect when he was hypnotizing me. It is easy to see when a Dacian is using hypnosis if they are hypnotizing someone else, because your mind is thinking correctly and you can recognize the shiny things in their eyes.

I think Aurora was angry because Thule tried to hypnotize me, but I was not angry about it because it is something all Dacians do. I do not get angry at the normal things that species do. Vorck are strong, so we use our strength. Humans have many feelings, so they use their feelings. In the same way, Dacians have hypnosis, so they use hypnosis. If I had hypnosis, I would use it. This is why I was not angry at Thule for hypnotizing me.

"Reprehensible human," said Thule after Aurora left. I predicted he was talking about her because there were no other humans there, but I did not know what *reprehensible* meant.

"Aurora is a human," I said, because I did not know what to say.

Thule spoke to me but his eyes stayed on the window that showed space. "How can you tolerate the presence of their kind? They are insufferable."

I knew what those words meant, so I knew that he was saying bad things about the humans. I think that maybe he just did not know them, so I said, "They get less bad with prolonged exposure."

"I admire your patience, Vorck. It is a trait we do not share."

Most species do not have Vorck patience. Patience makes species strong because they continue to do things when most species give up on them. It is a word that humans call *perseverance*. They talk about it a lot but I do not see them practice it a lot.

Thule made another fluttering sound. Then he spoke again. "What is one to do when they must start again?" He talked some more without giving me time to answer his question. That was okay, because I did not know what he meant. "I had a purpose for my people: to bring revenge upon the vile Broodmasters for their treacherous acts against us. But my ship is gone, and my people now consider me traitorous. Do they not understand that I had no choice in the matter?" He crossed his legs across his chest like humans do with their arms. "Now here I am, a captive to humans, a pariah to my own people. What kind of life is there for me among the stars? Where shall I go in my people's territory where I am not hunted? Where shall I go elsewhere in the cluster that I am allowed to peacefully exist? There can be no peace for me now. I have given my life to my people, and for what? To be discarded? I am in the twilight of my ages. I may as well die!"

Even though he said he may as well die, I do not believe he really wanted to die. I think he just had sad and angry feelings. I understood them, because those are the feelings I have the most, but for different reasons. "Can you fix things good or kill people good? Maybe you can stay on the *Illustré*."

I think that most times, I would not want a new crew member. I did not want Defoe to be on the ship because he made Elyse spend less time with me and that gave me sad feelings. But I also saw Defoe save two people. The first was Elyse when Thule was going to kill her. The second was Velistris when she almost broke on the bridge. I have learned that the best parameter to judge a lifeform's goodness is to see what they do when they must make a decision fast. This is when you see how they really feel. Defoe did not have time to think about whether or not he wanted to save Elyse or Velistris. He only had enough time to save them, so that is what he did. Even though I hate Defoe, I am glad that he did what he did. Maybe I do not hate him. I know that I do not love him. I think it is okay to not hate things and not love things at the same time. I think that maybe I do not hate or love Defoe. I think Elyse would say that is better than hating him.

I think that maybe my new feelings about Defoe were what made me say to Thule that maybe he could be a crew member on the *Illustré*. I think that in the past, it is not a thing I would have said. I think Aurora would say that that means I am growing. When she says it, she does not mean in my body, but in what she calls wisdom and maturity. It always makes me glad when she says that to me.

Thule said, "Of course I can fix things and kill people. I was the captain of my own spaceship! One cannot take to the stars without the ability to repair a spindrive, else they risk dying in deep space. But I do not wish to be a part of your ship or your crew. I wish to be free! How I despise the Broodmasters for what they did to me. How I despise my people for casting me out! I despise the whole universe."

Sometimes Dacians get very dramatic.

"Woe be to any who seek fulfillment, for this existence offers none! There is nothing good to be found anywhere in the stars. Nothing!"

"I think you are having many sad and bad feelings," I said. I wanted to be helpful. "I have many sad and bad feelings, too. Humans say that you should talk about these feelings and they will not be so sad and bad, but I have tried it and it does not work for me. What does work sometimes is when I think about other things that are not the things causing sad and bad feelings. When I am not thinking about them, then I am not sad anymore. Maybe you could try thinking of other things, too." It is not as easy as I made it sound. "I, too, struggle with it sometimes. There is a very bad feeling that humans call love. It is one that cannot be ignored and causes all kinds of feelings that do not make sense. Humans like love, but I do not think it is good for Vorcks. But you are not dealing with love, so maybe you can just think of other things."

Thule looked at me. "And do you think thinking of other things will make my problems go away?"

"Yes."

"Foolish imbecile."

I was not angry that he called me bad things. Vorck get called bad things a lot. I only get mad when Velistris calls me bad things because she is weak and missing one arm. "Try it to see if it works. Think of potato chips."

"What in Gormuth's Shadow is a potato chip?"

Gormuth was the first Dacian that ever lived. That is what the Dacians believe. They believe that his legacy stretches across the universe like a shadow. "It is a thing that humans eat when they feel sad and bad."

"Why would I ever think of that?"

"Or maybe you could eat them. One day after she had a bad talk with the human she wants to mate with, Aurora ate a whole tube of them. She sat in her big chair in her room and watched things on her video monitor and had pieces of potato chips all over her body. I saw it when I went to her room to give her a report, and she pointed to the lift and said, 'Get out!'" I thought about what I said. "Maybe it is not good to think about potato chips."

Thule was not interested in them anyway. "There is no hope for me, Vorck. Not in Gryamore, not in your starship, not in your human's potato chips. I am cursed! Look upon me and pity."

I did not like his age of bitterness.

"I wish to be alone," he said. "Leave me at once."

I did not think that Aurora would like me to leave him alone, so I said, "I cannot. I must watch you to ensure you do not create problems."

When I said it, Thule looked at me, but he did not say anything. For a moment, I saw the shiny things in his eyes that I liked, but then they went away. He looked at me for a moment longer then he looked at space again. "As you wish."

I think that Thule was going to hypnotize me but decided not to. I am glad that he did not do it. This means that he was trying to do a right thing even though it is not what he wanted to do. Maybe he did not think of it that way, but I thought of it.

He did not say anything else to me, and I did not say anything else to him. We only looked out of the window of the repair freighter at the stars. Nobody from the *Illustré* visited us while we were there. But that was okay.

I was happy to be with my new friend.

Chapter Thirteen

"THAT IS OUTRAGEOUS!"

Aurora's words resonated through the audience chamber of Point Maven, the respective onlookers from the Dacian and Broodmaster delegations watching and listening as the latest quarrel broke out between my captain and the ambassadors. The right side of the chamber was lined with Broodmaster representatives. Never before had I seen so many gathered in one place. Truth be told, I had never actually seen one in the flesh. But here, there was not one Broodmaster, but almost a dozen, their black, gelatinous forms quivering as their child caste literally buzzed about them like subservient flies. At the forefront of the chamber was Corvus, the liaison Aurora had spoken with from the *Illustré*. That it was present was no surprise—it is the liaison, after all. But I found it quite shocking that its ilk had accompanied it. Broodmasters do not customarily put themselves in positions of exposed physical vulnerability, being as they possess no meaningful way to defend themselves from attack.

It was very much a high risk, high reward maneuver, but I suppose it shouldn't have been surprising at a negotiation of such consequence. The Broodmasters were allowing themselves to be placed in danger—something their cowardly species *never* does—in exchange for agreeing not to use their mind powers to manipulate the proceedings. With camera monitors in every direction as witnesses and with a better portion of the human armada in orbit, the Broodmasters stood little to gain but destruction should they attempt a hostile mental coup. It all went to show that Broodmasters were manipulators in every sense—not just through their telepathy. Their physical presence was intended to be a show of goodwill, which they hoped would sway Aurora's judgment toward them.

On the other side of the chamber, and much more boisterous, were the Dacians. A short, stout specimen, who went by the name Lavimtelek, championed their arguments and rebuttals with shouts of venom and vigor. The irate Dacians seemed scarcely able to control their outbursts of vehement emotion.

I still preferred them to the Broodmasters.

"We have determined our solution to be fair and equitable for both parties," said Corvus in the same hollow, translated rasp we'd heard in the *Illustré*. "It is the only means by which we can all be satisfied."

"That would be tantamount to selling the Dacians to you as slaves," Aurora said. "That you would even offer such a solution is extraordinarily offensive!"

The solution Corvus was suggesting was anything but one. They would grant the Dacians full ownership of Gryamore V, and in exchange the Dacians would pledge their undying loyalty to the Broodmaster species. In essence, they would give themselves up as slaves.

"What then would stop you from ordering them to abandon Gryamore V the moment the agreement takes effect?" Aurora asked. "What would stop you from ordering them out of the system entirely? With all due respect, Corvus, this 'solution' is repulsive and will *not* be considered."

Corvus's body throbbed. "Do not consider it merely an agreement. Think of it as an alliance—one in which both parties stand to benefit. In order to show our honorable intent, we would call it the Freedom Alliance—an alliance that promotes liberty to all species in this cluster by showing the advantages of peaceful coexistence."

A preposterous proposition! Thankfully, Aurora realized it. "Be offended if you must, but I do not consider your efforts to manipulate these talks by sending us a mind-controlled

Dacian to be an 'honorable' act. Words are frivolous. It is your actions that speak to your intent, and they do not shine you in an admirable light."

"*Frivolous!*" Corvus bellowed, its body quivering until it regained its composure. "If you do not accept this proposal, then we are out of options. All others have been exhausted."

Aurora was avid in its response. "Just because we have not yet found a reasonable solution, does not mean that one does not exist!"

Despite its optimism, I was skeptical.

The few days that had passed between Wither's birth and our arrival at Point Maven had been rife with frustration. I had purposed myself—demanded of myself, even—to speak with Aurora concerning the revelation that my interior was irreparably fractured. I found, however, that discussing the topics of mortality and imperfection were not nearly as easy as I'd presumed. As much as I'd set myself to discuss these things, it required an internal strength that I could not summon. Matters of the internal are so fraught with uncertainty. When one deals with external affairs, things are right there in the open—they cannot be hidden or avoided. But who can see the inside of one's body? Who has eyes to see the spirit? Does a Broodmaster, with its telepathy? Does a Blepharisma, with its enveloping, probing properties? I could not imagine discussing such important things with either species. I could, however, trust Aurora. It surprised me so terribly much that I could not bring myself to speak with it. Hank-is-Handy has always called me weak. I feared, at least in this instance, that it may have been right.

I have wrestled with the reason for why this must be, and I have come to but one unfortunate conclusion: speaking words seems to have a way of making them real. When one is considering the eternal state of their soul—and particular, the potential damnation thereof—it is quite difficult to willfully usher the prospect into reality. It is easier to pretend that one is okay. That all is well. That the truth will go away if one just ignores it. But the truth I faced was undeniable. I cannot attain the perfection required by Deity. No Zepzeg can. How, then, can any of us find the Life After? There are only three distinct possibilities: there is a way to find eternity, there is no way to find it, or there is no eternity at all. This was a conundrum for which no option could be confidently written off. No one has been to the Life After and returned to speak of it. Many proclaim to know the truth—to know *a* truth. But the only truth is that *no* one knows. They can guess. They can pontificate. They can boast of wisdom or education or superior intelligence to know the answer. They can even scoff or mock those with whom they disagree. But these scoffers and mockers know as much about eternity as Riley the dog. None of them have been there to confirm or deny it.

It was the fear, really. That accursed seed of doubt. How it'd affected every part of me!

Perhaps it was because of all of these thoughts and reflections that I'd approached the negotiation with far less enthusiasm than I normally would for such ballyhooed affairs. I scarcely had it in me to tolerate the Dacians' and the Broodmasters' collective foolishness. It was the same pattern, over and over and over again. One side offered a ridiculous solution, to which the other side balked. Back and forth they went, one side to the other, then back again with no ground to be gained. I understood Aurora's exhaustion. I felt exhausted, too. Between the shouting, the bickering, the stubbornness, and the bluster, there was little room for any hope for a successful resolution to arise. Even as Aurora spoke—even as it struggled to manifest some semblance of reason between the two rival parties—I found myself slipping further and further into cynicism.

Yet still, the struggle went on.

"What say you, then, Lavimtelek?" Aurora asked the Dacian

ambassador. "Has freedom so lost its luster that you might actually consider such a heinous 'solution?' I should very much like to hear your thoughts on this proposal of Corvus's!"

Lavimtelek snarled. "We would never submit to Broodmaster control! They are the least trustworthy of all the species in this cluster! At least we confess our intent should we be awarded Gryamore V: we will expel every last Broodmaster from existence until the cluster has been purged!"

Closing its eyes, Aurora sighed, running its fingers through its coppery curls. Its hands—nay, its whole body—trembled in exhaustion. It looked on the verge of collapse. "I declare a recess," it said. "I must speak with my counsel to determine a course of action." That counsel was, of course, me. "We will resume these talks in one half hour! Please, I implore you to discuss this matter amongst your own counsels with much haste. If we tarry, the Daldath will arrive before a decision can be made."

"Whichever side defeats the Daldath, to them the whole system!" Lavimtelek said.

Raising both of its hands up, Aurora said, "No! We must not allow these talks to go the way of brute strength! Should might and muscle be the determining factors, we might as well give the whole cluster to the Zevolt. Now, please. Discuss this with your counsels and we will reconvene in one half hour. Do not delay! A decision *must* be made before the Planet Smasher arrives." Turning off its microphone and earpiece, Aurora stepped from its central podium before anyone could protest. It said nothing to me as it marched past me toward the preparation chamber assigned to it. The only sound it managed at all was a beleaguered *ugh*, voiced with considerable passion.

Following it into the chamber, I pressed my hand to my chest—for I did not have a second hand's worth of fingers with which to intertwine them. "I do not believe these talks are going well," I said.

"Astute as always," it spat back at me, before it lowered its head and blew out a breath. "I'm sorry."

"No apology is needed," I said.

It placed its hands against its hips and stormed from one side of the room to the other. Humans call this *fast pacing*, and they do it under strenuous situations in order to help them think clearly. There is a biological component to it, I believe, but it is not one I am familiar with. "Do they not realize the threat is at their doorstep? Do they not realize what will happen if the Planet Smasher arrives? The Dacians speak as if destroying it will be no large task, but there are Daldath warships with that Planet Smasher—and possibly more if they've called in reinforcements! This would be a multispecies battle the likes of which this cluster has never seen."

Its words were well-intended, but untrue. The Lernaean Cluster has seen numerous conflicts on a far grander scale than what could possibly have come of this looming confrontation. Humans are masters of hyperbole, so I allowed the captain to have it for its own comfort's sake.

"The Freedom Alliance. Have you ever heard of something so ridiculous?" it asked me.

I had, though it served little to confess it. "It is surely a ridiculous proposal."

"What do you see in that chamber that offers a glimmer of hope? You must tell me if you see it."

"Both sides have offered many solutions, none of which would be adequate in any civilized proceeding."

It placed its hands against the table in the center of the chamber and leaned forward. Its head was down, its coppery curls hid its face from view. For several seconds, it simply looked down and breathed.

I do not often see my captain so visibly flustered. Quite the contrary, it prides itself on the maintaining of outward composure. Of keeping its wits about it. I had no doubt that, despite its tortured state, it would find a way to gracefully navigate these turbulent, diplomatic waters.

Then, calamity! Aurora shrieked, sweeping its hands across the table and sending the floral arrangement at its center flying across the room, where it smashed into pieces against the wall! I jumped back, startled—I could not restrain it! Had my captain gone mad? Never had I seen such a torrent of emotion. "Captain!" I proclaimed.

It raised a trembling hand to its forehead. When it spoke, its words quivered. "Velistris, I am crumbling." Once more, it looked not at me, but at the table's surface. "These proceedings could not have come at a worse time for me. Chaos and doubt consume me. I am cornered at every turn!"

Its words described me so perfectly that for a brief moment I was flabbergasted, thinking it was speaking on my behalf. But then I realized that was not possible, for I had mentioned nothing of my troubles. Aurora was speaking of itself.

"I cannot do this."

"What ever is the matter?" I asked, drawing a step closer, albeit with caution.

Standing upright, it lifted its hands to cover its face, its fingers once more pushing back through its hair. "These talks demand rationality, and I am far from a rational state. I have tried to suppress it, I have conjured up every ounce of composure I have in me, but I am *failing*."

I was stunned. I had no words for what I beheld. Naturally, it demanded them of me.

"What shall I do?" it asked. "What choice shall I make? I am not strong enough in this moment to make this decision."

I did not believe that for one instant. "Captain, what vexes you so? What events have you so flustered?"

Once more, it fell quiet—as if it did not want to speak its vexations aloud, lest they be made ever more real. It was a sensation I had grown all too familiar with. At long last, and thankfully, it spoke. "I have lost everything."

"What have you lost? The *Illustré*? It will be repaired as good as new."

It shook its head. "Not the *Illustré*. I could not care less of the *Illustré*. Not in this moment."

"Then what ever could you mean, my captain?"

A pause, then an answer. Nothing could not have surprised me more than the words it spoke. "I have ended my engagement."

There are few times in a Zepzeg's life when surprise is permitted to show. We are a species keen on maintaining composure—of unflappability in the midst of chaos. To show surprise is to show a lack of expectation and control. One must never allow it. But I could not help it. Its words, its confession, struck me like current. "What?" was the lone word I could muster.

"Why did this negotiation have to happen now? Why could they not have battled out their differences without any outside involvement? Why did they *have* to ask for mediation?"

I took a step closer and reached out with my hand. Not a touch. Just a gesture, to express my desire to help. "You must tell me of this development at once."

"There's no time. I am only expressing to you the source of my dissonance. I only wished to..." It fought for the right words. It did not find them. "I don't know." Its eyes rose to meet me. "I cautioned them not to tarry, nor must we. My personal crisis is my own to deal with. We must focus on a solution to this dispute."

I nodded. "Indeed, we must. But your personal crisis is affecting *you*, and you are the mediator. We must speak of it, and we must speak of it quickly. If it brings you the measure of mental stalwartness required to fulfill your obligation in these talks and make a sound decision, then it is of the utmost importance than we discuss your situation."

It shook its head. "Velistris, I cannot."

"It is not a matter of can and cannot. This is a matter of what *must* be done. You have always trusted me as your counsel in all affairs, diplomatic or personal. You must trust me again."

"I have been horrible, Velistris. To you, to my nieces. To dear Hank-is-Handy."

Its words were not untrue. It had indeed been in a bad way as of late—though I also knew that the fault was our own. Mine, its nieces, Hank-is-Handy. We had all failed it in our own ways. "You have been human."

Laughing gently, it looked away. "And what do you know of being human, that you may guide me in this matter? I do not need my hair fixed. My engagement is ruined."

"Perhaps I know more than you realize."

"If you make the claim, you must prove it."

That courage I'd lacked earlier—how I felt it swelling within me now. Where I could not find the words before, they now came to my crystalline lips like captives desperate to be freed. What was once so hard to say now came easier than I'd ever expected. "I am damaged, Aurora." I felt it best to use its name instead of its title. The use of one's name in human communication often promotes consideration. I prayed it would do the same for me. Indeed, it did look at me. "Irreparably."

It looked at me strangely. "Your arm will regrow in time. I would not call it irreparable."

"I do not mean my arm." I pressed my hand to my bosom. "I mean, I am damaged deep within. Through the display of a translucometer, I beheld my very lifeveins in my quarters." The look on its face shifted. I now had its attention. "They were not what I imagined, Aurora. There was no beauty about them. They were shriveled, sinewy. They looked like something you would pull from the ground to discard. And all about them, in every which way, I was fractured. My body—the inner part that cannot be fixed—is riddled with cracks and imperfections. I saw them myself. Do you realize the ramifications of this?"

Its eyebrows parted. "Oh, Velistris."

"It means that I can never be perfect in the eyes of Deity. I can never match the standard that a Zepzeg must match to reach the Life After. We have been tasked with the impossible."

"Velistris, I—"

"I am speaking." It is only on rare occasions that I find the courage to interrupt Aurora. I wagered that it would not take my interruption as disrespect but as emphasis as to the importance of my words. It fell quiet and listened on, as I had hoped. "I do not know what one must do to live eternally. If it is perfection that is required, then no creature can reach it. We are born incapable. Does this mean that there is no Deity? Does it mean that all things eternal should be relegated to myth? I had hoped to ask you for your insight. Indeed, I had. But I could not find the strength within me to do so until now, at a most inopportune time." I could not think of a worse one. "I am terrified, Aurora. I have heard you recite the story of the mustard seed as an allegory for faith. The moral of the story, as I have understood it, is that the tiniest bit of faith can lead to extraordinary things. For me, the experience has been quite the opposite. It is not a seed of faith that has been planted, but one of doubt. And it has taken root in a most soul-fracturing way. Whereas once there was impeccable faith, now only doubt remains. I fear it has destroyed me."

Still, it listened, and so I went on.

"You asked me to support my claim that I understand what you are going through, and I now have. You say you have lost your engagement, and I have lost my reason to strive and to exist. So now I ask you, Aurora, from one struggling being to the next, to please explain to me why you have lost your way. Perhaps it is only through each other than we can find our ways again."

The eyes with which it looked at me were different from how they'd been before. Ours has always been a relationship of unspoken but understood hierarchy. I serve it, and I am aware that I serve it, so there is no need for the matter to be emphasized. But it did not look at me that way now. It looked at me in a way that was quite the opposite. It looked at me as I have often seen Delta look at it—like a human child seeking guidance from a parent. Though I did not know what its words would be, I knew they would not be chastising. It appeared, at least in that moment, incapable of the nerve. Indeed, when it finally addressed me with its eyes trailing to the floor, its voice was uncharacteristically submissive. Perhaps uncharacteristically honest, too. "I do not wish to stop living my life the way in which I live it now. I spoke to Bryce recently about my wanderlust, and indeed, it is what I have. But my problem runs much deeper." It paused for a moment—a sign I took as indicative of hesitance more than dramatic effect. "I do not like to fail. Oh, Velistris, how I despise it. You know this to be true of me." I did. "It is of note, then, to consider that every marriage in the Ultraviolet family has failed. Corinda is praised for her deeds, but what is never mentioned is that she had three husbands. All of her children suffered the penalty of divorce for their misgivings toward their spouses. You need look no further than Elyse and Delta to see the impact it has had. Elyse has never met her father, though it has not stopped her from idolizing him. And Delta would never have taken residence with me if not for the spiteful manner in which her parents ended their marriage. They are running from the sins of their parents. As am I.

"The *Illustré* is more than a spaceship for me. It is an excuse. With it, I can say, 'I cannot marry you, for I must roam the stars.' It keeps me safe from failure. Should I marry Bryce and our marriage fall apart, then I shall be just another Ultraviolet in a long line of terrible wives and husbands. I shall be an example of love that does not endure. That title, I cannot bear. So I have run away. How ironic it is that you should mention my stories of mustard seeds. There is no mustard seed of faith to be found within me. I am a coward and a hypocrite, Velistris. I have let my fear of failure ruin the greatest chance I ever had to experience love." It lifted its eyes to look at me—the first time it had done so during the entirety of the talk. "I did tell him. That I wished for our engagement to end."

It said nothing more, which prompted the obvious response, "What did he say in return?"

"He implored me to reconsider. More than imploration. He practically begged me. He said he didn't understand. He said that if I feared change, he would help me. He said all the things that a well-mannered and proper fiancé should."

"Did you tell him that it had to do with none of those things?"

Its silence indicated that it had not. "I couldn't bring myself to do it. I simply said, 'I'm sorry, Bryce. I'm so sorry.' Then I ended the call. He tried to contact me several times, both that day and in the days that followed. I did not answer. I have humiliated him, and in doing so I have shamed myself. I became the cautionary tale that I sought to avoid: that one should not bestow upon Corinda Rhea's descendants their love—they will all betray it in the end. I am such a fool."

There was no question that it was correct. I had always thought it and its human companions foolish. My error was never to recognize that I was among them. "Do you wish to marry him?"

It paused, no doubt in preparation to say the customary words of human bondage. "I do."

"Do you regret having broken off the engagement?"

Though its pause was longer, its words were no less uncertain. "How I do, Velistris. How terribly much I do."

The answer was clear. "Then you should reach out to him.

Relay to him your fears and the reason for your termination of the engagement. Many humans are forgiving when presented with the truth of one's intentions, provided they are well-meant. He will likely accept you back."

"And he may not. I cannot bear to hear his voice angry with me. It would be a wound the likes of which I may never recover."

"It is hard to imagine you tormented more than you are tormented now."

"It is not hard for me."

I thought hard on how to answer, for I felt it was prepared to confound me at every turn. Ultimately, the words I found to confront it were its own. "How much faith does it take to move a mountain, Aurora?"

Its eyes stayed on me for but a moment longer, then they shied away. "Faith the size of a mustard seed."

"How much does it take to salvage a marriage?"

Eyes lifting, it offered the faintest of placating, false smiles. "I understand what you're saying."

"I wish you to say it."

Pausing but a moment again, it said, "Faith the size of a mustard seed."

"And how much, Aurora Ultraviolet, does it take to change a family legacy?"

I have found that many times, humans must hear themselves say things several times before they begin to believe them. There was a method to the repetition that I demanded. With each time Aurora said the words, I beheld as their meaning—their purported truth—became clearer to it. "Faith the size of a mustard seed." Perhaps now, it would believe the words to be true.

"I know nothing of this story or its origins," I said, "and what I do know of it, I have learned from you. I know there is a spiritual connotation that I am unfamiliar with; therefore, I can only address its logical ramifications. That is, that the smallest thoughts can grow into consequences that are vastly larger. For you, the story is intended to provoke a belief that one can attain what was thought unattainable if one applies even the smallest bit of faith. It is *your* application of this story, and not my own recent experience with doubt, that I believe is most beneficial. I look up to you. I have learned much from you." The words were true. "I do not like the seeds that have been planted inside of me, despite the truthful revelations they have led to. I feel doubt has a purpose, but only for so long—at least, until a choice must be made as to what one must do with that doubt. Doubt has become for me both a learning tool and a sickness. It has brought me to a place where it is no longer a help, but a hindrance. It prompts me to cling to nothing. What I mean to say is, I much prefer your mustard seeds to mine."

"There are no mustard seeds within me," it said quietly— almost at a whisper. "If there are, they are most certainly not of faith."

I related to its words. "Might I make a suggestion, then?"

"You may always."

"Might we plant some together? You and I, right here? I am lost, Aurora. I have never felt it so strongly as I do now. I need the faith that your story speaks of—and if I may be so bold, so do you."

Its eyes continued to look down at the floor, its head canted in a way that insinuated deep reflection. I knew that it agreed with me. "I would very much like to instill such faith in each other," it quietly replied.

"Then let us, for we need it now, more than ever."

"I fear that we are in a scenario in which we cannot win," it said.

It led to the inevitable question from me. "How much faith does it take to negotiate a planetary dispute?"

Eyes flickering up to me, it flashed the briefest of smiles—if at nothing else, I presumed, at my cleverness, as momentary as it may have been. "You have taken me to task quite well enough, dear friend. I hear your words."

"I will find my way in this universe," I said. "You will find your way back to Bryce Lockhart. And now, together, we will find a solution to Gryamore V. Though I may not believe these things in my heart, I may choose to believe them in my mind. That, I feel, is an acceptable beginning."

It nodded its head. "As do I."

"Do you have any idea where in the negotiation we should go from here?" I asked.

It laughed, but just barely. "I do not."

"Then let us go and find our way in front of a live, galactic audience."

With the hint of a smirk emerging, it told me, "Yes, let us. What is the worst that could happen?"

It is a question I have learned is never wise to ask. Together, and with no idea as to how we should proceed, we returned to the audience chamber.

I appreciated Aurora's truthfulness with me, and I understood how a matter as seemingly unrelated as a broken engagement could impact the negotiation of Gryamore V. Aurora was troubled, and so long as it was troubled, it would never be able to think clearly enough to bring the talks to an acceptable conclusion. However, there is something that humans do often called, *getting things off one's chest*. Dare I say, I was beginning to feel the value of this concept myself.

Within minutes, the audience chamber was filled again. Representatives of the Broodmasters and Dacians took—or in the case of the Broodmasters, were taken *to*—their seats. It would be Aurora's job to call the talks back into order. As Aurora took its place behind the central podium, I wondered what it would say.

Turning the knob to indicate the call to order, Aurora sent a loud, resonant hum throughout the chamber. What little chatter was there died down, and all lifeforms turned their attention to the captain.

I could not help but feel that this moment—with all eyes and ears once more on my captain—was something pivotal. Perhaps even the precipice to a turning point. There was a tense eagerness to the crowd—I could see it in the Dacians' erect ears and the Broodmasters' sheer motionlessness. All were waiting to hear what Aurora would say. To see if the recess had birthed an epiphany. I was eager to see, too.

It stood silent over the chamber, its head downcast and its eyes closed. It did this often when in a prayer state. I hoped its prayer would not take long! Thankfully, it did not. When Aurora lifted its head again, it surveyed the audience with an almost supercilious expression that I quite admired for the confidence it conveyed. I did not know if it knew what it would say or if it would allow the words to come to it in the moment, as humans are often apt to do. But I do know that when it spoke, it did so with authority that had been lacking up until that point. It was good to hear my captain at its best again.

"There is a story in my faith," it said. "It is called the story of the mustard seed. The story states that if one has faith the size of the *smallest* of seeds, they may order a mountain to move and it shall move—nothing shall be impossible."

Though I had heard the story many times before from it, I listened with renewed focus. I wished to learn its lesson.

"You need not know of my religion to comprehend the story's meaning. It simply states that if one is willing to extend the smallest granule of belief, then the impossible becomes inevitable." It stood more erectly. "For a human of my religion, the story is an allusion to the faith one places in God. But the principle can be applied to the secular just as well. If we extend such faith—as tiny as it may be—to each other, think of what we could accomplish! For us, in this chamber, that faith must take the form of trust. Trust in one another, trust in the processes that have led us here, to Point Maven. The conditions of this negotiation state that I must declare a winner, but I do not wish to do so. In declaring a winner, I also declare a loser, and it is not my wish that anyone in these talks stands to lose. Yet, Gryamore V must be granted, and it is I who must grant it."

Such eloquent words! Were they prepared? They could not have been. This was Aurora Ultraviolet at its best. Was this the faith it spoke of, being lived out before me?

It continued. "We must all move mountains today. Mountains of doubt, mountains of distrust. Mountains of greed, and envy, and bitterness. We must do this in order to reach a solution in which all parties stand to profit. And so I ask you all, my friends among the Dacians and Broodmasters, to summon that faith from deep within you. And with that challenge— with that declaration of what *must* be done if anything is to be done at all—I ask you to present to me proposals in which we *all* stand to gain. Discuss them further if you must, but if you must, do so quickly. The Planet Smasher is coming. Our time shall soon run out. I stand here ready to hear you— and ready to sow seeds of faith of my own. I turn this floor over, now, to you."

Brilliance! Sheer, determined brilliance. This was the captain I had come to admire—one that, if I must confess, learned a great deal of its diplomatic tact from me. This was what the audience chamber needed to hear. I will not hesitate to admit that even within me, I felt seeds of faith begin to take root. This would work. This *had* to work. I believed, truly, that it would. I eagerly awaited the Dacian and Broodmaster response.

"The Daldath must die!" Lavimtelek bellowed. All around it, the audience chamber erupted in raucous shouting. "To the army that defeats them, the spoils of Gryamore V! To the loser, *expulsion from the stars*!"

So much for mustard seeds.

As Aurora lowered its head and set its hands on its hips, I could practically see its deflation take place. These talks, it seemed, had a long ways to go.

Chapter Fourteen

I KNOCKED ON the door to Elyse's room on the repair freighter. I did it very hard so that she would hear it. Then I said, "I am Hank-is-Handy!" because I wanted her to know who it was. I knew she would not think it was Aurora because Aurora was at Point Maven with Velistris, but I thought that she might think it was Delta. I did not want her to think I was Delta, because me and Delta are very different. I thought that saying my name was a smart choice and I was proud that I did it. Elyse opened the door. I did not see Defoe or his blue Slarb or his pink Gralb behind her. This made me glad. "I said my name when I knocked," I said.

"I heard," she said. She did not sound happy or sad when she said it, but I think she was probably impressed.

"Can I enter your room?" I was proud of myself for asking that question, too. Elyse stepped out of the way and moved her arm in a wave thing. This meant that I could go in, so I did.

I was glad to see Elyse with no hair. I was not worried as much about an enemy cutting off her head as I was before. When I walked into her room, I said, "I like what you've done with the place." I do not know what it means, but humans say it when they enter a new room. She thanked me after I said it, so I knew that I did it correctly. "I would like to talk to you about an important thing."

"Yeah, what is it?"

"I miss you."

She performed a head tilt like Riley does, then she said, "You what?" I think she must have tilted her head because she did not hear me, so I said my words louder.

"I miss you!" When I said it this time, she jumped. This is how I knew that she heard me now.

"Good grief, you don't need to shout! What do you mean, you miss me?"

I was surprised that the term was unfamiliar to her because it is a term that humans use, and she is a human. I decided to explain it. "When we do not spend time together, I get sad. It makes me think of the times we used to spend together, and I get more sad. I like it when you spend time with me and not Defoe or his blue Slarb or his pink Gralb." That was another reason why I was glad that she did not have hair anymore. Maybe she would not need Defoe to make it look good for her.

She did not say anything or make a reaction for four and a half to five seconds. Then she made a reaction. It was a strange reaction where she pushed her lips together and made a smile that looked sad. "Hank-is-Handy…"

"Yes, I am Hank-is-Handy," I said, because I did not know why she said my name.

Elyse came close to me and put her arms around my torso. Then she said, "I'm sorry that I've been so out of it." I did not know what that meant, either. She continued to speak. "I've just had a lot of things going on. I have a lot of…demons. Aunt Aurora's been helping me deal with them."

I did not know that she had demons. Then I thought of the times when I thought she was looking at something that only she could see because she had different vision than me, and I wondered if maybe she was seeing the demons. I predicted that this was the case. "If you show them to me, I will kill them."

"No, not those kinds of demons. I mean like…just things I struggle with."

My prediction was incorrect.

"Hank-is-Handy, I'm kind of a mess," she said. This was something that I knew. "I also know I've been spending a lot of time with everyone else. I know you may not understand, but it's been good for me. I didn't realize how much I… well, I guess that I needed it." Her muscles got tense and she hugged my torso tighter. "But I don't want you to have any doubt in your mind that you're my best friend, because you are."

What she said made me have good feelings. They were the first good feelings that I felt in a long time. I put my arms around her because that is what humans do when they have good feelings with each other. Then I said, "You are my best friend, too." Her muscles got tense again.

There is a lot that I have to learn about good and bad feelings. The feeling that has been hardest for me has been love. I only know that I love Elyse because she tells me that she knows I love her. But I have always thought that it would be good to feel love myself. I have felt the bad feelings that love makes, but I have not felt many of the good ones. But I think that maybe it was the good part that I felt when me and Elyse hugged. It felt more good than the bad feelings felt bad. I liked it very much. I did not want it to stop. I decided that it was a good time to talk about it. "I am sorry that I loved you, then I did not love you, then I loved you again. I think sometimes that I do not know what love is."

She leaned back and looked at me, then she shook her head. "You're not the only one."

"What are the symptoms?" When I asked it, I saw her mouth go into a smirk. Then she answered me.

"I really want to say something funny right now, but I know you're trying, so I'll refrain. Love isn't always something you feel. Sometimes you can love something without even liking it. I'm sometimes that way with Aunt Aurora and Delta."

I did not understand. She continued.

"But more so than what you feel, love is what you do. It's being there for someone, it's never giving up on them. It's holding them in their worst moment to make sure they're okay. Those are the 'symptoms,' as you put it."

"I do not hold people often."

"Well," she said, "you do. I just don't think you realize it. You've been after me to cut my hair off forever, and it finally happened. I know you wanted that to help me."

Elyse with no hair made me happy. "You made a good choice. It is one less thing on my list of things you are not good at." I took the new list I wrote from my waist strap and gave it to her. "I made the list again. I put not having hair on it and then I crossed it out so you could see your improvement."

Her eyes got big when she saw the new list. I predicted it was because she was happy to have another one. "Oh, joy." My prediction was correct. She took it, then was quiet for four seconds. "Well, just so you know, I miss my hair. A lot. That was probably one of the dumbest things I've ever done, and I can't wait for it to grow back." That made me sad. She gave me a smile that looked sad, too. "Sorry. But I know you wanted it to help me, and that means a lot. It means the whole universe. So thank you, Hank-is-Handy."

Her words made me both happy and sad, but I think I was more happy than sad. I did not know what to say or do, so I took a step back and put my hands beneath her armpits.

She said, "Hey!" I picked her up, and her voice got loud. "What are you doing?"

I said, "I am holding you."

"Yeah, okay, so I didn't mean hold people like they're an *item*."

As I was lowering her back to the floor, an alarm happened. It was very loud and coming from all of the walls. A voice came over the speakers in the repair freighter. It was like the voice that talks in the *Illustré* but a male instead of a female. "Warning! Warning! Threatening fleet entering system. Warning! Warning!"

Elyse did the thing humans do when they get surprised and

their eyes get big. Her mouth opened, but she did not speak for almost three seconds. Then she said, "The Daldath!"

That was my prediction, too.

Elyse ran out of her room very fast. I followed her. There were many humans running through the halls when we went into them. Most of them were security guards. Ahead in the hallway was the window that Thule liked to look out of. There were security guards standing by the window looking out of it. This is where Elyse ran. Sometimes when humans run too fast and they try to stop, they perform an act called a skid. This is what she did when she got to the window, except that it looked like a scared skid. I stopped behind her and looked out the window myself.

Elyse's prediction that it was the Daldath was correct. But I believe that if someone had asked us to predict how many Daldath ships were there, that prediction would have been incorrect. I would have predicted ten warships. The number of ships I saw was much more than ten. It looked more like a hundred or maybe a hundred twenty-seven and entering the system at a rate of one warship every four point six seconds. It was not surprising that they were close enough to see, because the Planet Smasher that had been following us had been using the same hyperspace vector.

"Oh my God!" said Elyse in a voice that sounded afraid. At the same time, she performed a gasp. "Hank-is-Handy, we've got to get off this freighter!"

Flapping sounds came from down the hall. It was Thule. His wings were spread out and he was flying. His big claw feet clanked into the ceiling above us and he looked out of the window upside down. Then he looked at us. "The Daldath are here!"

I do not consider a prediction correct if it is made after something happens.

"We need to get to the *Illustré*!" said Elyse. "Where's Delta and Defoe?"

I thought they were probably in their rooms, so I said, "They are probably in their rooms."

"We need to get them, *hurry*!"

Thule let go of the ceiling and landed by us. "Since Aurora is planetside, I will go to the ship and prepare it for flight!"

I did not think that was a good idea to let Thule go. I do not think Elyse thought it was a good idea, either, because she said, "No way, we're staying together! You can't start it without the access key anyway, and only Delta has one! You go get Defoe and his companions!" Thule made an angry snarl sound, then flew in the direction of Defoe's room.

There is no access key to the *Illustré*, which meant either Elyse was lying to make Thule stay with us or she had gotten confused. She did not sound confused, so I think she was lying. I thought in this case, it was a good idea.

"Come on," she said to me, "hurry!" So I went with her.

It did not take long to get to Delta's room on the repair freighter because it was not far from us. I got there first, so I punched on the door with my fist. "I am Hank-is-Handy! Can I enter your room?" I kicked the door down and entered. Delta was standing next to her bed with Riley and it looked like she was putting on clothes very quickly. I predicted that she had been sleeping when the alarm sounded. "I like what you've done with the place. The Daldath are attacking. We must leave."

"Leave where?" Delta asked with a fast voice. "Can the *Illustré* even fly?"

I had been observing the repair process so I knew the answer. "All vital systems on the *Illustré* are in working condition. All hull breaches have been repaired. The strike craft are operational." The only thing that was not fixed was Elyse's room, but that would not make the ship fly better or worse.

"Thule is getting Defoe and his pets," said Elyse, making fast gestures for Delta to follow her. "Come on, we've got to move!"

Delta zipped up the front of her silver jumpsuit and grabbed Riley. "Go, we're right behind you!" The words she said were true and she followed us into the hall.

I knew that the Daldath had come for Gryamore V. I also knew that when the Daldath decide to go after a planet, they will do everything in their power to get it. This means that even though the Dacian and Broodmaster armadas were in the system, the Daldath would not be afraid to fight them.

Daldath warships are some of the most dangerous spaceships in all of space. The energy missiles they fire are very destructive and can track engine components. It is very hard to survive a fight with a Daldath warship. Because there were over a hundred warships with the Planet Smasher, I did not predict that a fight would go well for the Dacians or the Broodmasters, or even the humans if they fought, too.

When we got to the dock where the *Illustré* was connected, no guards tried to stop us from entering it. I predicted they were too afraid of the Daldath to care what we did. I did not wait to see if my prediction was correct. I just went into the ship with Elyse, Delta, Defoe, and Thule.

Aurora has talked many times about emergency situations when she is not on board the ship. When a situation like that happens, control of the ship is to go to Delta. That is because she spends a lot of time teaching Delta how to captain the ship and what to do. I do not think Delta is as good as Aurora, but she is better than me. If I was captain and I saw a Daldath warship, I would ram it. I do not think the rest of the crew would like that idea.

There is one thing about Delta that is very good, and it is that she is faster than Aurora and Elyse. She got into the captain's chair very fast. Even though her eyes were very big and her voice was shaking a lot, she did the things that a captain was supposed to do. "Hank-is-Handy, detach us from this freighter! Elyse, how are our screens?"

I activated the emergency override on the docking clamps and detached the *Illustré* from the freighter. Behind me, Elyse said, "Screens are functional!"

"More Daldath warships are entering the system," I said. "Sensors detect two hundred and eighteen."

"Holy zin," said Elyse.

Thule was not at a station but instead was by the front of the bridge at the monitor. He pointed to the ships. "We must leave this system at once! The Daldath will destroy every vessel!"

Delta did the thing where humans ignore people they do not like to hear. "Get Riley and Defoe's pets into the holder!"

I think she was talking to Thule even though she was not looking at him, because he said, "Are you listening to a word I'm—"

Her face got angry colors. "*I said get them in the holders!*" Her breathing got a lot faster. I predicted that it was because she was getting more scared.

Thule flapped his wings and flew across the bridge to me, where he landed in front of my station. "Listen to her voice— she is frantic! This *child* will get us all killed!" His eyes did the shiny things that I liked. "You should put me in command."

I was beginning to think it was a good idea, then I could not see anything. This was because Elyse jumped on my back from behind and put her hands over my eyes so that I could not see. "Hank-is-Handy, *no!*" I did not think Thule's idea was good anymore.

"*Vile wretch!*" I heard Thule say. Then I heard his body move fast. I think he was about to try and kill Elyse, then take over the ship.

I did not think that was a good idea, either.

When Elyse uncovered my eyes, Thule was not looking at me anymore. Instead, he was flying over my head. His sharp claws were out. I predicted that this was because he was going to kill Elyse, then make me look at his shiny eyes again. I did not wait to see if my prediction was correct. I reached up very fast with my hand and grabbed Thule by his ankle. I heard him make a snarl sound, then I threw him forward and onto the floor in front of my station.

This is when Defoe attacked, too. "You hurting my friends!" he said to Thule. "You being bad, bad, bad!" He made his long tentacle thing come out and wrap itself around Thule's neck from behind. Thule made a sound that was like, *urk*, then he reached up with his sharp claw toes and tore Defoe's tentacle arm off. Defoe made the kind of sounds animals make when they are in pain. Thule threw Defoe's severed tentacle arm to the floor and it moved around.

Everything started to happen very fast. Defoe moved backward and all over very quickly. I think it was a reflex action to having his tentacle arm torn off. Elyse screamed, "Hank-is-Handy!" because I think she wanted me to attack Thule, which I thought was a good idea. At the same time as these things, Delta ran out of her captain's chair and jumped on Thule from behind. All of these things happened in approximately one point seven nine seconds.

I did not have time to pick up my phase hammer. Instead, I left my station very quickly and moved to where Thule and Delta were fighting. Just before I got to them, Thule grabbed Delta by the torso and flung her across the bridge very hard. Before her head could splatter against the bulkhead, Defoe leapt in front of her and opened his big plant mouth to catch her inside it, like he did with Velistris.

Thule turned around quickly to face me, then he kicked up with his wing hands and flew to the ceiling. I tried to grab him, but he performed a spin like a drill that made his wings tuck in very tightly. When his claws dug into the ceiling, he looked at me and hissed.

"Warship!"

I looked behind me. Elyse was pointing at the bridge monitor, so I looked at it. A Daldath warship was getting close to the repair freighter. I predicted that it would soon shoot at the freighter and destroy it, but I did not want to wait to see if the prediction was correct. I reached over to the captain's chair and pushed forward the joysticks that Aurora and Delta use to fly. The *Illustré's* engines went very quickly to maximum thrust, and the ship went forward very fast. Momentum made everyone on the bridge, including Riley and Defoe's blue Slarb and pink Gralb, come off their feet and fly to the back of the bridge. I did, too. My back hit the frame of my control station very hard and I heard it make a crack sound. I predicted that my back was broken.

A Vorck can move with a broken back, so it is not as bad as when it happens to a human. I got up to fight Thule again, but the forward thrust was too much and I could not stand. When I looked up, I saw that Thule was flying in the air toward the captain's chair. The momentum of the forward thrust seemed to be making it difficult, but he flapped hard and made it. When he reached the chair, he pulled back on the joysticks that I had pushed all the way forward. The forward momentum stopped, and everyone on the bridge fell to the floor. Defoe must have let Delta out of his plant mouth, because I saw her sliding forward across the floor in his plant slime. I looked up at the bridge monitor, where there were many more Daldath warships in front of the *Illustré.*

Delta tried to get up, but she could not because of the plant slime. I thought about helping her, but I knew that I had to make Thule dead first. This was when I reached for my phase hammer.

"*Incoming!*" said Elyse from her station. I looked at the monitor and saw several Daldath energy missiles coming toward the ship.

Thule screamed from the captain's chair, "Hold on if you

want to live!"

I knew that Thule said it because he was about to take evasive action with the *Illustré*. I did not care if I lived or died, but I did not want Delta to die. I did not think she would be able to hold onto anything because of the plant slime on her, so I moved very fast to reach her even though I felt my spine shifting where it was broken. I think that when I moved, the broken part got worse. I could even feel some pain in it, which is unusual for a Vorck, but I ignored it because saving Delta was more important than hurting. I got to her just as Thule engaged the downward thrust. I put one of my arms around her and held her close to my body, and I used my other arm to grab one of the railings. The downward thrust engaged and we flew hard to the ceiling, but my hand stayed on the railing and we did not fly up. I heard another crack sound, but this one came from my arm. I predicted that it was because my arm was broken now, too. My spine moved more, too, which I think was probably bad. I let go of Delta because the *Illustré* stopped its downward thrust, and she grabbed hold of the communication station console. She strapped herself in it.

I looked down at Defoe's tentacle thing, which was on the floor by me. It began slithering across the floor back toward Defoe. If we were not under attack, I would have had thoughts about it, but I did not have time to think about anything. I saw my phase hammer sliding across the floor, and I reached fast for it with my arm that was not broken.

"*Hold on!*" shouted Thule. He moved the joysticks fast again. I looked at the bridge monitor very fast and saw more Daldath energy missiles coming after the ship.

"Hank-is-Handy, strap in!" said Elyse from behind me. She was strapped in, too.

I looked back at her. "I must kill Thule!"

"That's not important now. *Strap yourself into your station!*" she said.

Delta spoke, too. "Hank-is-Handy, do it! That's an order!"

I do not know why they wanted me to not kill Thule, but Delta is in charge of the *Illustré* when Aurora is not on it, so I listened. I bent my knees and made a jump to the engineering console, which was hard to do because of my back that was now broken. I grabbed the strap with my good arm and locked myself into place. Two seconds later, the *Illustré* broke hard to the port side. I heard my back break more during the move, but it stayed together, which was a good thing for me. My bad arm was hanging and I could not move it.

When the *Illustré* stopped moving fast, Thule said in a loud voice, "Call out your stations!"

"I do not listen to Thule!" I said.

"Communications!" said Delta. Then she looked at me. "Listen to him, Hank-is-Handy! He's all we've got."

I did not think she was correct, but she was the temporary captain, so I listened to her. "Hank-is-Handy is on weapons and sensors!"

"Screens and power diversion!" said Elyse behind me.

"Are all stations manned?" Thule asked.

Delta answered, "All essential stations, yes!"

There was a problem. It was that I could not work my console with only one hand. I did not want to tell Thule that my arm was broken because I did not want to give him a tactical advantage if we got into a death fight, so I kept it to myself.

"Hank-is-Handy, what's wrong with your arm?" Elyse asked.

I did not want to tell the truth, so I came up with a good lie. "I am giving it a rest for a while!"

Delta looked back at me. "Hank-is-Handy, is your arm broken?"

I did not know what to say, so for a moment I did not say anything. Then I decided to lie again. "No."

"This is so not zin," said Elyse behind me.

At the same time, Delta said, "Defoe, can you help Hank-is-Handy at his station?"

"I helping!" Defoe said. I looked where he said it. He was moving fast with his slug foot to my station and his tentacle was attached to his body again. For a moment I wished I had time to make a thought or a prediction about it, but I did not. He grabbed the console with his tentacle and held to it tightly.

Delta asked him, "Do you know how to work weapons and sensor systems?"

"I knowing a lot on my Darkboat!" Defoe answered. "But on this bridge I not knowing anything!"

That would not help us.

"How quickly can you learn?" Delta asked.

Defoe did not say anything. Instead, he opened his big plant mouth and it came over me. The next thing I saw was darkness.

Seconds passed, but I could not count them. Feelings came over me, but I could not identify them good. I felt suction and heard loud sucking sounds. The next thing I saw was the bridge again, and I felt Defoe's plant slime all over me. I reached up with my good hand to wipe it off my face.

Defoe said, "Now, I knowing." He got next to me and his tentacle arm grabbed the weapons stick. "I being on sensors! Hank-is-Handy can using weapons with his good arm while his bad arm is resting."

"Is everyone on board ready for battle?" asked Thule very loudly. He was still moving the ship side to side very fast to not get killed by the Daldath missiles.

"You know there's no way we can defeat all these ships, right?" Delta asked.

Thule answered, "I have no intention of defeating them. We only need to get past them! Then we shall leave this star system far behind."

"No chance that that happens," said Elyse from behind me.

"Not with Aunt Aurora still at Point Maven!"

"Blasted child! It is as if you *wish* to die."

"Yeah, it wouldn't be the first time," Elyse said back to him.

A pair of Daldath energy missiles came close to the ship, but Thule maneuvered us past them. I thought for a moment that he might be a better pilot than Aurora, but I have never seen Aurora fight against the Daldath to compare it.

Thule got past the nearest Daldath warships that were firing at us, then he made the *Illustré* go fast. It went away from the Daldath warships, and they did not shoot at us or follow us. "They stopped firing," said Elyse. Her voice sounded surprised, but I was not surprised. I predicted that the warships only shot at us because we flew very close to them. The Daldath armada began to approach Gryamore V.

"We must contact Aunt Aurora!" said Delta. Her voice sounded scared and shaky and she was working the communications controls very fast. All of a sudden, the speakers in the bridge made a loud squealing sound. All of the humans and Thule reached up to touch their ears. Then the bridge monitor came on. It was not Aurora that appeared on the display, as Delta said she was going to do. Instead, it was the Daldath. I predicted that it was sending a message to all of the ships in the system and not only ours.

Elyse once described the Daldath as looking like an internal organ with crab eyes attached to a machine. I have not seen a crab before, but I have seen many internal organs from the lifeforms I have opened with a gun or with my hands. The Daldath body looks like many of the things I have seen, so I believe her description is accurate. We could see the machine at the bottom of the display that the Daldath was attached to, but we could not see all of it because the view was very close. The computer's translation thing interpreted what the Daldath said. The voice it used sounded mechanical. I think that the translator thing did a good job of matching the Daldath's sounds. "Analysis of System: Gryamore indicates strong concentration of desirable minerals at: Gryamore System Planet Five. I have deemed it necessary to harvest: minerals at this location. All sentient species are asked to assist in harvest of: minerals at this location. Payment of service to Daldath will consist of: valuable components and galactic credits."

A voice came over the channel. It was from one of the humans. "This is Commander Rigel of the Royal Armada. You are trespassing on an owned system in the middle of a planetary negotiation. Please depart from this system immediately and return to your system of origin."

"Insufficient response. The target planet: Gryamore System Planet Five is necessary for Daldath consumption. I do not desire: bloodshed and violence. Please assist with the harvesting of: minerals at this location. Such action will be mutually beneficial."

"If you do not desire bloodshed and violence," asked the human, "why do you show up with an armada of warships?"

The Daldath answered quickly. "Long-range scanners indicated: large mass of space fighters belonging to multiple interplanetary species. Military escort deemed necessary."

"We will not surrender this system to you, Daldath," the human commander said. "I repeat, leave this system at once or face military resistance."

I did not know who would win if the Daldath decided to fight the Humans, Dacians, and Broodmasters together. There were more ships in the system that did not belong to the Daldath than ships that did, but Daldath ships are very strong. I predicted that if they fought, a lot of people would die no matter what side won.

The Daldath spoke again. "Time allotment of: ten minutes will be provided. Please depart from predetermined system or face destruction." The monitor went black because the Daldath stopped broadcasting.

Thule spoke from the captain's chair, and when he did he

sounded mad. "We must leave this system immediately! Chart the course, Vorck, or I will chart it for you!" I do not think he knew that he could not chart it from his chair.

"I need to speak to Aunt Aurora," said Delta as she began to hit buttons on her panel. "She must know of all this!" A few seconds later, Aurora's face appeared on the monitor, but there was much static and it could not be seen clearly.

"Delta!" she said. "Why are you calling me? We're in the middle of—"

Delta spoke before Aurora finished. "The Daldath are here!"

"*What?*"

"They've arrived with an armada! There must be *hundreds*! They're saying everyone has ten minutes to leave the system or they'll attack!"

Aurora looked at Delta, then she looked at Thule, and her eyes got big. "Thule? Are you in my chair?"

"Remove this woman from my sight!" Thule said.

"I made him temporary captain," Delta said.

I decided that I would speak. "Thule tried to kill us and take the ship."

"Don't worry about anything on the *Illustré*!" Delta said. "You need to figure out a way to stop the Daldath from attacking!"

I did not know how Aurora would stop the Daldath from attacking while she was at Point Maven. I do not think Aurora knew how she would stop them, too. I thought this because her face looked confused, like how humans get when they are told many different and important things at a single time.

Thule spoke again. "I said *remove* this woman from my sight! We are leaving this system!"

I had a good idea. I decided that while Thule was not looking at me, I would attack him. I could not use my phase hammer because I only had one arm that worked, but it is a strong arm and can throw things good. So I bent down, picked up my phase hammer, and instead of shooting him with it, I threw it at his head. I predicted that I had a sixty-six percent chance of hitting him. It hit him. The phase hammer made a loud, mushy sound when it hit him in the back of the head. Thule fell forward and out of the chair. When he hit the floor, he did not move.

"*Hank-is-Handy!*" said Aurora, Delta, and Elyse at the same time.

I pointed at Thule. "Thule was a bad Dacian."

The bridge monitor got full of static again. Aurora tried to speak, but it was too hard to hear her words. "Aunt Aurora?" said Delta several times, each one louder than the last. Then the static got too bad and Aurora disappeared. Delta turned to look at me. When she did, she had an angry face. "Why did you attack him?"

I was surprised that she did not know. "He was going to make us leave the system."

"Not by himself! He would have needed the rest of us to cooperate!"

"I am wounded bad and he was not. He could have killed me, then made you run the ship under his hypnosis. You are an inferior physical lifeform and could not have fought him off."

She got out of her communications chair and ran over to Thule, then she knelt down by him. "He's not dead. We need to get him into the brig! If he wakes now, he'll be livid."

"I will move him," I said.

"You can't move him! You've only got one arm!" She bent down to try and pick him up, but he slipped out of her arms because they were slippery. "My goodness, Defoe, you couldn't have saved me without covering me in this *gunk*?"

Elyse left her station to help Delta. Together, they put Thule into the seat at the communications station and strapped him in. I think they did it because he was too heavy to carry all the way to the brig by themselves. After Delta finished strapping him in, she looked at me with an angry face. "Completely unnecessary, Hank-is-Handy!"

I did not agree. "You are the captain of this ship when Aurora is not here. Thule is not." I usually like to obey orders, but this time I felt like disobeying them was good because Thule was bad. I did not have the bad feeling that humans call *guilt*.

"But we were surviving with him!" Delta said. "He might have been bad, but he was really good at flying!"

I decided to argue. "We are not fighting now. There was no reason for him to continue to be captain."

"The Daldath are *right there*!"

"I think that the Daldath attacked us because we flew too close to them." There are some species that do not like it when other ships get too close. This makes them attack. The Daldath are one of these species. "They did not shoot the repair freighter, even though I thought that they would. I do not think we will get attacked by the Daldath again. If they engage the Humans, Dacians, and Broodmasters, they will ignore the *Illustré*. There is no reason for them to fight us because we are not a warship."

Her angry voice stayed. I was not scared of it, though, because it is not as bad as Aurora's angry voice. Aurora's angry voice makes me sad. "That's a pretty big gamble, Hank-is-Handy!"

"The Daldath will not attack us," I said. "I promise you." Humans like promises, even if they are not true. But I knew mine was true.

Beside me, Defoe said, "I detecting more ships entering the system!"

"God, how many warships do the Daldath *have*?" asked Elyse as she went back to her station. I think it was one of the times when humans ask a question they do not want answered.

"These ships not being Daldath!" said Defoe. I looked at the sensor display. I knew what the ships were right away when

I saw them. It made me have a very bad feeling, because the things I saw on the display were the Vorticella.

"Oh, you've gotta be kidding me," said Elyse when she looked at the display. "Do these things ever stop?"

If I spoke like humans do, I would have said the same thing.

"They can't be here for us," said Elyse, then she said it again because she must have thought someone did not hear. "They *can't* be here for us!"

The bridge monitor changed and the Vorticella ships appeared. It must have been Delta who put them there from her station. "Oh, come on!" she said as she strapped into the captain's chair.

Elyse quickly put Riley, the blue Slarb, and the pink Gralb in the bridge kennel. "Defoe, what did you *do* to these guys that they won't stop chasing us?"

The bridge monitor changed, and the Vorticella appeared again. They spoke in the same way they did before as their eyestalk bodies moved up and down.

"We have found you!"

"We have chased you across the stars!"

"You must realize you cannot escape us."

"Turn over the Blepharisma!"

"Or face a glorious eradication."

Delta looked back at Defoe with her same angry face. "Defoe, seriously, *what* did you do to them?"

Elyse spoke, too, but I think she was talking to herself. "This could not happen at a worse possible time." I agreed with her assessment.

"I not doing anything bad!" said Defoe as he moved his tentacle thing back and forth. A few times it hit me, but I did not care. "I only finding information from them!"

"What kind of information?" Delta asked.

"I knowing the location of their secret base."

When Defoe said it, I understood why the Vorticella were

after him. Pirate species all have secret base locations that they do not want others to know because they may destroy them. The Vorticella were probably trying to kill Defoe before he told someone powerful where they lived. I think that Delta and Elyse thought the same thing, because they did the thing where their mouths get open but they do not say anything.

The Vorticella spoke again. "Stole from us, this creature did!"

"His knowledge must perish with him."

"Turn him over, pink-skins."

"We will destroy you if you do not."

I did not know what Delta would do. One thing I did know, though, was why she was angry that I knocked out Thule. If we got into a fight with the Vorticella, I think Thule would have given us a better chance to survive than with Delta as captain. Knocking out Thule was a bad choice.

Delta looked at the Vorticella again. "What can we offer you to leave us alone? There must be something we can provide!"

"You may provide the Blepharisma."

"For immediate execution!"

"We will give you ten seconds."

"While our vaporizers charge!"

I looked at Delta to see what she would do. Aurora has been in many hard situations before and she always knows the right way to handle them. But this was the first time that Delta was ever in a situation like this. Also, she was alone, which made it double bad. Everything in the bridge got quiet. I began to count the seconds. Every few of them that I counted in my head, I heard Elyse say, "Delta...*Delta*..." But Delta did not move. I predicted that she was in shock because she was only sixteen years old and not used to these situations. I predicted that she was frozen in fear.

My prediction was incorrect.

When there were only two seconds left, Delta made her

body sit very upright in the captain's chair. Humans do this when they want to look stronger than they actually are. They call it confidence. She wiped her hair back and out of her face and then spoke. "You think you're so tough, Vorticella? How would you like to put that toughness to the test?"

I did not know what she was doing, and neither did Elyse. I knew that because Elyse said quietly, "Delta, what are you *doing?*"

The Vorticella spoke. "We are eager to hear—"

"—of your suggestion, puny human!"

"How do you wish to test—"

"—the might of the Vorticella?"

Delta said to them, "We will fight you. If you destroy us, then you won't have to worry about the Blepharisma ever again. But if we defeat you and you are forced to retreat, you will *never* again seek out Defoe *or* this ship!"

I thought this was a bad idea.

"*Delta!*" said Elyse.

The Vorticella answered quickly. "We accept your challenge—"

"—oh noble and courageous warrior!"

"Yours shall be a most glorious epitaph—"

"—written among the stars!"

"Our vaporizers are charged."

"Our screens are at full strength."

"We detect that your battle systems are ready."

"Let us begin."

The Vorticellas' words were correct. All of their battle systems were operational. From behind me, Elyse shouted, "Delta, we can't take on the Vorticella by ourselves! There's no way we—"

Delta turned her head back very fast and looked at Elyse. "*Not* what I need right now!"

I looked at Elyse. Her mouth was open and her eyes were wide, like humans do when they get scared. For one second, she did not say anything. Then her mouth closed, and she nodded her head. "Okay. Okay!" Her voice changed. I believe she was trying to have confidence. "All right, if we're gonna do this, let's do this! You got it, sis!"

Delta spun back around in the captain's chair. She grabbed the armrests very tightly. "Give me full power to forward screens, now!"

"I counting twenty-one Vorticella fighters!" said Defoe. "They being in three squadrons of seven!" I did not look at the display to see if he was correct. "They being firing!"

"Call the Royal Armada for help! It's right there!" said Elyse.

Delta answered her, "No! If we don't do it ourselves, they'll *never* leave us alone." I believed that her prediction was correct.

"Human creator!" I said loudly. "Delta is a bad pilot. Make her good!"

Delta pushed forward on the joysticks very hard. "Everyone, hold on!"

"What are you thinking?" asked Elyse.

"Everyone…" Delta said again, *"hold on!"*

I held on with my good hand. Behind me, Elyse said, *"I'd sure love it if I knew what you were thinking!"*

For almost one second, Delta was quiet. Then she said, "I'm going to try and ram them."

The human creator heard me!

"What?" said Elyse very loudly.

"I'm giving them something they don't expect! Breaking them out of formation. Hank-is-Handy, put Defoe on weapons!" Delta said. "You take over sensors!"

I did not know why she wanted me and Defoe to switch, but we did. It was easy because we were at the same console station.

"Defoe," Delta said, "do not miss!" The *Illustré* got very fast. The Vorticella fired, but most of their shots missed. Delta turned the nose of the *Illustré* toward the first of the three squadrons of fighters, then went fast to ram them. The fighters broke out of formation so they would not get hit, just like Delta said they would. The next thing that Delta did was very fast. She made the *Illustré* spin so that plasma cannon on top of it would be aiming at the fighters that she had tried to ram and that had broken out of formation. "Elyse, full screens to the underbelly! Defoe, fire *now*!"

I did not look to see what Elyse was doing, but I heard her hands hitting the controls very fast. Next to me, Defoe fired the plasma cannon. I did not think he would hit the Vorticella fighters because they are very hard to hit, but I was wrong. When the squadron she had tried to ram tried to reform, Defoe blew up three of them. The other four that were left went in four different directions.

"Divert all power from the spindrive to screens—switch them to the topside!" said Delta. Elyse did it, and I saw the screens increase to two hundred percent. "Defoe, don't stop firing!" Delta made the *Illustré* spin again so that the plasma cannon was facing the other side, where the second of the three squadrons was attacking. Their shots hit the *Illustré* but they did not penetrate the screens. Defoe fired at the fighters and hit three of them before the others dispersed. The four that were left went streaking past us. Delta turned the *Illustré* to follow them. Defoe fired, and two more fighters got dead. The last two in that squadron broke off on their own. "Elyse, launch Castor and Pollux! Make them track the two remaining fighters from that grouping!"

"Castor and Pollux launching!" Elyse said.

The third squadron of Vorticella fighters was approaching, and the ships in it began to shoot at us. The *Illustré* shook as some of the shots hit the screens. I heard Elyse's hands hitting her console station hard again.

"Screens down to..." She laughed very loudly—I do not know why. "One hundred and seventy percent!"

Delta tried to do the same thing that she did with the other two squadrons where she made the *Illustré* fly toward them like it was going to ram them, but the Vorticella fighters broke away before she could do it. "These guys aren't falling for it!" she said. "We'll have to beat them the old-fashioned way! Disperse screens equally across the whole of the ship!" She turned the joystick to make the *Illustré* follow the third squadron. All the while that she followed them, Defoe fired the plasma cannon.

The Vorticella fighters were now swarming around the *Illustré* much like they did when we fought them the first time and almost died. The ship was shaking a lot because it was getting hit a lot.

"Screens are dropping *fast*!" said Elyse. As she said it, Defoe hit one of the fighters in the third squadron and it blew up. Then he blew another one up.

"Hank-is-Handy, what are you seeing?" asked Delta.

I looked down at the sensor console. "Eleven fighters remain!" On the corners of the bridge monitor were the cameras for Castor and Pollux. Both of the strike craft were pursuing the two fighters that were left from the second squadron. Castor began shooting at the fighter in front of it.

"C'mon, Castor!" said Delta very loud. "*C'mon, Castor!*" The Vorticella fighter got hit. Two and a half seconds later, it blew up. Delta performed the thing that humans call a fist pump. "*Yeah!*" Castor rerouted itself because it had no target. On the display, we saw it aim for the fighter that Pollux was now shooting at but not hitting. Castor flew past it on an intercept course and fired while the fighter was dodging Pollux. The Vorticella fighter got hit, and it blew up, too. There were now only nine fighters left. They formed together in a single squadron behind us and began to pursue.

"Where do you want the twins?" Elyse asked.

Delta answered very fast. "Bring them around! Put them behind the enemy formation, then command them to auto-engage!"

The voice Elyse used did not sound confident. "You really think the Vorticella will just let the twins pick them off?"

"They will for a little while! Put all screen strength to the rear of the *Illustré*!" I watched as Delta pulled back on the throttle, which made the *Illustré* slow down a lot. "Fire at will, Defoe! I'm bringing them in closer."

"I firing!" Defoe began to shoot the plasma cannon behind us at the Vorticella in pursuit. At the same time, the Vorticella shot at the *Illustré*. On the sensor, I saw Castor and Pollux pull in behind the Vorticella. The *Illustré* began to get hit a lot. Delta did not try to dodge any of them. The whole ship shook, but only the screens took damage.

"Come on, twins, *do some damage*!" said Delta.

The same time that she said it, both strike craft hit Vorticella fighters. Defoe hit one, too. That meant there were only six left. All of the ships engaged in the battle shot lots and lots. The Vorticella fighters shot at the *Illustré*. Castor and Pollux shot at the Vorticella fighters. The *Illustré* shot at the Vorticella fighters, too. Every time a Vorticella fighter got dead, the screens dropped at a slower rate. Defoe hit another ship. Pollux hit two ships. There were only three fighters left.

"Screens holding!" said Elyse. She laughed again for a reason I did not understand. "Holy zin, Delta, you're going to do it!"

The last three Vorticella fighters broke off from their formation. Two went up and one went down relative to the *Illustré*. Castor and Pollux followed the two that went up. Delta rotated the *Illustré* so that the plasma cannon could shoot at the one that went down. Defoe shot at the ship that was going down and it got dead. Delta stood up from her chair and looked back at us behind her. "Order the twins to disengage weapons! Defoe, hold your fire!"

Elyse spoke next. When she did, she sounded surprised. "Uhh—what? Why?"

"Just do it!" Delta said back. She moved quickly from the

captain's chair to the communication station, where Thule was. She pushed him out of the way, which she could do because he was not conscious. I do not know how to work the communication station, but I believed that I knew what Delta was doing. I believed she was hailing the Vorticella. I was correct. "This is Captain Delta Bluewater of the *Illustré*! We have destroyed your pirate fleet and we have the rest of you in our sights! On my command, you will *all* be destroyed. You are beaten! Honor the agreement and leave us alone!"

The whole while that Delta spoke, I watched her body. It was moving up and down a lot, which is something humans do when their bodies require more oxygen than normal. It is associated with a human thing called *adrenaline*, which turns on when humans are fighting to survive. Vorck do not understand adrenaline, because we fight to survive all the time. If I had adrenaline, I would never turn it off.

I did not know if the Vorticella would answer her. Every time we spoke with them in the past, they talked like they did not care if they lived or died. They seemed to like combat a lot even if it meant they might be killed in it. But I also knew that if the Vorticella were all dead, then none of them would survive to tell the other Vorticella in the cluster not to chase the *Illustré*. So it would not be cowardice for the Vorticella to stop fighting and answer her. It would be acknowledging defeat and honoring the agreement. I predicted that they would do it.

My prediction was correct.

The two Vorticella that were left appeared on monitor, and they began to talk, one after the other. "Oh powerful captain!"

"We the Vorticella abase ourselves before your might."

"We beg permission to serve you!"

"Your potency in battle is recognized."

"You must continually enforce your will!"

"Go forth—"

"—and explode all challengers to your preeminence!"

Delta sat back down in the captain's chair to look at them. She put both hands on her head and pushed back her hair, which was still sticky with Defoe's plant slime, but not as much as it was before. She then did the thing that humans do when they think they are in a strong position and they cock their head to the side. "You are worthy adversaries, noble Vorticella. Depart from us at once and tell all of your brethren in this cluster never to cross our paths in hostility again."

The Vorticella spoke. "There is, of course—"

"—the matter of the Blepharisma—"

"—and the location of our secret base."

"If we may be so bold—"

"—as to ask you not to disclose it."

"You would have our endless gratitude."

Delta reached up with one hand to touch her chin. "I thought only the threat of vaporization made one's existence meaningful?"

For six seconds, the Vorticella got quiet. Then one of them spoke. "You, of course, are correct."

She cocked her head to the other side. "Fear not, noble pirate. I will not disclose the location of your secret base, nor will Defoe. Though we may visit you from time to time if we require your...assistance."

"We are honored to serve!"

"You need only tell us of your request."

"The noble Vorticella will be there to assist you!"

Delta lifted her chin. "Be gone now, pirate. May you remember this day well." She pressed a button, and the monitor went black.

I looked at the sensors. The Vorticella fighters were going away, so I said, "The Vorticella fighters are going away."

"*Ugh!*" Delta's body got limp and she flopped down on the chair. Then she slid out of it to the floor. I believe that if Aurora had been there to see it, she would have called it *dramatic*.

Behind me, Elyse got loud and high-pitched. "Delta!" I looked back. Elyse was running away from her console toward Delta. "That was *incredible*!" Elyse seemed happy, so I predicted that Delta would be happy, too. But she was not happy. She tucked her knees into her chest and did the thing humans do when they cry. Elyse put her arms around Delta and performed a human-to-human hug. "Delta, I don't know how you did it. I don't know how you did it."

I also did not know how Delta did it. The only explanation I had was that the human creator heard my request. I turned my head to look for him, but I did not see him. Perhaps he was hiding in Aurora's room where he could hear the bridge. I do not know.

Delta sucked in a sniff breath and looked up at Elyse. "Castor and Pollux?"

"I've already got them docking." I watched her wipe away water that was coming from Delta's eyes. "Sister, everything's fine. Everything is fine. You saved us." When she said it, Delta cried harder. Elyse performed her human-to-human hug again.

There are many things that I did not understand about what happened. I did not understand how Delta became a good pilot and tried to ram the Vorticella fighters. I did not understand why she made Defoe use the weapons, and I did not understand why he was good at shooting. I did not understand why Thule tried to take over the ship. I thought he was a friend. In fact, there was only one thing that I understood. I understood that I did not do anything. All I did was get a broken back, get a broken arm, and let Defoe do my job with the weapons. I believed that what had just happened was very important, and in a very important moment, I was not handy. I thought this was a problem, because my name was Hank-is-Handy. The feelings I was feeling were the bad ones again.

Delta said, "We need to contact Aunt Aurora! We must tell

her what has happened. Our first message to her may not have been clear."

"We'll contact her," Elyse said as she performed a head nod. "We'll do it right now." Delta got up from the floor very slowly and turned to the communications console, but Elyse put her hand on her shoulder. "Hey—I've got it." I saw her give Delta a smile. "I'm not afraid to work comms. Besides... you already have a chair." I saw them look at each other again. The smile that Elyse had got bigger. Then I saw Delta smile a little bit, too. They nodded their heads, then Elyse went to the communications console, where Thule was still unconscious. She looked at me. "Hank-is-Handy, can you drag Thule to his quarters with one arm?"

They did not know that I had a broken back, too, but I did not tell them, even though I heard it break a lot during the battle. I did not want them to think I was not handy. I did not know if I could carry Thule with a broken back and one arm, but I said, "Yes," because I wanted to be handy again very badly. I did not want Defoe to be more handy than me. But I did not hate Defoe. I unstrapped from my console and walked over to Thule, who fell to the floor when Elyse unstrapped him. I grabbed him by a foot with my good arm and began to drag him out of the bridge. I felt my back break more as I walked, but I did not say anything. When I was almost out of the bridge, I heard Delta speak to me.

"Hank-is-Handy?"

I turned around.

"Thank you," she said, "for holding me when Thule was flying the ship. You saved my life."

I had forgotten that I held onto her. It was why one of my arms was broken and why my back was broken very bad. "I did not want you to die."

"I know," she said. Then she did a smile. "I love you, too."

They were not words that I expected Delta to speak. I did not know what to make of them, because one says, "I love you, too," only when someone else has first said, "I love you." But I did not say those words. I did not know what to think, so I looked at Elyse. She was looking at me. I saw one side of her mouth smile a little, and she performed a single head nod to me. Humans do this when they seek to acknowledge something that is mutually known without actually saying it. I thought hard about what she meant by it.

Then I remembered.

Love is what you do. It's being there for someone, it's never giving up on them. It's holding them in their worst moment to make sure they're okay.

They were not my words. They were Elyse's to me before the Daldath arrived. During the small Daldath battle, I held onto Delta before Thule took evasive action that would have hurt her. I think if I had not, it would have made her dead, which might have been her worst moment. So I held onto Delta in her worst moment to make sure she was okay. It was what I did. I realized in that moment that I loved Delta like I loved Elyse. Now I knew why Delta said it back to me.

The good feelings came back.

I thought a lot while I dragged Thule to his room. There is much I do not know as a Vorck. But I am learning. I have felt the bad feelings of love, and I have felt the good feelings of it, too. I think I was wrong when I thought the bad feelings were stronger. I had never seen Delta look at me like she did when she thanked me. I wanted to see her look at me like that again. It made me feel like a good Vorck.

I hope to someday learn all of the good feelings that humans feel. I know I still have much learning to do. But I believe I am on a good path.

When I got to Thule's room, I stopped dragging him when I reached his bed. This is where I was going to leave him while I locked him in his room. When I looked down at him, I was surprised to see that his eyes were open and he was looking up at me. His eyes were very shiny, and I liked them very much.

looking up at me. His eyes were very shiny, and I liked them very much.

Chapter Fifteen

THIS WAS NOT where we were supposed to be. It was not how everything was supposed to have gone. Yet as I stood behind Aurora as it paced behind the podium, offering the cacophonous crowd of Dacian and Broodmaster delegates a rare glimpse of the visible uncertainty that permeated its flesh, all I could think was that we truly *were* on the front lines of an event the magnitude of which would be discussed for millennia.

We had received the frantic call from Delta while in the midst of hearing another proposal. We could scarcely believe the words that it spoke. Not only had the Daldath entered the system earlier than we'd expected, but they'd amassed an armada the likes of which the galaxy had never seen from them! For a situation rife with horrible turns of events, the timing of this one made it quite possibly the worst of all. Delta's words, as static-filled and frantic as they may have been, were soon validated by both the Dacians and the Broodmasters. Ten minutes—that was all the time the Daldath were giving the Dacian, Broodmaster, and human fleets to part for their arrival at Gryamore V. If a parting did not come, then they would attack.

That was six minutes ago.

"Please!" Aurora pleaded with the delegates yet again. "We *must* set aside these differences for the sake of what's at hand! The talks can resume afterward. We must work in harmony or countless lives will be lost!"

From the moment the Dacians and Broodmasters heard word of the time limit the Daldath had laid down, they began posturing to gain an advantage. There would be no harmony between the two sides—that much was certain. The Dacians wished for a battle. They proposed that whatever fleet survived to defeat the Daldath could lay claim to the planet. On the surface, such a notion may have sounded fair, except there is nothing fair about allowing another species to take the brunt of the damage before stepping in to mop up after them. Dacians are known opportunists. It is easy to imagine their nimble fighters avoiding conflict until the Broodmasters' forces were ravaged by the Daldath warships.

The Broodmasters, of course, were no nobler, and were stuck on their notion of a so-called "Freedom Alliance" between themselves and the Dacians. They would agree to nothing— not even defending the world alongside the Dacians—unless the alliance was endorsed by Aurora. Everywhere poor Aurora looked, there was posturing and bluster. Pleading desperately for civility, my flustered captain's words fell on repulsive, deaf ears.

Three minutes now remained. Abandoning the microphone, it turned to me. "What shall I do? Neither side listens! Both are determined to use this crisis to their advantage. Do they not realize that by doing so, they are punishing *themselves*?"

Its communicator chimed. It was Commander Rigel of the Royal Armada's flagship. The commander's had been a constant voice in Aurora's ears after Delta's message. "Ambassador, please advise us if you've reached an agreement! If we step in to combat the Daldath without the help of the Broodmasters and Dacians, our forces will be eviscerated."

"I need more time," said Aurora desperately.

"We have no more time, ambassador!"

Two minutes remained.

Closing the channel, Aurora turned to face me. "I must decide. Whichever side I choose, the other will certainly not assist militarily. They may even step out of the fight to allow the Daldath to take the planet out of spite! Whichever side I choose, there will be so much loss of life!"

I had no solution to the problem. All I had to offer were my own useless commentaries. "How ironic that the Daldath are the only ones offering a solution without bloodshed! Granted, that solution is for all others to abandon the planet, but the fact still remains."

It was right then, in that moment after I'd said the words, that Aurora stopped pacing. Slowly, it turned its head to me. Its eyes locked onto me.

I have been around humans long enough to recognize epiphanies—the sudden bursts of inspiration that make them seem so scrappy and ingenious. I realized instantly that I had triggered such a moment. It took but an instant more to realize why. Covering my crystalline chest with my one hand, I stepped back from it. "Aurora, no! You *cannot*!"

But it would. Even then, I knew it. I saw that determination in its eyes. Without a word, it stepped away from me and turned for the podium. In the midst of the shouting between delegates, it spoke with authority. "I have made my choice!"

One minute remained. Less than one minute! The auditorium fell silent as all eyes—even the vestigial ones—turned to it.

"I, Aurora Ultraviolet, arbiter of the planetary dispute surrounding the planet Gryamore V in the Lernaean Cluster, hereby bestow rightful ownership of said planet to…"

It was coming. Even as I could not imagine the words being spoken, so I heard them.

"…to the Daldath."

Aghast! The collective gasp—the collective pulse of stunned telepathic energy—permeated the chamber. Before any could speak, it picked up its gavel.

"By the prior agreeance of all parties involved, my word is binding, my word is final. This negotiation is closed." As it slammed the gavel down, the uproar began. But it did not hear it. Turning around as quickly as possible, it raised its communicator and spoke to Commander Rigel. "Commander, hail the Daldath! Tell them to hold their attack, that we've reached an agreement. I will be boarding my ship shortly to discuss it!" Even as the commander acknowledged, Aurora began running for the exit. "Hurry, Velistris!"

"My captain, what have you done?" I asked. "You cannot award the planet to a species that isn't part of the negotiation!"

"I can and I have! There is nothing in the stipulations that says I *must* choose the Dacians or Broodmasters. It simply says that whatever decision I make regarding ownership of Gryamore V, it must be respected."

"But the assumption is clear! This was a negotiation between two species!"

"And I awarded it to a third!" It stopped to face me. "What are we, Velistris, but two broken women trying to make the universe right? We have our misgivings about the Daldath, and rightfully so. But if there is anything I have learned as of late, it is that I am not immune to misgivings myself. I believe you would say the same."

I would've.

"We have talked much of the value of faith—I believe it is time to extend faith to the Daldath. That story of the mustard seed, that parable, is about God doing the impossible. I can think of no more impossible task than using the Daldath as harbingers of peace. Neither the Dacians nor Broodmasters offer any hope of that. Only one species has made peace an option, as you yourself have said. We must trust that your wisdom was providential."

I knew not what to say. "But—"

"We must trust!" With those words, it turned around again. "We must also hurry! I fear we shall not be liked, here."

With that, I wholeheartedly concurred. As fast as my delicate legs could carry me, I followed my captain to our assigned transport.

As we entered it, Commander Rigel's voice boomed over the cabin speaker. "By God, Ultraviolet, what have you done?"

"I assume, then, you've heard," Aurora said.

The commander was unamused. "We will never be trusted to handle a negotiation again! The Dacian and Broodmaster embassies are fuming. This is sheer chaos!"

"Did you hail the Daldath?" Aurora strapped into its seat in the transport's cabin—it and I its only two passengers.

"The Daldath controller is on the channel, waiting to hear from you," Rigel said.

Aurora looked at the monitor at the cabin's front. "Put him through to the transport!"

Seconds later, the display flickered to life. There, before us both, the disgusting Daldath appeared.

The abomination. The scourge! There is nothing—no species, real or in mythos—that I despise more. For destroying the planet I called home, I shall never forgive them. For their twisted forms alone, I could never condone their existence. They are wretched and vile. Aurora once had a saying that I myself championed with it: Death to the Daldath. Yet it was not death that we were offering the Daldath now. It was faith. It was trust. I felt nothing but self-loathing, for it was my errant verbiage that prompted this terrible turn of events. What had I done? What had Aurora done? I found no words within me horrible enough to describe it.

"Daldath controller," Aurora said, its voice laced with urgency, "as arbiter of the negotiations concerning the rights of ownership to Gryamore V, I have bestowed said ownership to you. None will attack you, lest they incur the wrath of all those who adhere to galactic civility. Please, call off your warships!"

Its mechanical voice resonated through the speakers. Oh, the chill its dreadful words sent through my core! "Threatening presence detected around: Gryamore System Planet Five. Unable to call off warships at this time."

"But you must not fire first!" Aurora said. "If you are fired upon, then no one will blame you. Your attacker will be in violation of the agreement. Promise me, controller, *promise* me that you will not attack! I have entrusted ownership of this planet to you. All I ask is that you trust me in return."

"Our arrival at this system was deemed undesirable by: native species to system."

"And it will continue to be undesirable…but they *will not* fire. If they do, they will face not only yourselves, but the might of all civilized species in this cluster for breaching their agreement! You must trust me, *please.* Call off your warships and the planet is yours!"

I watched as its four compound eyes, one of which was aided by some sort of augmented device, surveyed Aurora from the monitor. Several seconds passed before it spoke again. "Human aid to Daldath Planet Smasher: unexpected. Why have you assisted us?"

It was a question I myself did not know the answer to. I could never have brought myself to aid the Daldath—not in a thousand lifetimes. It was a sentiment I thought Aurora and I shared. Yet I did not feel anger at it. I felt nothing at all.

It took Aurora some time to reply. All the while, I saw a strange mix in its eyes—one of both disillusion and inspiration. As if the latter was overtaking the former before my very receptors. "I don't know," it finally said, exhaling in exhaustion. "Perhaps the same old thing can only work for so long. Perhaps for there to be any progress, there must first be change. Or perhaps I am simply…" It shook its head and, briefly, looked down. As I observed its gaze become momentarily lost, I realized that it was not solely speaking to the Daldath. Its words were also for itself. "Perhaps I have not trusted enough. Perhaps I am too guarded, too cautious. Perhaps I have been unready to put my life in the care of someone else." It spoke of its fiancé. "Perhaps it is I who must trust. I choose to trust you now—to extend to you faith that maybe…that maybe you don't deserve. That maybe no one does." At long last, it turned its eyes to the Daldath again.

"Take this world, controller. I give it freely to you. There will be no battle, there will be no loss of life. Under no other scenario could I have accomplished that. In return, I only ask of you this: that you might never again take a world that belongs to another. That when you pass the many inhabited systems in this cluster, you might truly pass them. There are so many untouched stars. Seek those out. Make them yours. Reduce them to husks, it matters not. Just do not make me regret this decision by cementing your status as the scourge of the stars."

What would it say? I found myself feeling what humans refer to as *pins and needles*, a reference I do not understand physically but a sentiment I have witnessed many times in moments of urgent uncertainty. Would the Daldath accept its proposal? Would it call off its warships and take the planet that was freely given to it? Would it promise to leave inhabited systems alone? No one had ever attempted to negotiate with a Daldath. The only responses that ever worked were either to fight, agree to its own lopsided proposals, or get out of the way. For it to change ways that had been untouched for eons...I saw no reason for that to occur. And so I did something in that moment that I had never done before. I belied all reason. I believed in spite of. Reaching out with my remaining hand, I took hold of Aurora's, as Delta had reached out to take mine. Very gently, I squeezed.

Faith. That seed-sized faith that my captain had spoken so passionately of. I dimmed my receptors and summoned it.

This would work. This would be our miracle. This would be our solution for Gryamore V. The Daldath would accept the proposal. It would take heed and listen. In the midst of all the outrage and all the anger and all the hatred that was being thrust Aurora's way from the Dacians, Broodmasters, and dare I say, some humans, there would sprout peace. It would work. It had to. And it would. When the Daldath spoke its words, the suddenness of it made it almost imperceivable.

"I have assessed your proposal as: beneficial to Daldath and species: native to this system."

I reopened my receptors. I felt Aurora exhale.

Then the Daldath continued. "Additional request to circumvent owned planetary systems deemed: impossible. Minerals required for survival of Daldath species. It is impossible to predict what or when minerals will be required." The bottom fell out of us both, until onward it went. "I offer a counter solution. We need worlds to mine. You can find such worlds. You will search for us. We will pay you well. We will avoid extinction, you will avoid bloodshed. Do you accept?"

"Yes!" Aurora proclaimed. "A thousand times, yes! If you need a world, seek me out. I will help you find one!"

"We give thanks to you. You will help us much. You are a friend to the Daldath."

I could scarcely believe my receptors! A friend to the Daldath? Never in my most vivid of imaginings would I have conceived it! Yet there this entity was before me, its compound eyes staring at Aurora and me as it accepted our terms. As it agreed to seek us out for direction. As it erred on the side of peace.

There would, of course, be unforeseen ramifications to this. How often would the Daldath require us? Was this burden one we were capable of bearing? Were we now at its beck and call?

What would happen if we failed it?

They were questions for another moment. In *this* moment, the imminent threat of war had been mitigated. I do not know what prompted the Daldath to listen. If it was a god, a matter of statistics, or an as-of-yet-undiscovered principle of fate. I only know that in the moment that Aurora and I gave way to faith, the impossible occurred. I cannot explain it. I can scarcely comprehend it. Yet I cannot deny it. I was at a loss when I heard Aurora choose the Daldath to possess Gryamore V. I had thought it frazzled beyond rational comprehension. Yet I realize now that it followed a guidance that I knew nothing of—that had nothing to do with beauty or perfection, but belief. It believed in something. Perhaps now it was my turn.

As the Daldath disappeared and the display faded to black, Aurora and I sat in silence. No words seemed appropriate. None could explain the feeling we shared. What a tremendous and wonderful feeling it was.

Aurora and I said nothing on the way back to the repair freighter from which we'd left. The captain only collapsed sideways against me, lowering its head as I felt the full weight of its relief. As its burdens released, one by one. Lifting my arm, I placed it around my captain's shoulders—another human gesture, but one that in that moment felt right. That in that moment, felt so incredibly warm. I felt inseparable from it. I felt akin to it. I felt taught by it.

How foolish I'd been to ever think it my pupil.

Chapter Sixteen

I DO NOT LIKE sickbay. That is because Vorck do not like to be hurt. I did not think I was hurt bad, but after the battle with the Vorticella, Delta and Elyse decided that I needed to be brought to a medical ship because of my broken arm. I did not agree, but they did not give me a choice. After the battle was over, they took the *Illustré* to a human medical ship.

Many things happened between defeating the Vorticella and docking at the medical ship. The biggest thing that happened was that Aurora gave the planet that the Dacians and Broodmasters were fighting over to the Daldath. This is something I did not predict. But I think it is a good idea. This is because now the Dacians and the Broodmasters will have the same number of planets in the Gryamore System and they will have to get along. Or maybe they will fight each other anyway. Whatever they do, it does not matter to me.

I think it is good that the Daldath did not destroy any ships. Many people do not think that the Daldath are a good species, but I do not hate them like many others do. They are doing what they must to survive, just like all species in the universe do what they must to survive. Sometimes a thing that one species must do to survive is a thing that will hurt other species. In this case, I think the two species should fight and whatever species is strongest should get their way. This is how the concept that humans call *natural selection* works. Humans like to talk about natural selection a lot, but they do not like it when nature selects a species other than them.

I am glad that the negotiation is over, even if it made

everyone mad. It will be good to do other things in space besides talk to the Dacians and the Broodmasters. Maybe we can go find a broken ship and I can fix it. That would make me happy, I think.

But right now I am not happy, because I am in a hospital bed on a medical ship. It is a bad place for a Vorck to be. I got to talk to Delta and Elyse for a little while before they did a thing to me called *surgery*. Vorcks do not like surgery, but Delta made me do it. I would have liked it better if I could have just healed. But Delta found out that I had a broken back in several places and did not give me a choice. She was very angry that I had a broken back and did not tell her. So I had to have surgery. Many species go to sleep during surgery, but Vorcks do not. The surgeons worked on me for many, many hours. Most of the time, I was bored, but sometimes I hurt a little, especially when they did things on my spine. But then I got bored again. I tried to talk to pass the time, mostly about things I liked to fix or my favorite lifeforms to kill in combat, but the surgeons said I needed to be quiet, so I got quiet. I was very glad when the surgery was done and they brought me to my own room. Then I could talk as much as I wanted about the things that I liked. But they left because they needed to speak to Aurora. So mostly, I just thought.

Before the surgery, I asked Delta why she made Defoe use the weapons, and she told me that it was because of a prediction that she had. She predicted that because he is able to read minds when he puts a lifeform in his plant mouth, and because he had read a Vorticella's mind once, that maybe he would have knowledge about how they moved in combat. I think that her prediction was very good. I do not know if it was correct, but Defoe was able to shoot a lot of Vorticella, so maybe it was. Or maybe he just did better than I would have because I only had one arm that worked. I do not know.

I am glad that Defoe was able to do something useful on the *Illustré*, like blow up the Vorticella with the plasma cannon. It made me think of him differently. I like things that do useful things. I like my phase hammer because it does a useful thing, like fix components in the engine room and kill bad lifeforms in combat. Now I like Defoe, too. I am not angry that he is Elyse's friend anymore. Maybe I will be his friend, too.

I am glad that Thule was with us during the battle. When I brought him to his room, he told me that he was an important part of the victory and that I was mistaken in thinking that he tried to take over the ship. I think he was right about both things. He thought it would be a good idea to bring Delta, Elyse, and Defoe to his room one at a time to tell them the same thing, and I thought that was a good idea, too. After they talked to Thule, they agreed with everything that he said like I did. It is good to agree with everyone else, except when everyone else is wrong. But I am glad that we agree about Thule. He said that there was no need to tell Aurora about what happened. We agreed with that, too. So I thought about Thule a lot while I was in my recovery bed.

But mostly what I thought about was Elyse. I thought a lot about the conversation we had before the Vorticella attacked and how she told me without words after the attack that I loved Delta. I think it made me think about love in a very different way than I did before.

I do not think love is as much of a feeling as I thought it was. I did not feel anything when I grabbed Delta to stop her from getting dead. I did it because it was a good thing to do for her. It was a choice that I made for Delta.

That is what makes me think that maybe love is different than a feeling. I think that I have been trying to feel good feelings about love to understand it, but now I think that maybe love is in the things that you do to make someone else's life better, and it is these things that cause the good feelings. It was not until after I saved Delta from getting dead that I felt good feelings. The choice to do a good thing made me have good feelings. There are many times when this has happened for me. I felt good feelings after I gave Elyse the list of things she was not good at. I do not think getting the list made her have good feelings, but I had them because I was doing something good for her. I think the act of doing something good for someone is making the choice to love. With this new variable, I can calculate many times when I have loved someone else on the *Illustré*. I think that there may have even been times when I have accidentally loved Velistris, even though I hate her. It is a little bit confusing, but I think I am starting to understand it.

I was still thinking about these things when someone made a knock sound on the door. The door opened and Aurora came inside. When she saw me, she did a smile that looked a little bit sad. She closed the door behind her, then she said to me, "Hi, Hank-is-Handy."

It is customary to stand up when the captain is present, but I had many tubes and other things attached to my body as well as a full-body brace, so instead I said, "I am standing up in my head."

Aurora made another smile. "That's okay." Her voice was very quiet and soft. She walked up to my bed and pulled a chair up next to it. "How are you feeling?" It looked like it was hard for her to talk, but I did not know why.

"I am feeling very good," I said, because I was not feeling bad. "I do not like this bed."

I think what I said was funny because it made her laugh. "Yeah, I bet you don't." She reached out her hand and put it on my arm, then she squeezed it. It is a thing humans do to relay a thing they call *compassion*. I do not know what compassion is because I have never felt it. "Oh, Hank-is-Handy."

Sometimes humans say a lifeform's name when they have feelings for them. That is something else I do not feel, but I understand that sometimes humans do it, so I did not say anything. I predicted that she would talk again soon after she said it. My prediction was correct.

"Thank you for saving Delta's life."

"I love Delta," I said.

What I said made her smile get big. But it still looked a little bit sad. "I know."

"I also love you."

"I know."

"I also love Velistris sometimes when I hate her."

She performed a pat on my arm. "I know, Hank-is-Handy. I know you do."

It made me glad that she knew. Humans like lifeforms that love a lot.

"I'm sorry that I haven't been particularly loving, lately," she said.

It was okay, so I said, "It is okay. I know that you love Hank-is-Handy."

She did the thing with her face that humans do when they look happy and sad at the same time. "I do. I do, so very much." Her eyes got wet a little. "You have done so much for us, and you've asked nothing in return. I know you may not understand the significance of that, but it is of vast, vast significance. The love you have given us…is the greatest love there is to give."

To hear her say that surprised me. I did not think I was loving because I was not good at knowing what love was until now. It gave me a funny feeling to hear her say it. "Am I a good Vorck?" I got in trouble a lot lately, so I wanted to ask her. I do not know why, but the question made her eyes get more wet and they leaked out.

"Hank-is-Handy, you are the best." Aurora stood up from the chair and got close to me. She leaned her head close to mine and kissed me on the forehead. She put her forehead on mine and put her hand on my cheek. "Thank you for always giving us your best. For loving us even when we don't deserve it, even if you never knew you were doing it at all. And for being so incredibly…incredibly handy."

The good feelings came again.

"We will always be with you. I want you to know that. I want you to hear me say it. The *Illustré* will not leave this station until you are back on it."

That made me glad. I did not want them to leave without me. It was a good thing to know.

"Just promise me one thing, Hank-is-Handy," she said.

Some humans do not like to make promises, but I do not mind them. It shows that you can be trusted. I did not say anything because it sounded like she would continue speaking. I was correct.

"Let us hold you, as you have held us."

I did not think they would be able to hold me because they are weak humans, but if it made them happy to try, I would let them. "I promise," I said.

"Thank you, dear friend," Aurora said to me. "Thank you so much." For a little while, she did not say anything. Then she stood up and said, "I'm going to get the two girls. They both wanted to come in." She walked to the door and opened it to get them.

I think that sometimes I do not always understand things that are going on that humans understand, even though I try very hard. I did not understand why Aurora wanted me to promise that I would let people hold me. Usually I promise to fix things in certain time frames or to fix some things before I fix other things. I also did not understand why Elyse and Delta's eyes were wet like Aurora's when they came into my room. I know that humans get tears when they feel a lot of feelings. Sometimes the feelings are good and sometimes they are bad. Sometimes, I think they are both. The first thing Elyse and Delta did when they came in was hug me, and hugs are good, so I think that their tears were good, too. That made me glad. I saw Velistris by the door, but she did not have tears because she is a weak and breakable rock. Velistris looked at me but she did not come in.

Elyse lifted her head to look at me, then her eyes got more wet. She said, "Hank-is-Handy, I love you so much."

This made me happy. "I am getting good at loving people."

"You were always good at it."

"Ha. Ha. Ha. Ha." I did a laugh because I thought it was a joke. They looked at me funny, then they laughed, too. This also made me glad because I finally understood what jokes were. It felt good to know what jokes were. But it felt better to feel loved. It was the best feeling I think I ever felt as a Vorck. When humans have best feelings, they often say that a day is the best one that they ever had. I think today was the best day I ever had, too.

It is not very often that there is nothing I have to do. But today it was a good thing, because it meant that I had time to talk about things I liked to talk about with Aurora, Elyse, and Delta. The surgeons told me they wanted me to be quiet, but Aurora, Elyse, and Delta said I could talk about whatever I wanted for as long as I wanted. I got to talk about all of my favorite things, like the spindrive, my phase hammer, and my favorite wall in my room. I also talked about how the human creator heard me for the first time, because I asked him to make Delta a good pilot. I thought that they would eventually want to talk about something else, but they did not. It made me have many good feelings that they now liked what I liked. Maybe they were becoming more like me. I do not know if that would make me happy or sad. Maybe I would not have any feelings at all about it. But I think it would be better if they stayed like humans. I decided that the next time we talked, I would listen to them talk about all the things that they liked. I think it would be fair and that they would enjoy it. But for now, I would enjoy talking about my favorite things. I enjoyed the feelings it gave me that they listened.

There is much about humans that I do not understand. But I am glad that I understand their good feelings. I have always wanted to experience them like they do. I have always wanted to feel what they felt. Today, I think that I felt it. I did not want it to ever go away. But I am not a human who feels feelings all the time. I am a Vorck. I am not Hank-has-Feelings. I am Hank-is-Handy. I am strong, just like my friends. I am glad that I have them. I think they are glad that they have me, too. One day, I think I will understand all of the things they understand. I think that day will make me very glad. I look forward to it very much. Until that day comes, I will continue to be a friend and to be handy, even if I am in a hospital bed. I know I will not be in one forever. I look forward to not being in this one and to being in the *Illustré* again. Maybe that will be the new best day of my life. But if it is not, that is okay, too.

One best day is good enough.

Chapter Seventeen

Three months later

HUMANS, PARTICULARLY those with children, are fond of the saying, "the days are long and the years are short." I confess that until I came to the place where I became custodian of my own young fractureling, it was a saying that I had no appreciation for. As I watched Wither work haplessly on poor Aurora's hair, I found myself prone to correct it at every turn. Lifting a finger as it attempted to twist a clump of the captain's coppery curls into a sort of half-braid, half-dreadlock, I prepared to chastise its lack of form for no less than the hundredth time that hour.

Sensing my eagerness, Aurora shot me the sharpest of looks and spoke. "Shh. She must learn."

"It is not a style that flatters you. It is…not a style at all."

"It is an education."

It was not the word I would have chosen had I been in its shoes. I would have leaned more toward something like *humiliation*. But it is a captain's prerogative to be humiliated if it so desired as much. "It is attempting things it is not prepared for."

Once more, its emerald gaze found me. "Be honest, dear friend. In ten minutes, will it matter?"

Against that, I had no argument. "I suppose not."

"Then please, be still and let her learn." Closing its eyes as Wither reached for tusk oil mascara, it leaned its head forward ever so gently to allow the fractureling to work.

I must often remind myself that at only a few months old,

only so much can be expected from my daughter. There would be some that would say that three and a half months is far too soon to begin cosmetic training, but they would most certainly not be Zepzeg. The craft of beautification is one that must be nurtured very early on, lest a specimen fall irreparably behind the other Zepzeg in the galaxy. Humans, for all of their curious merits, often forget that not all species are born ignorant. Despite being a fractureling, there are echoes of my own knowledge and ability pulsing through Wither's lifeveins. That is not to say that it was born in an advanced state. Far from it! But the knowledge and ability are still there, slowly seeping out in the form of subtle breakthroughs and recognitions. The fact that my new arm is only halfway grown has forced me to rely on Wither far more than I would have liked—but perhaps it is to the fractureling's benefit.

I will say that its skill has grown considerably in the scant few months it has existed. The first time I tried to teach it how to apply pretreatment, it dumped an entire bowl of avocado puree onto my poor captain's head. Aurora did not scream or shout, as I most certainly would've, but instead only said through the globs of green that fell to the floor, "Interesting choice. What else could you have done?" Such was also its response when Wither applied a generous dose of Quarisian shampoo to its face, then proceeded to scrub it in like it was some sort of exfoliant. Or the time it confused an acupuncture needle for a hairbrush and made my poor captain's scalp bleed. Even through the tears of pain that it struggled to hold in, Aurora implored me to be patient. "Let her play," it told me. "It is the only way to learn. I don't mind being an experimental canvas." I would not call it experimentation so much as I would torture, but to each its own.

"You're doing fine," it said as Wither brushed its lashes with the tusk oil. It was, of course, impossible for Aurora to determine that, as its eyes were closed the whole while. But indeed, Wither was doing quite well. Satisfied with its work on one eye, it moved right to the next.

Wither has not yet reached the age of speech, but it has occasionally made small chirping sounds that the humans find quite adorable. I, of course, find it utterly grating. But if one must learn to properly beautify, I suppose one must also learn to properly speak. All in due time.

Finishing up on Aurora's other eye, Wither leaned away and allowed the captain to look. Opening its eyes widely at first, then blinking several times, Aurora offered Wither a smile before looking at me. "Well, how do I look?"

A typical human would likely have marveled at the job Wither did. All I could see was imperfection. "Like you were beautified by a three-month-old." It was the politest way I could speak the truth.

"Fancy that," it said, before looking at Wither again. "Well done, my little darling." Wither chirped, which made Aurora's smile widen. "Please remind your mother that you are scarcely two feet tall, have twigs for arms, and have yet to be sculpted into any reasonably dexterous shape."

All of it was, of course, true.

Picking Wither up—another thing the humans simply love to do—Aurora set it down on the floor, then sat back in the chair. "Now, watch how your mother fixes my hair."

I was not in the mood. "Must I go through the effort? As you yourself said, there is no purpose."

"And deprive the girls of the satisfaction? I would never."

"Have you no pride?" I asked as I stepped behind it to undo the mess Wither had made of its hair.

Aurora offered what humans call a *harrumph*, a distinctly ineloquent noise. "It has served to better me not to take myself so seriously. I suggest that you try it. Besides, they've been begging for this day forever. I might as well give them a show."

"How ironic. It is a day that I dread."

"Doll me up, you old prune." Leaning its head back, it offered me its curls. "I don't want to be late."

With all protest in vain, I began my good work.

The months that passed since the frantic conclusion of the negotiation were of a most strange variety. Aurora stated, quite understandably, that it needed a break from the hustle and bustle of being a spacefaring dignitary. It'd taken no jobs since the negotiation, and discussing it brought it no joy. Things with Gryamore V went as they were supposed to, I suppose. The Daldath harvested the planet for minerals, leaving it a cold, lifeless husk that was of little use to any interested party. Then they promptly moved on to who knew where, presumably to contact Aurora again when they needed a new planet to harvest.

As for the Dacians and Broodmasters, their fate in this affair was perhaps the most shocking, the bitter rivals coming together under a mutual and newfound hatred of humanity to form, of all things, the very Freedom Alliance that the Broodmasters had been talking about. Mercifully, it was not an alliance geared at attacking humanity, but at "ensuring that all citizens of this cluster are given equal opportunity to flourish." Or at least, that was how Corvus so sleazily stated it. The repercussions of Gryamore V would be widespread, we were certain, and would most *certainly* birth unforeseen aftershocks. With Aurora at front and center of what so many deemed a debacle, we were sure we would feel some of those aftershocks. But those were troubles for another time.

Running my delicate fingers through its strands to tussle them about, I said to Aurora, "There. That is as good as what can be done."

It eyed itself in the mirror. "How modest, Velistris. I look stunning!" It looked at Wither and smiled. "And I have *you* to thank for that as much as your mother, little one."

Now it was I who harrumphed, though I must say it sounds far less intolerable when I do it. "Must we proceed with this foolishness, captain?"

"Oh, we must," it said. Its eyes and smile widened. "So let us get on with it!" Opening its mouth, it gasped, then looked at me. "That was my shocked face. How was it?"

"Ghastly."

It smirked down at Wither. "Remember, child, insult is a symptom of envy."

"And masochism is a symptom of madness," I said.

It scoffed. "Masochism? Do you hear this, Wither?" Bending down, it picked the fractureling up. "Might this be a lesson you learn at a young age: no one likes a stick in the mud—even if they're made of crystal."

I'd have rolled my eyes had I had them.

"Now come," Aurora said as it flashed its eyes at me. "We must not tarry." Out of the door it strode. "Important business is at hand!"

Out of duty and duty alone, I followed in step.

Despite my misgivings toward this one particular adventure we were about to embark on, the changes in my captain since Gryamore V had been quite positive ones. We squabble more, of that there is no doubt, but it is of a much looser, more casual nature. I feel that we have grown closer, considerably so. And that makes me feel glad.

I am quite pleased to say that its engagement to Bryce Lockhart is back on, the captain having forgiven itself enough to muster up the courage to contact Bryce and ask for *its* forgiveness. In an act that surprised neither Aurora nor me, Bryce graciously accepted. And just like that, the engagement ball was back on—to be held the day after this very day, in fact. That was primarily the reason why Aurora was succumbing to the peer pressure of its nieces. As the date had approached, it'd grown cheerier and cheerier. To say it was a pleasant change was an understatement. It was a needed one. I, for one, was thrilled that their engagement had been restored. It brought a satisfying end to what had been a strenuous season in our lives.

Halfway down the hallway, I paused. It is a place on the ship where I have paused with considerable frequency over the months, at a level of which has surprised even me. It is near the entrance to engineering. It is a photograph of Hank-is-Handy. Beneath it is a plaque that bears its name, followed by the words, "Greater love hath no man than this, that he lay down his life for his friends."

Hank-is-Handy died on the same day it had its surgery for a broken arm and severed spine. It was the latter ailment, as it turned out, that sealed its fate. Unbeknownst to the crew, at some point during their run-in with the Daldath and Vorticella, the Vorck suffered several traumatic back injuries. As typical for Hank-is-Handy, it never said word of it—it merely went about its duties in the midst of a crisis as if nothing was wrong at all. The wound was not discovered until it arrived on the medical ship and was given a full-body scan, by which point the damage had been done. The hours we spent in its room after the procedure were the last in its life. Mercifully, the Vorck was unaware of its condition. Even as its organs failed one by one, it prattled on merrily about the most mundane of affairs, until at long last it simply fell asleep. Its last words were scarcely worth mentioning. "Can someone charge my phase hammer?" it asked. I do not know if it even registered an answer.

A portion of the Vorck's ashes were transferred into the *Illustré* via a receptacle and then poured into the spindrive coolant tubes. The gesture was done so that it might "be a part of the ship forever," as Aurora put it. I will confess to vastly underestimating my own feelings toward the creature. Even I occasionally feel a strange, sad comfort when I think of its remains circulating the heart of the *Illustré*. A time or two, I have even placed my hand against the wall as if to feel its presence there. I dare say, I somewhat miss it. But as humans are keen to remind, life must go on.

Indeed, it must.

Sashaying into one of the vacant guest suites, Aurora feigned trepidation as its eyes surveyed the audience. Delta, Elyse, and, of course, Defoe were all present—as were Riley, Slarb, and Gralb. Thule, as to be expected, was not present; our new Dacian crewmember was as antisocial a being as I've ever come across. There are moments when I cannot blame it. This may or may not have been one of them.

The center of the room had been cleared out quite appropriately for the occasion. The grins that were plastered on Delta and Elyse's faces could not have been wider. "Hello, nieces," Aurora said, setting its hands on its hips. Its eyes shifted to the Blepharisma, which was situated at the center of the far wall. "Defoe."

"Welcome, Aunt Aurora!" said Delta, its eagerness threatening to burst it at its seams. Standing next to it and holding a capture device was Elyse.

Aurora angled its head warningly. "You are not taking pictures of this…"

"Are you ever going to do it again?" Elyse asked.

Narrowing its eyes in calculation, Aurora answered, "Maybe."

"We're taking pictures, because I *know* you'll never do it again."

Reaching up, it bounced its hair playfully in its palms. "I suppose it depends on how I look afterward, though I confess, the thought of putting Velistris in the unemployment line depresses me." It eyed me, also playfully, though I was not in the mood. "Whatever would she do if she were not ship beautician? Dust the ventilation shafts, I suppose?"

"Your wit is second only to your sense of self-respect." I

have taken some time in the past months to experiment with sarcasm. I must say, the results have been…satisfying.

"Well," it said, its gaze shifting to Defoe. "Shall we begin?"

The event, if one were to call it that, was one that Delta and Elyse had petitioned for for a very long time—a *just deserts* of sorts, to steal a silly human term. You see, for the entire span of time since the negotiation, Delta and Elyse have insisted that Aurora subject itself to the humiliation of one of Defoe's "beauty treatments." I have come to suspect that their concern is not for the eventual quality of the treatment—which I confess, much to my chagrin, is exceptional—but for the more immediate gratification of seeing their aunt covered in slime. I shall never understand what humans enjoy about seeing their own tormented in such ways, but to each species their own. It all seems to be well-intentioned.

With its flagellum waving, Defoe said, "I being ready!"

Truth be told, that Aurora waited as long as it had to give into its nieces is something I appreciate. It has insisted that despite the enhancing quality of Defoe's natural fluid, *I* am its beautician. I suspect the reason it gave in when it did was because of the imminent engagement ball and the potential to combine both Defoe's saliva with my expertise to achieve a hairstyle the likes and luster of which could never be rivaled. I had the utmost confidence that after this frivolous little aside, it would be back solely under my care again.

Crossing its arms tightly across its upper body, Aurora winced. "Okay, I'm ready. And you're *sure* this is something we must do?"

Oh, the actress it was!

Elyse was already taking photos. "There's no backing out now!"

"Very well, then. Am I standing the right way?"

"You're doing great."

Eyes flashing to Defoe, Aurora said, "Enjoy this, dear nieces. It will only happen once!"

"Shall we count down?" asked Delta.

"A lovely idea," Aurora answered, "why don't you count us down?"

The teenager was happy to oblige. "Five! Four!" Aurora winced. "Three! Two!"

"Get her good, Defoe!" said Elyse.

"One!"

Lowering its head, Aurora offered Defoe its coppery curls.

Defoe wasted no time. The Blepharisma rose up and its gaping plant mouth opened wide. As it came over Aurora, I heard my poor captain scream.

It was not the first time I had witnessed Defoe envelop another lifeform—I myself was even enveloped by the creature—but it was the first time I could observe it under a situation that was controlled as opposed to chaotic. I must say…it is disgusting. I could see the ooze flying as it sucked on Aurora's upper body. Several globules even splattered my own delicate form. I cannot imagine why Delta and Elyse would subject themselves to it willingly!

I do not know for certain, but it felt as if Defoe enveloped Aurora longer than most. I suspect this was much to its nieces' liking. But, of course, all things—I would hesitate to call this little endeavor *good*—must end. Defoe pulled its body back. With a revolving *slurping* sound, Aurora was deposited back on the floor with minimal struggle beyond what would be expected with the instinct to fight off an attacker. Standing there, mouth agape and covered from head to toe, was my poor, poor captain.

Its coppery curls! Gone was their beauty. They now slid down in all directions atop its head, weighed down by the plant monster's dribble. I could have moaned in lament for them.

Naturally, its nieces laughed in hysterics. The next thing I saw was Elyse's camera taking photo after photo like it was doing some journalistic report. It was all quite unnecessary.

"Oh my God," said Aurora, lowering its head so that its sticky strands hung down. With an effortless flip, it tossed the strands back and over its head with a splat. There was no need for it to attempt a shocked face. The look of horror it displayed was quite real. "I can't even move."

But its nieces could. And oh, how they did, prancing up to it, bending down to scoop up handfuls of slime, then depositing them mercilessly on top of its head.

"A gorgeous look!" said Delta.

"Defoe missed a spot!" chimed in Elyse.

I would have slapped them. But of course, Aurora only laughed and allowed them their fun, much as it does with Wither. It even went so far as to pose with various otherwise-impossible-to-achieve hairstyles for Elyse to snap pictures. Were it not for the horror of the act, it would have all been quite festive.

Humans.

At the very least, they were happy. I have come to recognize the value in that. If a small bit of foolishness is all that it takes to keep the hallways of the *Illustré* filled with good spirits, then it is worth it. I suppose, if I were them, I would partake in it myself.

Several minutes into the jubilation, a strange and noticeable lull fell over the females. Averting my mind from my thoughts, I turned to them. It was Elyse. The smile on its face was still there, but its lips were held tightly. In its eyes, I detected a shimmer. Canting its head to its elder niece, Aurora asked, "Elyse, what is the matter?"

It exhaled a hard breath. "I was just thinking that Hank-is-Handy would have laughed at you if he'd been here. Or tried to laugh, at least."

At word of the Vorck, all three went silent, the bittersweet sentiment shared between them. I suppose I felt it, myself. Holding its arms out, Aurora beckoned its nieces closer. No care was given to the mess on the captain's body. Delta and

Elyse took its embrace.

"My dear, dear nieces," it said softly. Then it looked at me. "My dear friends, all of you. Our memories are our most precious commodities. When all else is gone, they are what remain. And if that is our currency, my loves, then we are *rich*. We are rich beyond our wildest dreams. I am so very proud of you all. You have grown before my eyes. Even you, Velistris."

I bowed my head reverently.

"I hope that you have all seen that same growth in me. I am far from perfect. I confess it, and you have seen it. But I do hope that your time with me is cherished while it lasts. I want you to remember fondly these days when I am gone, as someday I will be. I hope that my love for you is evident, even if I do not voice it as often as I should. For that, I am sorry. I am striving to be better.

"This season of our lives is one we shall never forget. We have seen the most trying of hardships, each in our ways. But we have also seen the greatest of loves. Let that love inspire you. Take it with you. Give it freely to those around you. You never know how they may desperately need it."

I watched as they embraced. I took in the love they had for one another. I dare say, I felt it myself. I have learned the wisdom of listening to words of value. Of staving off my own preconceived notions of what is right and proper. I am far from perfect in that regard—but as I have learned, perfection is quite literally not what it's cracked up to be.

The tears passed, as I find they always do, and once again, the *Illustré* resonated with the joy and laughter of family, of which I was privileged enough to be included. I am looking forward to seeing how Wither fits in with that family. I am looking forward to seeing how I turn out as its mother. It is a challenge I am prepared to face, as my friends on the *Illustré* have each faced their own. I hope my journey is as uplifting as theirs.

The next day, we attended the engagement ball. It was as splendid as we'd all imagined. No one's hair was more breathtaking than Aurora's, and no one stole more of the spotlight. And of course, Delta at long last got to perform its dance wearing the garments I'd prepared for it. It had put so much effort into practicing for it, and I was so incredibly proud. The performance itself was far, far from perfect. But perhaps that's okay. Perhaps perfection is merely a goal to be striven for, not actually attained. Perhaps its unattainability is the point. Perhaps in the end, it is the point we are purposed to learn.

How wonderful a lesson would that turn out to be.

ACKNOWLEDGEMENTS

God, for the indescribable opportunities You provide, for giving me the endurance to see them through, and for the Grace You give in abundance every single day.

Lindsey, for your never-ending support and encouragement as I live this crazy #WritersLife. I am so blessed to call you my love!

Levi, Lawson, and Linden, for your boundless enthusiasm and entertainment! Don't ever grow up too much. Daddy loves you!

Mom, Dad, and Mr. Tommy, for never failing to believe that I can actually pull these things off.

The Petersen family, for welcoming us into your home, treating us like family, and trusting me with the universe you created. I loved every moment of this.

Everyone at Petersen Games, for making this a seamless process and a fantastic experience. It's easier said than done.

Jody, for your influence on every single published page I write. You bring order to my chaos!

Kasia, for lending me your unbelievable talent time and time again. I can't wait to see what we hit next.

Luke Jansen, for turning old Hyperspeed midis into the most rocking remix album ever created. This helped me so much.

Peggy and Georgie, for being amazing supporters and for your incredible and honest feedback—you made this book better.

Theresa, Racquell, Nicole, Angel, and Stanley, for subliminally implanting in my brain the urge to write a novel about hair care.

Blepharisma, for being my friend. Told you I'd be yours.

ABOUT THE AUTHOR

Born and raised in Cajun country, Lee Stephen spent his childhood paddling pirogues through the marshes of South Louisiana. When he wasn't catching bullfrogs or playing with alligators in the bathtub (both true), he was escaping to the world of the imagination, creating worlds in his mind filled with strange creatures and fantastic journeys. This hasn't stopped.

Author of the award-winning Epic series, Lee has made it his mission to create science-fiction that relentlessly addresses the human condition. He is a resident of Des Allemands, where he lives with his wife and three sons.

Information about the Epic series can be found at
www.epicuniverse.com.

EVACUATE

A survival game set in the
HYPERSPACE
Universe

It's too late! There is only one escape transport left and you must lead your people from a shelter to claim it before the others get there first. **Evacuate** is a community deck-building game where players use social deduction to outwit the other players and reach the Evacuation Transport with the most Survivors.

PETERSEN
—GAMES—

IN THE BELLY
OF THE BEAST

Contained in this book are eight short stories and a complete novel. The short stories are all inspired by the factions and cults of the "**Cthulhu Wars**" game, and the Cthulhu Mythos of H.P. Lovecraft and his collaborators.

The novel, **In the Belly of the Beast**, tells the story of a small group of human survivors trying to find a safe haven amidst the ruins of civilization. While traveling through a treacherous mountain pass, they find themselves caught between rival cults, and discover there are worse things in the cold places of the world than frostbite.

Made in the USA
Middletown, DE
15 November 2021